Derek Jewell has been in the communications business all his life. After Oxford he worked in Liverpool as a journalist and joined the *Sunday Times* in 1962, where he ended up as deputy editor of the Colour Magazine. In 1962 he became publishing director of Times Newspapers Ltd., which runs both *The Times* and the *Sunday Times*. A regular broadcaster on radio and television, he has also edited two books – *Man and Motor, The 20th Century Love Affair* (1966) and *Alamein and the Desert War* (1967). He has been jazz and popular music critic for the *Sunday Times* since 1963.

SELLOUT

DEREK JEWELL

SPHERE BOOKS LIMITED
30/32 Gray's Inn Road, London WC1X 8JL

First published in Great Britain by
Macmillan London Ltd 1973
Copyright © Derek Jewell 1973
Published by Sphere Books 1975

for
Juan Carlos who showed me
and
Nicholas, Sarah and Liz who let me

Set in Linotype Plantin

Printed in Great Britain by
Hazell Watson & Viney Ltd
Aylesbury, Bucks

CONTENTS

THE PRINCIPAL CHARACTERS

In England

Sir Bernard Grant:
    Chairman, The Prospero Group
Michael Grant:
    Chief Executive, The Prospero Group

Harold Armfield
Lord Bender
Earl Sanger:
    Directors, The Prospero Group

David Travis:
    Principal Assistant to Michael Grant
William Oldershaw:
    Managing Director, Brasserton's Ltd
George Lovelace:
    Managing Director, Lovelace Cars
Alison Grant
Sheila Travis

In the U.S.A.

Kerridge: Chief Executive, Kerridge Steel
Ed Corsino

In South America

Dr Jesus Enrique Cantania Garcia (Cantania): A Minister
Colonel Antonio Hernan de Vargas (Vargas): an 'asesor'
Palindo Juan Perez Armand (Perez): agent, the Prospero Group
Carlos: site works manager, Brasserton's Ltd
Francisco: a guerrilla
Delano Martin: project director, Kerridge Steel
Derek Quant: project manager, Brasserton's Ltd

In France

Claire Debrais: Director, Debrais et Cie
Lars Koringen: a racing driver

THE SUPPORTING CAST

Vernon Morton
Lionel Westbrook
Barry Prosser
Frank Bartram
Sir Harvey Jardine:
      Directors, The Prospero Group

Colin Hardy: Principal Assistant to Earl Sanger
Tom Colley: General Manager, Brasserton's Ltd
Philip Lovelace: Director, Lovelace Cars
Freddy Mailer: arms salesman
Charles Prat: Director, Debrais et Cie
Maria Koringen
Marjorie Corsino

The action of this book takes place
in England, the U.S.A., Ecuador
and France

AUTHOR'S NOTE

When direct-speech conversation is preceded by a
hyphen, like this ' — . . . . ', it indicates
that the speakers are talking in Spanish.

ACKNOWLEDGEMENTS

My thanks are due to many people for help with
this book, and particularly the late Juan Carlos
Teran Camacho and other citizens of Ecuador, as well as
Michael Banfield, Maxwell Boyd, Max Boyer,
Michael Brown, Janet Drummond, John Hathrell,
Louis Herchenroder, Elizabeth Jewell, Bill Jupe
and Charles Stewart-Hess. A reading of John Hemming's
The Conquest of the Incas helped notably in understanding
South American history.

'It was the best of times, it was the worst of times,
it was the age of wisdom, it was the age of foolishness,
it was the epoch of belief, it was the epoch of incredulity.'

Charles Dickens: *A Tale of Two Cities*

I. WHO NEEDS ENEMIES?

1

No; the small brown bundle of Indian lying at their feet was unlikely to die. The oil company PRO said so. Carlos obviously agreed. David Travis could relax a little. But there was only the river to look at.

It was brown and bloated, starved of sun, but not angry, moving with the insolent sloth of volcanic lava. Clumps of vegetation and fat tree-trunks, nudged forward on the smooth oily surface, were its prizes and witnesses to its power.

It was not a river to fall into. Certainly not in the middle. For although it was only a tributary, 4,000 miles from where the Amazon oozed through many mouths into the Atlantic, it was at this point more than a quarter of a mile wide. David speculated what its bland exterior might conceal. Like all strangers in exotic places, he remembered only the bad bits of the guidebook. And in this place, piranhas and crocodiles could not be regarded as supernumaries for James Bond movies in friendly neighbourhood picturedromes.

'Jesus,' said the oil company man. 'They're taking their time.'

'Does it happen often, then?' asked David, wondering whether criticisms from himself, a visitor and guest, would be regarded as hostile.

'It happens,' said the oil company man, a New York City geologist turned PRO; in this wet heat, even talking was an effort.

The injured Indian reached out a hand to take a lighted cigarette. Why he didn't faint or shout or even moan was baffling. To lie there with a bloody tangle of flesh and bone and boot where once a foot had been, smiling gently as though the Almighty had done you a service, wasn't normal. Such behaviour must be what the Embassy people, back in

11

the capital, meant by the natural dignity of the Indian. This one, poor devil, knew how to suffer.

David exhaled damp air impatiently; it was the feeling of helplessness which disrupted him the most. Once they had eased the Indian's foot out from under the bulldozer track, there was nothing any of them could do except wait for the helicopter. David and Carlos and the oil company man and the labourers just stood there, occasionally flapping rags or, in Carlos's case, a panama hat to keep stray insects away. The enforced passivity, when plain human need demanded some more useful response, was what gave the sardonic edge to his thoughts. It was a distracting safety mechanism of the mind which he had grown gratefully used to.

The injured Indian was only part of David's concerns, however. He would have been less uneasy had he been coping with his problems in one of the quiet air-conditioned conference rooms of Prospect House, the organisation head-quarters back in London. Instead he stood beside the Aguarico river, feeling every sweat-drop prickle under the impact of one hundred Amazonian degrees fahrenheit as he pondered precisely how he was expected to deal with a multi-million contract that he knew was going wrong.

'This is one hell of an operation,' he said, only because the silence was more oppressive than the heat.

'Yeah,' said the oil company PRO. 'And so is yours. What are they aiming to produce at that plant?'

'God knows,' said David.

'I hear you've had trouble.'

'A bit. That's partly why I'm here.'

'The same old rules, I betcha.'

'Huh?' said David.

'The impossible we can do. Miracles take a little longer.'

It was an old joke, but David laughed.

These were the times when he wished he'd never heard of the Prospero Group or its chief executive, Michael Grant, who had sent him here. On the other hand, how many Cambridge graduates (or Princeton or Sorbonne or Yoko-hama alumni, for that matter) were earning as much as he was at the age of 32? So now he accepted, but with irritable discomfort, the condition of his corporate existence, and worried: about what was happening in Prospero while he stood doing nothing particular in this other jungle; who was

12

making the running; who might be undermining him. He worried whether Sheila, his wife, had really meant it when she said she'd get drunk or laid or worse at the Carson's party if he didn't make it home within a fortnight. And, most immediately, he wondered what the hell he was doing in the rain forests anyway. The real action for him had to be back at the coast or in Quito, the capital.

Carlos had stopped attending to the injured Indian and was giving him that look again: cool, yet definitely impatient. Carlos was respectful – just – but resentful. Carlos hadn't wanted to turn his back on the coast either. At the coast, at Esmeraldas, where the plant was being built, Carlos had a big job to do. Why should he be made to leave it, even for a day or so, to show some dumb gringo where they were sucking the oil up from beneath the jungle? The oil was certain, already flowing through the pipeline; unless the guerrillas emerged boldly enough in Ecuador to start sticking dynamite on the pipes.

Carlos couldn't do much about that even if they did. His job was to help create the miracle, flatly called a petrochemical plant, which could alchemise the black gold in the pipes into different gold. It would cost a quarter of a billion dollars to build. But one day it would turn out thousands upon thousands of tons of plastics worth many millions of dollars more than had ever been spent in its construction.

David understood how Carlos must feel. He also knew why Oldershaw, who had come with him on the trip from England, had said David could bloody well swan off down the festering Amazon if that's what London wanted him to do.

That was typical of Oldershaw. He did not respond obliquely to frustration as David did. He simply exploded. And Oldershaw exploding was a comically fearsome sight. He was small and wiry. In anger, his whole body coiled like a spring and then, suddenly, let go. His cavernous face, clipmoustached, would distort and redden in a parody of an old-fashioned drill sergeant unleashing his rage on some clumsy rookie. Even his ears, out-thrust like handles on a jug, turned scarlet. Raging, Oldershaw would spatter his speech with the ancient wartime phrases that somehow went with the way he looked.

I haven't time for that kind of bullshit, lad. Perez isn't even genned up. Call him a flaming agent? He can't get half

13

*the first load out of customs. I've got to sort out the import
licences. I thought there was enough sodding red tape back
in Prospect House, but this lot . . .*

Oldershaw had reason to sweat. There was a hot fifteen
million pounds of Prospero Group business riding on their
share of the contract for the petro-chemical plant. If it went
wrong, Oldershaw would get the bullet first.

No, David conceded, not true. Oldershaw, edgily proud
of the engineering plant he ran, would be kicked, perhaps
chopped. He might even die of a broken pride. But that
would be a sparrow's fall. If this deal were a disaster, how
could Michael Grant himself survive? For Michael it was
who had chosen Oldershaw's company from the host of
Prospero subsidiaries to tackle this complicated project in
South America. It was Michael, too, who had pushed
through the Ecuador deal, when Prospero might have put
their money more safely into furniture or fruit machines.
The clinching of the contract, indeed, had been one of the
coups which lifted the younger Grant into the chief
executive's chair at Prospero.

Michael Grant depended on Ecuador, without doubt; and
David Travis knew he depended on both. He was Michael's
man. God help them all if Ecuador went wrong.

*See all of it, David. Get the feel. The men who run it,
how it works, the politics. Bill Oldershaw can't do it. He'll
look after the engineering, but he's no diplomat.* He remembered how Michael had urged him to go to the jungle.
*The consortium men and the fixers like Perez – they're fine
in their way, but I want it straight from someone I can trust.
Before this thing is through, you'll need every bit of information you can pick up, every contact you can make. Cover
our end at the plant, yes – but nose around elsewhere. Go
and see the oilfields . . .*

Oilfields? That was a laugh. It made you think of deserts
and sheikhs with fleets of gold-plated Cadillacs and platinum-
plated women. Here the oil lay 15,000 feet below the most
claustrophobic forest in the world. Flying over the jungle,
it looked black-green and evil, as if nothing could breathe
in there: impenetrable and unbroken, except for the brown
and yellow rivers which twisted and turned, formed dead-
ends and sandbanks and whirlpools, sliding through the
vegetation like gigantic serpents. Billions upon billions of

14

trees, embracing each other, embraced themselves by the wrist-thick vines called *ligana*, choking lovers. Trees rolling from the Oriente, at the eastern foot of the Andes, where the oil was, four thousand miles to Brazil's Atlantic shores.

Fields. Very funny.

The PRO picked up the conversation where it had bogged down in the heat a couple of minutes earlier.

'We had plenty of trouble too,' he said.

'I can imagine,' said David.

'What a crazy climate. I wouldn't like to have been the guys who got here first. Someone guesstimated they'd moved a million trees.'

Only a decade or so ago, men said the oil could never be got out economically from the jungle. That was before wars and disasters showed what could be done with the helicopter. Now there were queues of oil companies standing in line for the privilege of moving out the oil, at the back-end of the biggest helicopter operation in the world outside of Vietnam.

Wasn't it simple? First, get your gear in via those Amazonian tributaries. If there's no river handy, then get men to hang at the end of rope ladders from helicopters and start chopping at the trees. Hack away long enough, with the birds screaming and the anacondas sloping off to quieter parts, and you've got space for the helicopter to land. Then, roll out your bulldozer and push down a piece of jungle. Later, you can start drilling.

No wonder it was all costing the oilmen a billion, more or less. Maybe two. And was it pounds or dollars? He'd forgotten.

'Won't they ever get here?' said the PRO even more plaintively. Delays, disasters and acts of God were not on the itinerary.

They all looked up at the grey skies, bruised with the rain that could hurtle down at any time, as if this action might make the aircraft come sooner. But all that appeared was a forty-foot dugout canoe, with outboard motor, nosing in to the platform of logs beside the river where, in a few weeks, there would be a Bailey bridge.

'He won't end up at the camp,' said the PRO.

'Why not?' said David.

'No point. For this kind of injury, I figure the transportation guys will have been told to ship him to Quito. Better

15

hospital facilities there, the very best. We look after these guys well.'

David nodded. *We look after them well, even the goddam Indians.* Was that what the PRO meant? It needed no special insight to know that Indians rated lowest in this society, below the hybrid *mestizos*, even below the Negroes on the coast, and lived in a totally different world from the more or less pure-blooded descendants of the *conquistadores* of four centuries earlier. Even *The South American Handbook, 47th Annual Edition*, and John Gunter's *Inside Latin America*, which had been David's main preparation for grappling with the continent's matured fabric of greed and graft and ancient prejudice, had told him that. His correspondence course Spanish hadn't proved much help.

This, though, was a lucky Indian. Able to earn more than a dollar a day, if not the three or four dollars of the men on the drilling rigs, who worked up to their waists in bubbly mud when the rains were really in spate. That was good money for these people, but he'd been told that the Indians of the high sierra often died in the Oriente because they couldn't take the climate.

The lucky Indian on the ground, with five splinters of bone jagging through pulverised flesh, smiled even more broadly when he heard the chop-chop of the helicopter. It settled in the clearing, whipping the dust and bending the leaves. The PRO said, 'Leave it to them.'

'*Claro*,' said Carlos, and spoke in dialect to the labourers.

Three men in a sort of denim battledress came and took the Indian off on a stretcher. They were big men, but they handled him skilfully, almost tenderly.

The PRO drove David and Carlos back towards the camp. They passed some simple huts, wood and rusty sheet metal and roofs of palm leaves and bamboo. Outside the buildings played the children of the new colonists, Indians come to grow maize and bananas for sale to the camp.

The PRO kept pointing out the 'Christmas trees', the name which oilmen give to the five-foot hunks of metal that stuck up out of the ground, a bit like space-age village pumps. Each one of these markers was numbered. They showed the spot where drilling had taken place, the well at present sealed off until its oil was needed. Very unspectacular, really, these midget 'trees' that prevented the wells

16

from gushing. At one million dollars a well, the pipes going down maybe 18,000 feet, David felt the surface stuff should have looked more grand.

Soon the saw the twin pillars of rich black smoke, from a small oil refinery burning off surplus gases, which marked the camp. In the main office, the superintendent awaited them, a red-faced easy-moving Texan, middle-aged, with grey stubbled hair. David found him extremely likeable; straight, very competent, unhurried. He sat with boots hoisted on his desk.

'Have a good day, son?'

'Great. I'd like to have gone down to one of the drilling sites, not just flown over them.'

The Texan smiled. 'Your boots ain't tall enough for the mud.'

David laughed. 'Okay.'

'Heard about that guy's foot. I'm sorry. Poor guy.' He swung his boots off the desk. 'Plane's ready for take-off.'

David looked disappointed. He had been promised lunch. The PRO was anxious to molify him. 'Sorry, David, but they're expecting rain in Quito later. And that could stop you flying in.'

'Whatever you say,' said David. 'Thanks for everything.'

The Texan waved a hand, easily. 'Besides, your guy Oldershaw was on the line. He wants you back. I think he's having trouble over your plant. Hey, now maybe we've all gotten trouble. Something's movin' back in Quito. The Cabinet's in special session, and there's a whole heap of soldiers in the streets.'

He flashed a copy of a newspaper in front of them.

The headline read. *GOBERNO CONTROLA SITUACION.*

'I didn't know there was a goddam situation to control,' said the superintendent.

'Good luck with the plant,' said the PRO.

Luck, David was certain, he'd need.

2

They flew towards the capital. David didn't much like it. In a small plane it *feels* like flying. He felt resentful. Why hadn't Michael Grant come out here himself if the thing was going to get nasty? He was supposed to be the big expert on Ecuador, wasn't he – him and Ed Corsino, the American who had persuaded Michael that the Prospero Group could make another fortune if they put their engineering subsidiary, Brasserton's, into the consortium to build the petro-chemical plant?

David suspected, as did others in the Prospero Group, that Michael was so hooked on pushing the new Lovelace prototype sports car into a place at Le Mans in June that he didn't want to leave London. Michael wouldn't be the first businessman, David thought, to let a diversion become an obsession. The Lovelace company, acquired a year earlier, was scarcely essential to Prospero's fortunes; and he couldn't see why Le Mans was so crucial to selling automobiles anyway. Michael might once have been a sports-car racing driver too, but why couldn't he let the works team prepare the car without being present while they adjusted every bloody nut and bolt?

David knew this was probably unfair, but it was too near the truth for comfort. It had been a good year for David Travis. After five years with the Prospero Group, serving in its subsidiary companies and finally arriving in the central marketing unit at Prospect House, he was usefully positioned.

Maybe he was lucky to have been appointed Michael Grant's principal assistant the previous year when Michael became chief executive in succession to Sir Bernard Grant; but he'd taken his chance, survived that first year well. He had no desire to see it all go to pieces because Michael had given him, out of misjudgment, an assignment too tricky.

They were flying higher now, the jungle behind them, beginning to weave across the snow-draped volcanoes of the Andes. Once the Beechcraft C50 Excalibur, specially modified, hit 12,000 feet the passengers were gagged with oxygen masks. The main trouble, David thought, was that he had no idea what his next move, down there in Quito, should be.

The Prospero situation wasn't difficult to assess. During Michael's struggle to persuade his father to resign as chief executive and be satisfied with the nebulous position of chairman of the board, the battle lines had been sharply etched – progressives against conservatives. Now, instead, there existed only an uneasy neutralism. Michael would always be embattled in one sense, for he was surrounded by men of sharp ambition. But all the confused yelping of the pack-followers meant nothing so long as the man who was effectively the chief shareholder, Lord Bender, remained aloof and neutral.

David knew it was because Bernard Grant (Sir Bernard since the last Honours list) had forfeited Bender's confidence that Michael was now running the Prospero empire. Presumably Bender too had believed that Bernard Grant might have been a genius at property deals in the fifties, and reasonably sound as the purchaser of a multitude of other businesses in the sixties, but was no man for the subtler and stressful seventies. Besides, Bernard was 67 and had his first coronary only just behind him.

Now, everyone was waiting to see if Michael's performance matched his promise. Bender, phlegmatic and grey, would not wait for ever. Bender demanded profits, however broadly he might smile at board meetings. To the insurance company that Bender ran and the pension funds he advised, only tangible returns would justify the huge investment he had made in Prospero.

They were also waiting to see if the new chief executive over-reached himself. That was what really troubled David. Michael was good, no argument; far-seeing and fair, sometimes too honest for his own good. But he had weaknesses, and the chief of them was his apparent inability to get his priorities right. Obsessive about certain things he could be, unwilling to delegate them – the Lovelace business was a prime example. Yet with other tasks he appeared not to know the difference between delegating and dumping.

David cut his train of thought abruptly. The pilot seemed to be flying too close to the mountains. He could see the snow blowing like a white dust-storm away to port. They changed course subtly. He relaxed again.

In one way, Ecuador was just another assignment. In the past few months David had been to Paris, Hamburg, Cairo (and Tel-Aviv – involving the usual manipulation of passports in Cyprus), Barcelona, New York, Wigan, Chicago, Aberdeen and Green Bay, Wisconsin, on organisation business. Sheila hadn't liked all these absences, with their child

Kenwyn in his first year; very different from the nine-to-seven London headquarters slog which had preceded it. David had tried to persuade her that it wouldn't last long and that the inconvenience was the price they paid for a shimmering future of, of – well what? Bigger car, better house, school fees for the kids assured, Chivas Regal on the sideboard?

But it must be more than that, mustn't it? He still wasn't certain exactly what. It could be a matter of pride, an intangible mark of achievement which had nothing to do with possessions. It could be the human need to create *something*, even a factory in Tulsa, Oklahoma, or a foolproof filing system in London E.C. 4. For the moment, though, all he could tangibly assess from the past and allegedly successful year was two raises; one au pair girl; a four-bedroom house in Weybridge, instead of three beds in Orpington; a Rover 3500 V-8 instead of a Cortina 1600 GT; and uneasy peace with Sheila. He supposed that many men in other countries – an American executive moving perhaps from Riverdale to Greenwich, Connecticut, or from Detroit's inner city to Bloomingdale Heights – must experience similar feelings.

It was the air travel, the flaccid non-experience of modern flying, which he viewed with most distaste. How could the world have so mutated the adventure of aspiring to 35,000 feet that it became like living in a prison? There were, of course, pre-release movies for the good-conduct men, as well as Lolita fantasies – the air stewardesses – to imbibe with your dinner. But what did that add up to? Flash a thigh, flash a tit, flash a smile, all with no substance, no meaning. See-through people, sometimes in see-through dresses.

At Panama City, travelling with Oldershaw on the run down to Quito (beyond to Lima and Santiago), he'd seen backstage. Virtually the only passenger who hadn't got off for an hour to stretch his limbs, he'd been sitting at the back-end of the 707 when the new crew boarded the plane, in petunia costumes, like lascivious schoolgirls. They talked too loud, one of them pulling up her skirt to show her companions the mosquito bites, angry red welts on white thighs. They complained about the passengers – *only a few of them, but just look how they're spread out the whole length.*

Later, the wallpaper music began – soothe-us aspirin for the take-off, stirring strings and castanets (*isn't this the Latin run, for Chrissake?*) – which suddenly was interrupted by a curt voice: *Passengers boarding.*

The girls, sprawled wearily in the last two rows of seats, stood up, smoothing out breasts, thighs, hair and smiles. *Jeeesus! How many oilmen did you say?* Oilmen, especially Texas oilmen, meant calls for Scotch or bourbon every five minutes and, probably, stud poker and noise all night. No fun for the servants, even if they are called hostesses.

Swallow the air travel, though – and David on the whole did, like bad medicine, in a mixture called temperature change, time change, pace change — and who couldn't be a jet executive given stamina, a minimum IQ of, say, 125, and a portion of either cunning or insensitivity, depending on the negotiating style favoured? David, with neither cunning nor insensitivity in noticable measure, had found he possessed a flair for it. He was healthy enough to stand it and, provided it didn't stretch beyond his thirty-ninth year (so he said), was willing to endure the strain.

He had helped Prospero subsidiaries to buy powerboat hulls in New York, oranges in Israel, valve patents in Paris and Illinois without fouling things up. He had met one fantastic woman in Tel Aviv (fantastic performer, that is – if you like sexual gymnasts), arguing that he'd had no option but to grapple with her, since the man with whom he was dealing had laid her on and might have been insulted had he chickened out. He had also suffered one disaster in Hamburg when feeling depressed and vulnerable. The Hamburg girl came, as it were, to pieces in his hands: false eyelashes, wig and built-in foam breasts.

He was, however, no womaniser. He saw his wife seldom enough to make sex with her still very exciting and, somehow, new. The Tel Aviv and Hamburg girls he put down to the hazards of the way of life. He had still to learn that wise hosts do not take umbrage if the women they offer are refused, since they know that guests are flattered by the availibility of gifts rather than the consumption of them.

Nevertheless he had, in one short year, licked the foreign business bit and, in this sense, Ecuador wasn't special.

Oh, but it was. It was bigger by far than anything he had yet been mixed up with. The Prospero investment was very large indeed, and, like every deal in South America, relatively chancy. Brasserton's, the Prospero subsidiary which

Oldershaw managed, had a 15 per cent share of business in the international consortium which was building that huge petro-chemical plant on the coast. Their clients were an Ecuador-based company in which the country's government had (but naturally) the crucial stake. The plant was meant to use up some of the oil which now made the finds in the Oriente almost as spectacular as Venezuela, or Alaska. It was also intended to increase the value of what was produced *in* the country. The desire of all under-developed countries is to turn their people into industrial workers; Ecuador was no exception.

Inside the consortium which had negotiated the £100 million price for building the plant were chiefly American, French and British companies, and of these the Prospero Group was the British leader. Specifically, it was down as Brasserton business; but everyone knew that in truth it was Michael Grant business.

An optimist, Michael; a bit of a gambler. He'd pushed Oldershaw to take on a bigger job than Brasserton's had ever faced before. They were building and installing the process control for the plant. David smiled. Process control was a deceptively flat phrase for the intricate network of computer and cables, instruments and valves which would ultimately create competence or chaos among the tanks, towers and chemical convolutions of the whole operation. Even to attempt it, Brasserton's had needed to organise an army of sub-contractors. The control logic of the whole operation (one of the dandier phrases of the day, David thought) had kept the systems team brought in by a computer company happy and highly paid for nine months. As for the intricate financial structure which supported the operation, David preferred not to think about what could come unstuck.

There were times, usually after he'd been reading about refugees in Pakistan or those dire forecasts on world population or pollution, when he considered seriously whether it mattered at all if deals like this came unstuck or not. Who really cared whether an enterprise like Prospero made or lost a few millions? Who gave a damn whether Michael Grant kept control?

But in the end he dismissed such thoughts as fit only for the dialecticians of the left-wing weeklies or book critics writing their reviews from the neuter safety of country cottages in honeysuckle villages. If Prospero hit hard times, it could mean ten thousand more men standing in line at unemployment counters in bleak northern towns. If Michael Grant weren't there, then some worse bastard would be – and there were a few of those in Prospect House.

Of course it mattered. Ecuador mattered. His work mattered. Those who believed otherwise lived in Noddy-land. You couldn't change the world merely by rejecting it or existing on smoke dreams in some drop-out commune. The rough part was to be inside the organisation world and still to find a rationale for behaviour, standards, near-honesty.

Thus David argued to himself, often over-dogmatic, since no man can exist without self-justification in his own mind.

Carlos was signalling to him, pointing. There, looming up to port, was a monstrous peak, higher than they were, snow glistening in the sun.

Carlos took off his mask momentarily. 'Cayambe,' he said.

David jerked his head up and down. The sight of the volcano was worth a show of appreciation. Carlos wasn't bad. He seemed to have thawed a bit.

For a gringo, okay, Carlos decided. That pink face they all had, which the gringos seemed to admire. Brown wavy hair; a tall man, strong and confident, but not acting as if Carlos were a child. Yes, he could take David Travis. Not like that misbegotten Quant back at the site. Quant was the project manager sent out by the gringo's company from Britain to take charge of some of the plant installations. He did not like Quant, but Travis was different – an acceptable man. He spoke Spanish, too. Not well, but he tried.

Carlos had lost 48 hours at the site, which was not good, but now he would rest in the capital for the weekend as he deserved. Esmeraldas was too hot. Quito would be cool. The woman would be there. And he would be spared for three days the pressure from the two men who, knowing the secret radicalism of his student days, were becoming too insistent.

Carlos was not displeased with life. He looked down from the plane and considered that, had he not done so well, he might have been condemned to an eight-hour drive for a weekend in the capital, instead of riding like a politician in the luxurious plane of the oil lords. The road journey from Esmeraldas to Quito he did not appreciate. First, the

23

more or less flat run, just a few small hills, through green country, jungle and the banana plantations. Reaching Santo Domingo de los Colorados, where the Indians of that tribe still painted themselves crazy for the tourists, you were at 500 metres.

Then, leaving pot-holed and dusty streets, the drive really began. Up and up, temperature plummeting, through gorges, water pouring down the hillsides, along a twisting road which sometimes crumbled at the edges, was holed, bombarded by landslides. That might be good terrain for guerrillas to set ambushes one day – if the guerrillas ever came. You would be well over two miles above sea level by the time the climbing was over, and the road was continually deceptive. Often it would be covered in floating mist, the trucks and buses bucketing along above uncertain precipices.

Madmen, were they not, those drivers? They were Carlos's countrymen, but he believed they were fools. He was also a good Catholic, but he thought that the banners shouting *Jesus de la Gran Poder* with which such men festooned their vehicles would not save them. Was it not disrespectful to God, indeed, to behave with such lack of reason. He rode now in this fine aircraft through his own efforts – and those of his mother. God be praised for such a mother; an Indian, of the Cañari tribe, but half-educated through her friendship with a priest. A failed Spanish clerk, an outcast of his family, for a father, which made Carlos *mestizo*, of mixed blood.

Had it been left to his father he could have joined the rest of Quito's ragged boys, following the tourists and visiting businessmen in droves to shine shoes at 2 sucres a time – scarcely a dime in American money – or sell them lottery tickets. But his mother had somehow saved the fees for his education at a small private school. He was bright. The Catholic university had later accepted him too, a rare exception to the children of Spanish families and other successful ones in politics or commerce who usually went there. University, and pupillage, in Guayaquil, had made him *Ingeniero*, an honoured title which assured his future. He could do the job they'd given him at Esmeraldas with only half his brain, although, dear God, some of the workers they gave him were not fit to sweep the streets. Carlos would never forget his mother. Whenever he visited the capital he always went to La Compania, the church of gold, to light two candles for her.

But he could see that his own ascent did not remove the valid criticisms of his country's society. It was traditional to believe that *mestizos* despised Indians. He did not. How could *mestizos* despise or deny part of what had made them? He felt a great sorrow for the Indians, those who scratched in the fields on the cold plateau for a pittance or lived without pride in the towns.

At university, his sorrow had been an anger, hot but subtle. He and a few friends had, despite the dangers, looked beyond the boundaries of his country for the answer. One of them went to work for a summer in Cuba, but had not come back.

Now, as he told the two men who had been coming to his house at Esmeraldas with increasing frequency – worrying his wife, approaching him in *cantinas* and even, once, at the site – Carlos was wiser. He would work quietly and steadily for justice, believing that with increasing wealth – which oil would create – the old inequalities would in time be erased. The politicians were changing, and so was the mood of the country. Slowly, without doubt; perhaps too slowly. But how, in this society, could change be made faster without creating something much worse?

—*For dear Christ's sake, comrade, revolution in this country is inevitable, as it is in all of South America,* one of the men had said.

—*How,* said the other, *can even the Indians in the remotest villages sit much longer in church and hear the priests say, Blessed are the Poor in Spirit, when they discover every hour that such words are lies?*

—*Join us,* said the first. *Have you forgotten what you believed when you were twenty years of age? We need those like you. Men of education, of power, of access.*

—*To teach you how to blow up bridges or lay ambushes for politicians?* said Carlos, with sarcasm. *That is not the way. And,* he added, wanting to show he knew more than they, *not all the priests are saying the system is right. Some are working for change You insult the Church.*

—*Priests!* The answer was vibrant with scorn. *We shall be in hell by the time they change. Our way is the only way, comrade. Or do you believe we can wait one thousand years? People are coming across the border to join us. We have guns. You will be left behind if you do not join us now.*

—*Nonsense*, said Carlos. *The police pick up those who come. They rot in jail. A woman from Colombia was captured only last week. For four days, I am told, they kept her staring at an electric bulb, her eyes taped open. Even if what you wished to do was right, which I do not accept, do you truly believe you can overthrow the army, the police, the politicians – you and a few men with Czech guns which sometimes do not even work?*

One of the men spat. —*The men of power are the lackeys of the Americans.*

—*You gossip like old wives*, said Carlos. *We need gringo money and their skills to develop our country faster. This the politicians have learned. But when we have grown strong, then no one – not Americans, nor Chinese, nor Germans – will control us. What you wish to happen will happen in God's time.*

—*God*, said the second man, as Carlos left the cafe, *is dead. Only the revolution lives.*

The pilot signalled that his passengers could take off their oxygen masks. As the plane lost height, rain hissed against the windows. They came out of cloud and could see the lower slopes of the mountains, green and brown, with fields patchworked between them. David strained to glimpse the slopes of the volcano called Pichincha, near the city. That was where Sucre, who had given his name to the national currency, had beaten the Spanish in 1822. He had been aided by British mercenaries. David liked the idea.

'First time I came in here was in a 707,' said the mud engineer who was hitching a lift. 'We went into the soup and out again and I saw one peak a mile away and another maybe half a mile – and we were lower than them. Then we went into the soup again, and I turned to the guy beside me and I said, "Are you as shit-scared as me", and he said, "Yes – and I'm a goddam pilot!" Jesus!'

The pilot grinned; but as he brought the plane on to its final descent path, with a grey curtain of rain sweeping in over the hills around Quito, he was whistling. He always did that for the tricky bits.

At the airport, everyone was being searched by soldiers

26

in grey uniforms and white steel hats, carbines slung. David was not surprised. He'd already grown used to the idea that the invention of new problems for travellers was a South American industry. He lifted his arms to be patted from shoulder to ankle. The soldiers were slow, neutral, not especially imaginative. It was 20 minutes before he and Carlos rode into the city together, through streets that in places were ankle-deep in streamers of mist. They really had made it only just in time.

3

At the Hotel Quito there was a message from Oldershaw asking David to wait until six. He walked up to his room and found himself a touch out of breath; that was the altitude – 10,000 feet. He stood on the balcony, overlooking the pool. The mist was rolling in from the west in clinging banks. Of Cotopaxi, all 19,000 feet of it, and the other fabled volcanoes, there was no sign. Even the Amazonian parrots in the little zoo beside the pool had stopped screeching.

He was hungry after forfeiting lunch at the oil camp. He took a shower, and the room service waiter – very friendly, always hinting in pidgin about women – brought him a *ceviche* of shrimp and a *tortilla* spiced with crab. David, a fish-lover, thought that the Ecuadoreans must have the best in the world. He even heightened the piquancy of the *ceviche* sauce by adding some of the red-hot *salsa de aji* which came on every tray. Afterwards, he lay on the bed and closed his eyes.

When he awoke it was seven and dark. The mist had vanished. Down at the reception desk they told him that Oldershaw had not yet returned. When the clerk saw the note, he smiled.

'Hora Ecuatoriana, senor?'

David knew the joke. *Hora Americana* meant the appointment would be on time more or less. *Hora Ecuatoriana* – well, whenever your visitor arrived. He was debating whether to ride to the seventh floor and take a drink in the *Techo del Mundo*, overlooking the garlanded lights of the city, when Oldershaw steamed into the lobby trailed by

27

Perez, looking elegant and predatory as ever. The Ecuadorian's profile had not yet become blunted by good living, though Perez had seen plenty of that.

'How goes it?' David asked.

'Christ knows,' said Oldershaw.

David glanced at Perez. The answering look from Prospero's local agent was bland. Perez was not committing himself yet; just like a fixer.

'The Oriente. It's fantastic – yes?' said Perez to David as they waited for the elevator.

'Yes.'

Perez looked smug. Ecuador was on the way up, and that could only be good for Perez; especially if he found more clients as good as the Prospero Group of Great Britain.

'You had a good time, eh?' grunted Oldershaw.

David didn't like the tone. Oldershaw might have had a rough day, but his hadn't been exactly a rest cure.

'It was hot,' said David. 'Around a hundred humid. But they laid on everything. You should fly up there.'

'Some bloody hopes, the way things are going this end,' said Oldershaw sourly. 'It was hot in Guayaquil too. And wet.'

In Oldershaw's bedroom, David said, 'What's up, then?'

Oldershaw sat on his bed and assumed what he imagined to be control of the meeting. He did not like the set-up at all. Nothing personal against David Travis. A nice lad, Travis; straight, quite good at his job, no side to him. But you had to face the fact that Travis was one of the management boys from Prospect House; not like Oldershaw, a toiler in the field. The boy was there, Michael Grant had said, to help Oldershaw – which fooled no one, did it? David Travis wasn't *responsible* to Oldershaw, was he? He was Michael Grant's man. He'd keep a close eye on how well Oldershaw managed things and then tell his boss. What else? What did David Travis know about engineering and the mucky detail of the job which Oldershaw, managing director of Brasserton's in grimy Staffordshire, had to bring off?

It was sometimes no fun at all being boss of a subsidiary in a giant organisation like Prospero. Oh, he knew that without Prospero money – pumped in many years ago by

28

Michael's father, Bernard – the firm of Brasserton's probably wouldn't exist at all. Poised uneasily between controllable smallness and real bigness, desperately needing capital – and an executioner to get rid of Brasserton junior, the incompetent son of the founder – the firm had been in a mess ten years ago. Even if it had kept going alone, it was unlikely that William Oldershaw Esq., J.P., would have ended up its managing director. The theory, often propounded by Bernard Grant in the days when that silver-haired golden-tongued old monster had ruled the roost, was that Prospero provided the finance, the stability and the opportunities while Oldershaw got on with the job of actually running the machine-tool factory. But Christ, they'd had a lot more fun in the old days, sweating in the thirties for what was *theirs*, then picking up real money in the second world war. Today, the reality was that London interfered increasingly, often without knowledge of his local problems. He had fought many times, angrily, and not always discreetly, to keep control in the way he felt control should be exercised.

Who was it who'd caused the only strikes they'd had in the past three years but London, buggering him about over the production computer which some smart alick had said was necessary to increase output? There was that smooth Welsh git of a personnel director, bloody Prosser, who'd come fussing up to the Staffordshire works to interfere. And who had landed Brasserton's in this Ecuador business but Michael Grant?

Oldershaw didn't object to the contract – it was the big league stuff he'd always yearned for – but he would have arranged it differently if he'd had the signing of it. He'd have kept the computer people out of the contract for one thing. Bloody computer men. Slick and know-all. Bloody Quant. He'd bet that Carlos – a sly one, that Carlos – didn't like Quant either.

He knew, couldn't deny it, that they had to have a computer built in to control the plant at Esmeraldas. But why couldn't the Prospero brains have let the computer firm take care of installing the intricate control centre on the site themselves, with Brasserton's simply supplying all the stuff to hook up to the computer according to specification? Instead – the Michael Grant way – Brasserton's were responsible for the whole thing, using the computer company as a sub-contractor.

It was this arrangement which had meant sending out the snotty kid Quant as Brasserton't project manager. Hell, he didn't even *work* for Brasserton's, didn't Quant. He was the nominee of the computer company, a systems expert, and Oldershaw had known he had no real choice over the appointment. In a job as intricate as Brasserton's had taken on, the computer and systems men would have to be kings.

And now Quant wasn't even around when the going was getting sticky. He'd gone off to see their American design people in Michigan about corrections to some valve mechanisms. More trouble.

'What's up, lad,' he said to David, 'is import licences. We've spent all morning arguing with the customs people at the port. I've *seen* our stuff. Just lying in one of the sheds on the quay. They won't let it out.'

'But I thought all that was fixed,' said David. 'We've got our licences.'

'They're splitting hairs,' said Oldershaw. 'The customs say some of our stuff could have been manufactured locally. Some of the castings, for instance. That's not covered by the licences. They're only for special equipment that needs to be made abroad. It's a load of cock. How can you separate the castings from the bloody mechanism of a valve?'

David wasn't sure. He waited for Oldershaw.

'I know what it is. Those buggers haven't had their handout, have they Perez?'

Palindo Juan Perez Armand examined his manicured fingernails and spread his hands. The gesture indicated both pacification and the slightest hint of distaste. This man Oldershaw was very crude.

'It is a matter which can be arranged,' he said.

'Why wasn't it arranged before?' said Oldershaw. 'We've paid away a small fortune already. How many more bums are we expected to grease with butter?'

Perez winced. 'Mr Oldershaw – William. We must make *correct* arrangements. Where in the world do you not have to pay for service, for the favour of those with whom you deal? The principle is the same, only the means or the people are different. In your country, if there is a strike, you pay your unions for their favour in a way which I would think excessive. In this country, we send in tanks or troops or police and get things moving again. We do not pay the unions as much as you, but it is the custom that service is ensured in other ways. It is the *custom*, you understand. Everyone accepts it.'

Oldershaw was, David had to admit, being rather obtuse. Obnoxious, too.

'We've got to be realistic, Bill,' he said. 'But Palindo' – he chose the forename deliberately – 'I still don't understand why we get trouble now. I thought the Minister had made all the arrangements.'

Perez rose from the cramped cane chair, stretching his long and exquisitely tailored legs. He was tall for a Spaniard, around six foot, with a sharp nose, curly black hair and a waist thin as a toreador's. He liked the comparison to be made, especially when El Cordobes came to town each year on his annual tour of the ex-colonies. He danced, smoothly and dramatically, as a bullfighter might. He loved to walk around with no jacket on, particularly when there were women present, so that the tightness of his waist and the smallness of his behind – and even the hint of genitals – could be appreciated. It was something of a waste, therefore, that he had no jacket on now, with only two Englishmen for audience. But he went through the motions just the same: useful practice.

'The Minister, my uncle, has great power,' he said. 'He signed the contract with the consortium. He has a vision for my country. But he is not God. He has enemies, those who do not believe that his arrangements for the plant are the best ones. There were, you will remember, the Japanese.'

'Bloody Nips,' said Oldershaw, who had never forgotten that his brother died building the Burma railroad in 1943.

Perez did not hear him. 'So some men would wish to see my uncle fail or, at least, be discomfited. The Japanese still have hopes.'

'The Minister does not have the loyalty of the customs at Guayaquil,' said David. 'Is that it?'

'I made the arrangements personally,' said Perez. 'But the situation has changed. It happens.'

'Is that why the Cabinet has been meeting?' David asked.

Perez smiled his appreciation. David Travis understood these matters; an intelligent man, one with whom he could establish a relationship. This weekend, if things allowed, he would like to eat privately with David, tell the Englishman about his hopes and ambitions. Perhaps the Englishman would appreciate an hour or two at the Unicorné or Maxy's with a girl. That was easy, girls. Just for the discotheque, or afterwards if required. And often, unusually for the country, their mothers did not come too.

It was a good life, to be handsome and relatively well-connected. He had enough first cousins in Quito to make his entry into the world of business relatively painless, even if he would need to wait before he could make it into politics. He had, however, the example of his uncle, Dr Jesus Cantania, the Minister, to guide him. Before he had turned politician, Cantania had found it necessary to be a successful businessman too, as befitted a native of Guayaquil, which had overwhelmingly been *the* city of commerce in Ecuador before the oil oligarchs set up their headquarters in Quito. Perez dreamed that one day he – Perez, not his uncle – might be President, the most handsome president in South America, not like those granite-faced generals or feeble academic revolutionaries who so often ascended to power. Meantime, however, he would watch his uncle like a humble disciple, seeking always to learn.

'There are many rumours about,' he said. 'The one which is true is that a group of officers at the military college believe the regime is too *maleable*. Too soft, too easy. They also believe that my uncle has too much power – but that is envy.'

'Christ,' said David. 'Will he go?'

'No, no.' Perez was laughing. 'The officers have only themselves and, perhaps, a few hundred paratroops. No tanks, no armoured cars, nothing. The army is loyal. So too is the air force. They have been discovered in time. Seven of them are in gaol.'

'And the Cabinet?' said David.

'Powers may be rearranged a little. My uncle may have to concede something – as a gesture, you understand. It is not wise in this country to have too much the iron fist.' Perez smiled.

David said: 'Assuming that's what happens, then how much?'

'How much?' murmured Perez, enjoying his feigned puzzlement.

'How much more money will we have to spread around?'

'I will need, perhaps, another fifty thousand. Dollars – American dollars. Maybe more.'

'Bloody hell,' said Oldershaw. 'Do these people want a petro-chemical plant or don't they?'

David gave him the beady eye. It was not a lot of money, in relation to the size of the contract. If Oldershaw wasn't careful, he'd offend Perez so much that the price might go up.

'Your company will make a profit, will it not?' Perez said coldly.

'The way costs are going, I doubt it,' said Oldershaw.

'Come on, Bill,' said David sharply, 'we'll have to ask London, anyway.'

'It's *my* contract,' said Oldershaw. 'I'll be held responsible.'

David felt the need to soothe him. 'Let London take the decision, Bill. It's their can, not yours. You're here to make sure the technical side goes smoothly.'

'I don't do business that way,' snapped Oldershaw.

'This once, you'll have to.' David's words were equally crisp and much more final. He stood up, decisively. 'I'll need to send a cable, Palindo.'

Oldershaw rolled over sulkily on the bed. Perez smoothed the trousers over his hips. He admired the way David had played the end of the scene.

'Let me advise you. Wait at least 24 hours before sending your cable. Then we will know more certainly. It is now the weekend, anyway, and surely even your company will not work tomorrow. Let us go and change and then we will eat dinner.'

When David went down to the main lobby half an hour later with Oldershaw, who was still grumbling, they saw that there were two soldiers standing at the entrance. This was new, although the sight of soldiers at doors by night in Quito was not out of the ordinary. A number of private office buildings, Perez's among them, had such guards.

'Have you seen Del Martin about all this?' asked David as they waited for Perez. 'Maybe he can help.'

Delano Theodore Martin, project manager for the con-

33

sortium building the plant, whom Brasserton's and all the other partners would ultimately need to satisfy about their work, would certainly have to hear about what was going on.

'No,' said Oldershaw crossly. 'He's another one who's never around when he's needed.'

David judged the remark to be unfair, but let it pass. He would get Perez quietly to put him in touch with Martin over the weekend. Martin, a Chicagoan, placed in the job by Ed Corsino and the American organisers of the consortium, was a man to have on your side. Besides, David already liked him. A realist was Martin, as David believed himself to be. A vast man, gingerhaired, giving a feeling of physical and mental command, but with a lurking sense of tough humour. When he laughed, sparingly but with conviction, the dime-sized strawberry mark below his left eye disappeared into the lined flesh of the upper cheek. It made Martin easy to remember.

Perez was only a few minutes late, but immediately excused himself to go and talk with three men who were loitering gloomily with martinis, behind palm leaves, in a corner of the marble-floored lobby. He spoke with them for five minutes, with much gesturing of hands and body.

Finally, he strutted back to them. 'Fine,' he said, as if he'd just put a few thousands more into his Panamanian account, which was one of several he had overseas. 'Now we can eat. Excuse me for my neglect, but they are worried too.' He lowered his voice. 'They are also English, from one of your biggest marine construction companies. They hope to build fast launches, perhaps even some frigates for our navy.'

'What are they worried about then?' said Oldershaw with wasted sarcasm.

'The situation,' said Perez. He offered them the confidential tombstone smile of a salesman. 'I have, however, reassured them.'

David looked back as they walked towards the doors. One of the men was chewing hard on a cocktail stick, the mid-twentieth century's substitute for fingernails. He had seen it all before in foreign bars: men washing their ulcers in gin and vermouth for hours on end wondering whether, when the tanks were back in barracks again, there would be a new set of faces behind the desks and a new list of pay-aways to be made.

4

Dr Jesus Enrique Cantania Garcia did not look like a man who had just saved his neck. He sat smiling and immaculate behind a heavy mahogany desk in a room oppressed by dark and ancient furniture, musty with the odour of history's injustice. Only his long pale fingers, teasing the edge of a whisky glass, betrayed any residue of anxiety after the two days and nights during which he had scarcely slept and had never been completely sure the orders he gave to the soldiers outside the room would be obeyed.

'There is absolutely no danger to your enterprise, Mr Martin,' he announced. 'You have my word.'

Del Martin squared his muscular shoulders, pushed a hand through stubbly ginger hair, and considered how much value he could place on the word of a South American politician who had, he reckoned, just managed to pull out a shaky flush against an opponent's high straight. Years of dealing with foreign politicians, first in his country's diplomatic service, then in a succession of commercial contracts from Malaysia to Morocco, had made him wary. But he was no defeatist. Because he could weigh the balance of power in a situation like this keenly, the jobs which Martin took on usually took off.

'The President is secure now?' he said.

'Certainly,' said the Minister, and Martin believed he knew why.

'I suppose there will be some new appointments,' he said.

'Will you have more whisky, Mr Martin?' said the Minister. Without waiting for an answer, he rose and un-stoppered a square-cut glass decanter which had been carried across the Atlantic from Venice more than two centuries earlier.

He was a tall man, like his nephew, well-dressed in smooth grey, with hair that had become silver before he was 40. He liked dark rooms, which were kind to the marks on his left cheek, where hoodlums in Miami had once smashed his face as they robbed him. He liked quiet rooms too. Silence grew in this one like fungus, nurtured by the five-foot-thick walls which encased it. The Spaniards had built it to be a fortress, 400 years ago. Outside, its grey walls were smooth deterrent cliffs, sweeping down to a street in the old town. There were no indentations into which Indians might slot themselves to sleep like bundles of black rage at night, and the soldiers who stood on guard discouraged people from walking nearby. Even if sounds could have found a way around the walls, there were no *cantinas* to spew out music within a wide radius of the place.

Martin pressed his question – 'The new appointments, Minister?' – and Cantania did not really object. Habit made him sidestep direct questions on subjects which grieved him, but he would not dissemble with Martin; besides, he wanted the petro-chemical plant as avidly as Martin did. He had done the deal. It would have to succeed.

'I'm afraid that Colonel de Vargas will be one of them,' he said. 'It was inevitable.'

'I understand.' Martin gave no gleam of concern to Cantania, but his stomach shrivelled. Colonel Antonio Hernan de Vargas was right-wing and hard, no friend of the more liberal Cantania, and no friend of the consortium either. Martin didn't know whether the Colonel's enmity was simply pique that he hadn't been cut into the deal on the plant, or a result of his frequently professed belief that his country should spend the huge oil royalties in future on strengthening its armed forces against incipient revolution rather than on turning out textiles and fertilisers to make the lower orders more uppity. To have him in the cabinet again could be awkward.

'The Colonel,' he said. 'What position will he hold?'

Cantania laughed derisively. 'What will that matter? He will meddle with our soldiers, whatever post he is given. For what else has he been trained? These army politicians.' Cantania represented himself in this continent of soldiers as a professional civilian.

'Will he be in the Cabinet?'

'No. He will be *asesor*.' Again, Cantania snorted. Martin knew about *asesors*: their positions might be nebulous, but their power was not. A bit like ministers without portfolio, yet stronger, paradoxically, because they were *not* ministers.

Asesors had muscle enough to move and manipulate ministers. They were elusive, difficult to combat.

Martin asked: 'Will he – will he be able to . . .?'

Cantania slammed a fist on the desk. 'No, Mr Martin, he will not be able to stop us. He will try. We will, perhaps, have to make certain new arrangements. But trust me.'

'It will be more expensive.'

'A little.'

'How much?'

Cantania shrugged. 'Who can say? But you will build the plant, Mr Martin, and I will protect you. Your people now have too much to lose, and I – I will do it because I too am committed, and because I have faith.' He looked up at a picture of the President with an expression which Martin had seen elsewhere; the yearning public face of a politician who had translated dreams into blueprints and wishes his audience to appreciate his devotion without being too specific. Martin knew it was the best insurance he would get that night.

'Your nephew has had trouble at Guayaquil,' he said, but the Minister might not have heard him.

'Ecuador needs what you have to offer, Mr Martin. Capital, knowledge, knowhow.' He was proud of his English. 'And you need us. Your people dare not throw this continent away. We are natural partners, and those who believe that either revolution or sabre-rattling against our neighbours will achieve anything are morons. So let us drink to that.'

Martin left by a discreet door leading into a forgotten alley. He thanked God he had someone as relatively straight as Cantania to deal with. He almost liked the Minister – certainly liked the Minister's kids, whom he'd met once on a visit to the family *hacienda*. That was as far as the hard-gut realism in Martin's make-up would let him go. He thought of his own kids, the boy 13 and already a growth-prospect quarterback, the girl six years younger, still clinging to a doll as a totem of the father she too rarely saw and the mother who had died when she was scarcely out of diapers. Back in the States, both of them, getting their education. Martin looked forward to his leave, four long months away. Must give them the chance to make out better than I did. All that Martin's father had given his son was the names of the two Roosevelts and twelve years of blows and bullying before a Packard mowed him down near the *Tribune* Tower where he, drunk, had wandered wildly off the sidewalk. Why had Diana died? Martin missed her. Still, after five years.

Outside his apartment, a soldier stood on guard.

'*Buenas noches, senor.*'

Martin answered in Spanish. The soldier had an Indian face. There was a time, long ago, when Martin had almost become a soldier too, because that had seemed one of the few ways out of the West-side Chicago slum in which he had been condemned to live. Just like the Indian's motive, he suspected. But Martin had stuck it out, made college, even made the diplomatic service despite (maybe because of) his engineer's degree. He had quickly tired of the ineffectual yak-yak of that world. *New York Times liberals*. It was a favourite expression of his. How would their kind of talk on the cocktail circuit ever help an Indian get more maize in his belly? You needed to work to get the factories moving, the wealth created. Let the corporations make their profits, maybe, but a lot of it rubbed off on the peoples who helped provide the profits, didn't it? And you had to grow a tougher hide to take the fixers, the politicians, the gangsters who, in societies like this, were inescapably part of the machinery. Swallow the system, then digest it.

Martin was too tired to argue further with himself. He stood, rubbing the back of his neck, a seamed neck that looked like it had seen a lot of sun, a maze of pale riverbeds in the skin. Then he threw off his clothes and slept.

5

At about the same time, Derek Quant was wide awake. He sat in a room at the Dearborn Inn, close to Detroit, talking to England on the telephone.

'Sure, they can correct the design of the valves. No problem. But what the hell were Oldershaw's people doing when they agreed the specifications? That man's a pain in the ass.'

'When is he coming back to London?' said the voice from England, but in American not British intonation.

'Next week, I hope. He just gets in the way out here.'

'How?'

'Come on – you know him. He's no dealer. He's ruining relationships it's taken me months to build up.'

'I'll try to get him out of your hair.'

'Thanks.'

'And Travis?'

Quant leaned back on the bed, smiling the expert's smile of superiority. 'Useful. Distinctly useful. But he'll be able to tell Michael Grant far less than I tell you. Watch him, though. He's a very devoted young man.'

The fact that David was a year older was irrelevant to Quant. Quant was sharp, technically highly proficient, cocooned in the faith of his own intellectual superiority. He was the kind of man who had asked for a briefcase on his 11th birthday when other kids were demanding footballs, had worn his first pinstripe suit at 13, and was middle-aged at 15. He believed he was destined to be a commander, but not necessarily a leader. He had carved out for himself the area in life which he wished to control, an area of particular scientific and commercial expertise, now concentrated on the application of computers and computer systems. It would, he judged, keep him in material comfort for the rest of his life and enable him to destroy with confidence the credibility of any competitor who questioned his decisions. Beyond this, he had no ambition. David Travis he regarded as his inferior, his junior and no threat at all.

'How goes it for Cantania?' asked London.

Quant paused. 'When I left, dicey. But I think he'll pull through.'

'Are you saying Cantania could lose power?'

'Not necessarily. But we may need to have the help of people other than him. The Army, for instance.'

'I want to know it all, understand?'

Quant told the man in London all, or nearly all, about the latest political situation, part of which he, of course, did not yet know.

'Look, my plane leaves in two hours, I'd better go.'

'Hold it a minute. The labour set-up. What about that?'

'No better and no worse than I expected. We've a good man at the site. Carlos, he's called. He's prickly. Doesn't like me. But he does as he's told, thank God.'

'Stay in touch.'

'Of course. Goodbye.'

In London, the man who had been speaking rose and went to his apartment window to lap up the Sunday morning sunshine which carpeted Hyde Park seven floors below. The cat, black and over-plump, was curled in the window, enjoying the sunshine too. He bent and stroked the animal, which he'd found in the hallway below one night, wet and bruised and apparently lost. Sometimes he felt guilty about not being able to let it out to roam the park.

He sipped a glass of water, then wiped the moustache that curved down on either side of his mouth almost to the tip of his chin. It was a startling moustache for, without aid of cosmetics, it was deepest brown, whereas the hair on his head was frizzily crew-cut and blond. Jet black hornrims emphasised the surprising contrasts.

He pondered Ecuador. Messy. Damn right. Still and all, he could at least congratulate himself on having Quant as his fount of inside information.

6

Carlos knelt in the church of La Compania, speculating whether he could possibly expect forgiveness when he knew that soon he would undoubtedly commit further sins. But habit dies hard. It was here that he always came before he began a weekend in the capital, feeling the duty of honouring his mother, caring for her soul, and also believing he was somehow atoning for past sins, whatever might happen after he left the building.

He opened his eyes. He knew every carved figure on the painted pulpit – cherubs with puffed stomachs and chests; cherubs praying or waving or just looking; cherubs with no arms or with two heads, and one of two bent double like men in agony on the rack. He looked beyond to the high altar, framed in a scene maybe 15 metres high and 10 wide – the Father, the Son and the Virgin gigantically created in a riot of gold, much of it solid gold, whose glitter could burn your soul when the lights inside the church were switched on.

And that was only the beginning of it. The whole church

was a tangle of gold leaf and columns gorgeously painted in gilded gnarls and twists. There were ten chapels, all with altars plated in gold. Carlos thought about the further treasure stored in bank vaults and brought out only for special festivals: the painting of the Virgin Dolorosa framed in emeralds and gold, said to be worth eleven million American dollars.

There were those who called this the most magnificent church in the world, its eighth wonder. Carlos came here, he knew, not only because it had been his mother's church, but because he wished to be near the touch and the sight of gold. It represented an aspiration of self, such treasure, as well as honour to God. He suspected that this feeling of his also constituted a sin.

Ill at ease, he rose. An Indian woman, wizened, with shawl and hat and straggling black pigtails, was weeping quietly as she knelt to his left. It reminded him, uncomfortably, of his mother. Sometimes, when he saw such sights, he was forced to question whether his own belief in gradualism was right. Such treasure; so much misery. He thought again of the two men, ever more insistent, back in Esmeraldas. They had some arguments in their favour, he conceded. But he distrusted the guerrilla philosophy. He did not see how the killing of ambassadors or businessmen from foreign lands could lead to greater justice.

Walking towards the doors, he became aware of the sounds of the world, automobiles and street cries, which penetrated even this sanctum. He paused before the glowing red painting of Hell which reared up as a final ghastly reminder to departing congregations. The creatures in the painting were being tortured with spiked wheels and the forks of demons. There were men with daggers through their heads and bodies, men entwined by gigantic snakes, men being bitten by dragons. There were women with unspeakably loathsome insects crawling on them, women being boiled and beaten simultaneously, women sprayed with fire from the mouths of demons and forced to drink burning liquid through funnels. The names of the seven deadly sins, adultery and the rest, were written at various points.

It had several times been pointed out to Carlos that the torturers looked like Spaniards and the tortured like Indians. Not that he needed history lessons. He knew that four centuries ago it had not been uncommon for Indian tribal elders found guilty of heresy to be condemned to have their limbs torn off by unbroken colts. Doubtless the bishop who gave the Catholic order prayed for their souls.

Outside he felt better, leaving the grey sculpted facade and the fat woman selling mementos behind him. Soon it would be dark. Walking the cracked pavements towards the Plaza de la Independencia, he passed several Indians, squatting to cook food for sale over small fires. The sight and the smells tugged him back towards his childhood. Irrationally, he stopped to buy some *chiflés*, thinly-sliced crisps of plantain. Then, knowing that his stomach might now reject such dubiously hygienic objects, he threw them away. He passed through several narrow streets, along which Indians silently carried boxes against their chests and babies on their backs, before he turned into a house with cracked white walls and closed shutters.

The woman was waiting for him, as always on these occasions. It was a comfortable place, with soft seats covered in brightly coloured blankets from the Indian weavers in the villages and carpets just as rich and garish on the stone floor. Because the nights could turn cold at this time of year, wood was already burning in the open hearth.

She had prepared him dishes mainly of fish: *sopa de almejas*, the liquid plump with juicy clams, and *calamares a la gaditana*, with *humitas* made of sweet maize and a variety of nuts and seeds on the side. They drank Chilean wine.

She was, like him, *mestizo*, but in her the Indian strain predominated. Her face was very round with a flattish nose, eyes wide and brown in many shades to their depths, and her body was ripe. In another few years it would begin to run to fat, but now her full breasts still sat high and undrooping. Not a startlingly beautiful woman, but obedient and sensuous and with one characteristic which never ceased to astonish him. When finally she led Carlos into the bedroom, he pulled the loose white blouse down over her shoulders and looked at the surface of her almost wondrously.

Her breasts shone, as if she sweated, but they were dry to the touch, the nipples stiff but not large, with the aureoles spreading huge across the soft skin like purple wine-stains. The rest of her body was equally unblemished: a smooth

42

glowing surface, with swelling hips which were firm beneath his fingers and thighs unusually long for one of her blood. This skin, silken and shining, captivated him.

They made love without haste, without pain. Stroking her broad and slightly protuberant belly, savouring its texture, Carlos found himself thinking about the painting in La Compania, contemplating pain. He knew that Europeans and North Americans, to judge from their literature and their talk, often added the element of pain to their love-making. How could anyone insult a body as perfect as this by bruising it or striking it? To Carlos it was almost blasphemous. She gave him pleasure with hands and lips, gently, and after he had entered her and their various climaxes were attained, he was surprised to find – for the first time in his experience – that she was crying.

He awoke to silence and darkness, reaching out for her and finding nothing. He sat up and called her, received no answer and, walking naked, his eyes adjusting to the dim light, could not find her in any of the rooms. His watch said 2.30 and he perched on the bed, drawing, puzzled, on a cigarette, before he rose and pulled on his trousers. He was thinking of going out into the street when he heard a faint noise of whispering beyond the outer door. Instinctively he sought the protection of a corner, away from the door.

Two men whom he had never seen before entered. Menace, like a shroud, moved with them. He was afraid.

Carlos waited until they were very close to the bedroom door and then, flinging his body forward, he wrenched the outer door open and leapt down towards the street. He heard a shout from both men and their footsteps pursuing him.

It is not easy to run in many of the back alleys or, indeed, some of the main streets of Quito. The surface of roadways and sidewalks is often holed and splintered, and repair after the heavy rains of March and April takes time. Even to walk requires care. So Carlos lurched and scrambled as he ran barefooted, sometimes sliding on vegetable refuse, his frightened eyes looking for someone who might help.

Where were the police, the soldiers? Usually you could scarcely turn a corner without bumping into them, stepping out of trucks, directing traffic from little platforms, or simply standing with that curious dead-eyed air of possessiveness which lawmen exude everywhere in the world. Where were they?

Carlos blundered round four corners without meeting anyone, twisting indiscriminately, trying to lose his pursuers. He swung into a wider street, where a market had been held during the day. There were skeletons of stalls, squelching leaves and skins underfoot, a dog sniffing. He had no precise idea where he was, but knew that the Plaza de San Francisco could not be far. At the end of the street, half-hidden, he glimpsed blazing light from a kiosk. Thankfully, he dragged his aching legs and bleeding feet towards it. Lights meant people, probably a *cantina* or a food store. Safety.

Long before he reached the kiosk, he knew he was mistaken. It was circular, an island unto itself, a harsh pool of light, locked and empty of people, stuffed with flowers of all kinds – but especially white arum lilies – price-tagged for the faithful who could afford to take them to church over the weekend. Carlos leaned against the glass, heaving, straining for the sounds of pursuit. He could detect none. Then he began to trot down yet another slit of a street, but he had not gone far when he saw a blank wall rearing before him. The street was a dead end.

He had no breath even to curse. Suddenly aware of the blood on his feet he turned and there, plain in the glaring light of the kiosk, were the two men. As they began to walk towards him, he could see with awful clearness the machetes they held in front of them.

2. HAPPY FAMILIES

1

'WHY was he killed?' said Alison Grant.

'God knows. Lots of theories. But no real answers,' said Michael Grant.

'What does David Travis think?'

'Political reasons. There's talk he was mixed up with some kind of revolutionary party.'

'But you don't think so. What then?'

He shrugged. 'I'm inclined to look for simpler reasons. Like money.'

It was natural that Michael should think that. He had fought hard to keep down the so-called commissions on the deal. Too hard, perhaps. Michael accepted the need for bribery, but did not like it. So he had been mean. He had, for the past 24 hours, been trying to repress the suspicion that Carlos might have died because particular palms had not been greased.

'How do you mean – money?' asked Alison.

'Perhaps he was trying to keep too much for himself.' Michael realised he was not being honest with himself. 'Maybe David's right. It's damn sticky out there. Our man had a hard job of it to survive, I think.'

'The Minister?'

'Yes – Cantania. The man called Jesus.' They both smiled quickly, in reflex. It was their joke from a year ago, when the Ecuador business was getting under way. 'There's a new man. a colonel. He's on Cantania's back now. So it might be a political murder after all. Or guerrillas.'

'But you said there weren't any guerrillas.'

'That's what Cantania claims. Maybe he's wrong. They can't keep them out for ever.'

'Do you wish we weren't mixed up with Ecuador at all?'

Not even to Alison could he give a simple answer. The

deal had seemed exactly the right one through which Michael might symbolise, a year or more ago, that the future of the Prospero Group and the multifarious businesses it controled was going to be different. He suspected it had finally swung Lord Bender on to his side in the dispute with his father for control of Prospero.

First, Ecuador was a big operation, big enough to transform Brasserton's from medium-size into major engineering company, and be seen as a model for similar Prospero minnows.

Second, it was international business, and it was Michael's belief that his father had been too insular in his approach as Prospero had expanded. It was understandable, of course. Five years in a concentration camp, which had been his father's experience during that distant war of 1939, makes a man suspicious of strangers, clinging to the country he can trust. For Bernard Grant, Hungarian émigré, Britain had become refuge, cause and factory, sufficient to itself and to him.

Third, it was business which had been somewhat too revolutionary for the conservatives on the Prospero board – Harold Armfield, the finance man, and time-servers like the late Sir Giles Lymington. His father had opposed him too, although that was more a matter of emotional inevitability than of rational business conviction. Bernard had seemed unwilling to accept that Michael could yet have acquired the capacity to dominate a business as big as Prospero.

Ecuador had indeed been the perfect issue for Michael to throw at Bender as proof that the new generation's vision, imagination and expertise were what was needed for prosperity in the decade to come.

Michael's victory had not been easy. It had taken a year of persuasion to convince Bender, sitting there so quiet and withdrawn, with all those pounds from his insurance company and pension funds to invest where he chose, that Bernard was failing both in skill and sheer physical stamina. His father's coronary had provided the first element of doubt; Michael's own energy and flair and (he had to admit to himself, not with particular pride) marginal conspiracies had completed the equation. With Bender leaning on Bernard to concede, it had been inevitable that son should succeed father as Prospero's chief executive. And, ironically, part of his troublesome inheritance was the Ecuador consortium, that tripartite and sometimes creaking alliance of American, French and British companies.

Leading it was Kerridge, the aged American steel magnate and industrialist. Kerridge's project management and design company had drawn up the master-plan. And it was Kerridge's steel mills that would turn out the pipe and plate and rod and bar metal which would, in turn, be fed to a myriad of smaller companies to transmute into tanks, vessels, columns, heat exchangers, nuts, bolts, flanges, structures and all the rest of the jigsaw of fittings which go into a petrochemical plant.

Not that Michael had ever met Kerridge. The whole arrangement had been set up by Ed Corsino. And how, precisely, could he describe Corsino? Fixer? Export-import man? Speculator? Wheeler-dealer? Corsino was all of these things. Above all, he had the knack of being able to make *arrangements* – God knows how, half the time. He was tough, heavy, fast-talking and, to Michael, fascinating. Michael had assiduously courted him since first meeting him at the Watkins Glen circuit eight years ago, in the days when the younger Grant was learning about the American way of business and racing sports cars at weekends for both kicks and cash. Corsino would do him a turn one day, Michael had decided, and he had been right.

Whoever it was, then – Kerridge or Corsino – there was over thirty million pounds of American money involved in the deal covering design and management fees and steel supplies alone, not counting the many millions more which it would take to erect this agglomeration of space-age artefacts, and the various financial guarantees which Kerridge Steel had made to get the whole deal off the ground. To Kerridge, also, were responsible the many sub-contractors who would make the machinery for the plant, its pumps and compressors.

The second partner, SAEF (Société d'Automation Electrique de France), was French and in Michael's view, foxy. This company, Paris-based, was responsible for the electrics. Corsino and Michael, searching for partners, might have chosen ASEA of Sweden, Siemens of Germany, GEC of Britain, or Brown-Boveri of Switzerland. But in the end a variety of considerations — including having a Common Market partner – had led to SAEF.

Although the making of around twelve million pounds worth of electric motors, starters, transformers, distributors and turbines had long since began, SAEF were forever spewing out problems. They kept questioning the precise meaning of various parts of the official contract between the consortium members, which was in English, and sometimes read ambiguously when it was turned into French. They pleaded difficulties with their bankers. They slowed down the whole operation. It left Michael queasy in the business stomach.

Finally there was Brasserton's, who would create the systems mechanisms to ensure the smooth operation of the whole plant, a so-called process control system stuffed with thousands of instruments and valves, computer-controlled. Not that Brasserton's knew much about computers. But it had seemed neater, and more ambitious, for them to produce the process control complete, using the computer company as a sub-contractor. It was this partnership which had shot Brasserton's share of the consortium business above the £15 million mark, making them bigger partners than SAEF.

Michael had at first enjoyed the feeling of triumph which the contract induced, though now he wasn't sure he wanted to bear so much responsibility in a new and untried field for Prospero. He was forced to acknowledge privately that the going had been tougher than he had ever imagined it would be. To draw clever organisation charts on paper did not reveal, for instance, that Bill Oldershaw at Brasserton's would hate on sight the guts of everyone in the computer company and loathe, even more intensely, the idea that the computer people would need to provide the project manager in charge of installing the process control out in Ecuador.

The vendetta which had grown up between Oldershaw and Derek Quant had added hours and, for some, ulcers to every stage of the job. There were problems of greater magnitude to worry him, but his dilemma over Oldershaw was typical of the whole situation. To change Quant, Michael admitted, would not remove the root-cause of Oldershaw's displeasure, which was the feeling that the computer company was overlording Brasserton's. They were, too, in a way. The computer boys had it made. They were on a straight-payment deal from Brasserton's for the machinery and the expertise they provided. No wonder Quant and his companions had a kind of sod-you attitude in their relations with Brasserton's, snug in their cocoon of technological superiority. There wasn't a thing Michael could do about it.

His wife still awaited his answer. Did he wish he was out of Ecuador? How could he, when it was the justification of so much he had done; cause and effect of his ascent at Prospero? And yet it was a bloody mess, undoubtedly, getting bloodier by the week.

Their conversation remained dead as he toyed with his last fragment of toast and she sipped coffee. They sat in April sun, mounted on a slightly raised alcove, looking out through a wide plate-glass window across the Thames. To their right, the commuter traffic was pounding in across Battersea Bridge from the south bank. Michael wanted to be off too; but if for this reason these morning conversations tended to be staccato, they were nevertheless important.

Alison understood his language, spoken or tacit, and he found it impossible to envisage being married to a woman who didn't. So these morning sessions had become as essential as confession to a believer: a compound of humiliation and comfort. Besides, Alison offered an intelligent comprehension of his subject-matter in a way that priests sometimes could not give to the preoccupations of those whose confessions they heard.

He was grateful to her and, if he had not distrusted the expression, would have said he was in love with her, body and mind. Love seemed an insubstantial, devalued word for what they had.

'Come on, Michael,' said Alison. 'Do you wish you'd never heard of Ecuador?' The only way, he decided, was to play it for laughs.

'Sometimes, yes,' he said, acting out a subdued smile. 'But don't tell Sanger – or Bernard.'

It was the first time they had mentioned the name of Earl Sanger that morning, but normally it was dropped more than any other except, perhaps, for Bernard Grant's and Lord Bender's. If Michael didn't bring it up, Alison did. Her dislike of the American director on the Prospero board had by now become pathological. He was Michael's enemy and, automatically, her own.

'Can Sanger use this to get at you?' she asked.

'He'll find a way'.

'But he was in on the deal. I remember . . .'

'Early on, yes. He persuaded Kerridge to join in. He was my messenger boy, and Ed Corsino's. But I did the final stages. Sanger will say I didn't fix the right price, didn't get enough safeguards. It's not difficult to dream up a case when it isn't your name on the contract.'

'But he can't blame you because a man gets killed.'

'He can. He'll say it was because we bungled the bribes.' Michael couldn't resist referring to his own feelings of guilt. 'Besides, there are other things.'

'Yes?'

'We're having to pay out twenty or thirty thousand pounds extra to fix the customs at Guayaquil. And that's probably just for starters. Oh, yes – he can have a field day if he wants to.'

She pushed at heavily-arched eyebrows with long fingers, her elbows on the table: it was her sign of unease. 'Do you regret Sanger as well as Ecuador?'

'Taking him on, you mean?'

'Yes.'

'We all make mistakes,' he said, but then let her see he knew this was a too-flippant answer. 'No, maybe it's still right that I needed him. I'm not sure.'

That was the truth, too. In the last days of his father's reign as chief executive of Prospero, he had needed shovers and scrappers. So Sanger had come, a short-haired American of the kill-or-cure persuasion, one-time classmate of Michael's at Harvard Business School: a man who knew how to reach objectives and wasn't too particular about how he reached them. A conniver, a plotter, a lover of espionage almost for its own sake. Bernard had been toppled, moved to the indeterminate eminence of chairmanship of the organisation, and Michael had climbed into the executive driving seat.

He had been surprised that, once he had won his victory, Bernard and he had become closer, seeking now to protect each other against possible threats from outside the family. He was, too, not even sure it had been a victory. The awareness of the ambitious Sanger at his shoulder had turned victory into a sort of desperate melancholy.

'Sanger,' she said, 'is a bastard. Be careful, Michael.'

'I'm working on it,' he said, not wanting even Alison to see how much it concerned him. No one on the Prospero board of directors liked Sanger very much. But liking has only a certain amount to do with why business alliances are formed. While Sanger was necessary to them, while Sanger kept bringing in the profits, it was unlikely that Michael could persuade the other directors to push the American off the board. He would have to live with it.

'How's the car doing?' she said. That was typical, too. She knew when to change the subject, and he was grateful.

'Fine. A month before it leaves for France again. I'm going down to Hampshire to see it next week.'

'Will it win?'

It was a naive question, but he was tender in response. 'If it's placed in the first five in its class I'll be happy, but I'll have to keep pushing old man Lovelace. Christ, he's stubborn.'

He looked at his watch, performed the usual pantomime of haste as he finished his coffee, and then walked round behind her. Leaning over, he kissed the copper hair that lay straight and thick on her scalp, placing both hands on her exceptionally full breasts. The hair smelt like hair, as hair should, neither scented nor lacquered. And her body, beginning to grow heavy with child, had the slightly lazy warmth and softness of early morning.

'Good luck with the board,' she said. 'Give my love to Bernard.'

When he had gone, she stood up, looking down through the window for the sight of him in the courtyard below. She was tall, with several features not special, but gratifying enough when added together to have encouraged men to desire her in marriage or for purposes less comprehensive during her twenty-nine years. A select few had succeeded in the latter – including, very briefly, David Travis.

Apart from the copper hair, there were her eyes, very wide and unusually blue-green. Even had she not been several months pregnant, her shape would have been, by fashionable standards, generous: not deserving to be called plump, but with breasts and hips pleasantly full. This morning she wore a loose-fitting top and trousers whose slim-fitting legs emphasised how long were her thighs. She had

51

been a beneficiary of mini-skirts when they were the fashion, as of everything which either revealed or pretended to hide her upper limbs.

Only one feature marred her looks: a thin white scar line which stretched from the edge of her right eye downwards towards the lobe of the ear. She fingered it now, a habit she had still not managed to break over the past year. It gave her face character without ugliness, though she did not think of it in that way. Few people who have such marks realise the advantages.

She watched Michael below, walking to the car. She worried a little, as only those who have experienced serious automobile accidents worry. It was the crash which had left her scarred, the one mark of several dozen which the surgeon had thought it inadvisable to try to erase. Until that moment, late at night on the Guildford by-pass, when a stray lunatic had driven without ceremony into the Jensen's near side – not Michael's fault in any way – no one had known of their relationship.

She still grimaced at the irony that this had been their first meeting which wasn't business. As a public relations girl in Prospero she had been useful to him – a sort of office sneak, not to put too fine a point upon it. Finally, on the brink of becoming chief executive, he had invited her out. Would he have married her if it hadn't been for the crash? She thought it might have moved that way, but she would never know for certain.

About her attitudes now, however, there was no prevarication. Until she married Michael she had been that species of intelligent girl which the contemporary world breeds so often: a girl who sidesteps marriage because the institution has become so suspect, yet does not really know why she is keeping her options open. To build a career? To live with many partners, simultaneously or in succession? To maintain flexibility in the pursuit of happiness, whatever that might turn out to be?

Alison had persuaded herself of all such motives, and many more, at various times. But she had also been driven by ambition: an ambition, however, of an idiosyncratic kind. Her ambition was to be needed; needed in a job, needed and admired by men – but only those men whom she herself coveted. In the end, that too had proved no basis for a plan of action, for she consistently failed to decide what or whom exactly she coveted. Realising this clearly, understanding how her lack of clarity led her ultimately to take the paths of least resistance in relations both private and public, she had been more grateful to Michael Grant than even he would know. His suggestion of marriage had enabled her both to exercise her power of short-term decision and thus to give her life a kind of settled long-term prospect.

She was herself surprised how this had changed her. To Michael she had become committed with a fierceness which was almost unnatural. It was not difficult to like him as well as enjoy him, for he could be a pleasant man, if as ridiculously over-committed as most men in senior positions of commercial power are these days. But her feeling went beyond loyalty, or even love. He represented stability for her, in a way which had nothing to do with the fact that he was very rich. He had become her cause.

He waved, as he often did, before stepping into the car. A year ago it had been a Jensen. Today it was a Lovelace, the finest symbol of power which the sports car company Michael had taken over in the previous year could produce. For the couple of miles to Prospero's headquarters at Prospect House, it would draw senseless envy from the several thousand people it passed. She waved back and, as a flight of starlings rushed past, she wondered if she hated Earl Sanger enough to wish him dead.

2

Sir Bernard Grant had been awaiting his son for more than half an hour before Michael slid the silver Lovelace carefully into the echoing underground car park at Prospect House. It was very unusual these days for Bernard to be at his desk as early as 8.30. As chairman of the Prospero Group he could now afford to relax a little, to wheel and deal in comfort.

He was not, however, idle – not by other men's standards. He had performed several useful functions on the fringes of Government recently and was welcomed on the Arts Council and other cultural bodies. He had the freedom to seek out enterprises ripe for Prospero interest and, by assiduous attendance at sales, had added significantly to his collection of post-Impressionists during the past winter. He could also watch more carefully the conduct of the other Prospero directors, so it was not that Sir Bernard had stopped running, simply that it was now not a continual sprint; and on mornings of grey cold rain he might, if he chose, lie abed to breakfast over *The Times*.

But today he had news, important news: and the knowledge of the power this gave him, even should it turn out to be merely the power of surprise, made him eager to be at his desk, waiting. He enjoyed the role of oracle.

For perhaps fifteen minutes he had been flicking through the sheaf of figures before him, occasionally adding marginal commentaries. Now he leaned back, troubled, but at least made comfortable in his preoccupation by the familiarity of his surroundings.

It was a good room, austere with that kind of luxurious bareness which only a few hundred thousand pounds can afford. The partner's desk was 1790, brilliantly restored. The stringed bronze upon it was Hepworth. There was a glowing Dufy on the wall.

Hugging the knowledge of his good taste around him like a blanket, he moved to gaze from the window at a view which was also not inexpensive. The twentieth floor of Prospect House – and there were many more layers above him – gave him a vista along several miles of the Thames. It was a good name, *Prospect* House. Suggesting vision, foresight, command, power. He was glad he'd thought of it; the name of the organisation on the building would have been too banal. Prospect was close enough, but better.

There were other tall buildings around this one, certainly, but only the Millbank Tower within a mile on either side really competed with the silvery needle-sharp pile which Bernard Grant had built as the headquarters of his empire. The Thames ran idly below him, throwing up pin-points of sunlight this clean morning, and the pretty pinnacles of the Houses of Parliament were suffused with a warm pinkness, as if the stone itself were soft and sugary.

Bernard Grant was no joke tycoon. He had, it was true, made his fortune from property development in the 1950s and, later, from all-round business hustling, which had turned Prospero into an almost wilfully diverse conglomeration of companies producing a turnover that thrust beyond

£200 million each year. As an intelligent and sensitive man, he realised that he was susceptible to the charge that those who fear they have created only profits, which are evanescent, will try to enshrine their memory in functional memorials of steel and stone. He would reply to such accusations that where others had defaced the skyscape of London, he had enhanced it. Honourable mentions for the style of the Prospero headquarters in several assessments by the nation's architectural pundits had confirmed him in his view.

At 67, he tended increasingly to look back at what he had achieved, but today was different. It might be a bad day, because the information before him could possibly be damaging to his own standing as it certainly would for Michael's; but it would be a good day if he could gain the satisfaction of being leader, mentor and prophet to his son. Bernard Grant, still believing his talents to be under-exercised, desired to be needed as much as, in her own way, did his daughter-in-law.

Eager for Michael to arrive, he stood fidgeting with the slim grey tie which sat snugly inside a maroon waistcoat with pearl buttons. His tastes had been formed in the late 1950s and coloured waistcoats worn with impeccable suits – dark grey this morning – were still his affectation. He could survive even this peccadillo, for he was a man of striking enough presence to create his own idiosyncratic style. Well over six feet tall, he had no more than a suggestion of a paunch. He retained his hair, and any suggestion of over-sleekness was removed by the spiky shaggy eyebrows which cartoonists had always seized upon and which Sir Bernard now encouraged with upward-sweeping fingers each day before his looking-glass. Here was a face and form which had overweened chairmen of better education and more substantial background down the years. Michael, Bernard secretly hoped, would do the same.

He suffered in no sense from illusions about his son. Michael's manoeuvrings a year or so ago had, in retrospect, been almost innocently transparent, and Bernard now believed he could smile at some of them. Son of his father – yes, that was part of it. How, too, could Bernard, who had so often demonstrated the art to the world in the past, complain at the clandestine nature of some of Michael's dealings?

The irony of the aftermath also appealed to Bernard. In becoming the executive head of empire, Michael had discovered in Bernard's view that he was only part-leader. He could not survive without his father's support, for in place of hostilities with Bernard he had simply substituted a long-running battle with Earl Sanger, an enemy far more dangerous, since non-familial, and American too.

In these circumstances, Bernard Grant was prepared to support the status quo, exacting only the tribute of Michael's acknowledgment that they were interdependent. Sometimes this was implied in the joint consultations they held before decisions were made, sometimes in the requests which Michael made for Bernard to use otherwise unapproachable contacts, and occasionally in supporting Bernard's ideas at board meetings with a fervour greater even than the progenitor would have thought they were worth. Thus they co-existed; and thus do the defeated, and especially the aged, learn by habit to rationalise the inevitable and live with it.

'Harold Armfield is very worried,' he told Michael when his son arrived. He was careful in laying the responsibility for concern upon the organisation's finance man, ignoring his own worry.

'You have to keep your nerve,' said Michael. 'These big overseas contracts are always full of minor troubles.'

'A million pounds isn't minor, Michael.' Bernard Grant spoke from the heart.

'It's £800,000, not a million. And it's a temporary shortfall.'

'How long is temporary? It could be expensive. You've been over-confident.'

Michael knew he couldn't win, and understood quite clearly that he would swiftly need to have guarantees of his father's support at the board meeting. But his nature drove him to fight just a while longer.

'That's scarcely fair, father. You saw the contract too. It looked good. We won almost everything we wanted. You know we did.'

'I saw it,' said Bernard Grant calmly. 'But it's not my

signature upon it. Had I been assessing the situation from the start, I might have viewed it differently.'

Michael chose his moment to concede. He encouraged the exposition which had to come. 'How?'

'Mainly I'd criticise you on the 10 per cent contingency figure. That may be all right for contracts in this country. Overseas, you need 20 per cent at least to cover yourself adequately. Especially in South America. Contingencies come in all shapes and sizes there – from revolutions to earthquakes. Admit it, Michael. You were too eager to land the contract. You let them drive you too hard.'

'I wouldn't have done it if I hadn't felt I was well inside the limit on the other figures. According to the specifications laid down by the designers I reckoned we had plenty to spare. So did Oldershaw. So did everyone else we consulted.'

'Designers!' Bernard was huffing, the sibilants loaded with contempt. 'They're always the same. They have a vested interest in making you believe it's going to be an easy ride. They want to set up the package, con the government concerned into delusions of grandeur, persuade the major contractors to come in, and then run the show as overall project managers. Don't be naive, Michael. You wanted this thing to go through and you cut corners to achieve it. You've got damn little margin for things to go wrong.'

Michael nodded, turning up the corner of his mouth wryly, and even that trick was enough to bend the tone of his father. He had done that when caught out in pranks and affairs more serious ever since he had been a boy. It was a trait surviving even their five years' absence from each other in the war, with Bernard in a concentration camp after being too late to escape the Nazis in Vienna, Michael safe in England, though apparently an orphan when his mother died in 1943. The father never failed to fall for that simple, charming nervous gesture of the mouth.

'All right, Michael, it was a risk. You have to take risks sometimes. But you have to live with the consequences.'

'I know.'

'I'll help if I can.'

'Thanks.'

'The worst thing is the cash-flow – and that's nothing to do with the contract, as it happens. What has Oldershaw been up to? He's paid out two and a half millions to his sub-contractors already, and so far we've only a million and a half of that covered by bank advances. Why?'

Michael was almost sure his father knew why, but he explained. 'We should have had almost a million more in the kitty by now. You know we get promissory notes from the client as each stage of the work is completed – progress payments, in effect. Well, the promissory notes aren't coming through because the whole job at the site has fallen behind. There's a long list of reasons for that. Cock-ups with local labour, not properly trained – that's one. We can only bring in a certain number of workers from outside Ecuador – the usual limited expatriate quotas – so we depend on local labour a lot. And masses of Oldershaw's stuff has been held up in customs. The clients say it's our fault for not complying with the terms of the import licences.'

'Do they indeed?'

'Naturally. The Ecuador Government are the major shareholders in that petro-chemical company we're building the plant for. They're scarcely likely to blame their own state officials. I won't bore you with the rest, father. It all adds up to the fact that we haven't reached the stage at which the next promissory notes ought to be forthcoming. That's why Oldershaw appears to have paid out too much.'

'He's a fool,' snapped Bernard. 'Always make people wait for their money longer than you have to wait yourself.'

It was a typical Bernard Grant over-simplification. Christ, thought Michael, he *knows* it is too. Working through batteries of accountants and serpentine channels of communication, modern business allows for few such simple rules of old-fashioned trade and barter.

'It's not his fault, father. If anything, it's mine. I'm driving him so hard to meet the dates for delivery that he encourages people to keep on time by being too prompt in letting them have their money. And he doesn't want to give the people at the site any chance to come back at him.'

Bernard shrugged, using his son's frankness as a lever to make the point he'd been saving up. 'If you're feeling so masochistic, you'd better let Harold hear you say all this too. Then confess your sins in not keeping him more fully in the picture. Then tell him how much you're depending on him to vet every damn digit in future. If you make him

58

feel important, he might be flattered enough not to eat you for breakfast.'

The tone was tough, the humour cruder than would normally have been to Bernard Grant's taste. English was not his native tongue, and like so many converts to causes, he was more meticulous in observing the niceties of the new creed than those to whom it was an easy, thoughtless heritage. But Grant, who had been born in Granowitz in Hungary, and made his living in Vienna, deliberately coarsened his approach to his son. This was the game they played, and both of them knew the rules.

'But' – the elder man's tone was still warning – 'whatever Harold may want to do, he sees no way out at the moment. We're at the limits of the borrowing powers the board has tried to observe. And a million is a million, even' (driving home his barb) 'when it is only eight hundred thousand. How are your friends in the consortium fixed?'

'The same as us,' said Michael. 'The French had to put their hands deep into their pockets at the start. They'll not lift a finger unless we can apply pressure in some way.'

And indeed that was true. Everyone in this game existed on borrowed money, hoping for the best.

Brasserton's had gone to the Export Credits Guarantee Department at the Board of Trade in London and got themselves an insurance policy to cover 50 per cent of the value of the equipment they would be exporting to Ecuador, just as SAEF had gone to Coface in Paris, and Kerridge Steel to the Eximbank in Washington. The insurance covered Brasserton's against the Ecuador petro-chemical company starting to repay the promissory notes in two years' time, at six-monthly intervals, with interest. In the case of revolution, political perfidy, changes of heart and other misfortunes, Brasserton's were protected.

And once the ECGD policy was shown by Brasserton's to their British bankers, the money men were bound to advance money at cheap rates to Oldershaw's company – provided the promissory notes were forthcoming . . .

That was only the start of the trouble however, as Michael well knew.

On paper the equation was simple. The plant was going to cost £100 million to build, and an extra £10 million was needed for working capital. Export credits in the various

59

countries covered half of the plant cost – £50 million – leaving £60 million to be found. Of that sum, £20 million was provided by a straight cash investment: half by the Ecuador government, half by Kerridge Steel and other interested American companies. The remaining £40 million had come in loans from various banks around the world, the whole sum underwritten by Kerridge Steel.

So far, so good – except that the Ecuador government had, as usual in these affairs, pleaded poverty. Their £10 million had in fact been provided by members of the plant-building consortium – strictly an under-the-counter arrangement, this, with the sum added to the price of the plant by careful manipulation of the invoices which would in due course be sent to the petro-chemical company in Ecuador for payment. So Brasserton's, in common with other members of the consortium – including SAEF, of course – faced heavy cash demands at the beginning of the contract. They had also to bear the cost of all goods and materials in production and in shipment prior to erection, as well as providing a 20 per cent cash down-payment before getting their export credits.

All of this was a familiar scenario in contracts arranged with under-developed countries. The Ecuador government didn't want to shell out a cent; nor did the private companies in Ecuador who had taken a modest stake in the petro-chemical company, but were hanging on to their money until the plant was actually finished.

No matter how you cut the cake, the consortium building the plant took all the risks. The customers simply sat back and waited. Bernard must know that their French partners wouldn't want to help Brasserton's if it could be avoided. They had enough troubles of their own.

Bernard persisted. 'SAEF wouldn't want to see us in trouble, surely? It would be disastrous for them if the project collapsed.'

'Certainly, father. But there's no danger of that yet. They'll expect us to sell assets to keep going rather than give us money.'

'Over my dead body . . .' Momentarily the elder man paused, scolding himself for being tempted into cliché.

'I don't disagree with you,' said Michael.

'What about Corsino? Won't he help?'

'He might, I suppose. I'll try him.'

'Make it quickly, then.'

Bernard looked at his son more warmly, allowing himself the luxury of admiring what he himself had in part created. Like Bernard, Michael topped six feet. Tautness of figure was Michael's too, not yet needing the regimen of careful greenery, lean meat and Evian water so essential to Bernard. Both men shared facial skin smooth as a child's, but Michael had not inherited the nose no more than faintly hooked which gave extra sharpness to his father's profile. The father, though, could not compete with Michael's handsome high-cheekboned leanness in the upper face, a slight legacy of East European forebears.

'I'll do what I can with the board,' Bernard said gruffly, uneasy at having to concede the point, yet delighted to be in a position where he could show magnanimity.

'Thank you, father.' Michael, understanding the protocol, duly exuded filial humility.

'How is my grandson today?'

Michael laughed easily. 'As far as I know, he – or *she* – is well. Alison does have almost six months to go, remember.'

'I'm not likely to forget. And don't talk to me about girls.'

Wisely, Michael stayed silent. He was learning to deal with his father's lures, not allowing himself to be baited as he had in the years when there was destructive tension between them. Not that he felt he could completely trust his father's judgment, since he retained a lingering suspicion that the instinct of treachery – which is within all men, and especially those of habitual loyalty – might one day obtrude upon that judgment. For Bernard had, in truth, reason enough to be resentful.

'I don't think there's anything else?' said Michael.

'Perhaps we'd better go over Harold's figures together and you'll appreciate just how tricky the cash-flow is. Then perhaps we can work out how you can fend off the perfidious Sanger.'

Bernard Grant smiled brightly, but switched off the beam just a fraction too early for it to carry conviction. Ten years ago, so consummate an actor would not have fallen into such mistiming.

Earl Sanger too was planning how he would play the board meeting, and he did it in a room as bare as Bernard Grant's, except that with him the sparseness was that of a monk's cell rather than of a tasteful sybarite. The chair on which he sat was hard and upright, the desk metal and functional and bare of papers. The walls were painted matt grey and adorned only with three charts of mysterious complexity.

For those who knew his habits the slow clicking of his ballpoint against front teeth was a sign as ominous as the sudden flash of shark's fin might be to bathers at Bondi Beach. More commonplace was the way in which he occasionally stroked his dark brown moustache – verging on the Genghis Khan rather than pure Zapata – in a downward direction or swept his hand over the top of his skull from which sprouted bristly blond hair. Not a speck of dandruff fell to mar the shoulders of his dark grey suit. Sanger shampooed daily to maintain his well-pressed image.

'It's a scandal,' he told his assistant, Colin Hardy. 'When the hell are they going to get into production at this rate?'

Hardy believed that nothing so minor as slowness in getting a production line for motor-cycle engines on the move merited the word scandalous. He screwed his mouth into a faint grimace, which could have meant anything, and pushed his Punch nose deeper towards his chin. He knew better than to disagree with his boss when Sanger was rehearsing indignation for board consumption.

'It would be worth making the point today,' he said.

'Damn right,' said Sanger. 'Remember how Michael sang about all the dough we'd make from those engines when he took over Lovelace? I wasted a whole fortnight setting up draft contracts with the guys who made the snowmobiles. They're still waiting for us to go back to them, six months later. They need *quantity*. And Lovelace can't give it to them. You know why?'

'Of course,' said Hardy.

'Michael wants to grow up.' Sanger rose quickly, adjusted his gleaming black hornrims. 'What the hell good would it do for profitability if he won goddam Le Mans?'

'Which is totally unlikely,' said Hardy.

'Right,' said Sanger scornfully. 'Just playing with his toy.'

Sanger wasn't the only director who'd said, or thought, the same thing. Michael Grant's background as a leading sports car racer in his twenties, at a time when amateurs might still hope to gain a specialist class position or two at Le Mans, was well enough known to draw the obvious barbs. When, the previous year, Michael had persuaded the board to effect an agreed purchase of Lovelace's, it was perfectly true that he had emphasised the profits which could come from the sports car company's sideline of motor-cycle engines – fashionably in demand for the new snow-mobile leisure industry in America. He had also dropped hints about the real estate value of the Lovelace property down in Hampshire. He had mentioned only lightly the future of the ailing breed of sports cars which had originally made the Lovelace name famous. Yet the suspicion that he really wanted to have a stake in motor-racing for its own sake was an obvious one. And, though Michael would have denied it, it was partially that desire which had motivated him, turning the mere pleasure of business into a prospect of business-like pleasure.

'You've got all the figures you need?' said Hardy.

Sanger nodded. He had figures enough, if only because Hardy had a seat on the car company board and now fed his American master a pre-selected flow of fact. He had cause enough to use the figures, too.

Michael had brought him to Britain 18 months earlier, aware of Sanger's reputation as a man who could really pull up ailing companies by their boot straps. Since then the American had received rewards which would have satisfied many men, a seat on the Prospero board among them. But it was not unnatural that he should now dream of occupying Michael's seat. Such is the everyday fantasy of most men near to the summit of power, particularly those who, like Sanger, have clawed their way out of poverty.

Sanger, however, was more complicated than that. He played the game of jockeying for position instinctively, although his actions would seem to be almost ritualistic in the face of Michael's strength as son of the founder. Now, it was different. Sanger's opposition to his one-time patron had grown desperately sincere – sincere by his standards, that is – for Michael had offended against the American's code of conduct.

Over the past several months, Sanger had been denied the confidence of the new chief executive, where once he had been a close conspirator. And though no word had passed between them, Sanger knew why. In the struggle to re-shape Prospero, Sanger had played the game too hard and too dirty for Michael's tastes. Thus he had been rewarded, as was his due; but the manner of the giving and his leader's tacit disapproval had robbed the gift of meaning.

Sanger was mystified, since his philosophy was simple. If a business objective was virtuous, then how one achieved the end was almost beside the point. And what could be more virtuous than the reinvigoration of a gargantuan corporation, the burgeoning of its profits, and the safeguarding of employment for its staff?

In the pursuit of revitalising Prospero, Sanger had pushed hard. Back in the Ohio steel town of his youth, you had needed to kick and scratch to survive. Fighting tough – dirty if necessary – came easily to Sanger. To save a major enterprise like Prospero you had to go the whole hog. Why should he alone be blamed for the suicide of Sir Giles Lymington, the ancient and effete diplomat who had been taken on to the organisation's board by Bernard Grant years ago as a contact man with Whitehall? Sanger wasn't to know that the digging supervised by him into Lymington's shaky business past would also reveal the old goat to be both a disastrously losing gambler and a discreet homosexual. He accepted Lymington's suicide almost too easily, arguing to himself that in pursuit of the greater business good, minor casualties might be inevitable.

Out of mystification at Michael's treatment of him after Lymington's death grew a sense of outrage. Sanger felt insulted by being so patently rebuffed, and in this he was almost Sicilian, though his father had come from Northern Italy. As deeply as any mafioso, Sanger demanded and needed respect from those around him, respect for beliefs which he deemed inevitable and right. He wanted not only to be right, but to be seen and acknowledged to be right. Denied this, Sanger began to display that malice which is rarely absent in those who are frustrated in the pursuit of prideful power just when they believe they have attained it.

Hardy was pushing a piece of paper across the desk towards him. He would have to watch Hardy. Hardy was clever. Hardy was cynical and independent too, knowing his own strength. Sanger realised that nothing in business is more dangerous than an alliance of convenience with an independent cynic.

He wished Hardy hadn't known about the piece of paper; but Hardy had also received it through the post. The sender had known his men.

'Do we act, then? It could be interesting,' said Hardy.

Oh yes, Sanger would act. Here was another means by which he might improve Prospero's fortunes, another of those demonstrations necessary to bolster his standing within the organisation. He would also act for less considered reasons. Sanger, pursuing profit and self-interest instinctively, moved fast, filling his days and nights with networks of conspiracies. He never gave himself time to ask why he was doing so. Perhaps he realised subconsciously that had he done so, he might have had no convincing answer.

He eyed the unsigned letter before him. It offered, in return for money, a list of the several thousand clients of a specialised offshore investment fund which was in close competition with a similar fund run by Prospero. It asked for a reply to be placed, phrased enigmatically, in the personal column of *The Times*. That method made monitoring by Hardy easy whether Sanger told him what he intended to do or not.

'How much do we offer?' said Sanger.

'Twenty thousand.'

'Fifteen.'

Hardy shrugged. 'If it's a dissatisfied clerk, he might take it. If it's a computer man with a print-out, he may have more sophisticated ideas.'

'It's not worth a cent more than fifteen. We might even try ten. That way I get the money through and no questions asked.'

'You're not discussing it with Michael?' asked Hardy, unable to resist sarcasm.

'Don't be bloody moronic,' said Sanger.

He pushed the letter back towards Hardy.

He slid open a desk drawer as Hardy left, pulling out a

sheaf of papers. In doing so he revealed a colour picture of a large black cat.

Sanger smiled in a way that was not him at all; almost sloppily. He must get his secretary to go out and buy the box of cat food he'd forgotten to pick up that morning. Sanger liked his cat. There had been another one. His father had booted it in the stomach, boozed as usual on a Saturday night.

For a week he'd wept at nights after it died. It wouldn't eat; just lay there with blank eyes, in a corner of his room, as life trickled away. For a boy with no friends, small and cowed and boss-eyed, a cat who liked him was important.

The second cat, the one he'd found in the lobby of his London apartment, was the only pet he'd owned since his youth. It had taken him twenty years to be able to face the feeling of having a cat again, to be able to enjoy it without being reminded of his roots, dragged back in spirit to the ugly poverty of his Ohio boyhood.

Yet he cosseted the animal obsessively, as if trying to repay some debt to the younger fearful years. The cat to him was a pampered yet touching symbol of what had made him. If anyone had hurt that cat, Sanger might have done him grievous bodily harm.

3. GAMES PEOPLE PLAY

1

MICHAEL GRANT was the first to arrive for the meeting of the Prospero board. He sat at the circular steel and plate-glass table waiting for the other nine directors, curiously glancing at his papers, wondering exactly how Sanger would attempt to undermine him this time.

Ecuador and Lovelace were his two most obvious weaknesses. But the real danger was that Sanger would pitch his curviest balls on neither of these issues. Sanger specialised in unsuspected dramas, fabricated from careful perusal of the latest trading accounts or information gleaned from secret sources, and the nature of the Prospero board encouraged such idiosyncrasies.

It was not that kind of board which is dominated by prestigious part-time directors, who tend to rubber-stamp the decisions of the working executives who really run the organisation – except, that is, at times of faltering profits or proliferating scandals, when these worthy outside guardians of corporate probity tend towards noisy pomposity and flatulent indignation. Nor was it a board composed purely of working managers, those who get called vice-presidents in America and executive directors in Britain and are usually a worrying kind of men, feeling at different times neglected or needed, threatened or bullet-proof, according to outside circumstances and the state of their stomach linings.

Reflecting the wayward growth of the corporation, the Prospero board was a hybrid animal, although it was certainly the full-time executives whose point and counter-point of dispute dominated its proceedings. Its meetings were, in other words, lively, explosive, entertaining, surprising, and continually devious. Sanger was the star turn on every count.

Michael remembered a dozen surprise titbits which the American had pulled out of his briefcase for these occasions: takeover suggestions, investment chances, profit improvement programmes, or simply sparkling anecdotes of pure malicious

67

gossip about business acquaintances. Once, Sanger had glee-
fully told the sad story of the Rolls Royce Silver Shadow
of a rival company chairman. It had, the previous night,
been savaged with a crowbar – windows shattered and every
inch of elegant bodywork dented – by the enraged husband
of a woman secretary to whose bed the chairman, most un-
wisely, was no stranger. Bernard Grant had been very tetchy.
He'd planned to tell the story himself. Sanger had not yet
acquired the tact to check out before the board meeting
whether his chairman had heard, and wanted to retail, the
adventure personally.

'Good morning, Michael.' It was Lionel Westbrook who
had entered; a man just past 40, running to fat, but still
struggling to stay abreast of modish suiting and hair styling.
His sideburns ran an inch below his ear lobes and his
medium-brown jacket had wide lapels and a thick white
chalk-stripe.

His promptness meant no more than did the amount of
noise he would make in his next two hours, although it is a
common misapprehension among those who have not sat
around boardroom tables that the sound and splutter emanating from individual directors is commensurate with their
influence. Rarely is this so; nor is real influence to be
measured in terms of the column-inches gained by directors
in newspapers, nor yet by the number of speeches made to
quasi-professional societies (especially to advertising conventions or operational research luncheon clubs), and certainly not by the weight-volume of memoranda produced
and distributed.

The plain fact is that only three or four men on any
board – including Prospero's – sway important decisions; the
rest of the directors are the chorus, acting only as commentators to the deeds of the genuine leading actors or as
clowns in the Shakespearian sense, offering those witty
maxims or sententious passages which have the useful function of relieving tension when it has grown unbearable.
Westbrook was in the chorus.

'How's Ecuador?' he said. 'Is David Travis back?'

If Westbrook had been on the ball, he would have known
how Ecuador was; and that David had been back in London
almost a week. But for the past year he had been sulking
because he had not been made Michael's deputy, which post

had gone to Harold Armfield, the corporation's finance man. Westbrook, strong on imagination but weak in judgment, had been in decline ever since, a slide hastened by his wife trouble. He might even have to be replaced as Marketing Director before long. Sanger's Special Projects department had already taken away most of the important work from Westbrook's shrunken empire.

'Ecuador is good and bad,' Michael said. 'I'll be making a full report. Those damned South American politicians!'

'And David?'

'He's fine,' said Michael. 'He's had a few days off. He did the best job he could.'

'Good,' said Westbrook.

'You trained him damned well,' said Michael, desperately wanting to be fair to a man who had been a faithful ally in the struggle for control over a year ago. But didn't Westbrook's recent behaviour confirm that Michael had been right not to make him deputy chief executive?

Westbrook nodded and walked to the gleaming hotplate on a side-table, poured himself black coffee, ladling in three spoonfuls of sugar. He had always eaten well. Now, with an excess of sugar, he compensated for the disappointment of his life, feeding his girth and his neuroses.

There were many such brief exchanges during the course of the next five minutes as the other directors assembled, those who mattered least continuing to arrive first, as if forming an audience to greet the latecoming stars, the men who would really decide every important issue that blustery April morning.

Among these supporting actors, Barry Prosser, the Personnel Director, dark and squat and black finger-nailed (which might have been a gesture to show he was still in touch with the toilers) carried with him the newest tome on industrial relations, as pedantic as had been his schoolmaster father in the Rhondda. He talked, after greeting Michael, with Frank Bartram, Manchester-born and long-time associate of Bernard's in property deals up north, now remaining on the board for old times' sake.

They paired off naturally. Bartram, like Prosser, had spent most of his life in the mud and guts of commercial life, tramping scruffy building sites, scuffing his shoes on the oily concrete of factory floors. The attempt, some years earlier, to turn him into a desk-bound managing director, running a clothing subsidiary called Supergear from a trendily designed office, had been a failure.

No one had yet summoned up the nerve to question his continuing place on the board, for it was accepted that Bernard Grant could play benevolent *grand seigneur* to his associates from the good old days. Bartram, an anonymous man in a blue suit, retained only one tangible asset; on this board he had a vote, exercised unfailingly on Bernard Grant's side. He talked with Prosser about the problems of overtime agreements and wage rates and productivity bargaining and the wild or wily characters of labour union leaders they had met. They nodded their heads and moved their lips in unmeaningful greeting to Laurel and Hardy, who next entered the room.

Laurel and Hardy was, it should be explained, what the brasher middle-rank executives at Prospect House had christened this new pair over their canteen lunches on the day the joint appointment to the Prospero board was announced. One was thin, short, hawk-nosed, with a monocle dangling down his waistcoat; Sir Harvey Jardine, formerly of Her Majesty's Foreign Service. The other, heavily-built, moon-faced and with a toothbrush moustache, was Vernon Morton, a merchant banker. Both were old friends of Bernard Grant and both had become linked with Prospero only in the past year.

Michael, with whom they chatted now, had offered no objection to their appointments. They were sound and sensible men, with excellent contacts, if insufficiently committed to the corporation for his taste. Bernard's reasons for bringing them in had been, officially, that following the death of Sir Giles Lymington, they needed Jardine as eyes, ears and voice in Whitehall, whilst Morton would give them much-needed extra influence in the City. The real reason, appreciated fully by Michael, was that Bernard had imported friendly voting power to the board to counter-balance the thrustful ambition of Earl Sanger and the unpredictable behaviour of Lord Bender.

'Good morning, gentlemen,' boomed Bernard Grant. 'I hope I haven't kept you.' He entered explosively. From under tufting brows, his eyes devoured them all. 'No – I see we're not all assembled.'

He knew, as well as anyone, that the three absentees were those who would give the meeting its point and balance of power. He stood, still a strikingly vibrant figure, the feeling of command flowing from him almost tangibly. These days he summoned up such moods only for special occasions like today's. He had resolved to drive the difficult meeting through to Michael's advantage. He was going to be determinedly cheerful.

'Ha, Vernon. Are you going to win?' he asked Morton, referring to the contest for control of a sizeable hotel chain in which his friend's merchant bank was advising the giant corporation which was bidding.

'Of course,' said the banker.

'You'll need to raise your price again,' said Bernard. 'That damned family don't want you. They're so full of virtue about their innkeeping tradition, you'd think they invented log fires and serving wenches.'

Very good, father, Michael thought as the room relaxed into smiles.

'Yes,' said Morton. 'Very stiff upper lip.'

'Not so much stiff. More like deep-frozen,' said Bernard, and there were more smiles. 'Well, *will* you make a better bid now you've been turned down again?'

Morton shrugged. 'Doubtful. We'll continue buying on the open market.'

'And writing letter to all the shareholders who *did* accept your offer first time around?'

Morton looked very cocky. 'Something like that. I'm lunching the owner of thirty thousand of those damned shares tomorrow.'

'Who?' said Bernard, and Morton whispered a name.

'Interesting,' said Bernard, markedly sardonic. 'He's susceptible to flattery, and to the profit motive. You might need a special arrangement with him. A touch more than market price.'

'Hush,' said Morton. 'Whatever are you suggesting? The rules don't allow that. Compromising my virtue again.'

Bernard reached forward expansively to grasp Morton's arm, for he was a man who touched people a lot, naturally and without offence. He guided the banker to a chair at the table, both of them chuckling.

It had been typical of their conversations, Michael

thought: topped with brittle humour, urbane, with hints of sharp practice which, since they were framed in mockery, no one knew whether to take seriously or not. Michael still marvelled, though, at the openness of the conversation in front of so mixed and uncertain an assembly. Security in business was still sometimes a joke, however seriously corporations might nowadays pay it lip-service; it foundered on the inability of particular men to hold their tongues in company. In his experience, too many businessmen were gossips.

It was perhaps a few seconds past ten-thirty when the three remaining directors arrived. Their immaculate timing reflected one of the few traits they shared. They were all utterly confident of their positions, so they needed not to fear that the meeting might start without them. Everyone knew, of course, that they were too well organised in their daily routines to be late accidentally.

Only one of them took coffee with him to the table, and that was Sanger. Coffee to Sanger was an accompaniment to most of his waking actions, and he drank it at once, greedily, which was a legacy of his bread-line youth. He tended to grab what he could get before anyone else took it away, and was dabbing a handkerchief at his startling moustache almost before he'd mumbled 'Good morning, gentlemen' to the others.

Lord Bender did not take coffee, because his doctor had suggested it might irritate his stomach linings, whilst Harold Armfield – old enough to have fought at Alamein, in taste conservative, a rosarian in his spare moments – scorned it as an unfortunate incursion into British life showing how much Americans and Continentals had in recent years undermined the country. He had, however, already drunk a cup of weak China tea in his office. Thus fortified, he was ready to go through the hand-wringing account of Prospero's trading statements which he knew would be expected of him.

Armfield sat down on Michael Grant's left, hands neatly interlocked across his files, and registered bland neutrality through his gold-rimmed spectacles. Bender, who sensed trouble, moved in next to Bernard Grant, and immediately fell to rubbing his right temple with one finger, a signal of his unease read clearly by both Grants. Sanger spread five blue folders in line before him, like a sniper laying out ammunition for later use.

72

Bernard Grant played the first fifteen minutes well. He acknowledged that in one or two areas, Prospero had problems. There was the sit-in strike at their convenience food subsidiary in the Midlands; he was confident, however, that the local management would win. Two new ventures, in data processing and greetings cards, had as yet failed to meet their budgets, already set at a loss since they were infant companies. One overseas contract, in Ecuador, had run into trouble due to the country's uncertain political climate.

'Well, gentlemen,' he said, smiling, 'we know that such ventures always contain an element of risk, but that the rewards can be very high.'

In choosing to place the Ecuador contract among matters as mundane as frozen peas and get-well cards, Bernard was trying to demote its importance. He had raised the issue, so no one could complain, but he was not going to push it. The meeting allowed Bernard to proceed.

He dealt with fourteen more companies in 7 minutes; assumed, beaming, that the board would take the rest as not needing comment; interspersed, with appropriate gestures, a joke about one-armed economists ('all the economists I've ever known have said "On the one hand this, on the other hand that"'); and, finally, offered two acquisition possibilities for Sanger's department to explore. Then he leaned back, smoothing maroon waistcoat (he did not like it when Sanger called it a *vest*) over scarcely protruding paunch.

The ploy was familiar to Michael. They thought, most of them, even those who knew him best, that he had finished, that the jokes were the signing-off piece, like a song at the end of a comedian's act. They were waiting to jump in on what Bernard had missed out. But he did not make elementary tactical errors.

'Gentlemen,' said Bernard, 'I'm glad we can smile. Why should we waste our time on this treadmill if it does not sometimes stimulate and amuse us?' He sat stiffly upright, shaggy eyebrows at attention too, using all of his six feet four to dominate the meeting, and in his mouth the words lost their pomposity. 'But there's one problem we can't smile about. The overall stance of our enterprises is good. Yet because several minor crises have arrived simultaneously, our cash-flow is strained. Harold – perhaps you'd talk about that.'

Harold Armfield wasn't going to be rushed. He pushed his spectacles firmly on his nose and lovingly he went through each paragraph of the monthly financial report which all his colleagues could have read with perfect ease from the copies in front of them. But this was Armfield's method – a man of infinite patience, solid, dependable, underlining every digit. No one objected, except perhaps Bernard Grant and Sanger, who masked their impatience because they both wished to court Armfield's favour later.

His monologue on loans which had been arranged, the timing of interest payments, the success or failure of Prospero's subsidiaries gave the men around the table a chance for private communion. Golf, roses, wives' charge accounts, a holiday in Monaco, a mistress's rent, a medical report, a cat, a fear of blackmail, a secretary's thighs, a chance to buy a Picasso cheaply, the length of Westbrook's hair, annoyance at having forgotten to ask a PA to arrange theatre tickets ...

'So everything I can do has been done,' said Armfield finally. 'Barring emergency action, that is. There are no obvious lines of credit open, and frankly even if there were, I'm dubious about borrowing more. We're dangerously close to our agreed limit.'

'What's in back of what you're saying?' said Sanger. 'What mostly worries you, Harold?'

His tone was sweet, almost demure. He was inviting Armfield to fire the bullet.

'Ecuador, without doubt,' said Armfield. 'I'm sorry, Michael, but it has to be said. That contract is really going wrong.'

Michael had known before the meeting how he would play the situation. And nothing which had so far happened had caused him to change his mind. Sanger was stroking his moustache like a Victorian statesman. Who would have thought that line of hair would came out black when the American's skull was blond? It didn't seem to deter Sanger, who had decided that moustaches were in and, accordingly, had followed the fashion as if it were a hot stock market tip.

'Yes,' said Michael. 'I can't argue with you, Harold. It's not good. Let me fill in the background.'

He explained about the politics in South America. He explained about the crises which no one could control. He reminded them that the decision to go ahead the previous year had been that of the whole board, though he admitted that his and Sanger's and Westbrook's had been the most urgent voices. But the rationale of the contract had been that this was a major opportunity for a Prospero company to break into a potentially very profitable overseas market.

'We all knew it would be to some extent a calculated risk situation. I fully agree I may have underestimated some of the risks. Now, gentlemen, I want your help – your advice on our possible courses of action.'

He looked around the meeting with a frank and steady gaze. Bernard, still uncertain whether he would give un- qualified support to his son if the pressures of the meeting became to uncomfortable, thought that Michael could scarcely have handled it better. No attempt to dump the main responsibility, yet a nice buttressing of acceptable pleas for partial pardon. Given arguments so finely balanced, would any of them, in Michael's shoes, have made a different decision over the contract 18 months ago? Michael's method – total candour – could still be the most disarming of all weapons.

'Yeah, well, I'd like to get a few things straight for the record, chairman,' said Sanger.

He was about to get himself off the hook upon which Michael had neatly hung him.

'There's nothing wrong with the general concept of that contract. I supported it. Still do. But I didn't write the small print. Nor did the rest of the board. That's where some of the hang-ups are.'

He selected a file, opened it.

'Point one. The contingency sum – it's too small. South America can be hell. I made the point when we signed the contract.'

No one remembered whether he had or hadn't, except for Michael and, perhaps, Armfield. Neither was going to argue the point now, though. It would have been undignified.

'If we'd increased our costs we wouldn't have got the con- tract, Earl,' said Michael.

'I can't go along with that,' said Sanger. 'Ed Corsino's a reasonable guy.'

The words were vibrant with meaning. Sanger had wanted to go over to New York City and negotiate the final stages of the contract with Corsino. Michael had gone instead. Sanger had been furious.

'No one can really know the answer to that, Earl,' said Michael coolly. 'I had to make a judgment at the time. I decided I'd pushed Corsino as far as he could be pushed on terms and price. Besides' – he pushed at the hank of black hair which curved over his right temple – 'the contract was open for the board to inspect. I remember well the general discussion we had about the pros and cons of a deal like this. No one made an issue at board level about the detail of the contract.'

'I think I wrote a note on it,' said Sanger, and placed one hand on a file as if to start a search.

'That's beside the point, surely,' said Bernard Grant, who knew that carbon copies of memoranda meant nothing; they could always be manufactured after the event. 'If the board had no chance at the time to know of your reservations and take them into account . . .'

The unfinished sentence, trailing, emphasised his cool hostility.

Sanger was not deterred. He had not totally lost the point if some of the men around the table retained the notion, however muzzily, that he had questioned Michael's judgment when the contract was signed. He moved swiftly to the next firing position.

'Point two, Sir Bernard. The payments made to us. It's a bad schedule.'

The way he pronounced the final word, the hard American 'k' cracking in the quiet room, always grated on Bernard. It epitomised for him all the abrasive, pushing hostility of Sanger's position in the organisation.

'Why, Earl?' he said. 'Surely it was acknowledged to be one of the strengths of the contract that we got our promissory notes from Ecuador as we completed each stage of the work?'

'Not if the client has the power, either wilfully, or through negligence, to delay completion of the stages after we've spent our money making the equipment. We should have had a fall-back position.'

'How precisely?' asked Michael.

'By insisting we got paid on delivery of equipment rather than on its erection at the site.'

'It wouldn't have been on, Earl. Clients aren't interested in looking at cratefuls of instruments lying at the docks. They want the bits and pieces put together.'

'I don't accept that,' said Sanger. 'And there's an alternative even so. We could have fixed a latest date for each promissory note to be due if work had been delayed because of constraints laid on us by the client.'

'We'd never have achieved that either,' said Michael. 'Who could judge who was to blame for delays?'

'In some cases, that's not difficult,' said Sanger. 'Stacks of our equipment are held up at the dockside in Ecuador simply because their goddam Customs people won't run with the ball. Whose fault is that but the client's? The Ecuador Government hold the biggest stake in the corporation we're building that plant for, don't they?' He knew they did; all 55 per cent of it.

Michael marvelled at the accuracy of Sanger's information. Where did Sanger get it? 'Sitting in London, that's how it looks. But the Ecuadoreans would claim the delay is our fault – because we haven't complied with the terms of the import licences.'

'Well, have we?' said Sanger, curtly.

'By our standards, yes.'

'It's their standards that count. What's the local agent doing for chrissakes?'

'The local agent, Perez, was recommended by Ed Corsino,' said Michael. 'David Travis, as well as Oldershaw, has been out to see him. The situation is under control now.'

'Oldershaw doesn't strike me as the kind of guy who'd know what time of day it was in fixing a deal like this,' said Sanger, still shooting straight for Michael. 'He's a good engineer, but politically – well, forget it. And Travis has got a lot to learn.'

'David Travis has successfully brought off three major sets of overseas negotiations in the past six months,' said Michael evenly. 'I sent him along specifically to hold Oldershaw's hand. I believe I know the strengths and weaknesses of our people.'

'I hope they know enough to have kicked Perez's ass – and checked out his bank account,' said Sanger.

The mention of money aroused Armfield. 'What do you mean by that, Earl?'

'We pay Perez to fix things. Either he's been keeping too much for himself – and I've known a lot of greedy guys in my time – or he doesn't know who are the right people to fix.'

Armfield considered whether to tell the room that the sums in the accounts for the Ecuador contract under the headings of 'Special Commissions' had increased sharply in the past week. He decided against it. He wanted the meeting to force discipline upon Michael. He wanted a larger involvement in the Ecuador business in future. But that was to be a matter between Michael and himself. Armfield liked to cultivate in board meeting an aura of careful, responsible neutrality. Besides, he had not forgotten that it was the Chairman's son who had confirmed him as the sole deputy chief executive. It would have been easier for Michael to ensure the warm support of Sanger or Westbrook or some newcomer to Prospero by maintaining the *status quo* of the time and naming a second, joint, deputy. Michael and Armfield had, in the days when Bernard Grant was chief executive as well as chairman, held such twin posts. In abandoning the tandem situation, Michael had knowingly made life difficult for himself, since most of the executive directors believed they had a claim to promotion and now nursed resentment.

Armfield appreciated all this and, in truth, Michael could only earn Armfield's ill-will when he denied the financial controller the opportunity to exercise power. And this, foolishly, Michael sometimes did, believing that in many ways his judgment was superior to Armfield's.

Whether this was so or not was beside the point. He needed Armfield, and Armfield knew it. So today, Armfield would support any tendency of the meeting which thrust the chief executive towards the constraining disciplines of the balance sheet. He wanted to be *the* man who ran Prospero along with Michael. At 56, that would be enough to last him the rest of his time. Bernard Grant could enjoy himself talking to prime ministers and presidents and authors, according to taste; a useful function, but not the heart of the matter. Michael could have the glory (and the stresses) of being front man in the shop, who sold the goods at the profit margins Armfield suggested and chatted up the customers. Armfield wanted simply to be known, in other important boardrooms, as the man who really ensured the continuing prosperity of Prospero. The role of *eminence grise*, so long as it was outwardly recognised, would be sufficient both to Armfield's life and to his obituary in *The Times*.

As for Sanger, the American was not a man to whom Armfield could warm in any way personally. Scratch a British or European businessman, and it's a better than even chance you'll uncover anti-American prejudices. Armfield, a traditionalist in business and in personal tastes, living in a green-belt Tudor house stuffed with antiques, confirmed the odds. He would put up with Sanger because Sanger produced profits which made Armfield's financial statements the more resplendent; and to be a bringer of good news can never do the messenger harm. Sanger was fireproof, in Armfield's view, so long as he continued to perform. But Armfield would join no plots, public or private, with him. Given the chance to score a point off Michael, Armfield therefore stayed silent.

'Perez will be all right,' said Michael. 'He is well-connected. His uncle is a key minister in the Government.' Michael did not mention the threat of Colonel Vargas to Cantania; nor could he resist a final thrust at Sanger. 'We understand the whole situation better now – largely thanks to David Travis.'

'Yeah,' said Sanger, affecting resignation. 'I heard about Travis. I guess he knows all about the murder of our local site manager too.'

Murder is not a word which features much in the vocabulary of board meetings. In the soft-carpeted warmly-wooded context of Prospero's boardroom, where discreet telephones murmured rather than rang and the various artefacts of Chippendale, Picasso and Turner reminded visitors of the civilisation they inherited, Sanger's sentence was almost obscene.

'Who's been murdered – you don't mean Oldershaw?' The questioner was Sir Harvey Jardine, the one-time diplomat. Affecting the general view of business, he was never one for the detail of Prospero's affairs.

'No, Sir Harvey,' said Michael. 'This is the local Ecuadorean man – the works manager at the plant site.' His tone was conciliatory. Disturbed that Sanger should know so much, since the death of Carlos had not been brandished around Prospect House as a case of murder, he had no wish to antagonise Jardine or any other uncommitted director. 'I expect you know the kind of man I mean. One is forced to employ nationals of the country in a number of positions.'

'Of course,' said Jardine, pleased at the public acknowledgement of his expertise. 'But murdered? By whom?'

'No one knows,' said Michael. 'Or why.'

Sanger bounced his ballpoint slowly on a thumbnail. 'He's believed to have had links with a revolutionary party there. Maybe he double-crossed them. Maybe the secret police knocked him off.'

'South America is full of damned guerrillas these days,' grumbled Jardine. 'How was he killed?'

'With knives,' said Michael. 'Something like that.'

'Typical,' said Jardine. 'In Colombia they'll kill a man by cutting his throat from ear to ear with a machete. Then they pull his tongue through the slit. They call it a Colombian necktie.'

It was as if Jardine was the chorusmaster for all those directors who had sat mutely while the three or four principal soloists were performing. Once he had told his interesting but essentially irrelevant anecdote, the whole table was suddenly clamouring to speak.

Westbrook moves fastest. He had, as befitted a marketing man, been looking into the world prospects for petrochemical products. He bounced around the names of Shell, Texaco, Burmah, B.P., Occidental and others less familiar. He salted his monologue with multi-million figures.

'So you see,' he concluded, 'there's a lot of uncertainty here, mostly because there could easily be over-production in the world across a wide range of plastics and fibres and other synthetic materials. It's all very well to say that South America – or India or Africa for that matter – *needs* these things. Everybody needs boots and shoes and plastic pipes and fertilisers. The point is; can the people afford to *pay* for them yet?'

He sat back with an air of satisfaction which masked the anxiety within. Those who had absorbed what he'd said – they included Michael and Sanger – thought it interesting but largely irrelevant. If Prospero had been thinking of investing in the petro-chemical business it would have been useful background. But since Prospero was simply building a plant for a client, with no direct involvement in how the plant's products would afterwards be sold, it was largely an academic exercise. Too much of Westbrook's work nowadays was like that. Stuffed with useless detail, not suited to the particular job in hand. It was sad, because he was fundamentally a nice man with an agile mind, whose chief mistake had been to become obsessed with trying to understand everything in the world of commerce.

Prosser was next on stage, pushing stubby fingers on to the glass table to emphasise his points, leaving smears; pushing to the idea that he ought to go out to Ecuador to see if he could sort out the labour problems.

Not your scene, Michael thought. A good man to have around, Prosser – good with labour unions he understood, speaking the same language, watching the pride and vanities of the officials he dealt with. But Prosser was not a skilful enough politician to cope with South America. His presence was not commanding enough, nor his appreciation of the new forces in the world sufficiently sophisticated. In the current vogue phrase, he lacked credibility.

As the discussion dragged on, with Jardine and plump Vernon Morton joining in, Michael looked hard at his father. But Sir Bernard, slightly pursing his lips, indicated that it should continue. Michael understood the signal. Let them go on, boy, Bernard was thinking. Let them exhaust themselves with talk, feel important. In the end they will be the more willing to let you have your way.

And about most of the men at the table, he was right. But not about Sanger, of course; nor yet Lord Bender. Everyone, subconsciously or not, was waiting for Bender. He never spoke much at board meetings. He sat there and listened, occasionally disturbing the dandruff on his grizzled temples with a probing finger when the talk grew too flamboyant or too disturbing, a small man in his sixties, with a face like parchment, his bony frame shuffled into an old grey suit.

He was an ascetic, who ate little and carefully, drank nothing but water and weak China tea, and indulged the fortune he had made with Mondor Insurance and many other companies only in his weakness for good cigars. He was no automaton, nor heartless, and he could be very kind, especially to children, himself having none. The only socialising he ever did was in the service of the five different charities on whose boards of trustees he sat. For the rest, since the death of his wife five years earlier, he had devoted himself almost entirely to two objectives. First, to the task of remaining alive, sleeping ten hours each night. Second, to the affairs of both Mondor, the huge insurance company of which he was chairman, and of Prospero. He was also pleased to spare occasional moments for the use of the six other corporations who had invited him to become one of their non-executive directors.

Him and his money, that is. In Bender's gift lay the disposal of such weighty sums that he had no cause to disperse his energies on unnecessary display or on courting the powerful. Instead, the powerful courted him. He dressed without care, since who was there to impress? And he spoke little, since there was no necessity for that either.

Power had made Bender introspective and seemingly casual, a trait which some men mistook for coldness. He was not cold. He believed in business with humanity. He took his responsibilities with deep seriousness. He was proud of his creations. But he made no fuss about his creed. When at last he did speak, the voice was low and tired; but it stopped the barrage of sound at once. To control 35 per cent of the stock in an organisation as large as Prospero is a devastating conversation killer.

'Michael, you said you wished for our advice on how the money needed to get over the Ecuador hump might be raised.'

That was the point, of course. Bender was dismissing the last half-hour of talk as of no account. Michael was glad the moment had come.

'Yes,' he said.

'I'm afraid I can't help at my end,' said Bender. 'In my view this organisation should not borrow to the hilt and I'm sorry to see, Harold, that the safety cushion of three million pounds liquidity which used to be one of your ground-rules has already been seriously eroded.'

He flicked a glance at Armfield, a headmaster beginning to chastise his errant pupils, one by one. Armfield did not interrupt him.

'Now, Michael,' Bender went on. 'If one of your solutions is that we sell off an asset or two to cope with the cash

82

shortage then I must tell you that you will not have my support. We need more profits in this organisation, not cash from selling companies we control.'

His gaze, steady and stern, moved on to encompass the whole table. 'If the market learns that this Ecuador contract is going sour, our share price could be seriously affected. Security about what we have heard today is crucial.'

'I agree with that,' said Michael, who had been saving up the point to make if finally he had to fight off Sanger.

'Certainly,' said Bernard Grant, offended that Bender was stealing his thunder by summing up in a way which should have been left to him as chairman. He was much more ambivalent about Bender that once he had been. For over twelve years they had been friends, with Benjamin Bender's money backing every move Bernard Grant had made in building up his empire. Never once had Bender seriously questioned his judgment. He had believed he could rely on Bender for ever.

That faith had vanished when, following Bernard's coronary, his son had begun pressing for his retirement as chief executive. Bernard had learned now to live with his partial retirement; in fact, he frequently felt tired these days, and his appetite for working long hours had gone, all of which he supposed was the aftermath of the coronary. In retrospect, therefore, Bernard did not regret the change, nor even the manner of it. If Michael had pulled a trick or two in easing power away from him, then he understood that. He could argue to himself that this showed Michael to be son of the father in a way which was not displeasing. He had even tried, not entirely successfully, to persuade himself that Michael had been at least partly motivated by concern for his father's state of health.

His attitude to Bender was quite different. Michael could never have succeeded had not Bender thrown his weight against Bernard. He remembered their lunch at the Savoy, sitting miserably among the steaks and the cigar smoke, looking at the other dealers shaping their various worlds. Bender's words had been measured and deadly.

What would you sooner have me do? Try to persuade you to give up being chief executive – or let things slide and, in the end, pull out Mondor money? You'd be finished if I did that. The market would murder you.

It had been naked blackmail. He would never forget Bender's disloyalty, nor excuse it. Almost fifteen years of friendship, and the millions he had made for Bender, ought to have insured him against such treachery. He did not consider that if the decision had been right for Prospero and for himself, then Bender had shown a certain kind of friendship in lining up with Michael. Men and women often expect logic to be denied when it comes to friendship.

Bernard Grant looked at Bender now almost with loathing. He disliked the way in which his former friend was seizing control of the meeting. He thought, too, that Bender's voice might have been influential in the background discussion which had doubtless gone on before he received his knighthood. He had expected a life peerage – and had he not deserved it, being free down the years with stunning gifts to charity and to the arts? Instead, it had been only a K, which was the reward for actors and football managers and even the most bumbling ambassador in Her Majesty's service.

He had, for a whole week, debated whether to turn down the honour. Perhaps Bender had used his influence to keep Bernard one status step lower. Perhaps he had been treated so shabbily because he was only a naturalised Englishman, Hungarian by birth. It could even have been a slight against his Jewishness. He believed he had grown to understand the Englishmen's deep-rooted xenophobia, disguised and controlled certainly, but always to be reckoned with. Foreigners were tolerated, encouraged, flattered – but never quite accepted.

'At this stage, it is pointless to go over the past.' Lord Bender had moved on. Now he was, without looking at Sanger, reprimanding the American. 'Perhaps the Ecuador contract could have been drawn up with more safeguards. But in my experience, it's rare to gain complete immunity from risk in transactions of this kind. The size of risk generally matches the size of profit you hope to make.' It was a kind of defence of Michael, and Michael felt good. He should have known better. 'What we now have to decide is how to make the best of what we've got. And that, Michael, is your responsibility. You persuaded the board into this business. Now you must see it through.'

Michael said: 'I propose first to approach Corsino. Our American partners may well help us with cash. The consortium can only succeed if each part of it succeeds. To this extent we all sink or swim together.'

Bender nodded. 'Mr Corsino, whom I have not met' – he made this sound like a reprimand too – 'organised all our contacts in Ecuador, did he not?'

'Yes,' said Michael.

'Then he must feel some responsibility for our problems,' said Bender, and Michael thought that at times the chairman of Mondor could be extraordinarily naive. Did Bender not realise that time – in South America especially – could change everything? Had he never heard of revolution, of elections, of guerrillas urban and rural, of kidnappings, of coups?

'I'm going to approach our French partners, SAEF, as well,' said Michael. He had also intended to mention a subsidiary company, even two, which Prospero might have sold to raise cash, but in view of Bender's earlier remarks he said nothing.

'There may be finance to be had in London,' said Bernard. 'Money we don't have to borrow. Government money.'

'Overseas aid?' queried Jardine.

'Yes. The allocation for a country is made dependent on the money being used for a particular purpose involving a British company. But it's usually arranged *before* a contract's signed – to encourage exports. Now, it's going to depend entirely whether there's any money remaining that's earmarked for Ecuador or South America.'

The meeting pushed that idea around for a bit. When Sanger implied that he thought it hadn't much chance of succeeding, Bernard was driven to rating the chances higher than prudence dictated. Sanger's words reflected adversely upon the Chairman's influence in Whitehall, which Bernard liked to believe was acknowledged without question by his board as considerable. One Minister, and several senior civil servants, he implied, owed him a favour. This begged the question as to whether they were the right lot; gratitude in one Ministry is not necessarily reflected in favours from another, for Ministers and Permanent Secretaries are afflicted with the usual human feelings of jealousy and pride, as Bernard well knew. Sanger's careful baiting made him ignore that obstacle, however. He heard himself virtually promising to bring succour from Whitehall to Prospero.

He was regaining control of the meeting, but only because Bender had subsided. The next moves on Ecuador had been agreed, so the chairman of Mondor Insurance could again become silently watchful. Sanger raised the subject of Lovelace Motors. He was trying to get the board to put pressure on Michael to free more resources – management and money – within that company to develop the production line for motorcycle engines.

'We have a fine opportunity to turn this acquisition into profit. Why the hell else did we buy it? We've lined up several prospective customers in America. They're going to slot the engines into snowmobiles. We can't keep them waiting much longer before we sign contracts. At the moment, there's too much effort going into the preparation of special automobiles.'

Sanger mentioned neither Le Mans nor Michael. He had no need to. No one failed to recognise his target. Yet – and this is one of the fascinating unpredictables of business and the ebb and flow of board meetings – not a single director moved to support Sanger. It was as though the meeting had been exhausted by the long discussion on Ecuador. They had experienced their catharsis for that morning, and now wanted only to push through the rest of the business fast.

As a result, the discussion on Lovelace was desultory. Michael pointed out the prestige value of ensuring that Lovelace cars improved their flagging reputation. It could even help in selling their two-stroke engines for snowmobiles. Americans he believed, liked to be associated with a name which had overtones of racing success.

Sanger disputed Michael's order of priorities; there were hums and hahs and even some actual words from the chorus. And then Bernard Grant said: 'We've spent enough time on this. I suggest it's decided outside this meeting.'

'I agree, Chairman,' said Armfield. 'We haven't budgeted this year for any great change in Lovelace's profitability. We can afford to wait.' He was satisfied that Michael had been sufficiently constrained over Ecuador. Indeed, he had an idea of his own on that front about which he was keeping quiet for the present.

They moved speedily through the other business of the

meeting. The tension had almost disappeared. Finally, Bernard Grant began pushing the papers in front of him together and, raising his eyebrows almost humorously, said, 'Any other business?'

Sanger said, 'Yes, there is something, Sir Bernard.'

He opened up a blue folder and quickly slid a typewritten sheet towards each director. Bernard fidgeted in annoyance, but Sanger held the initiative.

'This is a rudimentary summation of the assets and trading position of a French office equipment company called Debrais. Perhaps you know them. They are number two in the field in France. They make typewriters, desks, chairs, filing cabinets. They're not simply distributors. They also have several subsidiary interests including an employment bureau chain. Their turnover is approaching 500 million francs – say forty million pounds – and their annual profit around ten million francs. They want us to buy an interest in them. I think we could really push up their lousy performance.'

The proposition was a complete surprise. Michael quickly looked at the figures. Even Sanger didn't usually spring major ideas like this without warning.

'I think Earl should tell us more, Chairman,' said Lord Bender. 'We have time.'

Sanger sat back and hitched up his trousers, exuding pleasure. Bernard nodded sharply, a gesture of displeased surrender.

'It's the right kind of deal for us. Our British operation in this field has a lot of the right kind of knowhow – which is why Debrais came to us in the first place. We need more involvement in Europe, and this gives us the chance to get our feet wet. I figure we stake it out like this. We take a one-third interest in a new joint company. Maybe we get an option to increase that to a majority holding later. That would be perfect. We don't want to commit ourselves too heavily until we see how Britain gets on inside the Common Market. If that goes fine, then we'll be right there.'

Michael said: 'What's their motivation in coming to us?'

'They're scared,' said Sanger. 'The guy who started the company after the war died last year. His widow doesn't want the responsibility of it. And it's vulnerable. They're afraid of being taken over by the market leader in France.'

'Why do they prefer us?' asked Bernard Grant. 'The French are so xenophobic, it's not like them to ask perfidious Albion to come in.'

'It's a question of personalities, as usual,' said Sanger, his tone showing that he regarded Bernard's pedantic reference to the history of national sensibilities in Europe as irrelevant. 'The widow has a real phobia about the president of the other organisation. So do most of her top managers. He used to work for her old man in the early days, quarrelled with him, set up his own outfit, and did even better. She reckons he stole her husband's ideas. I think she even blames the guy for his death. Maybe she's right. She sure does hate.'

'Black widow,' said Westbrook, trying out a macabre pun. No one laughed.

'How much money would it need?' said Bender.

'We couldn't really get in at under four million, maybe five,' said Sanger.

'Pounds?' said Armfield sourly.

'I gave up talking in dollars for Lent,' said Sanger with a humour which was not usual to him.

Armfield, annoyed that Sanger should privately have taken so expensive a transaction so far without consulting him, was not deterred. 'I don't know how we could spare that kind of money just now. It's a touch precipitate, don't you think, Earl?'

'How come?' said Sanger angrily. 'Seek and find, seek and find – that's what this organisation is about.' He snapped the file in front of him shut. 'This is a great proposition.'

'Have you talked with the woman?' asked Michael.

'Once. Mostly with the senior men, though,' said Sanger 'The deal could be ours if we want it.'

'Perhaps we should have known about it earlier,' said Bernard quietly, wishing to appear statesmanlike, yet wanting to turn the mood of the meeting against Sanger. 'It's a very sizeable commitment you're suggesting. And private negotiations carried too far by an individual director can be embarrassing to the organisation.'

'Who's to say what *too far* means, Sir Bernard? It was my judgment. That's what I get paid for. This is ridiculous.' Sanger was almost shouting, his voice hard and angry, one hand pulling irritably at the waistband of his trousers.

It was a mistake. He was over-reacting. He was exposed because, desirous of carrying home to Prospero so rich a prize, he had been too greedy in wishing to keep all the credit to himself. He needed allies, and around the table it began to look suspiciously as though he might lack them. An excess of presumption is a sin which businessmen do not easily forgive.

'Not ridiculous, Earl,' said Bernard. 'Your concern for Prospero touches us all. But success is the art of timing.' He beamed blandly. 'Had we known this sooner, we might have been able to earmark organisation funds. Harold is right. Where *do* we get the money?'

Sanger controlled himself, laying his hands on the table, clenched. 'If we'd maintained the level of fallback money which Lord Bender mentioned earlier, we'd have no problem.'

That was clever. Bender sang on cue. 'Earl exceeded his authority, perhaps. But the prospect is a good one. We're unlikely to get a chance of entering the French market so easily again.'

'Right, sir,' said Sanger. 'It would be better if we didn't use our cash anyway. We could borrow in France or on the Euro-dollar market.'

'And run the risk that the borrowing may be called in and not renewed,' Armfield observed sourly.

'I think we should investigate this further,' said Bender. 'Despite our cash problems, it sounds promising.'

In the momentary silence which followed, Sanger was foolish enough to believe that he was a narrow winner, on points. Then Bender said, 'But I think it would be wise if we broadened the scope of our inquiries. Perhaps you might add that young man David Travis to the team, Michael. He seems to have the track record for affairs like this.'

It was nicely done. Bender had helped Sanger, but had put an observer on his back too. Preserving the balance of power.

Whilst words of agreement were spoken and Sanger fumed, Baron Bender of Kingsway was no longer teasing the angry patch of scalp above the right ear. Instead, he took an Uppmann from his cigar case, snipped off the end, and lit up. The last word which mattered had been spoken and soon all of them, winners and losers and passengers alike, moved off towards a nearby room for lunch.

All, that is, except Michael, who excused himself for five minutes. In his office, he placed a call to Edward Corsino, in New Jersey, for five that afternoon. Then he unlocked a drawer and took out the unsigned letter which offered – as it had, unknown to him, also offered to Sanger – the closely guarded client list of an offshore investment fund competitive with a similar Prospero subsidiary.

The morning's meeting had made him even less inclined to dabble in that kind of fringe activity. He disliked the sneakiness of it anyway. Now, temptation was removed altogether with the clearer understanding of what his priorities must be. As he walked towards the board dining room, he stopped at a small corner office. A shredding machine quickly swallowed the letter through its digestive knives.

2

That morning, Sheila Travis had lain in bed wanting her husband to make love to her, raging in silence at his exhausted form beside her, refusing the humiliation of even trying to arouse him.

At breakfast her eyes were bleak. By the evening she was still coldly resentful. As David slumped into the car she said: 'You might have tried to make the early train for once. It *is* bloody Friday night.'

As they drove from the station he explained that Michael Grant had called him in late to talk about a new errand for him in Paris.

'I thought you'd been promised a few weeks at home?'

'Christ, love, Paris isn't the end of the earth. Besides, it may not happen yet.'

'It still means you'll be away.'

'That's the job. What do I do? Tell him to get stuffed?'

'Sometimes I wish you would.'

There was no point in arguing. He understood her irritation. But as he subdued his own feelings at times, he wished she would more realistically keep quiet about hers when business got in the way of their cosier plans. He sat silently because there was nothing else usefully to be said, although he knew that the longer they remained mute, the more difficult it would be to start talking again.

The dusk was on the trees like gauze as they drove into their neighbourhood. In earlier years, the stockbrokers and civil servants had masked their mock Tudor mansions with walls and thick overhangs of elms, enslaved by the middle-class conventions of privacy. Now, there were colonies of new houses, each with its regulation quarter-acre of breathing space but, in American fashion, without fences around the front lawns.

On their better harmonious days, David and Sheila would joke about it. Her father might have been a don at Oxford whilst David's was a clerk in Falmouth, but they had both been nourished on the middle-class traditions which drifted on after the war from the thirties. Privet hedges, and the privacy they enshrine, are much the same at the fringes of the dreaming spires as they are skirting a cottage near a fishing harbour in Cornwall.

He looked incuriously at the landscape. In sitting rooms galore, the curtains were still undrawn. There were flickering television screens. A man tilted a glass to his mouth. A woman primped flowers on a table.

He didn't sneer in his mind at all this. Prospect House was one thing. This was his other world and, oddly, he didn't feel as rootless as the sociologists would have him believe a suburban dweller ought.

'I know you don't want to come to the party,' said Sheila.

'What are you talking about?' he said. Christ, don't push, girl.

'They asked us for 8.30. It's almost that now.'

'I'll hurry,' he said. 'I just need a shave.'

'We've got friends in this place too,' she said. 'I need them even if you don't. And they've got people along tonight especially for you.'

'Look,' he said. 'I'm sorry I'm late. I really will hurry.'

He wanted to mollify her. He enjoyed the odd local party – even the gropings in darkened playrooms while Sinatra and the Beach Boys ground away – as much as she did; sometimes, he suspected, more. But he had to have different priorities from hers. Why couldn't she understand that? Or, since he thought she did, why didn't she grow to live with the facts more peaceably? Now, however, he stamped on his pride, wanting only to keep the evening bright. He knew he owed her something.

'Come on, love,' he said, leaning to kiss her as she drove. She really was very dishy, even when her mouth was pouting.

'Not when I'm driving.'

'You look so good.'

'All right,' she said. Her long legs fiddled with brake and accelerator. She half-smiled. 'But you're still a rotten sod.'

'How's Kenwyn?'

'He was asking for you,' she said, still unwilling to forego scoring points. 'Karen was tucking him in when I left. He'll be asleep by now.'

'Tough on Dad,' he said.

'Tough on Mum, too. He's been a little horror.'

David felt like asking whether that had bothered her particularly, or whether Karen had taken the strain. Karen was 17, Danish, with fair hair down her back, breasts she hung so that they threatened to impale the unwary, and swivel-hips. Had she given him any encouragement, he might have been tempted, but to Karen a man of 32 might just as well have been 80. Her bedroom was plastered with coloured posters of Jagger, Led Zeppelin and Grand Funk Railroad.

If Sheila, then, had no cause to be envious of what Karen might do for David, then he – secretly and ashamedly – was jealous of what the *au pair* did for her. Karen gave Sheila freedom and time; time to see people, look into shops, talk, play games. So David, in his least likeable moments, thought. And he was the provider, of course. Life for Sheila was all right, he would argue to himself. God give *me* more time.

In the bedroom, David shrugged off his own quiet discontents and worked further to assuage Sheila's. Out loud, he admired her shape as she stood naked before the looking-glass, and that was no hardship to him. She was long and slim, with small high breasts and a belly narrow and flat despite the child. In tennis clothes she looked like one of the girls on the Wimbledon and Forest Hills circuit. Her body was firm as theirs too, and just as brown, for which the sun lamp in the corner by the Sony TV rather than winter sunshine was responsible.

Finally, encouraged by him, she chose a loose white trouser suit. White figured a great deal in her wardrobe.

With her tan and raven-black hair she looked marvellous in white, if in the context of their usual parties rather pre-meditatedly virginal. He zipped the back for her.

'Move, boy,' she said. 'It's almost nine.'

'I've shaved,' he said.

'Not that suit, David. You look like you're going on a management training course.'

'What, then?'

'Slacks and sweater. And your new belt. That's all they'll expect.'

He pulled on violet slacks, flare-legged, and far too expensive for the state of their overdraft, topped them with a jersey-wool roll-top in purple and slung a wide black belt loosely around his hips. The large silver buckle hung so low it was like a twentieth century codpiece.

'Okay?' he said to Sheila, who was absorbed in experimenting with a clutch of hooped and dangly ear-hangings.

She gave him a quick glance.

'Fine,' she said.

But he was not so sure.

When he saw two other men dressed like this it looked like middle-aged fancy dress. Yet everyone in the neighbourhood wore the same, except for the dreariest of accountants, solicitors and shop-keepers. Big-buckle belts and flare pants had that year become suburbia's fertility symbols.

When they hit the party it was almost 9.30 and the feeling between them was more comfortable. It was a big house, late 19th century, with steps leading up to the entrance, brass carriage lamps gleaming outside, and a monstrous brass knocker – a naked nymph – sitting expectantly on the yellow door.

The Carsons had made it, definitely. The husband had recently become a partner in a firm of Mayfair estate agents.

'Darlings,' said the hostess, 'how super. I suppose you've been slaving away as usual, you poor thing.'

She emphasised the point by thrusting her body against David's side and wriggling. It was an interesting sensation for him, like rolling in feather pillows. She wore a long black silk skirt, patterned peasant-like. Her belt was twice as wide as his, metal-studded. Above it her white blouse was split deep, her ample breasts unsupported, hanging beneath it like elongated melons almost to the belt. Upheld, she'd told Sheila, she believed they made her look like a school matron. This way, she fancied, she was a cross between Yoko Ono and Earth Mother, with a touch of Queen Boadicea. And that was okay.

'You look ravishing,' she said to Sheila. 'You must tell me what the diet is, I'll have to start again. It's a bore.' She swung her body with feigned heaviness.

'You look great,' said David. His mind began to sing, unwarned, *Don't change a hair for me, not if you care for me*, from an old pop song.

'You're a lovely man,' she said and Sheila raised her eyebrows.

The roar of conversational surf came from a room across the hall which was guarded by two carved wooden figures of blackamoors, early nineteenth century style, about four feet tall. David wondered if they were genuine (which meant about a thousand quidsworth) or copies. He could see mouths opening and glasses being raised.

'Do go in and sip a gin or something,' said the hostess. 'Then you must meet the Mailers. You boys can talk about the perils of the Amazon together. He's been out there too. Isn't that lucky?'

Once he'd got his first Scotch in his hand he soon lost Sheila, who plunged into god knows what plots and gossip with the women she knew. He always felt schizophrenic in situations like this, carrying on bitty conversations which he only half-heard, hoping his smiling face and nodding head were working at the correct moments. The blizzard of words hit him.

I'm dotty about her really. She's the most gorgeous daughter I've ever had . . .

So we left them to it. Twenty of his friends. The weirdest bunch yet. I said to John, I don't care what they do. So long as I don't know. I'm glad to be out of it. But I hope they're not sick on the carpet . . .

Heal's came into my kitchen. It's beautiful. A galley. I've got the name of a man there . . .

He went to the careers advisory centre, and they told him he should be an architect not an accountant. What use is that at 41 . . .

Then Jim Slater came in on it and all hell was let loose . . .

94

Don't buy in Portugal, sweetheart. You're ten years too late. Now, I've got a chum in town who's very well in with a chap in Athens . . .

He's cuddly, isn't he? But he never goes too far . . .

And I said to him – well, sex, I've got to take mine now. I was joking, of course . . .

It wasn't until everyone had got their moussaka and were sitting around in various rooms or on the stairs that David caught up with Mailer. He was in his late thirties, very brown, lean of face, wearing a dark-blue blazer with gleaming brass buttons. He was easy to look at and he smiled a lot, but not with his eyes, which were grey and melancholy. He'd been in Ecuador for a month recently, trying to sell frigates and fast patrol launches.

'I came back to see how much the design boys could shave off our price. Nothing will happen till the new balance of power sorts itself out.'

'Colonel Vargas?' said David.

'Check. Do you know him?'

'No. But he won't be good for us. Maybe for you, he will.'

'He wants to buy if he could get the money,' said Mailer. 'But we'll have to pay away a bit more on the side now there's a new set of faces around.'

'So will we,' said David, grimacing.

'How's your plant shaping?'

'So-so. The usual troubles. Stuff held up in customs. Costs too bloody high. Work behind schedule.'

'How's it been funded?'

David shrugged. 'Mostly British and American money. Commercial banks. In theory the set-up's fine. But we haven't seen much of our money back yet.'

Mailer nodded. His eyes grew more melancholy than ever. They looked as if they knew all about hanging around waiting to get paid. 'Weren't the Japs interested?'

'They were. They damn near made it too. We clinched it on the terms.'

'Bully for you.'

David laughed. 'We've got some useful guys up front. The main dealer was an American called Ed Corsino. He pulled us in. He's in big with Kerridge.'

'Kerridge Steel?'

'And the rest. Kerridge really fronts a conglomerate these days.'

'But steel's still the main prop, isn't it?'

'I suppose so,' said David. 'That's why Kerridge is leader of the consortium. His mills will make just about all the main equipment, or get sub-contractors to do it. And one of his companies is designing too. He must be in for 30 to 40 per cent of the deal.'

'And you've got how much?'

'Say fiifteen per cent. About fifteen million quidsworth, that is.'

'I didn't know Prospero were so big in plant construction.'

David explained about Brasserton's – and the computer people Oldershaw was working with.

Mailer twisted his lips derisively, presumably at the notion of computer people. 'And the best of British luck.' He put his plate down. 'Jesus. Those bloody officials.'

'Which ones?'

'All of them. I spent a month doing nothing except waking up every morning wondering which office they'd shunt me to next. And then the waiting. It's a status game with them. The more people an official has hanging around to see him in his front office, the more important he is. My arse learned it the hard way.'

'What was the trouble?'

'You tell me. I think the idea was to make me so pissed off with hanging around that I'd cut the price out of sheer frustration. I would too! But that's not the problem. They insist they pay through Eastern Europe.'

David had an idea what was coming.

'They've got a pile of balances in two Eastern bloc countries. From selling bloody bananas. And coffee. We've got to find a middle man who wants to buy really big behind the Iron Curtain. Then we provide the ships for Ecuador. Ecuador pays us in zlotis or roubles or whatever. The middle man uses them to buy his goods. Then finally he pays us in sterling.'

'Lucky old middle man,' said David.

'Right,' said Mailer. 'I wouldn't mind his cut. That's the trouble dealing one hundred per cent with governments. They can call the tune about currencies. How much of a stake has the Ecuador Government got in your plant?'

'Fifty-five per cent of the shares in the petro-chemical company our consortium's building the plant for.'

'Who else?'

'Ali-Chem has 20 per cent. They're big-league in chemicals in the States.'

'What's their angle?' asked Mailer.

'The usual. Protecting their South American market. Expanding it if they can. They're going to get tax advantages and some tariff protection, I expect.'

'It's still a gamble.'

David shrugged. 'These organisations have to take gambles sometimes, I suppose. So do we. So does Kerridge. He's going to hold 15 per cent of the petro-chemical company's equity as well as having built most of the plant for them. And he's underwritten a hell of a big slice of the commercial loans. He's supposed to be a cute old sod, so he must see big profits in there somewhere.'

Mailer nodded; but he still didn't look convinced.

'We've been screwed too,' said David. 'It was a hell of an initial investment we made.'

'Poor old you,' said Mailer. He laughed like a man who was about to begin the dirty jokes session. But Sheila came up to them.

'If you two boys will stop talking shop, I'll join you. Want some coffee?'

'Thanks,' said Mailer. He looked at her hard. She was better than a dirty joke. 'Black, no sugar.'

'Me too,' said David.

'D'you fancy Ecuador?' asked Mailer when she'd gone.

'Beautiful,' said David. 'Absolutely fantastic. I'd like to spend a holiday there.'

'Alone, if I'd the choice,' said Mailer. 'I met some smashing birds. You?'

'No time.'

'Sure.' Mailer laughed. 'One was an Indian. Fabulous.'

'I wouldn't care to be an Indian out there. You must've been lucky. The ones I met weren't having much fun.'

'One day those poor devils will saw the balls off the old politicians,' said Mailer. 'Like in Cuba. It must happen.'

'But not yet.'

'Maybe.'

Sheila returned, and the three of them sat while the men

swapped anecdotes of Indian villages and restaurants and the jungle. In a while, Sheila looked bored. Heavy rock music was hammering somewhere. The hostess lurched towards them. She looked drunk.

'David, dance with me,' she said, swaying gently. 'You've been ignoring me all night.'

'Okay,' he said.

The dancing room was unlit. As they went in, David could see from the light outside that about five couples were shaking to the sound of ancient Beatles, very loud. Then the music stopped, and as everyone wandered out, she put both arms around his waist and pulled him towards her, lips and teeth contacting his left ear simultaneously.

'Don't you dare go,' she said, nibbling. 'It's nicer music now.'

Slow and easy, the sound came from the speakers. Stan Getz, bossa nova, with guitars and the cool voice of Astrud Gilberto. They began to move in rhythm, and then she broke away to push the door shut and cut off the light.

'That's better,' she said, and she came back, pushing hard against him as they swayed together, scarcely moving their feet. There was no one else in the room. She giggled. 'I'll bet Sheila thinks I mean to do you a mischief.'

He had heard about her and once, at another party, had spent a quarter-hour comfortably pillowed on her soft bosom whilst dancing. But she'd never been so direct.

'Do you?' he asked.

'Do I what?'

'Mean to do me a mischief?'

'Give me the chance,' she said.

Her hands slid behind him, moving slowly and with greed. They wandered elsewhere. She thrust herself harder against him.

'That's nice,' she said. What the hell, he thought.

The skirt was smooth and soft on her skin, and he could feel the heat beneath it. Inside her blouse, the breasts were almost too soft, not firm like Sheila's, but her nipples were stone-hard. She sucked in her breath quickly as he touched her. The record whispered *Corvocado, oh how lovely* as she let her hands move more intimately, and then: 'Come and see our summerhouse. We had an extension built on this spring.'

'Too obvious,' he said.

'No one will see,' she said. 'I'm the only one with a key. Don't you want to come?'

She led him to a curtained window, opened a door, and they were out on a flagged patio. He could see lights from the house and a human shape or two through windows. She guided him into a white-walled alcove. He leaned against the wall and she paused to unbuckle her belt, laying it on a cane chair.

In retrospect, it was ridiculous. She led the way, persistent as a bulldozer, undoing and taking off almost by numbers, chattering, as sexy as the girls of St Trinian's.

'My skirt undoes. Buttons,' she said.

She was keen, full of instructions and explanations. 'I dumped my tights. You'd have spent all damn night finding your way in.'

The wall he was pinned against was gritty and uncomfortable. She said: 'I've always wanted this.' And he thought that *always* wasn't long; he'd known her for two years at most.

Finally her talk, like a running commentary on a wrestling match, turned into a low-voiced incoherent jumble. He wanted, one-half of his mind, to get away. The other half was as fascinated as a rabbit pinned by the stoat's stare. What was he doing here? It wasn't totally disenjoyable, couldn't be. But who would have thought it? Dear fat little Brenda Carson, the estate agent's wife, rampaging about like a blue-movie nymphomaniac.

It was over within three or four minutes, start to finish. She moaned and said that it had been worth coming for. Joke, he thought. Then she drew away and he could see the huge breasts, white and trembling, which had half-suffocated him as she sported on the slopes of his body. He suddenly felt cold.

'Great,' she said clinically. 'Let's do it again some time.' All matter-of-fact, like tasting a new coffee flavour. Then she bent down and pulled a box from under the chair. He couldn't help laughing. She even had the Kleenex handy.

They went back to the dance room, slid quietly in and resumed swaying with the couples who had slunk in during their absence.

'It's okay,' she whispered. 'We haven't been away ten minutes.'

When they went back into the lighted hall, he felt stupidly self-conscious, as if everyone must be watching them. The party had splintered into innumerable groups, bodies lying on the floor talking to the ceiling, glasses underfoot, cigarette ash everywhere. His hostess squeezed his hand, murmured 'See you, lover', and was calling to another man for a dance with the virtuous air of someone who'd just finished washing up the glasses. He couldn't believe that even she would repeat the performance in the summerhouse with someone else. Not for an hour, at least.

'Have you seen Sheila?' he asked Mailer.

'I think she's in there.' Mailer pointed to a closed oak door, down a passage.

'Thanks,' said David. He sat down, not wanting to move off immediately, in case he should appear the frightened husband. A woman he knew passed by, nodding brusquely, zooming towards the dance room like a neurotic spotter plane. He knew what she was looking for, too. Her husband would put his hand down any convenient dress-front as mindlessly as a salesgirl taking change from a cash register. At neighbourhood parties his wife flew regular reconnaissance missions, purely as a gesture, though.

Mailer said, 'Great girl, Sheila. You must come to dinner or the theatre or something.'

'Yes. I'd like to see that new Pinter. How long is it in the Old Vic rep. for?'

'I'll find out. And let's keep in touch about Ecuador. We might be able to help each other.'

David smiled. 'We're not in the war game – not yet. So let's.' He stood up. 'Sheila may be getting lonely.'

'I doubt it.'

He tried to look relaxed. 'What do you mean?'

'Smoking is a together thing, so they always say.'

'Smoking?'

'Yeah – that's the smoking room. Stupid bastards. She said she'd like to watch.'

'So would I,' said David.

Heads jerked up embarrassedly, trying to look neither guilty nor afraid, as he entered. Everyone was lying around on cushions, their faces in half-shadow from the four flickering candles which provided the only light. Sheila wriggled sideways to make a space for David.

'Well?' he whispered. Everyone else was whispering too.

'You'll learn something,' she said.

'I don't want to.'

'Don't make a fuss,' she said.

A man was sitting by a low table making joints. The room watched him in fascination.

'I think this is good shit,' he announced, American-accented.

'He knows,' said the hostess, who had a hand – not her own – on her left thigh. David was astonished to see her. She must have got the freeze on her latest summerhouse proposition.

It was brown-black and sticky-crumbling in a wrapper of silver paper. 'A block this size' – the American's fingers formed a small rectangle – 'will cost 200 dollars in New York City.'

An English voice spoke. 'If you get it from Morocco, it comes mixed in camel dung to hold it together. It's just the resin of the plant.'

'And you smoke the dung too?' said a woman.

'Sure.'

The American had laid out cigarette papers flat on larger pieces of ordinary paper. On to them he shook the shredded tobacco from regular cigarettes which he'd broken open. Then globs of the sticky stuff were laid on the tobacco. He rolled the joints crudely, twisting the cigarette paper in at one end, leaving the other open.

'Jesus, that's a bummer,' he said of one disintegrating joint. 'Could I have some cardboard from that pack?' He rolled a strip of cardboard into a tube, stuffing it into the open end of the joint to form a mouthpiece.

David said, 'Let's go.'

'No,' said Sheila. 'I'd like to try.'

'You don't want this kind of experience.'

She looked at him very coolly. 'You have your experience in the summerhouse, fine. I get mine here. Okay?'

'You're mad,' he said.

'Aren't we all?' she said.

The American lit up. 'Sit closer now,' he commanded.

101

'And watch that light. You'll find it interesting.' He pointed to one of the candles.

Many of the neighbourhood locals hadn't smoked before. Their hipper neighbours coached them. There was no noise except for the sharp, hissing intake of breath, teeth showing. A woman let out her smoke immediately, as she might have done with a cigarette, and was quickly reprimanded.

'Hold it, girl. Take it down.' The American had relaxed on the floor. Each person took three or four puffs, then passed on the joint. A second and third began to circulate. Sheila smoked. David declined.

'Man, you're all so easy here,' said the American. 'In New York everyone's watching you smoke. They want you to pass it on after only two draws. If you grab more, that's greedy. They're very uptight about it.'

'It's like everyone's floating,' said a woman in a surprisingly harsh voice. 'Sometimes with me it comes in waves. It can be very frightening if you're on your own.'

'Jesus. You don't do this *alone*. Come closer.' The American put his hand on the woman's thigh and pulled her towards him. She rolled over and kissed him.

'Hey, man,' he said suddenly to Sheila's neighbour. 'Keep that joint over the ashtray. That's why we got big ones. No ash on the carpet.'

An English voice. 'I'm high. Stoned.' Two or three people kicked off their shoes. Sheila wore a silly smile. She looked at David. 'I'm all right,' she said. He scowled.

'Don't be so bloody high and mighty,' she said.

He turned away and looked at his hostess. She didn't see him. She was lying flat, not a hand laid on her, looking neglected.

'This is good stuff, good shit.' The American again.

'That candle's floating.'

'Don't say that to her,' said a man, pointing dreamily to the hostess. 'She'll vomit.'

'No she won't,' said the American. 'She only vomited last time because she was in someone else's pad. She won't do it in her own.'

A shrewd hit, David thought. Were they all play-acting at being stoned?

Sheila lifted his arm to her waist. 'Don't be cross, lover. I feel fine. Honest.'

He was almost happy at what he took to be a signal of reconciliation. He knew of course that she was taking a sort of revenge on him. If she felt guilty about her stupidity – for taking pot must, in his book, be stupid – then it put him in a stronger position. He wanted to play it kind and easy.

'How?' he said.

'Kind of soft in my mind. Your skin is all glowing. I want to touch you. Do you know you look beautiful?'

The American was telling a long anecdote about a friend who'd had acid slipped in his drink at a Manhattan party. 'They found him two hours later wandering around the highway. God knows how he wasn't killed. And all the way home he was cursing and raving and crying out just like a kid *They're trying to kill me*. It was real weird. It took him three months to get over that. A prolonged nervous break-down. He said it was like he wasn't in control of his head. It really broke him up.'

'My God,' said a woman.

'So you stay clear of acid, ma'am.'

The room was full of peace, giggles, groping and whole-sale embarrassment.

Sheila said. 'I want to go home.'

'Are you all right?' asked David.

'Yes. I just want to leave. No fuss. Slowly.'

David crawled over to the hostess. She was wide awake beneath the dreamy guise. She leaned towards David's ear. 'Don't have me on the floor, darling. People might notice.'

'We've got to go,' said David.

'Spoilsport. We could try again.'

'Don't push our luck,' he said.

'If you say so.' She sat up, and anyone who wanted could see her nipples. He'd had enough encores for one per-formance.

In the hall, more formal, she exhibited symptoms of the middle-class ethic of fear. 'Don't ever tell anyone you smoked in *this* house.' Then, lowering her lashes towards David. 'Don't tell anyone *anything*.' It was a deliberate goad to Sheila.

'The cow,' said Sheila as they crunched across gravel to the Rover.

103

'I thought you liked her.' He couldn't keep the taunt out of his voice.

'She's all right. They're all of them all right. Kind in their way. They'll help. Do you a turn, any time.'

'You bet,' he said sardonically.

'But she really ought to keep her hands out of other people's trousers.'

'Definitely.'

'What did she do with you?'

'Everything and nothing. Mainly nothing,' he said, trying to keep it joky.

'All right,' she said. 'You don't have to tell me.'

In the car, he said, 'I didn't mind you smoking, but I still wish you hadn't.'

'It did nothing for me, except make me feel sort of warm and sexy towards you. You should be so lucky.'

'It's evil,' he said.

'Don't be silly,' she said. 'Just once. Where's the harm?'

'All those people, poncing about like they've found a new recipe for being one-up.'

She was riled, but controlled and lucid. 'Listen, love. Listen to me for once. I can't get upset at your poor Indians and their standard of living, or who's going to get a billion dollar contract, or which restaurant in Bangkok is the best. I don't *feel* it, because I don't *see* it. I've never been, so I'm not involved. Anyway, don't your Indians chew coca to make themselves happy? You told me.'

'Yes,' he said, defeated for a moment.

'So I can take these people because that's what I've got. I forget all their nonsense, all their bloody awful pretensions, because maybe we've got a few too. Underneath they're all right. They're just playing the game because it's the only game in town. Do you understand?'

'All right,' he said. 'I like some of them too.'

He had not yet discovered the motivation behind Sheila's frequent bouts of irritation and self-justification. Every woman wants her husband to be successful; but not *too* successful. If men do too well, they achieve an independence which is beyond marriage. Women know that the power they hold over their men, a hold compounded of convenience and love, of sexual attraction and legal complication, is weakened. During the past year or so, David Travis had done *too* well with Prospero for Sheila to be sure about him.

'Freddy Mailer,' she said, 'is he one you like?'

'Yes. We must see him again.'

'We will,' she said. 'He thinks you might be useful to him. Back to business, folks.'

He ignored the jibe. 'I don't mind the people, Sheila. Really. It's just that you make such a thing about it, and about me and what I do.'

She shrugged. 'What else is there to make a thing about? They're all I've got.'

3

Michael Grant didn't reach Corsino until almost midnight. He took the call in the sitting room, perched in the alcove watching the stream of lights on the Embankment below.

'Sorry I missed you at the office,' said Corsino. 'I've been up to New York City today. Now I'm on my third martini. How about you?'

'Strictly coffee, Ed. Then I'm for bed. How are you?'

'Fine. Just fine.'

'And Marjorie and the kids?'

Corsino leaned back in one of the cushioned cane chairs that adorned the indoor courtyard of his home. Behind him, water swished and gurgled softly as it ran over a series of coolly lit, natural rocks.

'Yeah,' he said. 'She's fine, too.'

That day she had paid almost five thousand dollars for a pastel mink coat, with the summer coming on too. And without telling him. And she'd paid retail when he could have saved a thousand at least through his wholesale connections. He had almost struck her in his anger. But it was her money she was using. That was mostly why he had married her fifteen years ago, using her assets to play himself into position. Now that he was in position, she had the interest of an empty bank vault to him.

'And how's Alison?'

'She's blooming, Ed. She's expecting a kid.'

'Hey, great, Mike. When you going to bring her over?'

'Maybe this year, Ed. Before the fall.'

'Any time, Mike. But you didn't call me to talk happy families. What's on your mind?'

Michael explained the problem of Prospero's cash flow.

'We're stretched, Ed – almost a million pounds adrift. Our operation shuffles money around so fast, we don't have that kind of liquidity.'

'What have you been doing, Mike? Playing Santa Claus to your sub-contractors?'

'We have to pay them promptly. They're mostly little guys, without resources. Did you know the promissory notes weren't coming through to us from Ecuador?'

'Sure I knew. But you're behind schedule.'

'It's not our fault, Ed. You know what it's like out there. Can't you push the Government a bit?'

'Listen, Mike, you know the contract.'

'Of course, Ed. But I didn't expect the Government to try and screw up its own damn petro-chemical plant.'

'They'd say they weren't. If you didn't like the small print in the contract, you should have tried to change it. You signed the goddam thing.'

Corsino's voice was hard and flat. When it came down to it Corsino would insist that Prospero did its job, on time, and looked after its own pennies. With business there was no messing. Michael couldn't object; he liked the directness of American businessmen when it came to the point. But Corsino might be a little more sympathetic.

'Our costs aren't shaping up too well either. If we have to start flying out parts to make up time, instead of shipping them, Christ knows where we'll be.'

'There's no sign of that yet,' Corsino scoffed. 'I've seen Del Martin's latest report. So don't try and pull that one, Mike. Anyway, you've got a contingency sum in there. We all have. If it's too small, go kick the ass off your accountants. How can I help you?' The tone was almost offensive. Corsino had his own troubles.

'Maybe by persuading the Ecuador Government to put in some of their *own* money. You know how much we've already slipped under the counter to them. Couldn't they ease up a bit on the contract terms for stage payments?'

'Number one, Mike, I don't want to go crying to Quito right now. They might think we're trying to blow the whole deal. Anyways, I don't figure Cantania would dare take the political risk. Number two, it's not only the Government who'd have to find that dough. Ali-Chem and Kerridge are involved in that company too. Thirty-five per cent of over sixty million bucks they're in for – and a damn sight more for Kerridge. That ain't peanuts.'

'Maybe they could help.'

'Listen, son. Ali-Chem have been pissin' all over me the last three months. They came in on the deal in a rush. Now they're regretting it. They've been seeing how petro-chem production is stacking up this year. They don't like it. There are signs of a goddam glut of product already. They're scared they'll end up selling to India or someone like that and getting a bellyful of soft currency they can't use. I think they'd want out if they could.'

'But they can't pull out, can they?'

'No way, Mike. But they'll be doing nobody any favours.'

'And Kerridge?'

'He's an ornery old bastard. Doesn't like being pushed around and mean as hell. You know that.'

'So we just stew, Ed, do we?' Michael was losing patience.

'I'm crying for you, baby, but what can I do? Surely your old man can pull something with your own Government? It's a damn big export order, and I know what your balance of payments is like. Try the French. Use your imagination.'

'All right, Ed. We'll give it a couple of weeks. If we get nowhere. I'll be back.'

'See here, Mike.' Corsino's voice was a shade softer. 'If you were really in the shit I'd have to help. You know that. We sink or swim together, right? But I've got to give the situation down in Quito a month to cool off. Try to sort out the dough your end. Remember what they say.'

'What do they say?' said Michael.

'When the going gets tough, the tough get going.' Corsino laughed ironically, and Michael kicked the leg of his chair in irritation.

'I get the message, Ed.'

'Then act like you've got it, Mike.' Corsino's tone was back to neutral matter-of-fact again.'

There seemed nothing more to be said. Michael spoke as warmly as he could. 'I'll be in touch, Ed. 'Night.'

Then he put down the receiver, switched off the scrambler

device with which both his home and office telephones were equipped, and slipped out the tape-recording of the conversation he'd made. He wasn't likely to play it to anyone, but in conversations about deals, you never knew. Then he poured out another cup of coffee and sat there, watching the lights prickle across the Albert Bridge, and wondering whether next week he had time to go see how the Le Mans car was shaping down in Hampshire.

Ed Corsino was more positive in action. He was a big man, barrel-chested, with a swarthy pockmarked face and thinning black hair. His head was just about the only place he didn't have much hair. Curly strands bushed thickly on his arms and thrust out of the open neck of his shirt. The cane chair creaked as he leaned forward to dial another number.

He listened to the call tone and let his eyes rest with satisfaction on the enormous spread of the courtyard. It was completely encased in glare-free glass. The floor was marble, exquisitely veined in careful browns and blues. The plants were the finest the best indoor garden sculptor in New Jersey could provide, a riot of palms and cacti and creepers. The rocks were genuine Shap granite, shipped in from England, and the water which ran among them was pure enough to drink. Dominating everything else was the bar, over 40 feet long, stacked with several hundred visible bottles of all hues and contents. The courtyard had cost, altogether, two hundred thousand bucks. There weren't many whole houses in this New Jersey town that were worth that. With the surrounding acres, he reckoned his would fetch a million. Not that he was aiming to sell. Ed Corsino had made it, and he wasn't going to let any English kid unmake him.

'Hello, Kerridge?' the old man to whom he spoke, sitting in a grandiose house, terraced and pillared, high in the Palisades National Park of Northern New York State, was leader of the consortium. But Corsino did not address him like a supplicant.

'Listen to me and listen good. Is this 'phone secure? Yeah, well if any of those Prospero gooks come sniffing around you for dough, it's no go, understand?' He paused and listened. 'Sure, they've got themselves screwed up over cash flow. Maybe we can help 'em later, maybe we can't.

But not now. Let them clean up their own mess. I've got my investment to protect and I don't aim to lose a cent of it. You got that?'

The old man fidgeted in his chair. Beyond the large window he sat by, the light had gone. The pines and the rocks and the lake were a black blur. He could hear a deer moving. One single light burned in a neighbour's house half a mile away.

'Yes, Ed. I understand.' The voice was untypically mild. It seemed not to suit the powerful straight nose which jutted from the crumbled, cratered face of Kerridge, or the pouches beneath the eyes which bespoke confident power, nor the hot brown eyes. It was a face strong enough to have made the cover of two issues of *Time* magazine in the last twelve years. But Kerridge wasn't going to quarrel with the man who pulled the strings of the syndicate which, in several complicated ways, held so major a block of stock in his organisation. He still, however, wondered how he had been so poor in stewardship as to allow Kerridge Steel to get into a position where a man like Corsino could tell him what to do. Ten years ago he would have trodden on Corsino like a beetle.

'And by the way,' said Corsino, 'what in hell's going on with Crewe's? They keep blaming the steel you're shipping them for why they can't get the goddam towers right. Have you seen Martin's report?'

'Yes, I've seen it, Ed,' said Kerridge wearily. 'But' – and the voice swiftly became firm and proud – 'there is nothing wrong with my steel. No one's complained in fifty years . . .'

Corsino interrupted. 'Sure, sure, I know all that history stuff. We'll get someone out there to Crewe's and kick their ass.'

'They were, I seem to remember, your choice as sub-contractor for that part of the job.'

It was true. There had been five competitors tendering to build the towers and vessels that would one day have to withstand unimaginable pressure and corrosion in order to work chemical miracles at the petro-chemical plant in Ecuador. But it was Crewe's who had offered Corsino the biggest kick-back in commission. Privately, of course. To be paid in Panama.

'Don't try to pull that one, Kerridge. You said they were okay too.'

'They had the experience. Their price was reasonable. But I didn't know them, I'd never worked with them before.'

'You're responsible for seeing they do the job – with your steel,' said Corsino coldly. 'And don't forget it. As consortium leader, it's your baby. The Ecuador people will screw *you* if anything goes wrong, not Crewe's.'

'I know that, Ed. And the Ecuador people, as you call them, also happen to include me. I've got a hunk of my money committed to the stock of that petro-chemical company I'm building the plant for.'

'*Our* money,' said Corsino.

'Certainly,' said Kerridge. 'And we expect a return for it, don't we? As well as on all the rest. So don't think I don't know what's expected of me.'

Corsino let it go. There was no point in bullying Kerridge further.

'One last thing, Ed.' Kerridge was tired. Now he was going to call the plays. 'There's a story in *Fortune* today about the SEC not liking our bid for Talsey.'

Kerridge was talking about another steel company, a keen competitor whom he'd decided to drag, willingly or not, into his conglomerate. *Fortune* hadn't seemed surprised that Kerridge Steel was finding the Securities Exchange Commission troublesome about the attempted takeover. Monopoly or near-monopoly situations, either nationally or in certain states, were the touchiest political landmine of the year.

'My syndicate wouldn't like that.'

'Nor would I,' said Kerridge. 'I don't want a hearing. Not now.'

'I'll talk with some people,' said Corsino.

Even on a telephone checked twice weekly for tapping, he would say no more. And Kerridge knew he had no need to. Sometimes Kerridge believed Corsino could fix anything, including whether a man six thousand miles away should live or die.

4. SPIES AND SINNERS

1

GEORGE LOVELACE glowered at Michael Grant across the oak table, slammed a fist slap in the middle of the magazine laid open in front of him.

'This is disgraceful. Surely your people can take action on this kind of ad?'

Michael looked at him sympathetically. Old man Lovelace's face was open, lined and brown, topped by a light frizz of grey hair. Even in this rather splendidly old-world office, heavy with oak and silver trophies and photographs of Brooklands in the 1930s, Lovelace wore blue overalls, stained with oil. Grease was grimed deep into the creases of his hands too. He was a likeable, hard-working man. Michael only wanted him to be happy and to build him a car that would one day murder the Porsches and Ferraris and Matras at Le Mans and the Japanese at Watkins Glen. It was an inconvenient nuisance that so silly a thing as an advertisement should upset Lovelace.

It showed a sleek red sports car, Japanese, beating the hell out of a clutch of other automobiles. Most of the also-rans were blurred shapes, but the leading loser was plainly recognisable as a Lovelace Special. The words of the ad. listed the plus points of the Japanese car very specifically against the minus points of other models. And every comparison in the ad. used figures lifted straight out of the Lovelace specification. It was dirty old-fashioned 'knocking' copy of a kind rarely used today, not even when a marque could justify it following a major race-circuit victory. The Japanese hadn't won anything that mattered. They were going to probably, and soon. But yet, they hadn't. It was a pushy, nasty ad.

'I'm very sorry, George,' said Michael. 'I'll see if we can take some action.'

'I'll not have my cars made mock of,' said Lovelace. 'We

were winning at Monza when those yellow devils were still making toy watches.'

'I know,' said Michael. When would people outside the East stop thinking about Japan as they'd thought 20 years ago? They were here to stay, building marvellous cameras, radios, cars, ships – and too damn cheap for Britain's overloaded, overpaid, underskilled and undercaring factories. Lovelace treated the phenomenon like a tropical disease which, one day, would go away. He was typical.

'Well?' said Lovelace.

'We can't stop them producing this kind of muck if they want to.'

'We can publish something that damages *them*,' said Lovelace.

'That's no answer, George. The game of tit-for-tat goes on for ever. And you're not on that kind of advertising budget.'

Lovelace almost blew up again. His eyes sought out his son, Philip, sitting quietly in a corner armchair, fingers carefully steepled, saying nothing. His son didn't look like a big-business smoothie; with his fair wavy hair, blue eyes and strong neck coming out of the rough-knit white poloneck sweater, he was more like a fisherman of England. Yet it was Philip who'd talked him into going in with Prospero the previous year. Before that he wouldn't have had to get Michael Grant's by-your-leave to spend money on an ad. He conveniently forgot that he wouldn't have had the funds to pay for the space, whoever made the decision.

'The best way, George, is to knock the stuffing out of the Japs at Le Mans next month,' Michael went on. 'Will we?'

Lovelace stood up brusquely, shoved an unlit pipe in his mouth, and spoke round it. 'Come and see.'

Beyond the brick office block, in a low hanger, mechanics were working on the frames of three cars. As George Lovelace led the way in, an engine on a test-bed clattered into life, and the roaring whine made speech almost impossible. The frames of the cars were a mass of metal struts and wires and pipes. Against the fat black tyres, the workmanship looked ridiculously fragile. Lovelace had had some success in Grand Prix racing as well as with sports cars earlier in the 1960s because the old man had dared to shave off millimetres of metal in vital places to lighten his machines where others had not had the skill or guts.

'That's the one,' screamed Lovelace, pointing to the only car which had its body in position. The other two machines were naked. The flimsy metal shapes which would dress the chassis and provide smooth surfaces for the air to glide over were propped unceremoniously against the walls. 'I'd hoped to have a back-up car for us, but we'll probably have to go with only one.'

Michael had been half-prepared for this, but he was still disappointed. Two cars gave you twice as many chances in a race as punishing as the 24 Hours of Le Mans. And he nursed a quiet dream that, with one car spare, as it were, he might even get a drive himself. A month earlier he had renewed his international competition licence with Royal Automobile Club. But under an assumed name. The officials had been very understanding.

'Is there no chance at all, George?' he shouted.

'Kill that noise for a minute.' Lovelace waited for silence. The mechanics looked self-consciously at Lovelace and the man they realised was the new boss.

'There's some chance,' said Lovelace finally. 'But I've got to get this one right first.'

'What's the problem?' asked Michael.

'Philip here' – jerking his thumb towards his son – 'had the car out at Goodwood last week.' Michael knew he had. There was little he didn't know of the day-to-day events at Lovelace's. But he said nothing. 'The nose lifts too much as soon as you get beyond 150. That's no bloody use for the Mulsanne Straight. We're trying to reshape the nose now, and we're working on the suspension a bit. The trouble is we might over-correct it. Then we'll be digging into some of those mole-hills if we're not careful.'

Michael knew what he meant. Eight years earlier he'd raced in the 24 Hour marathon at Le Mans. Past the pits, bear right on a climbing curve, down into the Esses, left, right, and right again and then, with Les Hunadieres Restaurant on your left, the Mulsanne Straight. They called it a straight, but it was misleading. You soon realised the straight was full of small hills and dips. As well, the road subtly changed direction to the right before you hit the 90-degree Mulsanne Corner where you tested your nerve every time, waiting for the last fraction of a second before you trod on the brakes and went down through the gears.

So Mulsanne was as much a shallow-angled V as a straight; and if you thought about it, riding up each of those little hills, you shook. To drive blind at a crest travelling at 220 m.p.h., as the bigger cars now did, took guts. Cars often flew at two of those bumps in the road.

A couple in recent history had overturned. Nasty.

They'd made Le Mans safer than it had been when he drove, true – building the Ford Chicane to slow down the cars before the pits straight. But the course could still be a killer. For one thing, there was the enormous difference in speed between the cars. Some were 100 m.p.h. slower at top speed than others. In addition, there simply weren't a hundred drivers in the world good enough for Le Mans, were there? Yet around a hundred raced each year. Michael would not admit to himself that he might be among the not so good.

'Let me try it,' he said.

'Get in there, Harry, and fix the seat,' said Lovelace.

On the day, pedals and backrest and harness, everything, would be tailor-measured for the driver. For the moment, Michael allowed himself to be approximately slotted into the centrally-positioned seat. It felt good to have the tiny leather-covered wheel in his hands. His feet moved lightly on the pedals.

There were as yet no periscope driving-mirror, no pieces of adhesive tape holding the body into place, no advertising signs, for Biostrath or Martini or Cibié, on the smooth green body. But for a moment Michael felt he was right there, sniffing the oil and the heat and the warm cloud of frying fat odour drifting in from the fairground at Le Mans. Next week he would tell Lovelace he wanted to drive the car at least twice at Goodwood before it left for France.

Back in Lovelace's office, he said, 'You've done a marvellous job, George. Now we've got to do the same on that bike engine production line.'

Lovelace plainly did not relish the subject. 'That's Philip's business. Ask him.'

For practically the first time that morning, Philip Lovelace spoke. 'We're getting on slowly, Michael. On present plans we should be able to hit a thousand units a month by, say, November.'

'Christ, Philip, what have you been doing?' said Michael sharply. November was another six months away. Sanger would go mad if he knew that his snowmobile customers in the States would have to wait so long. 'I thought you were aiming for July latest.'

Philip Lovelace shrugged. His father was apparently studying the detail of a sepia photograph on the wall. It showed a Lovelace – all headlights and running-board and serpentine outside pipes – winning at a track that looked like Nurburgring in 1929. God, Michael thought, I wasn't even born then, and this old man was already a boy-wonder mechanic in the thick of the circuits.

'It's a tricky technical job,' said the youngest Lovelace.

'You've got the money,' said Michael. 'For God's sake spend it.'

'It's expertise we're short on, Michael. And some of that you simply can't buy.' He looked for help to his father.

'You can't do two bloody things at the same time,' said George Lovelace. 'Either you want a new car fast, or you want to make money out of pleasure-mad Americans.'

He obviously disapproved of foreigners doing anything so trivial as wanting to travel fast on ski-clad buggies over the snow, even if his motor-cycle engines – a Lovelace sideline – were driving them. Lovelace always suspected the pursuit of pleasures which were not his own. Like many businessmen (even mechanics turned businessmen) he had a puritanical exterior. Puritanism in business usually comes cheaper.

'Why not both?' asked Michael. 'If the money's there . . .'

'Our best men have been on the car,' said the elder Lovelace tersely. 'That's what you wanted.'

Michael saw no point in precipitating more rough words. He would call Philip Lovelace up to London with his top engineers that week. He had to get that production line working at full stretch before November.

He looked at his watch. 'Keep at it, then, George. You're right. We need that car. And we need it to do well.'

When Michael had gone, Philip Lovelace said, 'Don't be so damned sharp with him, father. He takes a lot from you

115

considering he's paying the piper. Where would we be with-out him?'

George Lovelace growled. 'Perhaps we'd still be running our own darn show instead of jumping every time there's a bugle call from Prospect House.'

'That's not the way Michael works, and you know it,' said Philip.

'We could have found the money somewhere,' his father insisted.

'Don't be stupid, father. We needed him. By God, we needed him.'

'You'd better get back to your bloody toy engines,' shouted George Lovelace, slamming the heavy oak door of the office as he went.

He knew that every word his son said was true. He even liked Michael Grant. But the knowledge made the hurt of knowing he was no longer really the boss all the sharper. That was why he was so angry, futilely and childishly angry.

2

Colin Hardy was waiting for David, grinning, at Waterloo. He hoped it would look to David like an accidental meeting.

'Look at them all,' said Hardy quietly, pointing to the streams of commuters leaving the trains, as David had just done. 'Talking about holidays and the bloody unions and the way the blacks are everywhere, but what they're really worrying about is how this month's bills are going to be met. And that they don't talk about. Ulcers coming along nicely. How's yours?'

David grunted non-committally.

'First law of management, lad,' said Hardy. 'When in doubt, mumble. You're learning.'

'What's up?' said David. 'I thought you usually made it in earlier than me.'

'Used to,' said Hardy, mock-sadly. 'But where did that get me? You got the job, man. You got the job.'

That was unusually direct for Colin Hardy. David had been very close to him a year ago, but how can you stay friends with someone with whom you are in earnest com-petition? Business permits bonhomie rather than friendship.

116

When he and Hardy had worked for Westbrook, the Marketing Director of Prospero, their joint interest in upholding their master – and in helping to put Michael Grant into the Chief Executive's chair – had drawn them together. Hardy had in effect been David's mentor, a sarcastic but razor-edged intelligence. Now that Hardy was Sanger's chief aide, the American's rivalry with Michael inevitably placed the two men's retainers in different camps. Hardy was also jealous that David had been chosen as principal assistant by Michael. He showed it, whenever they met.

'Crap,' said David.

'As you wish,' said Hardy. 'Feel like a cab?'

David nodded. They stood in a queue, looking at a huddle of uniformed chauffeurs. It was the same every morning. Velvet-collared, bowlered men stepping self-importantly into Rollses and Humbers and Daimlers which the capped drivers polished incessantly and needlessly, since there is a limit to how gleaming a metal surface can be. They had nothing better to do. Cloth and chamois leather were to chauffeurs an equivalent of worry beads, nervous symbols of reassurance for hands and mind, used only to buff up the egos of those they waited for.

In the cab Hardy asked, 'Is your magic working in Ecuador yet?'

The news from Ecuador had got no better at all since the Prospero board meeting a fortnight earlier. Colonel Vargas had already made three speeches emphasising the threat to national security if the armed forces budget was not substantially improved. Jesus Cantania had been keeping his head down. Oldershaw's equipment was moving out of the docks, but only in dribs and drabs.

'You know we're still up the creek,' he told Hardy.

'Come and join us in sunny Europe,' said Hardy. 'That's where the future is. What in God's name did the son and heir want to paddle up the Amazon for?'

Hardy had learned Sanger's tune well. 'He ought to write the bloody Common Market anthem. "Europe is profits *now*," ' David said. 'South America may be something else. We might even help to prevent the world going up in revolutionary smoke, and our hopes for profits with it.'

'David, lad, don't give me that third-world scenario. If the guerrillas are going to happen, you won't stop them by

117

building petro-chemical plants for the old aristocracy to manage, and one day maybe nationalise. Business is profits. The only hope is that the profits get shared out in enough pockets. Then, and only then, will the have-nots become the haves and, perhaps, decide not to tear the world of our lovely tycoons apart.'

'Great speech,' said David. 'What do you want, Colin?'

'I want, this beautiful May morning, to find out when the hell you and me are going to get together on the Debrais business. That company's just dying to fall into our arms. Sanger told me to prepare a complete rundown along with you.'

'I've been briefed,' said David, who knew precisely why he hadn't approached Hardy. Michael Grant had told him to hold off for as long as he could. The board would expect the initiative to come from Sanger, who had done the negotiating so far. If Sanger did not move, Michael might escape blame for inaction at the next board meeting. And Michael wanted to go slow on drumming up money to buy a stake in Debrais. He sought to keep the organisation's resources intact in the next few weeks in case he had to squeeze more funds out of the Prospero kitty for Ecuador.

'Then let's meet this week,' said Hardy. 'Young Mr Sanger was distinctly tetchy with me yesterday.'

'Give me a ring when you get in.' David could always tell his secretary he wasn't available to Hardy. With luck, he could push the discussion on the French office equipment company past the weekend.

Hardy leaned back, smoothing his tan suit, single-buttoned and very chic. Since his elevation to Sanger's number two, he'd become a snappy dresser. He pushed his red face and Punch nose into the Personal columns of *The Times* and smiled.

'Something funny?' queried David.

'Something nice, not funny,' said Hardy.

'Show me.'

Hardy folded the paper shut and smiled an even more superciliously superior smile.

'Secrets,' he said, and only he knew how close he was to telling David the whole story of the coded answer on the offshore investment fund proposition which had appeared —

118

in the affirmative – in print that morning. Hardy badly wanted to be able to boast about his own cleverness.

'You're infuriating sometimes,' said David. 'What are you up to now?'

'Up to everything, dear boy,' said Hardy as the taxi drew up before Prospect House. 'Since all the world treats me like a deceitful and devious bastard, I might as well behave like one.'

Stepping out of the cab, he wondered how high Sanger would really go in the negotiation for the mailing list.

3

In the end, Sanger closed the deal for £11,500. He had offered only ten. The contact, who wore rimless spectacles above a tumbling dimpled chin and a crumpled grey raincoat, smiled damply and said that his principals required fifteen minimum.

Sanger talked about the risks they were taking, the lack of guarantees from the sellers of the lists he was buying. He kept the price down, he knew, because the lists were so specialised that the sellers would have a hard time unloading them on any company other than Prospero. Even at £11,500 he squeezed very hard.

'How do we know the lists are genuine?' he said.

They sat in the cafeteria of a large department store off Oxford Street, seeking anonymity among the smallish crowd of early-morning women shoppers. The contact began to unwrap the folded pink *Financial Times* which had been one of the recognition symbols.

'You must take our word, Mr Sanger. But I can offer you some circumstantial evidence of our quality. Here is a sample sheet of names and addresses.'

Sanger glanced at the sheet. It had the right feel to it. In alphabetical order, every name beginning with 'M'. Mostly individuals rather than companies, with addresses in a wide range of countries. For an offshore investment fund, an appropriate listing.

'Check out a few of those if you wish,' said tumble-chin.

'What else?' said Sanger.

Tumble-chin slid over three more sheets of paper, photostat copies. 'These you cannot keep. But examine them by all means.'

Two of the sheets were copies of internal office memoranda. One was headed SECRET, the other STRICTLY PRIVATE AND CONFIDENTIAL. The originals had plainly been torn up, but the pieces had painstakingly been pasted together to reform the document. The sums of money mentioned in the letters were both of six figures. The third sheet was also headed SECRET. It was a paste job too. It contained columns of figures. Each line was prefaced with a multiple code symbol formed of numbers and letters.

'What is it?' said Sanger.

'The first quarter's investment figures for the fund. Branch by branch.' Sanger looked at the total. Seven figures.

'Impressive,' he said. 'How do you do it?' The question was deliberately naive.

The contact did not smile. 'Professional secrets, Mr Sanger.'

Sanger needed not to be told. With the right kind of collectors, in the right offices, wastepaper baskets or IBM typewriter ribbons could always be made to yield secrets. There was no necessity to go into the more sophisticated areas of telephone bugging and long-range cameras. Systematically organised, this kind of espionage, enabling one to read every letter and document typed or originated from a chosen source, was not difficult. In the two years Sanger had spent at Prospect House, he had tightened up security – document shredders, scramblers or key telephones, special locks on files, a bug-detector search on a different day each month, and much more limited access to the computer room. But he still trembled to think what tumblechin's associates could do if they really tried.

'In what form are the lists?' he asked.

'Microfilm.'

'Give us three days.'

'Very well.'

'How will the money be transferred?'

'Five pound notes. Used. No sequences. We'll arrange the drop-point. You'll collect the goods at the same time. Can you take a call from me, say, Friday at your private number, seven in the evening?'

Sanger pulled out a pocket diary. 'Make it seven-thirty.'

'Then good morning, Mr Sanger.'

Sanger watched him move swiftly through the tables at which women were already showing each other the goods they'd bought. The contact seemed to float rather than walk. He did not look back.

Over a fourth cup of coffee, Sanger considered the proposition. For a little over £10,000 he would be able to provide a tool for Prospero's offshore fund subsidiary which, he believed, would get the company's name and image into the heads of 15,000 people with a known record of investment in such enterprises. Given the usual rate of conversion on direct mail letters to hot-prospect investors, he estimated that the extra business for the Prospero fund might be 5 per cent, perhaps even ten.

Altogether, he thought as he paid the bill, a good morning's work.

For Bernard Grant it was a bad morning. A cable from New York informed him that a Sickert for which he had been willing to pay $25,000 was no longer for sale.

He had other messages and calls. A friend who was, like him, a naturalised Briton told him during the course of a social telephone chat, about a splendid piece of business done in buying up a consignment of cheap textiles in Czechoslovakia, with the prospect of much more varied trade to come. But he gave no sign that he wanted to cut Bernard in. To know of such dealings without participation was always a source of grief to the Chairman of Prospero. Now, also by telephone, he was about to hear more unpleasant tidings.

'Bernard, good to hear you, old chap.' It was one of Her Majesty's Ministers on the line. He wasted no time. There were three hot questions on the Order Paper for him that afternoon. He was still, with the aid of his Parliamentary Private Secretary and a fat file of Whitehall statistics, working out the precise phraseology of his answers.

'Harvey Jardine told me about this Ecuador business.'

Bernard Grant knew that, of course. He'd been talking himself too: to two Ministers and three Permanent Under-Secretaries, for more than a fortnight. To push Sir Harvey Jardine into the front line as well had been a last gesture. It hurt his pride to think that he could not work the spell in Whitehall without assistance.

121

The Minister was still talking. 'If only you'd come even two months ago. This year's funds in that area are fully committed now.' He gave some details: banana research in the marshlands south of Guayaquil; a grant for building a tyre factory extension in Cuenca; money for helping re-establish natural rubber in the north of Ecuador.

Bernard impatiently plucked at the strings of the small Hepworth bronze on his desk. Excuses, excuses.

The Minister's voice bored impeccably on. 'So there's really no way. Not for an organisation as well endowed – pardon me, Bernard – as your own.'

The Minister was thinking: Why doesn't he sell something? He can afford to.

'We must keep our assets,' said Bernard. 'By year-end we'll be sufficiently liquid again.'

'Ah, liquidity,' said the politician, motioning to his PPS to pass him another document. For him, the conversation was at an end.

'Yes, Bernard,' he said at last. 'I really am deeply sorry about this. If there's any other way in which I can help ... yes. Goodbye, then.'

Bernard Grant flung a meticulously-sharpened yellow pencil on to the carpet. It bounced, lay still; the pencil point remained intact.

He looked down at the river from his window. A pleasure launch, awnings fluttering, was puttering below, its passengers appearing motionless in their seats from the height of the twentieth floor. Every year the launches started a week earlier, or so it seemed to him, as the American tourist invasion ate deeper into the early weeks of spring. He was torn between being flattered that they cared so much for his adopted country. To love England, as so many of them did, vindicated the rightness of Bernard's own judgment in choosing to live and work here. Besides a fraction of every dollar spent was good for Prospero. His profits from hotels and bookshops and consumer foods grew fatter with every incoming charter flight.

The news from Westminster was a blow. Bernard Grant must now appear to everyone on his board as a man of no influence with Government and Civil Service. The reaction was over-extreme, of course; but Bernard was deeply hurt when he added up the favours he was owed by a number of

Government departments. He could see Sanger's sarcastic smile. He could see, and was more concerned about, the unsmiling face of Lord Bender, locking away the memory of Bernard Grant's defeat carefully in the storehouse of his brain, waiting for the time – perhaps months or even years distant – when it might become relevant after being multiplied with other disasters.

He had no heart, and no courage, immediately to go to Michael. Perhaps Harold Armfield would help. He pressed a buzzer below his desk and asked for the deputy managing director.

Armfield carried a sheaf of financial papers when he came. But he had no answers.

'If anything, Bernard, the situation is worse.' He pushed his gold-rimmed spectacles hard against his nose until the blood left the bridge. 'The promissory notes are still outstanding. Bills from Brasserton's are positively flooding in. I know that Michael has had no joy of either the Americans or the French. From a lunch conversation the other day, I believe the City may be on to our problem soon. Michael will have to go to Ecuador and put the screws on the client.' Bernard waved a hand as if the gesture could dispel the bad news.

'We must push him to make up his mind,' said Armfield. 'Isn't he due to go to France the week after next for that motor-car race?'

'He is,' said Bernard tartly.

'Then we haven't much time.'

It was good that Bernard, as in the old days, needed his counsel on a matter of importance. But Armfield felt no sense of disloyalty to Michael Grant. It was his task to force Michael again to accept the disciplines of the possible, the constraints of financial reality.

Besides, he had not been idle on Michael's account, though he would keep the fact of his good stewardship to himself until a moment more dramatic and more rewarding than this. He had, yesterday, brought to finality a matter he had worked on for several months – a professional indemnity insurance on the whole process control which Brasserton's were installing in the Ecuador plant. He remembered well that a steel fabrication company, of which a friend was a director, had recovered almost £2 million through such an insurance when the sub-marine gas pipes they had laid would not do the job they were intended for. That was the point about such insurances. They guaranteed constructors against inability to achieve results technically. If Oldershaw and the computer men failed to make a system which actually worked out there in Ecuador – and could not be blamed for bad workmanship – then Prospero might at least limit its losses.

Sweeping up his papers, Armfield felt positively virtuous at having the means within his power to assuage the Chairman's misery at a later date. Meantime, Bernard would have to suffer, for was that not the inescapable condition of all men who had the rewards of leadership?

4

Two weeks after the Carson's party, the Mailers came to dinner with David and Sheila. It was, in the English sense of distance, a long evening drive for the visitors: all of sixty miles from darkest Berkshire. Mailer's wife was dumpy, uncommunicative, elderly before her time and devoted to life in her village.

One week later, Sheila met Mailer for a pub lunch. That same afternoon, scarcely one mile from where David was talking with Hardy about the Debrais company, she went to bed with him. It was a kind of revenge on her husband.

There was a certain inevitability about it all. At the Carson house she had given Mailer the encouragement that springs from the eyes and from certain ways of touching. Normally she would have shunned such nonsense. But she was tired of not being served by David for, sometimes, two or three weeks on end. She was irritated by the preoccupations which came between them and love in marriage. And her husband's suspected dalliance at the party burned up her insides with envy and anger. By the time of their own dinner-party she had cooled, but the pressure of Mailer's hand on her thigh at one stage – and, very thrillingly, on her breasts when he followed her into the kitchen alone – maintained the momentum leading towards a more extended exploration.

When he rang and suggested lunch, since he would soon

be returning to Ecuador, she agreed. She felt too honourable to run the risk of being called a teaser.

She made the lunch coincide with a shopping excursion. They met in a quiet riverside pub on the South Bank and when it was over he suggested she might like a farewell drink elsewhere.

'I have to stay in town a lot, midweek nights. A friend lends me his flat on the Embankment. Super view from the balcony. Would you like?'

They drove there in Mailer's MGB. Her heart was pounding unnaturally. She had not felt this sense of anticipatory guilt for a long time. It was the risk, she realised, which made the experience so exhilarating. They went within a few hundred yards of Prospect House on the way and the apartment block was no more than a mile distant from the modern mausoleum where David worked.

Mailer wasted little time. He did pour a drink; then, handing it to her, he leaned over her and squeezed her breasts.

'Do you want to?' he asked.

'Of course,' she said.

She was incredibly clinical about it. She folded her red dress very carefully so that it would not be creased. She laid her tights and bra and red shoes neatly beside it as if she had a phobia about untidiness. Then she stretched out and waited.

He was a thoughtful lover. Before she could do anything for him, he slid down the bed and began kissing her ankles. He kissed her everywhere. She climaxed twice, even though she was only half-involved in this particular act of lust.

Afterwards they lay apart, smoking a shared cigarette; just like an old-time movie, Sheila thought.

'For the first time, fine, hm?' he said, sounding not displeased with himself.

'Fine,' she said flatly.

'It'll be some time before we do it again – if you want to, that is.'

'When do you leave?'

'Thursday. The crunch is very near. Is David going back?'

'No, not now. His boss will probably go instead.'

Sheila leaned on her elbow. She had covered her body

with the sheet because, oddly, she could not bear Mailer's eyes on her. 'David's got some French job to do now. So he'll be away again I expect. You bloody tycoons are hell.'

Mailer shrugged. 'That's how it goes.' He began to caress her breasts. 'But it's not all bad.'

'I've got to go,' she said.

He looked disappointed.

'I've a date for a dress fitting at 3.30,' she lied.

By the time she plunged into the crowds of Regent Street and Bond Street, picking up clothes and shoes and a pair of jade cufflinks for David – it was his birthday in three weeks' time – she had recovered her nerve. In one store, where she purchased five items, the salesgirl charged her for only four. Sheila saw the mistake in her favour quite clearly, but she said nothing, which was unlike her. All the way home the double guilt of her afternoon out made her tingle with a strange pleasure. At her station, she wanted to score a third time and shuffled through in the thick of the early commuter crowd without giving up her ticket. She slipped it into her handbag, ready to use some other time.

5

The detectives hit Prospect House on the last day of May.

Michael arrived just after eight to find two uniformed policemen standing by the revolving doors at the entrance, and a plainclothes inspector with a patient voice and around a dozen other CID men in tow seated at the desk inside his office.

He was outraged. He threatened to ring his solicitor, to bring an action for unlawful entry, to complain to members of the Government. He threatened damn near everything.

But the inspector simply spoke a touch more firmly, in a tone of infinite regret.

'I'm sorry, sir,' he said. 'We are only doing our job. We have all the necessary authority.'

He showed Michael the search warrant. It looked vaguely like a birth certificate. It authorised the police to look at files and documents and other things in Prospect House; there were further words about recovering documents relevant to police enquiries.

126

'I shall require keys to all the drawers and cabinets we have not already examined, sir, in the following offices.' He named Michael's office, Sanger's, Hardy's, David Travis's and finally, the computer room. 'We've no wish to do any damage.'

Michael thought of refusing. The inspector might have been looking inside his mind.

'I must tell you, sir, that refusal on your part can only be harmful to you.'

Michael looked at the heap of files and papers stacked on the floor, the bending figures and busy fingers of the detectives. Silently he went to his confidential cabinet, unlocked it, and slid open the drawers.

'Those papers are crucial to this organisation's business,' he said. 'Some of them contain information which would be highly damaging to us were it known to our competitors.'

'Of course, sir,' said the inspector. 'You may rely on our total confidence and discretion.'

'What the hell is this all about?' Michael asked angrily. The inspector said something about information having been laid, but Michael pressed him. 'What information? Tell me. I've a right to know.'

The inspector looked at him with rebuke in his eyes. 'We have reason to believe, sir, that certain stolen documents are in these offices.'

'Rubbish,' snapped Michael.

'Documents belonging to another commercial organisation,' said the inspector.

'Which organisation?'

The inspector hesitated, then named it.

'A complete slander,' said Michael angrily. 'Did they tell you that?'

'We are acting on information received, sir,' repeated the inspector non-committally.

'I'll sue them to hell,' said Michael, but as he watched the search proceed he felt less and less certain of his ground. The organisation mentioned by the inspector was the one whose client lists he had been offered in the letter he'd fed to the shredder earlier in the month. Had someone else in the building been sent the same letter he had?

Michael was not allowed to leave his office, except with a detective beside him when he went to the men's room,

127

for well over two hours. Nor, he understood, were Sanger and company when they arrived. He was asked whether he objected to a personal search. He shrugged, stood up, and submitted to the humiliation of turning out his pockets and being patted all over.

Finally, the inspector said: 'We've seen all the other people concerned now, sir. And our search is concluded. We're sorry to have troubled you.'

'And?' said Michael, still furious, feeling the cold dampness under his arms where the sweat of apprehension had slowly been soaking his shirt.

'We are removing some documents and some pieces of tape and microfilm for checking, sir. We'll be in touch,' said the inspector.

'I demand to see the documents you're taking.'

'Very well, sir.'

A sergeant who had been writing out a list of documents handed it to him to examine.

'I want Mr Sanger and the other gentlemen in here while I look at these documents.'

Sanger looked paler than ever, but as crisp as usual. There was a barely discernible curl to his lip which only those who knew him as well as Michael would have called victorious. Hardy looked faintly amused, David neutral, and the computer room executive completely nonplussed. There were only three files which Michael did not recognise when he examined the detectives' haul. Sanger explained one of them, David the other two. Only at that point did the relief begin to flood through Michael's frame. There was absolutely nothing here which was suspect. As the adrenalin churned, he grew angry again.

'Is this all?' he asked the inspector.

'Yes, sir.'

'This is all our property. You have no right, no right whatsoever . . .'

'We have the right, sir,' said the inspector, still unflustered. 'And the authority.'

'I'll find out who caused this if it's the last thing I do,' said Michael. Then he walked to his chair and pulled a pen meaningfully from his inside pocket. 'Perhaps now we can all get on with some work. Stay, if you please, Earl.'

As the detectives and the Prospero people filed out.

Sanger rose and shut the door behind them. He remained standing by it.

'Fine and dandy, Michael. A great show of righteous indignation. You did our image proud.'

'I don't think it's funny, Earl. What in hell have you been up to?'

'Let's not talk here, for God's sake,' said Sanger tetchily. 'Who knows what they mightn't have planted.'

They went to the boardroom. It was quiet, the dust flicking in the rays of the sun, almost museum-like. Sanger sprawled into one of the Chippendale chairs around the circular glass table.

'Well?' said Michael.

'Well what?' said Sanger.

Michael knew he had to be right. He backed his hunch. 'I got that letter too, Earl. I didn't think you'd be so stupid as to do anything about it.'

Sanger made no attempt to dissemble. 'Why not? I got those lists cheap. Very cheap.'

The sweating was beginning under Michael's arms again. 'If you land this organisation in a scandal, you'll be finished. I'll see to it.'

'Don't be so goddam naive. Do you think I'd leave stuff like that lying around the office?'

'You're just a thief,' said Michael. 'A cheap thief.'

Sanger kept his cool. 'I paid good for what I got. That's not larceny. Grow up, Michael. This goes on all the time – when it's necessary. And don't come the high and mighty with me. You've known about things like this before. Sure, I get your line. So long as you don't have to dirty your own hands, you go along with it.'

'Shut your mouth,' said Michael. Sanger's tone and language drew a brutality of speech from him which he did not like.

'I'll shut up when I'm good and ready,' said Sanger.

'The board would like to know about this,' said Michael.

'Yeah,' sneered Sanger. 'The board would like to know a lot of things. Like about Lymington.'

'Don't talk about Lymington,' Michael shouted.

'Like how you okayed me to spy on one of this organisation's own directors.'

129

'I did no such thing,' snapped Michael. 'That was your decision, done in your own dirty way.'

'Horseshit,' said Sanger. 'Westbrook knows as well as me. Everything was ay-one-okay till the guy killed himself. It was only then you didn't want to know. It may be just great for your conscience to blame me, but it's not my rap. Not alone. It's yours too.'

The impulse of anger drained from Michael. He pushed a fist in his mouth and just sat there looking at Sanger with an expression of cold unmoving loathing in his eyes. Sanger's accusations were too close to the truth for comfort. Sir Giles Lymington, once the organisation's contact man with Whitehall, had been suspected, with good reason, of leaking Prospero's repeats to a rival. They had never confirmed that; but the private investigator put to work by Sanger had turned up huge gambling debts and, surprisingly, Lymington's homosexual activities too.

So no one would ever know exactly why Sir Giles died early one April morning. The inquest verdict had been suicide. His wife had spoken of Lymington's fears about cancer. But was that why he took his own life? Michael thought he knew better, as he was sure did Sanger and Westbrook. Knowing, too, that Sanger's private investigator had vanished from the scene for good just before Lymington's death, Michael believed that the aged diplomat had been subjected to blackmail on the side.

The memory of Lymington, his pale waxy skin, the way his hands were always trembling in the last weeks of his life, would live with Michael Grant for ever. He had not directly instructed Sanger to employ paid spies. But he had never countermanded any of the exercises in which he suspected the American was indulging. For Lymington's death he was morally as much to blame, if blame there was, as Sanger. After this, he had resolved never again to abdicate responsibility: nor to allow such methods to be repeated.

Yet he knew that in business today – and probably yesterday – he might not be able to avoid them. Could anyone truly run a company and allow men criminally to damage the business without employing treachery in return?

'Earl,' he said finally, 'I won't argue. But by God, if anything comes of what happened this morning, I'll break you.'

'Go to hell,' said Sanger.

'And now you can't use the list anyway.'

'Maybe I can,' said Sanger. 'Just as soon as I've found out who laid it on us. We were set up, that's for sure.'

'Your responsibility,' said Michael. 'Bad judgment.'

Sanger looked offended. 'Luck of the game. If I struck out, it was because I was going for a home run. It happens.'

Michael had recovered his nerve. 'You don't frighten me about Lymington, Earl. If you put one foot out of line in the next few weeks, I'll tell the board everything. I mean it.'

Sanger still did not look or sound shaken. His voice had the same brittle insolence. 'Yeah, well, I'll think about that.' But Michael knew from the American's reaction that he believed what Michael said.

'Good, Earl. And you just think about the fact that I could even tell the police, too. The organisation couldn't be held accountable for the criminal act, which was totally unauthorised, of one individual director. And while we're talking straight, you also think about taking the heat off the French deal for a while. Stay away from Madame Debrais and her directors. I want to keep our options open.'

Sanger rose, hitching his trousers in nervous displeasure, then dusting at non-existent dandruff on his shoulders.

'You fucking English are fantastic,' he said. 'And to think you have the nerve to call *me* a bastard.'

'Don't forget, Earl. You will not use that list,' said Michael coldly as Sanger headed for the door of the boardroom. 'And that's an order.'

6

David and Sheila sat on the small flagged patio of their house, listening to the many birds and sipping sangria, a summer habit picked up from too many holidays in Spain. Only in the last week had it really become warm enough to sit out in the evenings, when David got home from the office. Now the sun had gone behind the trees at the bottom of the garden. Its rays pricked through the leaves and found their faces. It felt good.

'I had Freddy Mailer on the 'phone today,' he said.

Sheila's heart-beat increased sharply. Mailer had said he'd

131

be away for at least another fortnight, and that removed for a time the need for decision about seeing him again. The excitement of what she had done that afternoon last month, both with and without Mailer, still made her insides churn in the emotion of recollection. She liked the feeling, but knew how dangerous it was.

'Yes?' she said, exaggerated offhand.

'He's back earlier than he expected.'

'Has he got the order?' She was glad, for once, that the talk was all business.

'The price is no problem but the South Americans still want to pay in soft currency. Freddy sees no way.'

'Wonder why he rang you?'

'I don't know exactly,' said David. 'Maybe he just wanted to cry on my shoulder. Or perhaps he thought that with our connections over there we could help. I thought of telling Michael, but it's too late now. He's got other things on his mind.'

'I hope he doesn't want to take you to Ecuador with him,' said Sheila.

'No. He's playing this one solo. We're still in trouble over getting our money; the old man, Armfield and everyone have pushed him so hard he's got to go. Apparently he had a hell of a job persuading Ed Corsino to fly out to Quito to meet him. He says it'll be a miracle if the Government there give anything away.'

'Why's he going then? It sounds a terrible waste of time and money.'

David sipped his drink. 'What choice does he have?' he said. 'It's a long shot, but he's got to try it.'

'He'll miss Le Mans, I suppose.'

'Yes, he's pissed off about that.'

'He never asked you to go.' The words were flat, drained, but half-accusing.

'Next year, he says. Next year when they've got a real car.'

'I'll remind you of that,' said Sheila. 'Do I get to come too?'

'Could be, love. But I can't promise. The whole sodding company might be up the spout by then. Who knows? I've been told to lay off the Paris trip too. So you've got me all to yourself. For at least a week.' He raised his glass and struck Sheila's lightly. 'Here's to the times when the boss goes away.'

In their apartment by the Thames, Michael and Alison clinked glasses too.

'Good luck out there, darling,' she said. 'I'll miss you.'

He smiled at her. He had never seen her look more beautiful. It was pure pleasure to know that even in his absence she would be for him, willing him to success. The heaviness of her body seemed, somehow, to make her love for him and her support even more satisfying. He wanted no sex; simply that warm and infinitely exciting feeling that he owned part of her mind.

'You'll come to New York,' he said. 'If it works out and there's time?'

'Try and stop me. I want to strangle Edward J. Corsino personally.'

'Don't,' he said. 'I need him alive.'

'And Sanger. I'd like to throttle him too.'

'I'll survive,' he said. 'By the way. Bernard's asked you to lunch with him day after tomorrow. He worries about you.'

'If he wants to play nursemaid while you're away, I don't mind.'

He left his chair and leant over to kiss her, gently squeezing her breasts. Her tongue was busy and skilful, but the physical connotation of sex was not what mattered. It was their way of signing a contract in their minds.

The next day Michael took the DC8, National Airlines, early afternoon flight to Miami. He read the Ecuador contract for the twentieth time with the sunshine at 30,000 feet streaming in on him.

Halfway across the Atlantic a stewardess told him the captain of the aircraft had a message for him. Michael froze mentally, following the girl down the gangway like a zombie. The last time he'd taken a message in a transatlantic plane, well over 18 months ago, it had been news of Bernard's coronary.

This one was from David Travis. The Lovelace car, the only one, had crashed in practice that morning. The driver had a broken leg. The car was virtually a write-off. It could not be put together again in time for 4 o'clock on Saturday afternoon when the 24 Hours race would begin.

Michael walked slowly back to his seat and ordered a large Martini. Only an hour later, when the balm of three more drinks had softened him, could he find the heart to repeat to himself over and over a hopeless litany of comfort.

'Next year, next year, next year. Next year, you bastards, I'll really show you.'

It was not satisfactory. But it was the best he could do. He was too worried about Ecuador.

5. THE QUITO COMPACT

1

IN THE WEEK after he ordered that Carlos should be killed, more than two months ago, Colonel Antonio Hernan de Vargas had discovered other uses for the woman who was now without even a weekend lover. Not that the Colonel liked women. He had other predilections, and women to him were objects made to be humiliated. But this one could be dangerous. She must be bound in some way to Vargas, watched, bought, protected and, if it amused him, employed.

This evening, his mind sought such amusement. In an hour he would meet Dr Jesus Cantania. He was always willing to meet with his enemy. Vargas could use the opportunity to tempt him, test his resolve, dig for weaknesses. And nothing could be more diverting as an aperitif to this meeting than to have intimate contact with the person whose betrayal of Carlos had disrupted Cantania's timetable at Esmeraldas for many weeks. The damage to the petrochemical plant plan was sufficient justification for the death of one man. But even Vargas was no indiscriminate killer. In the end it was the further suspicion that Carlos was working with dangerous revolutionaries which had clinched the matter in Vargas' mind.

A guard let the woman into the room where Vargas sat alone, legs outspread, in a deep soft chair. She saw again the gentle glow of the gold and silver ornaments which were scattered around the room, burnished by the flickering flames of the wood fire. She looked fearfully at the dark portraits of ancient *conquistadores*, with pointed beards and ruffles and breastplates of dirty silver. Above the fireplace was a painting of Vargas himself, in military uniform, small black moustache set on heavy brown face, very slim and tall in carefully creased khaki and gleaming knee-boots.

The painting lied. Vargas was short and plump, but even though he was not wearing uniform now, he looked as if he was. His jungle-green shirt, pockets flapped and buttoned, was immaculate. He wore boots too, from which trousers puffed out at the knee. As she approached him she smelt the cologne. Vargas hated the smell of bodies, even his own, and drenched himself in sweetness at all hours of the day and night. She dug her fingers in her palms, hoping he would not notice she was sweating.

She sweated a great deal these days. When Vargas's men had put pressure on her to betray Carlos, the decision that she should agree had been a narrow one, taken by her friends in the Quito cell because they feared Carlos might in the end tell the authorities about the comrades who had tried, unsuccessfully, to seduce him to the revolutionary cause. She hated the betrayal, nevertheless, as she now feared the unforeseen life-pattern to which it had led her. She survived it; but she sweated.

Vargas snapped his fingers. She needed no words, for the drill which followed had become familiar. She slipped from her clothes and, naked, knelt before him. Vargas was already moved by the prospect of her subservience. She excited him with her fingers. He grunted. As he began to breathe heavily he dug his hands into her black hair and pulled her head towards him. Finally, she looked up with fear in her eyes, but he pushed her scornfully away, indicating that she could dress. There were angry marks on her upper thighs. Tonight he had been too tired to strike her either during or after her performance of submission. Besides, she had done well. Not once had he felt her sharp tiny teeth upon him, only her softness.

Her clothing rustled. Outside the room a dog barked. Vargas smiled at the thought of his own security. He had four dogs in the grounds, alsatians, imported already trained at almost one thousand American dollars each. Their howls were as powerful a deterrent as their teeth. At night, when the area of the house was always brightly lit, they could be heard half a mile away. Six guards were always on duty. Six more slept nearby. Most of them were tough, old campaigners who had pursued and killed guerrillas in the hard mountains of Colombia. A couple were young, slim and most handsome young men whose guard duties were more various. The fence was electrified and there were several guns in fixed positions. He wished he could believe that all Ecuador was so strongly defended.

Vargas's philosophy was simple. For years, his country had been surrounded by enemies. Colombia and Peru and Venezuela believed that so modest a nation, not much bigger than Britain and much smaller than the state of Texas, could easily be bullied. Ecuador had fought a war with Peru in 1941. Today, Peru would steal Ecuador's oil around the disputed border between the two countries in the Oriente region if she could. Now that both Peru and Chile had moved politically to the left, more or less, contact with them could in Vargas's view only encourage such tendencies in Ecuador. For this reason among several he looked upon the new Andean Pact, an arrangement for economic co-operation between these three and other South American countries, with cold hostility.

He lived, too, in deadly fear that a guerrilla movement of the kind which had infected so much of South America would become established in his own land. He did not like Americans, because he believed them to be economic colonisers. He distrusted intensely the current vogue among the commercial classes of the country for gradualistic liberalism. Far from accepting that this was necessary in the contemporary international climate, he was certain that such policies would open the gates to the guerrillas. To him, Dr Jesus Cantania represented everything that was wrong with the left-of-centre commercialists; one could expect no better of a Guayaquileno, a money-grubbing trader. Guayaquilenos were monkeys, born of the swamplands of the coast. Once, at an election meeting, someone had called Vargas a hillbilly, the usual insult shouted at the inhabitants of the high plateau by the monkeys of the coast. Colonel Antonio Hernan de Vargas, who could trace his pure Spanish line back four centuries and beyond, would like to have ordered that heckler to be shot.

He believed, indeed, that a certain amount of shooting would swiftly solve many of his country's problems. He would, if he had his way, shoot all suspected revolutionaries as well as all the student leaders who were always causing trouble in the University of Quito. He wanted to make the armed forces far stronger, and to do that he needed the royalties which would flow from the oil in the Oriente to be devoted to the defence budget rather than to unnecessary follies like Cantania's petro-chemical plant at Esmeraldas. Why bother about cheap shoes and shirts and plastic buckets for the Indians? Cantania was both foolish and presumptuous, undeserving of power. Vargas's class, who understood how to rule, were the natural leaders of the land and would bring it to its destiny.

The woman was dressed. She knelt and rearranged his clothing. He might find other uses for her, he thought, if only he could get at the Americans and the British men of power who were soon arriving to see Cantania. He handed her a 500-sucre note, since he was not ungenerous with bribes, which are themselves a form of humiliation.

She smiled as she left the room and not only at the thought of the money. She had, again, survived. And although she loathed Vargas, she knew she was doing her job well. Vargas lit a cigar and waited for his next visitor.

Vargas had 53 first cousins in the city of Quito. The man who arrived 10 minutes later, neat and dapper in business suiting, was one of them. He had built in the past 20 years a highly profitable business in natural textiles. He had needed no persuasion by Vargas that the establishment of a huge synthetic fibres plant within Ecuador would damage his interests severely. So he, like Vargas, wished the plant and Dr Cantania no good whatsoever.

Vargas offered him a glass of whisky. It was good whisky, flown in nightly on the contraband air routes which spread like a spider's web all over South America from Colon, 40 miles from Panama City at the opposite end of the Canal. In the Free Zone of Panama there are no taxes, no duty. The price to Vargas was a special one.

'—Let us drink to the downfall of our friends,' said Vargas.

'—It goes well?' asked his cousin cautiously, and Vargas nodded.

'—Well enough. The schedule of the plant is months behind. Materials are slow in arriving. The Americans and the British are so worried that they are coming to see our friend. I have suggested to the President that the whole time-scale for the project be revised. That is a first step only, which should at least divert some funds for the armed forces. If we keep up the pressure, we could force abandonment of the project finally or, at worst, a much more modest size for the plant. All of which should please you.'

His cousin still looked worried. '—I would be more pleased if construction had not gone so far already. I am doubtful if you can do more than delay the inevitable.'

'—Do not speak like a child,' said Vagras angrily. He was annoyed that a first cousin could doubt his power. His cousin had spent a year at the business studies school of Colombia University in New York City. He disapproved strongly. Such experiences softened the brain, made men forget the realities of their own society. '—I cannot begin to tell you how many things could go wrong at Esmeraldas.'

He detailed several. His cousin smiled at last. And within half an hour, Vargas drove out to visit Cantania in a large black Cadillac with smoke-brown windows, a white-helmeted outrider before and behind it. The old town was festive. Music spilled from *cantinas*. Foodsellers, crouched along the cracked sidewalks, were doing a brisk trade, even though the evening – as June evenings often can be in Quito – was cool. The neon signs were blinking along the Avenida de los Amazonas. Vargas frowned. The name of the avenue was good, he thought, emphasising the proud slogan which was stamped on all official letters: *El Ecuador ha sido, es y sera Pais Amazonico* – Ecuador has been, is, and always will be an Amazonian country. Vargas liked the avenue, in which area most of the major oil companies had established their Ecuadorean headquarters. The neon he disliked. *Horseshoe Saloon*, one read. He superimposed a grimace of distaste upon the frown.

High above the avenue, on the sixth floor of a new white building which had not been there a year ago, Dr Jesus Cantania awaited him. Cantania had deliberately chosen the central offices of the consortium for the meeting. He wished to emphasise that his business with Vargas had ramifications beyond the range and rivalries of government. He had been surprised that Vargas, with his concern for protocol, had accepted.

Cantania looked at the men around him. Apart from Martin, who kept touching that red mark on his face like a talisman, the two men who had arrived on the morning plane were present. Edward Corsino, the American, was swarthy enough to be a Spaniard, though his manners were not nearly fine enough. Michael Grant, the Englishman, lacked Corsino's heavy-handed assurance, he thought. But Cantania already liked Grant. The Englishman seemed to understand all that the Minister had told him about the need to create wealth and then to keep it within Ecuador for the benefit of everyone in the country, even the poorest Indians.

Cantania wasted no time. He believed that to put pressure on Vargas before the visitor had time to settle was the best tactic. He introduced the men in the room quickly, explained that Vargas would soon see why he had invited them, hoped that the Colonel would allow the unexpectedness of their presence not to inhibit frank discussion.

'These gentlemen have legitimate concern about the huge investment they are making in our country,' he said. 'That is why I have asked you to provide heavier protection for the whole area around Esmeraldas. Equipment has been stolen already. We must prevent that. I wish also to show them that sabotage at any stage would be impossible.'

Vargas licked his lips and sat plumply to attention in his chair. He wanted to walk out of the meeting. How did Cantania dare bring these men here without clearing it with him? But if he withdrew in pique, the President would not like it. Nor, even, would several of the men he viewed as allies within the Cabinet.

'We have so many calls upon our men,' he said. His English was rather more formal than Cantania's. 'If we are to keep conditions right for the plant to proceed, then the first priority must be to secure the state against violent revolution. The strengthening of the frontier forces is long overdue. We must also patrol the coast to guard against illegal landings. For that, we need patrol launches and frigates which we cannot afford. Such priorities must lessen the chances of doing as you wish.'

He pleaded with his hands. 'We have too small a defence appropriation, gentlemen. There, my colleague and I disagree, I know, but it is part of my responsibility to judge.'

He shrugged. 'So many things can go ill with a project such as yours which are beyond my control. Let us say, for instance, that a *brujo* in a village nearby should persuade the local Indians that what you are doing will offend the spirits. They are animals, some of those Indians. Soldiers alone will not help you, gentlemen.'

Michael Grant glanced at Corsino. The American gave him a look which said only *I told you so*. What the hell was a *brujo*? Yes, remembered. Sort of witch-doctor. Was Vargas threatening them?

Michael was still trying to adjust to the time-change. He'd slept all afternoon, but he still had a nagging headache. He objected to the timing of the meeting. It was too early. It was a rule for all sensible executives to take at least a 24-hour acclimatisation period in a foreign country so distant before beginning negotiations.

Michael was so unacclimatised he'd done nothing except ride from airport to hotel and, after a fitful sleep, climb into another automobile and come to this building.

Not quite true. He had asked Perez, who was full of generalised charm but few hard answers, to stop the car at a small supermarket. How stupid can you get, Michael had thought, to forget your toothpaste?

In the store he'd been offered a tube of toothpaste which was grubby, bent and dented all over, as if someone had been chewing it. He'd looked inquiringly at Perez, who had first laughed and then, conspiratorially, explained.

'Take it, my friend. It it perfectly okay. And only half the price you would be paying for a tube in a cardboard container. This is contraband. At the frontier, one pays duty by the crate. So the people who bring it in throw away all the packaging from the toothpaste. Then they cram all the tubes from three crates into one crate. That way they pay one-third of the duty only on each tube. This is why they are misshapen. But the toothpaste is good, very good. So have it, and I will pay, huh?' Perez, carefully adjusting his tie in the plateglass window of the store, seemed delighted with his story.

Cantania was trying to push Vargas. Michael did not believe that Vargas would be pushed. He was surprised Vargas was so small. He had expected a more masterful military man to fit his picture of the prime enemy of the consortium.

Vargas explained how the defence budget was already stretched. 'At this very moment we are prevented by currency problems from buying naval equipment we need –

from your own country, Mr Grant.' Vargas gave Michael a curt bow. 'You will see our difficulties.'

Michael involuntarily nodded back. Not because he agreed with Vargas, but because he assumed that Vargas was offering a deal. Give him guns and he'd play ball. Something like that. But how in God's name could Prospero help?

The talk drifted on. Vargas was so coolly non-committal about everything that Michael wondered why Cantania had bothered to call the meeting.

Cantania knew exactly why. When it ended, half an hour later, with all the civilities intact but no bargaining progress made whatsoever, Cantania bade his foreign guests goodnight with a sense of having attained one minor objective at least. Perhaps Grant and Corsino could now see how huge were the obstacles that he, as Minister responsible for the consortium deal, faced. Perhaps now they would realise that there was little chance of changing the terms of the contract in the consortium's favour. It would be enough, would it not, if he managed to thwart Vargas and provide conditions in which they could construct the plant on present terms?

If Michael did not, as yet, see all this, then Delano Martin was not deceived. He accepted the ritual of the meeting as a necessary chore. He had, indeed, scarcely listened to the conversation, for his mind was preoccupied with another problem. A man from Ali-Chem had been to see him that afternoon asking a lot of questions about a site on the coast to the south of the petro-chemical operation at Esmeraldas. The guy had apparently been surprised that Martin knew nothing about it.

'We'll be building there in due course,' the Ali-Chem man said.

'Building what?' Martin had asked.

'A chemical operation, what else?' said the Ali-Chem man. 'Subsidiary plants. Maybe to slot in with what you're setting up. I want your advice about local conditions.'

Martin's visitor had plainly been unwilling to be drawn further. What damn plants was he talking about? Slotting in? What kind of crap was that? If this second operation was meant to produce raw materials to go with the oil up at Esmeraldas, then Martin had thought so far that such products would be shipped in. Anyway, why the hell hadn't he been told?

They flew to Esmeraldas next morning.

'Goddam spicks,' said Corsino as the Excalibur pushed through the cloud that lay heavily on the mountains. Michael and Martin, the other two passengers, exchanged glances. The pilot, another American, was busy with his instruments and appeared not to hear. 'If they foul up this operation, I'll kill the both of them,' added Corsino.

Because it was a meaningless threat, born of frustration, his companions made no comment. But they were surprised. Michael had always known Corsino to be hard, but not crude; colourful, but not overtly vulgar. He had, however, never seen Corsino under pressure. As for Martin, he scarcely knew anything of Corsino's character in detail. His job had been arranged through Kerridge Steel. Corsino for him had been a shadowy figure who might have strings to pull. The more he saw of Corsino, the less he liked him.

Corsino laughed, an acid sound. 'Remember what J. Edgar Hoover said, Mike? He was never worried about the President being assassinated by Mexicans or Puerto Ricans. He used to say they'd never shoot straight enough. But when they come at you with a knife – then, watch out, baby.'

The pilot, now less occupied, turned his head. 'Right on. And they had to bring in a hired European guy to help knock off Trujillo in the Dominican Republic. I read it somewhere.'

Like Corsino, he was in no serious danger of winning a Martin Luther King award for achievement in the field of inter-racial harmonisation.

'Yes,' said Michael, as flat as possible. 'What's the river down there?'

'The Esmeraldas,' said the pilot. 'Hits the sea at the dump we're going to.'

The mountains were growing more distant on the starboard side of the plane. As they lost height the terrain below was a lusher green, but full of gorges and small hills, and then jungle. The sun lay like a warm blanket over the land.

'How good is this guy Quant?' Corsino asked of Martin. Michael thought it was scarcely up to Corsino to put that particular question about the man who was in charge here of the Prospero-Brasserton share of the contract — not in front of Michael, at least.

'Competent,' said Martin. 'He handles the government people in Quito well. He's not so good with the local labour. We miss Carlos.'

'We still don't know why he was murdered?' said Michael.

'Nope,' said Martin. 'Nor will, if you ask me.'

'I hope you've found someone who can get these bums to work,' said Corsino.

Michael shifted uneasily in his seat. Martin held back the words he would like to say. Corsino was beginning to live up to his worst expectation. He'd met the situation a dozen times on overseas contracts. He was used to the men from New York or Frankfurt or London arriving to take a look at their investment, men who wore like a badge what Martin thought of as the *Playboy* morality, whose commandments included bank accounts in Switzerland or Panama, property in the Bahamas or the Riviera or, just possibly, a neat chateau near Geneva and, inevitably, a private jet airliner. If wealth was virtue to such men, then poverty was sin – a heresy which was, however, not to be rooted out violently, as the Inquisition had once tried to dislodge another heresy in this country. Instead, poverty for them was a sin to be ignored, shunned and held in total contempt.

'We've just got to get this whole operation moving faster,' said Corsino.

That also, to Martin, was typical. Corsino, like many investors before him, regarded the 1500 men who were now sweating in the tropical June heat on the Esmeraldas site as so many units of labour who mindlessly would bulldoze the earth, dump shingle, drive piles, pour concrete, lay pipes, raise towers until, when a neat equation of hours used and equipment supplied was complete, they would have earned him his commission and put another wad of dollars into his several numbered accounts. Martin was compelled to see them as people who could be frightened by local witch-doctors, worked on by agitators, worried over the prospect of the eighth child one of their wives might be about to produce. He saw them this way because if he did not, the job – wherever and whatever it was – might not get done.

On his first stroll around the Plaza de San Francisco two years earlier, he had been intrigued by the rows of Indian women sitting on the steps near the oldest church in South America. They were dressed in bright-coloured skirts and shawls and all of them wore broad-brimmed hats, like men's, over the black hair which hung down their backs in long braids. Many carried babies slung on their backs. All had baskets stuffed with clothing or food.

When he aimed his Nikon to take a picture, every one of a group of half-a-dozen women put their hands about their ears or covered up mouths, noses and eyes, for they still believed or half-believed that if their likeness was captured in his box their soul would be taken from them too. What did Corsino know about people like that and what might motivate them to work or not to work?

Nor were Martin's problems confined to Indians and mestizos and Negroes. Down below at the site, in the camp reserved for foreign specialist labour brought in to cope with skilled tasks, an Irishman from Dublin had last week fought another from Londonderry. They'd half-killed each other – all over what the British Army was supposed to be doing in Ulster several thousand miles away. Martin was now as wary of Irish labour as he had come to be down the years of Italian.

'See that?' said the pilot, pointing. 'That's the pipeline. More than 250 miles long. Clear across the mountains. Goes up to 13,000 feet and more. Texaco-Gulf had it built. William Brothers of Texas did the construction in a year, more or less.'

His tone was flat. He had recited the astonishing facts too often. The pipes ran sometimes straight, sometimes angled, like a scenic railroad track towards the mountains. To the left the sea was now in sight. They dipped in towards the airfield.

Esmeraldas, named after the precious stones which once had lain around the place in some profusion, belies its title. It was never a pretty town even before the fire which devastated it in the 1950s. The buildings which, with United Nations aid, went up afterwards were strictly utilitarian:

regimented blocks of new houses in reinforced concrete and brick, very roughly finished, with aluminium roofs. The highways tend to be wide, rough and dusty. It is little more than 70 miles north of the Equator and, accordingly, hot. Even before the oil pipeline was built from the Oriente to the tanker terminal, it was a boom-town with a thriving trade in timber and bananas and the highest wages and prices in Ecuador. Oil, as well as the ongoing construction of the petro-chemical plant, made it even more expensive – and uglier.

The hotel they flopped into – the best – was crumby; no air-conditioning and a dank tropical smell about it. The porter was black. Michael remembered that a load of slaves had once found political asylum there from the British, after mutinying and taking over the slave ship.

It took 15 minutes of dusty driving in a Land Rover to reach the plant site along a road that could become a quag-mire overnight when it rained. There were armed guards in hard hats at the gates in the wire fence surrounding the site. One of them recognised Martin and spoke into a telephone hanging on the fence. Another man appeared from a shack and Martin shouted, 'Three passes and three jerries.' He turned and grinned at Michael. 'I've picked up your slang for pisspots. Jerries is what your guys call these hard hats.'

'How effective is the security?' Michael asked.

'Not bad.' This guy shoots straight, Martin thought. 'But we'd need a lot more men if there really were guerrillas around here. Anyone could get through that perimeter fence. You can't watch every damn inch.' He pushed a hand through his ginger hair. 'The guy they make damn sure doesn't know too much is me. I'm supposed to be building the place, but I've never smelt a sight of a flow sheet for what will go on here once we've finished. Christ knows what materials they'll put into the pipes or what temperature all the bits will work at.'

'Why's that?' Michael was genuinely surprised.

'The chemical industry is all cloak-and-dagger,' said Martin. 'If it's a new process they're going to use here, it could be worth tens of millions of dollars to keep it secret.'

'I know,' said Michael. 'But you work for Kerridge, and he has a big stake in the company that's going to run this place.' He looked questioningly at Corsino, who held out

146

a hand towards Martin, wanting the project director to explain.

'Sure, sure.' Martin was beginning to get enthusiastic. He had an engineer's love of an audience. 'But the people who call the shots on the technical side are Ali-Chem. They may only have 20 per cent of the stock, but their expertise is 100 per cent. So far as they're concerned the other stockholders – the Government here, Kerridge and the local industrialists – are simply financial and political partners. Ali-Chem don't trust them with their production process secrets any more than they trust me.'

Corsino nodded. 'Jesus, it's hot. I'll need to have this suit cleaned when we get back to Quito.'

Michael had already noticed Corsino's fastidiousness. In Corsino's hotel room his linen lay folded and uncreased, inside tissue paper, as if begging not to be worn even in an emergency. His suits were carefully protected against dirt with plastic covers. And most items – even the insides of his shoes – had his initials on them. He seemed frightened of forgetting who he was.

'Something came up with Ali-Chem that puzzled me,' said Martin.

'Yeah?' said Corsino.

'I had a guy in the other day asking about a site down the coast. Ali-Chem aim to build there too. What's that all about?'

'You know these people,' said Corsino. 'Once they get a foot in the door, they push.'

'But he spoke like it was part of the whole original deal.'

'I expect they've fixed something up in Quito, for Christ's sake.' Corsino sounded almost testy.

'They might have told me earlier,' said Martin. 'How am I supposed to advise them?'

'Leave it, Del,' snapped Corsino.

'But did you know?' Martin was quietly persistent.

'I knew something about another deal, yeah,' said Corsino angrily. 'But that's Ali-Chem's business, not yours. Why do they have to come bugging you? Next time they call, just tell them to go screw themselves. And you get this plant built here. That's what I'm paying you to do.'

'What Kerridge is paying me to do,' said Martin quietly. 'Okay, let's go.'

Michael sat prickling with embarrassment as they drove into the site. It looked a mess. They bucketed along on a road of crushed stone, past shacks, huts and temporary-looking workshops and store sheds of all kinds. In every direction the ground was a dirty yellowish shingle, mingling with the natural rich red-brown of the soil. It was scarred with the tracks of countless wide tyres and pitted with thousands of shallow depressions. Michael knew enough to understand that these were where the piles had been driven, casings of steel filled with concrete and steel bars to take the heavy loads of the towers and transformers and tanks and pumps and heaters to come. Out of these depressions, the reinforcing steel bars that American engineers call rebar and British know as starter bars, stuck up impertinently like sticks of twisted barley sugar.

'You should've seen it six months ago,' said Martin. 'Nothin but diggers, earth-movers and mud. It's nice and neat now.'

He told the driver to stop. 'Come and see something, Mike'

Michael followed Martin. In this part of the site, the work was much more advanced. Before them loomed a tall steel structure a hundred feet or more high. It enshrined, towering above them, a complex of large tanks, some rectangular, some globular. Martin beckoned him towards steps. Michael touched a handrail as he began the ascent, then snatched his hand away. The metal was painfully hot.

Martin laughed. 'Sorry, Mike. I should've told you. This is the Equator.'

Michael sucked his sore fingers and then they climbed again, boots clattering on the metal.

'Thought you'd like to see some of your stuff,' Martin said. 'And watch that decking. Bits of it are loose.'

Michael was panting by the time they reached the fifth level of the structure. There was no need to tell him that the valves, spaced at intervals in the twining network of pipes before him, linking the tanks, were the products of Oldershaw's factory in Staffordshire. Each valve was about 2 feet high, not unlike a giant bathroom tap.

'Good gear,' said Martin. 'I like the design.'

'It's partly American,' said Michael.

'No compliments,' laughed Martin. 'I like 'em whoever makes 'em.'

'Have you seen the really big ones?' asked Michael. 'The six-footers? They're all ours. Every inch British. Over three thousand dollars a throw.'

'Okay. I know you're making those bastards pay.' Martin's face, sun-brown, crinkled into a grin that took any offence out of the remark. His strawberry mark winked at Michael as his face creased and uncreased. He was, Michael thought, an easy man to like.

'Did you really mean what you said down there, Del? You don't know what they're going to be doing here?'

'Sure I meant it. Hell, I know this here is a complete process unit that'll change one chemical into another. I know your valves will stop the flow in the pipe at any given point – or simply control it. And I know that through there' – he pointed to a sight-glass set into one of the pipes – 'you'll be able to see if anything's going wrong. Apart from that, man, I just don't know nuthin'.'

'You could guess, though.'

'Yeah, and some of my guesses I don't like,' said Martin.

'What do you mean?'

'Take no notice of me, Mike.' He wiped his face with a large red handkerchief. 'Guess I'm just suspicious. It's mixed up with not knowing what Ali-Chem are planning on the coast and wondering what can go wrong next here. This is an edgy number.'

They moved away from the pipes and looked out over the site. Men in hard hats swarmed on the ground, helmets that were blue and yellow, red and white to distinguish the labour forces of the various contractors. Even in the harsh sunlight, the silver sparks spraying from electric arc welders slashed vividly across the air. Pipes in rows of dozens at a time were already uplifted over the site, nestling in racks supported by towers. Hundreds of cables stacked together in similarly supported trays followed their own paths above the yellow earth.

'That's a quarter of a million bucksworth,' said Martin, sweeping an arm to encompass the horizon. 'And that thing is a distillation column.' He indicated a tall cylindrical tower, dully glinting below them. 'Only one place in the

149

world that item comes from. Wouldn't you know it was Texas?'

Michael laughed. 'And what's that? It looks like the biggest H-bomb in the world.' It did indeed. Made of metal, too, the object he pointed out to Martin lay like a 40-foot bomb, minus fins, on its side.

'Heat exchanger,' said Martin. 'It makes one liquid hot and another cold. Say, it sure is sinister.' He spoke as if the thought had not occurred to him before.

The conversation stopped. Such a pause in the talk of people who do not know each other well, but who sense immediate affinity between themselves, is not uncommon early in a relationship. The special function of the pause is recognisable too. These men wanted to say something important to each other.

'Ed Corsino doesn't speak for me, you know,' said Michael at last. 'I don't know what the hell's got into him since he arrived out here. So tell it to me straight, Del.'

Martin fenced a little. 'Level with you?'

'Yes.'

'Which part of it?'

'You choose.'

'Okay.' Martin paused, but he'd decided Michael could be trusted. 'I'm used to all the sneaky deals on a job like this. The bribes for officials, the way the labourers get swindled by the middle men, the pay-offs for fixers like Ed. And for guys like Perez. Christ, he's a creep. That's the usual scene. I don't like it, but I live with it even if it is a helluva way to make a living. But there's something more going on here.'

'What?'

'Jesus, it doesn't make sense,' said Martin. 'I can figure the Government – they want this plant for prestige as much as for what it will make. It's like a new toy to shake in the face of Venezuela and Colombia and Peru and the rest. Maybe they believe they can be number one in petro-chem. in the Andean Pact. But I don't see why Ali-Chem and Kerridge have got 35 per cent of the action in the petro-chem corporation.'

'Insurance, Del, surely. Playing new markets.'

'Crap,' said Martin scornfully. 'If he had any sense Kerridge would grab his money for what he's helping to build

150

here and run. Fast. And Ali-Chem – well, they could be consultants, but I don't get why they want in for ever. The market here hasn't got enough dough in it for their products. And if ever it does get the dough, sure as God they'll be kicked the hell out of this country.'

Michael didn't want to believe what he was hearing. He pushed Martin for more reasons.

'Come on, Del. That's the same in developing countries the world over. The oil companies digging out the crude in the Oriente are taking that gamble too. But they can't afford *not* to take it, can they?'

'With them it's different,' said Martin, rubbing at his strawberry mark. 'They daren't miss out on new fields. But Ali-Chem? Making second-phase products? You gotta be joking.'

'What do you think, then?'

'Christ knows. That's what bugs me. But it sure smells. There's that coastal site. And Ed Corsino getting so sore when I asked about it. I can't put my finger on it.'

'Let me know if you do,' said Michael.

'Are you propositioning me?' said Martin.

'If you want me to.'

Martin roared with laughter and put his arm round Michael's shoulders. 'I'm kidding. Really. I think you and me will get along fine.'

They moved towards the steps again. But neither man made a start to the descent.

'Have you had much real trouble here, Del?' asked Michael.

'No more than usual,' Martin replied. 'Your stuff is moving out of Guayaquil now, and the whole power plant and control system is catching up on lost time. It's way ahead of the structural work. Quant will confirm that. I'd say that all the Kerridge end – the steel and the pipes – has been coming in even slower than the gear from Brasserton's.'

'Really?'

'Yeah. Say, I liked that young guy you sent out – David Travis. He's good.'

'He has to be,' said Michael.

'Pardon me, Mike, but I'm glad Bill Oldershaw wasn't alone. He's a prickly kind of guy.' Martin watched for

Michael's reaction. He decided to soften the words. 'Damned good engineer, sure, and that's what counts.'

Michael smiled. As if Delano Theodore Martin could tell him anything about Oldershaw's temper. 'Why do you think I sent David Travis to hold his hand?'

Martin nodded.

'What other trouble have you had?'

'That crane over to your left,' Martin said. 'It's a Manitowok. Costs over a quarter-million dollars and it can lift 300 tons. It's needed to shift the towers and columns and it sits on a circular concrete platform and runs on rails. Three months ago it fell over.'

'Christ!'

'Some goddam surveyor hadn't located a water-spring under the shingle before we laid the concrete down. It cost me a week.'

'Hell's teeth,' said Michael.

'I can take all that,' said Martin. 'Just so long as they keep the guerrillas away and let me get on with spoiling another patch of God's good green earth.'

'They call it progress,' said Michael, matching his intonation to Martin's.

'I don't mind filling this place with stink and steam and dirt,' said Martin, suddenly serious. 'So long as I can believe the poor goddam Indians might get a pay-off from it.'

Michael nodded. Martin made you believe it.

'After all,' said Martin, 'in our civilisation, you've got to have a few assholes somewhere.'

Derek Quant was waiting for them in the shell of the control room which ultimately would dictate the miracles of chemical inter-reactions throughout the whole plant. Already there were thousands of dials and instruments set in the kind of futuristic panel they always feature on space-age TV soap operas. And dangling from a dull-white suspended ceiling were shoals of silver and copper wires, like nerve-ends waiting to tingle. Right, Michael thought. This would be the nerve centre one day. There was a hush about the place, as if the building was practising to be the air-conditioned brain-cell it would become.

'Good to see you again, Derek,' said Michael, extending a hand. 'This is Ed Corsino, founder of the feast.'

Corsino didn't catch the reference. He looked quizzically at Michael as he shook hands with Quant.

'How's it going?' asked Michael.

Quant considered the question. He wore a white coat – a medical specialist greeting ignorant students. Martin was dusty and the sweat lay in dark patches on his jungle-green bush shirt. Quant was pale, dirt-free, immaculate, with his hair neatly brushed down to thin, short sideburns. He had not only shaved, but looked as if he had shaved.

'It's going slowly, Mr Grant. If only the people back home give us what we ask for when we ask for it, there should be no problems.'

Michael couldn't help smiling. How often had he heard it? The man in the field, ringing London from a telephone at a muddy, rainy, site where a wildcat strike had just started, cursing the bastards who sat and pontificated in their warm cosy offices with girls in miniskirts just around the corner. And, inevitably, the headquarters executives testily complaining in return about the way the yokels on the site couldn't control their labour costs. It was the old, old war.

'But,' Quant went on predictably, 'since not all those conditions have been fulfilled, there *are* problems.'

'Like what?' interrupted Corsino.

'Slow delivery, mostly. I may have to ask Oldershaw to start flying out certain items.'

'If we have to, we'll do that,' said Michael quickly. 'So don't worry.'

He spoke for Corsino's ears. Inwardly he swore at Quant for even suggesting so costly a procedure. Corsino himself laughed secretly at Michael's predicament. If this big-mouth Quant worked for him, he would have kicked his ass.

'Good,' said Quant. He didn't really dislike Grant, he decided; but he believed he was wisely backing two horses by sending confidential dispatches to Sanger back in London on the progress of the work. Quant intended to keep his nose clean.

'Is Perez looking after you?' asked Michael.

Quant looked around to make sure none of the local labour was within earshot. 'He's manageable, but unreliable. He doesn't much care for coming up here, in case he gets dust on his shoes.'

153

Corsino looked down at his feet. Then he flicked the lapels of his suit. He didn't care for this scene either.

'You've got all the men you need?' Again, Michael kept his question hard on the point.

'Labour is a cow,' said Quant succinctly. 'Ask Martin here.'

Del Martin grinned. 'No worse than usual. It's the final 3 months we'll have to worry about. Then they've got you by the short hairs. They know you've *got* to complete on time or the client will kick you in the balls.'

They talked some more. Corsino looked bored and started to smoke a cigar. He proudly pointed out the tie-mark in it, which showed it was the primest Havanna, since the best cigars are always placed on the outside of the tied bundle. Then they trudged off to Quant's office, a room as well organised as Quant. On the wall was a map of the site. Martin pointed out the camp for foreign specialist labour. 'It's okay. Cinema, bars, PX, you know. But God help them if they bring liquor on to the work site.' For the local workers there was a larger compound. No PX. Then Quant took over, explaining the neat array of bar charts and schedules, all in purple and green. By the time he'd finished, everyone needed a Scotch.

They were drinking, feeling good, when the explosion happened. The sound came dully to them but unmistakeably. Martin led them out into the still dazzling sunlight.

'There,' he shouted, shielding his eyes and pointing towards the distillation column he'd earlier shown to Michael. Black smoke floated lazily beside it. They could see a flicker of flame. A siren began to wail. Then came the sharp angry chatter of automatic weapons being fired.

3

'—This morning,' said Colonel Vargas, stroking his moustache, 'is the cinema show.'

He spoke to three men seated before him in his office in the old town of Quito. It was barely furnished, dominated by a huge map of Ecuador in which red and blue flags had been stuck. A fly droned beneath the blinds on the one window in the room, smashing itself angrily against the glass. Somewhere outside a bell was tolling. Apart from these sounds, there was only the creak of the cheap army-style furniture and the sharply expectant sound of Vargas's breathing. The men, dressed in denim trousers and second-hand combat jackets, unshaven, regarded him sullenly.

'—As a film it is interesting. It might even win a prize at a festival one day. Will you give me your opinion?'

Vargas paused. The men did not speak. Since they had been brought back from Esmeraldas the previous afternoon they had received two excellent meals, drunk two bottles of wine and had had the chance to sleep in comfortable beds in a room like a richly-endowed hospital ward. They had not, however, slept much. Such treatment confused them.

'—Ah, well. We shall see.' Vargas spoke almost reproachfully to them, smiling gently, and it was the lack of menace in his blandly reasonable expression which made it so ominous. For although his facial muscles moved, his grey eyes did not smile. He smiled like a man enjoying a private reminiscence which gave him pleasure. He added, finally. '— It is a very good film.'

Its quality depended upon the viewer's attitudes. But special it certainly was. Perhaps the rarest and, foot for foot, the most expensive film in the world. Very few people could clearly explain how certain of its sequences, since all were documentary, had come to be recorded.

The film was also revealing of the character of Colonel Vargas. About all suspected revolutionaries, troublemakers and guerrillas who threatened the state, he had a simplistic philosophy. They should be shot, out of hand. But the extraction of information before that clean, painless oblivion could be contrived, he regarded with distaste. He had, to be sure, certain sexual inclinations, which a libertarian society might regard as harmless titillations. He was not, however, a sadist. He knew what the Brazilians and the Americans and the Russians and the French were reputed to have done in the name of national security, but he himself recoiled at the prospect of inflicting such treatments, especially the more grossly physical kind. The very thought made him vomit. To twist flesh and maim bodies was not his style; he believed that the most effective agony must be stirred within the mind.

'—Let us go,' he said, smiling again after his chilling fashion. He was genuinely pleased that the men had chosen the plant to attack on the previous day. Such activity both damaged Cantania's cause and strengthened his own argument for military spending. But that the men were probably a guerrilla vanguard disturbed him deeply.

The prisoners followed him down a dark corridor. Three guards trailed them. The party walked into a small projection theatre with comfortable armchairs and sat down. The lights were lowered, but not so low that Vargas could not see the faces in the room, and the film began.

The first scene lasted but a few minutes and was played in complete silence until the end. A man, rather bruised about the face, but otherwise unmarked, sat in a stout high-backed wooden chair. Straps bound him to it around his legs, wrists, chest and neck. Another man, in shirtsleeves, approached him and placed small metal plugs, attached to wires, in his ears. Vargas knew that these were electrodes. He also knew that when they were activated, even the most resolute mind could be emptied of every name and truth and reminiscence it could dredge up. He closed his eyes to avoid the look of sheer disbelief, horror, and then unquenchable agony which he knew would be the next image upon the face of the man in the chair. But even though he put his hands to his ears, he could not blot out the scream which now intruded upon the hitherto silent soundtrack. The sound seemed endless.

Cautiously, he opened his eyes. The prisoners were unmoving, still expressionless. He flicked glances at the screen which was now filled with images of men and women entwined, in the most ecstatic and lascivious acts of lust. He grunted.

The film continued for 25 minutes. There was a scene of a man being shot, a dozen rifle bolts snapping on the soundtrack before the victim hung dead in the ropes that supported him. Then another, more peaceful passage of sexual activity. Yet a further man (a scene emanating from Brazil, he understood) was shown bound to a chair, but he was bloody, inhuman, vomit-covered and this time the wires led to his nipples and his penis. The reactions of undreamed-of pain were, however, not dissimilar to that of the first sequence, which had been quietly smuggled out of France and thence to the CIA headquarters in Washington before Vargas had managed to get hold of a copy.

Vargas heard one of the three prisoners vomiting. The guards did not move. The other prisoners had put their hands before their eyes but, like Vargas, they could not escape the high-volume sound in the room, both of agony and of the murmured endearments and blasphemies of lovers. There were still more scenes to come, and all were variations on the same theme, except for the last. After further thrashing of thighs and other members on the screen it showed, curtly, a man being castrated with one sharp single blow of a machete.

It was perhaps the most obscene film that human minds could conceive, but Vargas, rising to his feet, believed it justified if it could help save the state and prevent the necessity of tortures such as he had witnessed being implemented in his country.

The prisoners, hunched and ashen, began to file out. Vargas watched them go. He knew the one who, after a rich meal had been offered to him, would be best for questioning in an interrogation which would be peaceful and reasonable and painless.

4

At the same time, approximately, another Minister – Dr Jesus Cantania – faced three different men in a room more luxuriously appointed. Michael Grant, sitting uneasily amid the dark heavy chairs and faded gilt of the walls, wished that this final interview had taken place in different circumstances. How could they hope to obtain more money or better terms when the Minister's preoccupations were of another kind?

Michael was uneasy for another reason. He had never been pushed so close to the painful realities of another nation's politics.

'What will happen to the three men?' he asked.

'Colonel Vargas's department is examining them,' said Cantania. 'I will receive a full report.'

Corsino was angry. To see a few score thousands of

dollars of an investment going up in smoke was to him a personal affront.

'We want protection, not reports, Minister,' he snapped. 'What's the army doing about these guerrillas?'

'That word is too emotive, Mr Corsino,' said Cantania quietly. 'We have no reason to believe there is any organised guerrilla force within our borders. These men are probably a few isolated revolutionaries, from Colombia perhaps. Colonel Vargas will discover the truth.'

'How?' asked Michael, though he expected that the answer would be bland.

Now Cantania also was suddenly angry. 'We are not barbarians, Mr Grant, if that is what you are implying. We have no torture chambers. Would you care to see one of our prisons perhaps?'

Cantania was, in his own terms, not dissembling. The President had assured him many times on this point, and Cantania had always stressed how crucial it was that the regime did not become associated with the more horrific apparatus of a police state. His whole creed, the belief in gradual reform, would be undermined if the revolutionary forces within the continent really could depict the rulers of his country as sadistic tyrants.

'I apologise, Minister,' said Michael. 'But I have read reports of what happens in some South American countries.'

Cantania shrugged impatiently. 'Some are doubtless true. Most are exaggerated. Your newspapers have too much licence.'

Dear God, Martin was thinking. Did the arguments always have to be the same? He did not disbelieve that Cantania believed them, sincerely. But he'd heard them too often. Gag the papers, put a few people in gaol or twelve feet under, squeeze the poor – just until the country is strong enough to stand dissent, rich enough not to have to bend to either America or Russia or China. Then things will change. Except in his experience, the rarely did.

He wasn't fooled about the United States of America either. He viewed his homeland as a country of myths: myths that said its people cared about each other, that proclaimed the existence of equality of opportunity and justice and free speech, that alleged the envy of foreigners for its social and political institutions. The whole package was wrapped up in illusions about the luxury of American life. It was like a gigantic and fraudulent advertising campaign, so insidious that Americans consumed not products but, pre-conditioned, the reputation of the products. So ran Martin's views. Yet here on the Equator, with the heat cracking brains outside the window, beggars on the pavement and a cardinal on every government committee that mattered, he often wished he were back in Illinois with his kids for good.

Turning his head slightly, Martin considered that Michael looked as sick as he himself felt. He heard Corsino arguing about money, and it seemed irrelevant.

Cantania was shrugging again. 'Even if it were easy, I am not at all sure that I ought to help you, Mr Corsino. It is not our duty to provide you with a cast-iron insurance for profit. My job is to get the best bargain I can for my country. You must take normal commercial risks, and I have never hidden the truth from you. But these arguments are scarcely to the point. In the circumstances, how can I assist you?'

Corsino was stubborn. 'Spell that out, Minister. I want to be sure.'

'Hard currency is in short supply with us,' said Cantania patiently. 'We cannot even find a way to help Colonel Vargas get his warships and guns.'

'But there must be non-governmental sources of capital you could tap,' snapped Corsino. 'You have friends.'

'My friends have already supported the petro-chemical company to the hilt, Mr Corsino. Who else has taken up 10 per cent of the stock?'

'I know every damn one of them,' said Corsino. 'But there are other people with money. The textile guy I met . . .'

'The textile guy . . .' Cantania let the words float distastefully, then smiled bleakly. 'That man is not especially anxious to see artificial fibres manufactured in this country. He also happens to be related to Colonel Vargas.'

Corsino refused to be put down. 'When I did this deal you said nothing of Vargas. He's new on the scene. And he's your responsibility, not ours. Buy him, for chrissakes.'

Cantania rose and went to replenish his whisky glass. He did not offer any to Corsino, nor even to Michael and

Martin whose discomfort he discerned. He forced himself not to break off the interview; he remained determined that the petro-chemical plant would be built.

'Colonel Vargas is not for sale,' Cantania said, delivering his insult with precision. 'Not at your price, Mr Corsino. If you presented him with maybe one division on the ground and three squadrons of Lightnings in the air, he might perhaps do you favours. Have you that kind of money?'

He turned to face them. 'Your best chance of assistance, Mr Corsino, must still be Ali-Chem or Kerridge Steel. And those, of course are *your* friends.'

5

All the way back to New York City, Corsino griped. Especially about Cantania. A few months ago the Minister had been, to use Corsino's phrase, a swinger.

Michael had now come to expect this change of attitude. What worried him was that Corsino seemed to have no clear plan of action. Michael wanted him to fix a meeting for both of them with the Ali-Chem people next day, but Corsino was adamant.

'They're my baby, Mike. I can tell you we haven't a chance. They're really screwed up for funding.'

'But Ed – surely I can try. Where's the harm?'

'They like to know the people they're dealing with. You they don't know,' said Corsino bluntly.

It was raining and blowing a force 6 when they reached Kennedy in mid-afternoon. Alison had been waiting for Michael at the Drake Hotel, at Park Avenue and 56th, for almost 48 hours. He was never more glad to see her. They had scarcely embraced before a telephone call came through to their room from David Travis in London.

David wanted to know if he should go yet to see the Debrais people in Paris. Sanger had made no move towards Debrais since Michael had left. The American was keeping his head down in the aftermath of the police raid on Prospect House.

'Fine,' said Michael ironically; thank God something was going well.

'But the whole Debrais business is drifting,' said David. 'Perhaps we ought to move now.'

'Hold it till I get back,' said Michael.

'When are you coming?'

'Monday. I'm committed to a weekend with Ed Corsino in New Jersey. Nothing will happen over Debrais in the next three days.'

'I understand,' said David. 'Sorry to bother you.'

'No, that's fine. Good to hear you.' He meant it. 'But I'm screwed up at this end.'

'It wasn't good?'

'That's the understatement of the year.' Michael quickly painted the picture, and David made sympathetic noises down the line. He said he'd think what he could do. But Michael didn't blame his assistant for sounding as depressed as he felt.

'Top-secret, all this,' Michael said.

'Of course,' said David.

They said goodbye. Michael turned back, gratefully, to Alison.

She looked good, hell she did. Her whole body had a glow of ripeness. As he clung to her, he was thrilled by the softness of her shoulders and breasts, contrasting with the hardness of the mound that pressed against his stomach. He kissed her lips and her cheeks with a warmth which had nothing to do with sexual desire. He needed a supporter, and she was exactly that. Her strength seemed to flow into him.

'How bloody is it really?' she said.

'Forget it,' he said. Even the slight extra fullness of her face suited her.

They lay side by side on the bed and all he wanted to do was to run his hands again and again over her clothed body. He had no desire to do more.

Finally, she rose and picked up a glass of whisky, ice chiming freshly in the glass. She had prepared it whilst he was speaking to London.

'I thought you might need it,' she said.

'Thanks. I do.'

'What happens now?' she asked.

'The rest of the day is ours. I've promised Ed Corsino

we'll drive to him tomorrow. I'm sorry, darling, but we'll have to get back to London on Monday.'

'That's okay,' she said. 'Whatever you think's best.'

'I might just stay on – if he changes his mind about an approach to Ali-Chem. But I don't think he will.'

'What's all that about, Michael?'

'It doesn't make too much sense.' he said. 'Ed wasn't enthusiastic about coming to Ecuador anyway, though now there's this guerrilla trouble I think he's glad he did. But it's Prospero who are really struggling over money and terms, not his end of the consortium. So in a way he was doing me a favour trying to squeeze help out of Quito.'

'Which you didn't get,' she said.

'Too true.' Michael smiled sadly. 'But so long as Ed judges that our problems won't wreck the consortium as a whole – and he thinks we're able to drum up money if we're really desperate – then he's not much bothered. He'll let us stew.'

'And?'

'I want to see if I can get money from other partners in the company we're building that plant for. Apart from the Ecuador Government, there's Ali-Chem or Kerridge Steel. But Ed insists he should handle that end of the business alone. Doesn't want me poaching on his territory, I suppose. But I'd prefer to put my own case. He's a funny devil.'

'I thought he was a chum,' she said. Then, not wanting to imply criticism, careful of their alliance. 'I'm not having a go, but you don't seem very keen on him suddenly.'

He sipped his Scotch. 'Right. Perhaps I've never seen him when he was pushed before. In a tight corner, Ed's not very pretty. He scratches and he bites, and he doesn't much care whom he hurts. He's as racist as they come and I think he'd shop his own mother. I don't really trust him any more.'

'And we're going to spend a happy weekend with him?'

'Can't be helped,' said Michael. 'The proprieties will be observed. Sorry love.'

'How dangerous is all this to you?' she asked.

'Depends a lot on the board,' he said. 'Especially Bender. And Bernard.' He made a determined effort at cheerfulness. 'The hell with it. There's not much I can do at the moment. How *is* Bernard?'

'Absolutely fine. I had a great lunch with him. He was very sweet. He likes the prospect of a grandchild.'

She took Michael's hand, regarding him seriously. 'Let him help you, Michael. He really wants to. He won't let Bender and that bastard Sanger get at you if only you'll give him the chance.'

'Bender he can't do anything about,' said Michael flatly. 'If Bender wants to crucify me, Dad can't stop him.'

It was the first time she had heard him call Bernard by the shorter, warmer name in months.

'I think he'll surprise you,' she said.

He remembered the past, all the arguments with his father, his own behaviour to Bernard when he had fought for control of Prospero. He had believed it to be right that he should take over; but he had also known that his motives were tinged with revenge and pride.

'Yes,' he said slowly. 'I'll try. You know I'm tired of fighting Bernard. Things have been getting better, haven't they?'

Alison smiled, and the scar on her face creased white against the tanned flesh. 'I know. But let him win a few battles for you himself. Then he'll imagine he's won the war. That you could stand, couldn't you?'

Michael reserved to himself only the thought that he would choose the battles. He wanted no further to disturb his compact with Alison. They were allies as well as lovers, and that is a condition within marriage which is not always clearly understood. Lovers can often be competitors too.

'I'm not arguing,' he said.

The words tumbled on – about his father, about Prospero, about London. Suddenly, he said, 'This is ridiculous. How have you been getting on here?'

'I've been to Tiffany's,' she said. 'But I haven't bankrupted us.'

He liked the way she used 'us'.

'All I bought was a thing like a sardine can opener for you to put on the end of your toothpaste tube. It winds it up neatly. It's in sterling silver.'

He laughed. 'You've no sales resistance. Do you like it all?'

'Everybody told me so often I'd hate it – especially your

father – that I'm a bit disappointed I haven't been mugged, raped and offered my daily dose of heroin already. It's dirty, like they said it was, and Times Square is awful. Do you know I saw a poster in a shop there, six by six, of two hippopotamuses screwing? That I've never seen, not even in Soho. But the people seem all right. A bit twitchy, but all right. And Michael, it *is* exciting, isn't it?'

He knew exactly what she meant. You could see excrement on the sidewalks, garbage in the river, smog in the air, knives in guts, graft in City Hall and dope in the eyes of thousands. Yet it was like his friends who were *really* New Yorkers always said. Even as they admitted that their city was coming apart at the seams, they would say, well, but how can we leave? It's where we are, where we belong, where the good action as well as the bad is. That in his experience had been true.

It wasn't simply the cataract of money which Wall Street represented either. Some people didn't like the place. He did. He liked the way New Yorkers lived life as if it might be taken from them at any moment. He enjoyed the dazzling spaghetti strands of neon, the sharp light of day and of night, and the soft light of early evening when the impossible skyline of spikes and domes and turrets becomes washed in green and purple and pink. He could have catalogued a hundred items for her, but all these memories added up to the single fact that in New York City he felt that fantastic schemes – for happenings, for exploration, for good, for evil and, inevitably, for making money – might be dreamed up as in no other place in the world.

In Manhattan, in a hotel or apartment block, it is sometimes difficult to know what the weather is like. So many rooms face inwards into wells, and the towering walls kill the light. It was from a glinting window, the sun's dull disc mirrored in it, through a gap the architects had forgotten to fill, that Michael knew now the rain might have stopped.

'Let's go out,' he said.

'It's pouring.'

'The sun's coming out.'

'It's blowing like hell,' she said.

'Doesn't matter,' he said. 'I want to show you something.'

'Ring Bernard,' she said. 'Please.'

'Later.'

'You ought to get more sleep.'

'I've too much on my mind,' he said.

So they went out and found the streets already beginning to dry under the lash of a brisk warm wind. They won a cab and fought their way through the sticky trash of late-Friday afternoon traffic until, 25 minutes later, they were set down on the rim of Manhattan, at the end of East 82nd Street. The wind off the East River hammered their ears as they promenaded.

'What is it?' she said.

'The John Finley Walk. They built it during the war and they called it after some editor of the *New York Times*.'

'Why here?'

'I don't know. It's one of the nicer things about this city, that's all. I just wanted to see it again – with you.'

They walked into the Carl Schurz Park. There were a lot of kids in clumps of rock, climbing. There were dogs and owners and sandpits and playgrounds. They passed trees, which he said proudly were laurels and firs, and flowering things, which he called forsythia and rhododendrons.

She knew, but she didn't want to spoil his pleasure. He had his arm around her like a shelter. No one looked at them with any curiosity whatsoever. A long way below them, the river ran frothily and she asked questions, and he told her about the Queensboro Bridge to the right and the loopy arches of the Triboro Bridge to the left and she thought it was just like Americans to call it that because it linked three boroughs. Logical, like the streets. He pointed out Welfare Island, where the hospitals are, and she could feel the cars throbbing below her feet on East River Drive, and as he talked on about the ships slipping by fast and the flags and the cargoes and the people hanging over the railings in exhilaration and, for all she knew, distress, he made the city glow and tingle for her in a way she would be grateful for all her life. Christ, she thought, when he's like this he is a lovely man.

As for Michael, the freshness of the air and the warmth of Alison with him drove Ecuador and Prospero from his more immediate thoughts. After half an hour they turned towards the streets again, exchanging the blinding light of the water and the noises of dogs and kids and boats for the cacophony of car horns and the bleak scent of automobile fumes. As they tried to get a cab, a man, not ill-dressed, approached them. Michael stiffened. He wanted nothing to spoil their hour.

The man did not speak. He handed them a card. It read: *Please pardon me for intruding. I am a deaf mute. This card I sell for a living. Let me have whatever you wish. And may God bless you.* Michael turned over the card. There were verses on the back. He handed over a dollar and the man walked away.

'At least he wasn't pushing heroin,' said Michael almost apologetically.

That evening he tried three times to reach Bernard without success. They ate at the Drake, sitting beneath a dark ceiling from which lights glowed through small portholes, not saying much. At one point a tall careful girl came in, very clean, very shiny, with smooth long thighs visible.

Alison asked, did he like her? Privately she thought the girl looked marvellous. Michael said she looked like plastic; predatory as well as pretty. The sort you trade in every year for a new model, he said. When the waiter arrived, Alison chose escalope of veal, which was a meat Michael did not enjoy. He wanted lobster, which she believed was overrated. They smiled at each other, sharing the joke about their preferences. They believed now they would never make the common mistake of imagining that marriage partners ought to like everybody or everything in common. Every sound marriage includes exclusive and private areas of choice, thought and action.

They went to bed early, but it was well past noon when they finally got up. And it was an hour or more after that when – having apologised to Corsino by telephone – they rode west out of the city in a limousine through streets that were hot with the late June sun. They made the Lincoln Tunnel and then sat silently as they passed the scarred and ugly landscape of riverside New Jersey.

Corsino's house had had a giant extension, with indoor swimming pool and guest rooms, added to it since Michael had last visited it two years earlier. In the parkland surrounding it, he had laid out a nine-hole golf course. Corsino greeted them in a peaked cap which bore his initials, and yellow slacks which did not. He was waving a five-iron. He seemed to have regained his good humour.

'Say, Mike, but she's *beautiful*,' he shouted, hugging Alison like a long-lost daughter. 'Marge, Marge,' he called towards the open door of the house.

Marjorie Corsino looked five years older than on his last visit, Michael thought. The blue-rinse sat on her hair defiantly, but there were sad lines around her mouth and her eyes were mournful. She was dressed sloppily in smock and paint-stained slacks.

'Yeah, she's chasin' Picasso these days,' said Corsino. 'For some pictures she makes over a thousand bucks.'

Michael saw her flinch. He knew she didn't need the money, as Corsino had once explicitly told him. Corsino believed, when he married Marjorie 15 years ago, that he had linked up with a cash register. Her father had made millions out of nuts and bolts. But he, cunning fellow, had locked it up so tightly that it could only be used for their mutual benefit. Once over the initial surprise, Ed Corsino had accepted the situation. He had used her money, and made a fortune of his own. Now that her financial purpose in his life was fulfilled, Corsino needed only to use *her*, and that not often.

He allowed his wife to mix the drinks as they sat amid water, rocks and artful foliage.

'This is nice, Mrs Corsino,' said Alison.

'Thank you, my dear,' said her hostess. 'Please call me Marjorie.'

'Yeah – and Ed,' said Corsino. 'You feeling better, Mike?'

'Sure,' said Michael. 'Now I can be miserable without getting suicidal.'

Corsino threw his head back, gargling Scotch and Coke through laughter. 'Leave it to me, Mike. I'll fix those bastards. Today, we're gonna have a ball.'

'I'll try,' said Michael.

'We've got a little party early evening for you. Just some friends. And later we'll go out to eat. Somewhere special. Right?'

'Right,' said Michael.

'And I don't want to hear about those bums in Quito – understand?'

He turned to Alison, his gaze beginning at her ankle, working upwards. It was routine rather than real interest, for he at once started to talk about the subject he really knew.

'If you girls had to do business in South America, you'd know,' he said. 'They've gotten more uppity than the blacks in Africa.'

Alison's smile stayed fixed and bright. 'Have you done a lot in Africa, Mr Corsino?'

'Ed, dammit,' he said, almost bad-tempered. He swung back to Michael. 'Did I tell you how we used to play the tenders in Nigeria?'

Michael shook his head.

'When the tenders were opened, ours were always the best,' chortled Corsino.

'You had advance information on the others?' asked Alison, and Corsino looked at her in surprise. Marjorie Corsino was silent, eyes downcast.

'Better than that, girl.' Corsino was swelling about the face, like a turkey. 'I knew the guy who opened them. Met him at Harvard Business School.'

Michael said: 'And you got him to change your figures?'

Corsino laughed again. 'Jesus no. We left a blank space. He just filled it in for us. Nothing sensational. Just a modest three, four per cent lower than any others.'

No one spoke. Corsino gulped at his drink.

'Cryin' shame it didn't last. They shifted him out after a year and a half. Ministers don't stay long there. Still and all, he quite likes it in Switzerland. Mighty cold for niggers in winter, but he's got his numbered account and a few girls to keep him warm.'

Corsino told many similar anecdotes in the next 30 minutes. He was absorbed in the sound of his voice and the feel of his interests. Marjorie sat there regarding him sadly, with the look of a woman who knew that in the fulfilment contest she had finished a poor second to business, and probably to golf, football and liquor.

Finally, Corsino said: 'Hey, Marge. You wanna show Alison your studio?'

It was a command rather than an invitation. When the women had gone, Michael said: 'Ed, I'd like to ring my father.'

'Sure, Mike. I'll get Manuel to place the call.' Corsino kept Puerto Ricans to run his house. 'When do you want it?'

'Any time in the next hour.'

Corsino spoke into a telephone, then turned to Michael. 'I really mean it about not trying to play with Ali-Chem,' he said. 'Or Kerridge. That's my ball-game, okay? You'll just have to get yourself out of the shit, son. Your old man can stand it.'

It was blunt to the point of offensiveness. Michael admired the way American businessmen laid it on the line, but Corsino was too much. Frankness with him came out as a steaming brew of challenge and taunt.

'I'm not arguing, Ed. I'll do the same for you one day.'

To his surprise, Corsino only laughed. 'No hard feelings, Mike. That's how it is. Come and see my golf park.'

Half an hour later, Michael and Alison were in their bedroom, preparing for the cocktail hour. There were two bathrooms attached to it, with golden angels for taps. The initials 'E.C.' were set into towels, face-cloths, bath mats, cakes of soap and the floors of the sunken baths. The hangings were brocade and lace. A massive record-player was installed for their pleasure: Tony Bennett and Golden Strings cheek by sleeve with *The Sound of Music* and *Annie Get Your Gun* and art books with (Alison discovered) uncut pages and the collected works of Robbins, Hailey, the Book of the Month Club and Literary Guild.

There was a short, sharp buzz from the telephone.

'It'll be Bernard,' said Michael. He picked up the receiver, but said nothing. He waved his hands at Alison, wanting silence. Then he covered the mouthpiece and went on listening, intently.

'Listen Kerridge. When I ask you to call I don't expect to wait 24 hours.' The voice was Corsino's.

'I've been away.' This time the tones were old and grating, measured and not fearful. 'What do you want, Ed?'

'What I told you about Prospero before. Just to underline it. No deals. Understand?'

The old man sighed. 'Why waste my time, Ed? I don't have to be told twice.'

'Michael Grant's hotter than ever to talk with you. Just remember that. And remember Ali-Chem too. There's a lot of dough in that subsidiary plant. I don't want it screwed up.'

Michael's face had gone clenched and pale. Alison made as if to speak. Again he waved a hand.

'Goodbye, Ed,' said Kerridge. 'I won't forget.'

'Yeah – well, thanks.'

'Careful, Ed. You're being polite. I may think you're slipping.' Kerridge's voice was gravely mocking. 'And how are your friends getting on with the SEC in Washington?'

'I'll check that out Monday.'

'You'd better, Ed. That take-over is getting cold.'

'Yeah. I'll ring you. Cheers, friend.'

The line went dead. Michael put the receiver down very slowly. He was shocked, angered, but not really surprised. What he was, more importantly, was confused.

Before the telephone call he had assumed that Corsino was Kerridge's servant. The first few exchanges on the line had then made him assume the opposite. Finally they had seemed to be uneasy equals. And what was the talk about the SEC? Perhaps that had nothing to do with Ecuador. But the words about Ali-Chem almost certainly had. His conversation with Del Martin was still clear in his mind. The pieces fitted.

'Corsino's got something going with Ali-Chem in Ecuador I don't know about,' he said. 'Some plant they're going to build. I wish I knew what was going on.'

'So do I,' said Alison.

The telephone buzzed again and, when they made no move towards it, kept on buzzing. At last Michael lifted. It was the servant, Manuel, telling him there was no answer from Bernard's London number.

'So much for 'phone buzzers that shouldn't buzz and extensions that shouldn't be extended,' Michael said grimly. 'I didn't feel I ought to go on listening. I'm glad I did.'

She gave him a serious look and, absent-mindedly, resumed brushing her hair. It shone like beaten copper. 'This is sick,' she said. 'When can we get out of here?'

'We'll make some excuse to get back to New York tomorrow evening. Monday I'll set something going.'

'Do we catch that London plane?'

'If I stay, Ed will soon know. And he'll get suspicious. I'll have to get someone he doesn't know to do the digging.'

The cocktail party was like such occasions anywhere, except that here the women had larger diamonds and more predatory eyes, whilst the men were perhaps more neatly dressed and more gleamingly washed and toileted. Belligerently so. The after-shave on their skin assaulted the nose, mingling archly with the Martinis and bourbon on their breath.

At first, men talked to men about stocks and deals, and diets and golf and football. Especially football. Corsino had told Michael he was trying to fix a deal for a new franchise on a pro. team. Sometimes a blast of laughter would erupt and brows which were beginning to sweat would tilt back. Those were the jokes, about either sex or money.

Women, meantime, spoke to women. Some mentioned families and friends; some hinted at objects their husbands might buy them or which they might buy their occasional male friends. But many of them also discussed stocks and deals, and diets and golf and clothing, and the alimony won by women they knew and the grey hairs their long-tressed, apparently indifferent children gave them.

After an hour, the liquor had done its work. The company began to mingle. Then some of the men began to talk with members of the opposite sex, trapping them in corners with one arm propped against the wall like a gate, looking hard down the fronts of dresses if the view seemed promising and suggesting – like prospectuses for new company flotations – the advantages they could offer in future liaisons.

The women who still fancied their chance watched the various performances with calculating eyes. They were never convinced but somehow still wanted to be, very badly. None of them complained when the hands of the talker lingered playfully on a hip or even (in the case of one man, plump and really smashed) partly inside the inviting cleft of a dress front.

Some of the wives, knowing their husbands too well, hopped around the room like birds pecking at crumbs. They did it not out of hope that they might disturb their spouses' mating dance, but more from habit and, perhaps, to relieve their feelings. Alison was safe, more or less, because she was so obviously pregnant. The men were respectful, attentive. Michael, after weighing up the business scene, talked with various wives about London. They were nice

171

enough; but what can you say that has much meaning at a cocktail party when your mind is on other things? Finally, some of the guests followed them into the warm night, with the daylight only just fading, to go to dinner at the restaurant which Corsino had chosen.

His behaviour there was no revelation. He was known, and the fact – often repeated in his Silver Shadow convertible, driven with hood down and stereo blasting – was important to him. When the headwaiter greeted him with both hands, then placed an arm proprietorially around him, Corsino's whole body seemed to shimmer. Corsino liked having it made. Irrationally, Michael found himself remembering the story of the frigid headwaiter at the Hotel de Paris in Monte Carlo of whom, when he died, people were able to say, 'God finally caught his eye.'

The tables were ringside. The food was excellent. The cabaret was tolerable – Buddy Greco on a night when he played piano as much as sang. And, crushed as they were, ten of them around a table made for eight, someone had to get a table leg up the junction. It was, of course, Marjorie Corsino. She was a woman who, at an outer table for four, would always be the one who sat with her back to the restaurant. She looked like a person whose spirit Corsino had spent, leaving her only her father's money.

He had developed a skill for ignoring her, and the other guests did not offend the protocol, so that Michael was often left trying to make conversation with her. It was hard work. Removed for a time by the night air from the threshold of oblivion, she swiftly slid several glasses of Californian wine closer to it. Her elbow kept slipping from the table. Twice she sprayed sauce on the cloth when she tried to spear her steak. Her voice rose higher and higher.

Alison was on the other side of the table. She remembered best the moment when, apropos of nothing, an uncareful hand was laid upon her thigh and its weaving owner said gruffly, 'My wife, see, won't even look at any other guy. Lucky me. Wouldn't give a darn if she did. Maybe I wouldn't feel so guilty so often.' The hand squeezed painfully, which was the bourbon speaking.

Corsino fuelled this frenetic consumption of time with food, drink and loud commands. He drank mightily but never suggested drunkenness. Towards the end of the evening, he suddenly offered a toast to their English guests. Three of the company had no wine left in their glasses. Wouldn't Corsino have been exactly the guy to have saved some for just such an emergency, Michael thought? He was organised for sure; tight and compact and decisive as a snake's head striking.

They left finally when the waiter had finished shaking the crumbs out of the other tablecloths and the tips out of battered credit card holders.

'Didn't I tell you it was a great place?' Corsino boomed as they waited for the Rolls. It was a question which defied dissent. How could anyone present not share his tastes? No one appeared to notice that Marjorie was leaning against a wall, crying to herself, not for display.

Back at the house, Michael and Alison didn't want to talk, only sleep as long as possible. Next morning, at 11, Corsino persuaded Michael to leap into an electric buggy and race 150 yards to the first tee of the golf course, where they played 7 holes before brunch. Michael, who had little time for golf back in England, played miserably and lost badly. They never saw Marjorie Corsino again before they left.

At the Drake, there was a message asking Michael to telephone his father. He got through at once, his mind still numb from the weekend. Bernard's voice, strong and thick and cheerful, made him feel better at once. He would not have believed it could have so bracing an effect.

Bernard insisted on talking to Alison and he made her laugh, quite spontaneously. Then she handed the telephone back to Michael, and his father bubbled on as if he were enjoying himself. He saved the coup de grace till the end, though, like the wicked old actor he was.

'Michael,' he said, suddenly changing his tone to one of archness. 'That's a fine young man you have in your office.'

'David Travis?' said his son.

'Certainly. He's clever, intelligent. Not too proud to ask for help if he needs it.'

'Tell me, father, what's all this about?'

'On Friday afternoon, we had a cosy little chat, Mr Travis and I.' Still arch, still bursting with the effort of holding back his news.

Michael, however, experienced only a faintly chilling sense of alarm. He was still not sure he wanted chats, cosy or

173

otherwise, between David and his father. How could his assistant understand what Bernard might or might not know, even need to know?

'He told me you were having a little local difficulty persuading the Ecuadoreans to make the contract easier for us.'

His son stayed silent. It was, Michael thought afterwards, uncanny that Bernard could scent out immediately even over a transatlantic telephone his son's displeased unease.

'And don't be annoyed with him, Michael. Everyone knew that was the purpose of your visit to Ecuador. And could you have hidden your problems from me?'

'All right, father. I agree.'

'David told me about the problem of your Colonel Vargas,' Bernard continued. 'My understanding is that he wants certain goods, and that if he got them your troubles might be considerably eased. Is that correct?'

'Yes,' said Michael. 'It would help.'

'Then *I* can help you – and so can David Travis.' Bernard was chuckling, enjoying himself. 'Mr Travis knows the man who has been trying to sell those goods to Colonel Vargas for many months now.'

'Are you sure of that?'

'I have been away 36 hours on your behalf, dear boy.'

'That's why I couldn't reach you,' said Michael unnecessarily.

'*Naturlich*,' said Bernard. It was one of his joke middle-Europeanisms, a sly and confident acknowledgment of his roots. He only used such words when he was winning.

'All right, I'm grateful. But do you know there's a damned big snag? Ecuador can't pay for the bloody arms.'

'Hush,' said his father. 'Don't be so indiscreet.'

'But they keep talking about soft currency.'

'That I know. And I can fix it.'

'You're joking.'

'Don't be adolescent, Michael. I don't make such jokes. A friend I was talking with some time ago told me about a deal he had to buy large quantities of textiles and other goods in Eastern Europe. It was not really my kind of thing. Not now. So I did nothing about it. This morning, however, I reached him. The deal is going through, even more so now. And the sums of money match up nicely. He

174

will be delighted to allow your South American friends to use their branches in Eastern Europe to pay for *his* goods. Then he will pay the company to which Mr Travis's contact belongs the equivalent sum in sterling in London – less, of course, a commission. Then that company can give *their* goods to South America. Is that satisfactory?'

Michael could have done without the lecture in simple economics. But he was delighted. 'If you've really got that middle man, well – I don't give a damn what his commission is.'

'Don't be so generous, Michael. There's never any need to give more than you should. It gets us a bad reputation. You're too impulsive.' Bernard was having his fun and Michael didn't object.

'*Touché*,' he said.

'Good,' said Bernard. 'You leave the question of the size of commission to me. My friend does not realise how important the arrangement is to us. And he need never know if we make an agreement quickly. When are you coming back?'

'Tomorrow. Early.'

'Couldn't be better. We'll talk in the evening. Kiss Alison for me.'

'Of course, father. And thank you. Thank you very much indeed.'

'Thank David Travis most of all,' said Bernard. 'A good man, that. Bind him to you. Bind him. Good night.'

That evening Michael was busy on the telephone for two and a half hours, talking to several kinds of men, sending many cables in careful terms, summoning those who could carry good news and specific instructions to a variety of places, including Quito. When he went to bed he felt better than for many days. The deal for the frigates and launches should be enough at least to stop Vargas being bloody-minded. And now, surely, Cantania would keep his end of what, in Quito, had appeared to be an implied bargain.

The hope was back in Michael's bones, and that – in business as in all living – is what counts. Hope, and the expectancy it engenders, is the fuel of operators.

As he closed his eyes, he even found time to think about sports car races again and to believe in the Lovelace way of constructing winners. And David – yes, thank

God for David. Perhaps it was time to send him to start pushing the Debrais deal again. He had the touch, David Travis. One had to have it, too. Some people were like charms. Lucky. David was lucky. It was as crucial as loyalty.

6. TWO KINDS OF SACRIFICE

1

'First,' said Michael Grant, 'the good news.'

David thought that it was unlike his boss to be flippant. He waited, not wanting to spoil Michael's obvious enjoyment in explaining the document in his hand.

'The promissory note we've been waiting for,' said Michael. 'Cantania's come through at last.'

'He's taken long enough,' said David.

Michael laughed, not entirely with humour. 'By South American standards, three weeks is fast.'

'Vargas must have been pleased,' said David.

'Just wait till you meet him. He shows pleasure at nothing. He's simply kept his part of the bargain in an old-fashioned horse-trading operation. He's got the toys he wanted – his boats and his guns. So he's prepared to let Cantania play games with the plant for a few months. They've come up with the second instalment even though Brasserton's haven't got as far with the construction as they should have done.'

David looked more closely at the piece of paper. With this as security, the banks would be willing to advance more of the money which Brasserton's needed.

'Even three million dollars doesn't exactly make us all square does it?'

Michael shrugged. 'It helps. And Vargas is off our backs for the moment too. In this game you have to live from week to week.'

'If you're satisfied, fine,' said David. 'I still wish it was more.'

'We'd have got nothing without you,' said Michael. 'You did a fantastic job.'

Christ, David thought. If only you knew. Since Michael's return from New York more than three weeks earlier David

177

had never felt more wanted – in Prospect House, at least. At home, with Sheila, it was something else. She had been unresponsive to all his gestures of goodwill, almost furtive. Five days ago he had worked out why.

On the Friday evening last month when Michael had telephoned him from New York with the details of the abortive visit to Ecuador, he had told the whole story to Sheila. He had intended to act anyway, but was uncertain whether he should go to Bernard Grant.

It was she who had told him he must. It was she who had worked out as quickly as he that if Prospero acted honest broker, an arms deal could get not only Mailer but also Cantania and Michael Grant off the hook. Sheila seemed to know more about Mailer's whereabouts and time-table that David did. She protested that David had told her all that. He was near-certain he hadn't.

So he went to Bernard, and his success was now history. But Sheila, instead of revelling in it as she had every right to do, evaded his questions, sulking when he tried to involve her. His bafflement made him almost a bully, his questions and comments growing more pointed every day. Finally Sheila, with a recklessness which was not her style, conceded him every suspicion in an outburst over supper.

All right. I've seen Freddie Mailer. We had lunch. Are you satisfied? How could I have helped you if I hadn't? Why do you have to go on and on and spoil it?

She had wept, moaning. *It's not fair. It just isn't bloody fair.*

He had been too shocked – not morally, but out of surprise that he knew so little of her character — to do other than comfort her. For almost a week they had lived edgily. David had no more inclination to ask questions, perhaps from fear of what he might discover, perhaps from a sense of shame within himself. Sheila volunteered no statements.

He looked at Michael with what he hoped was intelligent interest. 'And the bad news?'

Michael pushed *The Times* across his desk. It was folded open at the facing-leader page. 'Have you read this today?'

The piece gave a rundown on guerrilla activity in South America. Most of it was about Uruguay and Brazil. But there were two paragraphs, ringed in red, on Ecuador. Five separate incidents had been reported from Quito during the

178

past month, including one referring to the explosion at Esmeraldas while Michael was there. It was assumed, said the article, that regular guerrilla units were now operating in the country.

'It's datelined Buenos Aires. How the hell can they tell from there?' David still wanted to offer what hope he could.

'Come on,' said Michael.

'Okay,' said David. 'Suppose you're right. How bad will it be?'

'I anticipate Vargas and his goons can contain them. So the plant won't suffer seriously. But trouble of that kind can only strengthen hard-liners like him and weaken Cantania. So . . .'

Michael stood up suddenly, squaring his shoulders, laughing like a man determined to find the bright side for his subordinate's consumption. Leaders lead – all that.

'All we can do is hope. Meanwhile, the money means we can start moving in other directions again. I want you to go to France and sort out the Debrais business. I can't hold the ring there any longer. Bender was really itchy at the board meeting yesterday. He wants some action, and he specifically named you.'

'I don't recall saying two words to him in my life.'

Michael smiled mischievously. 'Golden boys are always better if you don't meet them. Fantasies for old gentlemen to project themselves through. And that's what he thinks you are now – a golden boy. So Debrais is yours to work out. Earl Sanger won't interfere. He's walking softly.'

'Are the board still unhappy about the police raid?'

'Yes. But satisfied with my explanation that it was all a ridiculous mistake. All the huff and puff, though, has made Earl Sanger frightened I'll split on him. The board was very moral.'

David did not know how seriously to take his boss. He was faintly uneasy about the way his situation had changed in three months or so. He had done well for Michael. In return he had gradually become Michael's confessional. There was very little the chairman's son did not talk about to him now in uncompromising and even lese-majesty terms. The nearness of their ages had something to do with it, he supposed. He also imagined that all men at the summit, seeking relief from stress, need someone close at hand to

179

whom they can talk, celebrating their victories, finding solace in defeat. He chanced his luck farther.

'And you?'

'And me – yes, on that, I'm moral,' said Michael. His tone was serious again. 'Don't ever try to pull that kind of trick without my knowing, David. I'd chop you. No messing.'

'When do you want me to go to France?' David moved on fast from the other, fruitless subject.

'Soon. And I want you to see the woman.'

'Claire Justine Debrais. Forty-five. Two children.'

'Good,' said Michael. 'It's her feelings about not wanting the French competition to take over that gave us the chance, so deal with *her*. The managers can only do as she tells them. She's the majority stockholder. You can't start soon enough. In a few days they'll all be off to their Greek island or whatever. You know what August is like in Paris.'

'I'd like to be off to mine,' said David, smiling to take the edge off the remark.

'Don't worry – you'll get that holiday. Promise. You deserve it.'

David wanted not to appear uneager. 'Is there anything I can do about SAEF while I'm travelling?'

'I don't think so. They're still being unhelpful. They've got a pocketful of loose cash and they could bear some of our risk if they wanted to. It won't help them if we land in trouble in Ecuador. But they just shrug and smile and you know they're thinking why don't we just sell a company or two if we're short of money. Well . . .'

Michael spread his hands in an apologetic gesture. David knew too well that Michael dare not raid the conglomerate's subsidiaries. Bender would crucify him. And Sanger would hold the nails.

'Just keep your ear to the ground on SAEF,' said Michael. 'You never know.'

Michael's desk box buzzed. 'Your father is on his way, Mr Grant,' said the secretary. The door opened and Bernard Grant came in, pregnant with news. The beam switched on.

'Ah, David. Everything going well? When are you going to France?'

You don't change, David thought. Can't stop hustling.

Keeping up the pressure, just in case Michael might not be.

'We were just discussing it, Sir Bernard.'

'Good. Very good. Don't trust the French. Be careful. Worse than South Americans.' The beam hit full power. 'Not as bad as Hungarians, though. Do another Ecuador-style job and you'll be forcing me to resign. Good luck.'

The final words were a dismissal. Bernard had things to say that wouldn't wait. As soon as David had gone he sat crisply in one of the easy chairs. He felt his tight grey hair gingerly as if to make sure the waves hadn't come out in the sunshine.

'Well, Michael? What news on Ali-Chem?'

Michael walked over to join his father in equality – both in the same kind of chair, both at the same level. 'They're still digging. Nothing very useful yet.'

Bernard Grant expanded almost visibly, modestly examining the gold-shield cufflink on his left sleeve, created in Athens, 24 carat, purchased one holiday, duty not paid.

'My contacts have come up with two very important facts. I'd like you to be able to say they were wrong. Somehow I don't think so.'

Michael did not speak, mentally urging his father to move past the dramatics and give the detail.

'First, you're aware that Ali-Chem have a largish shareholding in the petro-chemical company we're building that damn plant for?'

'Of course.' Michael showed no irritation. He was learning, at last, to give his father the satisfaction of the teacher-pupil relationship. It did no harm.

'They haven't paid in a damn penny yet. They're committed to the holding. But they actually shift cash to Ecuador only *after* the plant is completed. And they're getting their shares at a bargain price. They get a discount because of their expertise – technical, marketing, and so on.'

'I knew they were buying cheap,' said Michael. 'But I didn't know they hadn't put in any cash yet.'

'That's not all, Michael. Ali-Chem went in only because they were frightened they'd lose their special position in the market there, and miss their chance in the wider South American market too. If they hadn't agreed to work with your friend Cantania, some other big chemical firm would have stepped in.' This, too, was not unknown to his son, but again Bernard had new information. 'So far so good. But I'm led to understand that they will continue to hold a protected position – favourable tariffs to them and no one else – until the petro-chemical plant is actually producing. You know what that means?'

Michael paused. It took him no time at all to work it out. It meant that Ali-Chem were quite keen for the plant to be finished, but that they stood to lose nothing if it were delayed – even, to put the worst interpretation on it, if the project were total disaster. While the plant did not exist, no one else could start flooding Ecuador with cheap plastics. So Ali-Chem were not bothered.

'No wonder your associate, Mr Corsino, didn't want you to talk with Ali-Chem.' Bernard loaded the words with almost melodramatic distaste.

Michael said: 'I don't see that, father. All the talking in the world couldn't shift them from a position as impregnable as that. Supposing I'd found out what you've just told me? Corsino couldn't be blamed. Perhaps he doesn't know the whole picture himself.'

Bernard's gesture expressed disbelief and disapproval of Corsino.

'If we're ever to get help from Ali-Chem – which personally I doubt – you'll need some very powerful leverage indeed, Michael. They're sitting pretty.'

'I'm still puzzled. Just as much as I am by how Ed Corsino managed to get his syndicate such a damn big stake in Kerridge Steel.'

'That was a good report you got done on the real position in that company, Michael. Everything we needed to know. I don't suppose you'll tell me who you used over there to provide it?'

Michael smiled. 'No more than you – yet – will tell me how you've suddenly become so knowledgeable on the American chemical industry. We'll pool *all* our facts when we're ready, I don't doubt.'

'Perhaps,' Bernard smiled back. 'Aren't you going to congratulate me?'

'Of course. And thank you. Very much.'

Bernard rose, moving to the door. He liked to hear compliments from his son. He was needed. He was proving rather good at being needed, too. That was enough.

'William Oldershaw's been trying to reach me on the telephone, Michael. Any idea what he wants? I don't want to get embroiled.'

'Wants to complain, I expect. I've been rough with him recently. His people have made some silly mistakes in the designs. God help us if Benjamin Bender or Earl Sanger knew the half of it.'

'Hmm,' said Bernard. 'So far as he's concerned, then, I'm not available. I feel sorry for him, responsible even, in some ways. But he wanted this job. Now he's got to see it through.'

'Fair,' said Michael. 'I'll try to play it cooler. He's a good old stick. Bloody infuriating and bull-headed sometimes – most of the time, come to think of it – but a decent man, doing his best.'

Bernard smiled. 'Michael, I do believe you're getting sentimental.' Then he was gone.

2

The office in which Oldershaw sat had not changed in 20 years. Bleakly and rather scruffily functional, it was full of old things: old metal desk and filing cabinets; old chairs with scuffed varnish; old worn leather; old, browning pictures and designs of yesteryear. It was a stroll down the machine-tool industry's memory lane. Today the souvenirs shook with the reverberations of Oldershaw's anger.

'You'll do as you're bloody well told,' he blasted into the telephone. 'Don't you realise we're spending thousands flying your parts out? You're weeks behind.'

He was silent for perhaps 15 seconds as a voice answered tinnily in his ear. Opposite him, his works manager, Colley, lifted a muscular forearm and indicated by slowly moving an open palm towards the floor that Oldershaw should calm the conversation. Oldershaw simply scowled.

'Don't give me that stuff,' he told the telephone. 'Just start to earn your brass.'

The telephone went down, hard, and before Colley could speak, Oldershaw was on to him.

'And, Tom, don't you bloody tell me what to do.' The tone was curt, flat, drained of warmth. Colley had been at the Brasserton's plant from the beginning, over 30 years ago. 'I'll not take it. Understand?'

Colley regarded his old friend sadly. They had sweated it out together to build this place, the blank walls and clattering machine shops set in a slumland of mean houses and weeds and discoloured canals. Built it from one shed with a roof of rotting corrugated iron in the late 1930s.

He had never understood exactly why it had been necessary for Brasserton's to be sold to the Prospero Group. They had needed capital, no doubt of it. Who didn't. But they could have struggled through somehow. If there had been no Prospero, there would have been no production computer. No careful young men with rimless spectacles, white coats and degrees from sodding Cambridge. No Ecuador contract, with work which was almost beyond his capacity to comprehend. No troubles, beyond the local union disputes that he knew how to handle. And, above all, no continual hassling with Bill.

Oldershaw no longer looked wiry, simply shrunken; his face, once brown, was now unhealthily sallow, with concave cheeks, dark rings around the eyes and a smear of breakfast egg on the almost painfully clipped moustache. When he was angry – and these days mostly he was angry – his hands often shook. The fingernails had been chewed to the quick.

'Sorry, Bill,' said Colley. He wanted no trouble.

'Twisters, all of them,' said Oldershaw. 'I don't know whether the bloody sub-contractors are the worst or those buggers at Prospect House.'

Oldershaw hadn't always spoken like that, Colley remembered. Six years ago, Bill had argued for the good sense of the take-over, especially when they'd made him managing director. He'd argued for the computer too, and welcomed the chance of the big-time which the Ecuador contract had offered. Well, maybe now he'd learned.

'I should never have given in on letting those computer bastards run the show.' Oldershaw was steaming on. 'I'm damn sure the mistakes on those tolerances are their fault. They don't know what work is. Bloody going home at 5 o'clock when we've got urgent stuff still to be done.'

Colley nodded. In the war, they'd worked till one in the morning sometimes, by gas light. Jesus. That was when he'd first had to start wearing glasses. He didn't like glasses. Cissy. He fingered the pair he usually kept in his breast pocket. He hated having to put them on to peer at work on the lathes downstairs.

'Well?' said Oldershaw. 'What do you want?'

Colley knew that Bill knew what he wanted. He'd waited patiently through Oldershaw's tirade about the computer men and the sub-contractors, even though he was sick to the stomach with that routine. All Oldershaw's raving would change nothing. But the ruling he now sought really did lie within Oldershaw's capacity.

'The sixteen bloody Tolpuddle martyrs,' he said. 'They want paying for Friday.'

'Stuff that,' said Oldershaw.

'They say they won't start work again until we give them a guarantee of payment – in writing.'

'Cheeky bastards,' said Oldershaw.

'They mean it.'

'I don't give a damn. If they won't work, give 'em their cards.'

Colley couldn't help sighing. 'Bill. That won't do. Not today.'

'What the hell do they expect? If they walk out on a sodding unofficial day off to join a protest march in sympathy with their brothers in the docks, then that's their lookout. We don't pay. What are you doing down there, Tom? Playing pat-a-cake with 'em?'

Still Colley kept his cool, clenching his first. But his voice took on a high note of sarcasm.

'They say their trade union consciences are outraged by the docks situation. They say any decent working man would have marched. They say . . .'

'I don't give a nigger's arse what they say. No money,' snapped Oldershaw.

Colley rose. 'Okay, Bill. That helps me. I told every man or boy in that shop on Thursday that if they stayed out, they'd be docked a day's pay. Forty-eight of them took me at my word. They clocked in.'

'Well?' said Oldershaw.

'Bill, the sixteen marchers include the seven best leading hands. Casey, Maiden, Tomkins . . . If they quit . . .'

'Bastards,' said Oldershaw. 'They know, don't they? They bloody know.'

'Aye,' said Colley. 'Without them, I don't think there's two buggers in that shop who could get the final stages of this job right. You know it. I know it. They know it.'

Oldershaw didn't rise. He seemed to shrink further into the dusty cracked leather of his swivel-chair. He didn't shout either. For five seconds his teeth furiously attacked the stub of a fingernail. Then he whispered.

'Bastards. All of them. Give 'em their money.'

'That's not what I want to hear, Bill. They shouldn't get paid, and you know it. I just wanted to let you have the full picture, that's all. We can't pay, Bill. Where the hell does it leave me with the rest of that shop? Next time, you'll lose the whole damn lot of them. They'll laugh at me.'

'Pay them, I said. If we don't keep up the schedule now, I won't have a job, nor will you. London will murder us.'

'Then tell London, Bill. Perhaps they'd understand. In the long run it'll do Prospero no good at all. The militants in their other companies will take it as a precedent.'

The laughter that came from Oldershaw was desperate and crackling. How could Prospect House be expected to understand that because they had not paid out a hundred or so pounds to a few awkward workers, an order worth millions might be further prejudiced?

'I wouldn't even try, Tom. Pay them. I'll carry the can if there's any comeback.'

Colley simply shrugged, rose, and made for the door. One thing about Prospero, he thought. They have a bloody good pension plan, which the old Brasserton's set-up hadn't. And Colley had only two years to go. He wouldn't have to take this kind of humiliation much longer. Maybe he could even swing an early retirement. Then he could forget it all and grow his tomatoes and beans. Weren't they all mad? Bill, Prospero, the lads down in the shop, all of them?

As Colley opened the office door, feet clattering on the metal grating outside, Oldershaw heard the machines sing at full blast, whining and grinding and clashing. That was his orchestra, better than the Hallé. But now, at Brasserton's, it wasn't the fun it had been being the conductor.

The sound became muffled again as the door closed. Oldershaw lifted the telephone and dialled.

'George?' he said. 'Bill here. Bill Oldershaw.'

They had met, George Lovelace and he, at a Prospero function for out-of-town executives in London nine months earlier. Both of them had felt out of place amid the soft carpets and the softer girls handing out sherry and unknown foreign meats on minute fragments of toast. They had come together immediately; two engineers who wanted only to get things done with their hands in the old ways they knew best. Since then, they had met four times.

'George, I've just about had enough.' Swiftly, he described his last few days. Finally, he said. 'What we spoke about – will you join me?'

'You bet your sweet life I will,' said Lovelace. He'd just lost two of his best men from making the cars. His son, Philip, had switched them to the snowmobile engine production line while he'd been off for ten days with a strained back. 'But Bill – not yet. We've got three races the prototype car's entered for in the next two months. I can't miss those. Let's get that out of the way.'

'I don't know if I can last another bloody week, never mind a couple of months.'

Lovelace said: 'I'm not going to bugger up the car. I can't. You know that, Bill. Wait. Then I'll be with you.'

Again, a finger went to Oldershaw's teeth. Christ, you never could win, could you?

Then he said. 'All right. I'll hang on. But by God we'll shake those buggers one day.'

3

Oldershaw wasn't the only man that day who was engaged in encounters and the business of persuasion. It was, indeed, a day for meetings, like most other days in the lives of giant corporations. In the honeycomb rooms of Prospect House various groups of men and women sat discussing how the Prospero Group might further its fortunes.

Sometimes the various meetings worked towards common objectives; sometimes, however, they did not. The reasons for the futility of certain of the discussions were various.

In certain cases it was simply lack of communication. It is incredibly difficult, as businesses grow larger, for the people within them to know what their fellows are doing in detail, without the disease of proliferating paperwork clogging the arteries of the organism.

On the other hand, some futility is quite deliberate in origin. Individuals have their own views, often sincere, of the paths towards profit and satisfaction and even morality in any given business situation. Thus, they may work inside meetings with honest zeal to frustrate the plans of others whose views differ from their own. Their motives may also be more ignoble. It is not unknown for a perfectly sound business plan to be frustrated for ridiculous reasons.

Imagine, perhaps that a thrusting young marketing executive has conceived a plan to launch a new flavour fruit drink, which a test marketing exercise has shown to be very well received by children under the age of 12 in the poorer districts of Milwaukee, Wisconsin. He arranged this project during the lengthy absence, on a long overdue sabbatical, of the company's ageing marketing director. But upon his return, the marketing director, neurotically fearful for his position, wishes to put into practice a scheme of his own, dreamed up while eating fresh pineapple in Honolulu during the 2-day stopover of his world-cruise liner. His plan, like his junior's, is simple: to launch a range of ice lollies *shaped according to their flavour* – pineapple, banana, raspberry, apple, orange, grapefruit and so on.

The marketing director is aflame with the brilliant simplicity of his vision. He is full of chagrin that a subordinate, whom he thinks desirous of his director's seat, should have gone ahead on a private plan without permission. Funds, too, are short. If a campaign to launch the new fruit drink is approved, he can say goodbye – perhaps for ever – to the pleasing sight of children in the sun-kissed cornfields of Kansas or the soot-roofed alleys of Wigan blissfully sucking upon cool ice, flavoured with pineapple essence and shaped in the chunky oval form of the fruit it imitates with, perhaps, a crown of rich green sugar leaves sprouting from its head.

The director will do anything to win his point. He honestly believes his idea is better. He does not wish the notion to grow that the new-product department can manage quite well without him. And, what is more personally upsetting, the young executive in question whisked from under his nose the most sensual secretary in the head office at the last Christmas party and, it is widely accepted, made her that very evening on the settee in the marketing director's own office, which was to have been the setting for a similar adventure of his own – with the same lady.

First, therefore, the marketing director attempts to undermine the validity of his junior's test operation. He argues that the sample (meaning the numbers and quality of people who gave their opinion on the drink) was too inexpertly chosen to make the results valid for a nation-wide or even state-wide launch. The advertising expenditure was, he believes, too heavy for the company to sustain in similar proportion for a mass sell-in. He manages to get a marketing man in another company (an old friend) to submit an article to a trade paper which argues the dangers of accepting test-market results in situations where the advertising of competitors was at a lower level of intensity than would normally be the case. He proves (fortunately for him, but not unusually) that no competitor was doing more than a low-level campaign in Milwaukee, Wisconsin, at the time when the new fruit drink was being touted.

And so on. In the end, being wiser and more versed in the arts of corporate skulduggery than his subordinate, he wins the day. It is even possible that the frustrated young executive then sneaks off to a competitor and gives them all the data on his own fruit drink product, which they then launch, with great panache and even greater profitability, six months later.

But that is not the point of the story, which is simply intended to illustrate that business can suffer from the human traits of vanity, fear, pride, envy and lust just as can other fallible man-made institutions.

Remember, however, that the marketing director may, although for unworthy reasons, find that his subordinate's work was indeed slip-shod in execution and thus, by foiling the fruit drink launch, save his company from making a grave error of judgment. Meanness of spirit is on occasions the fertiliser of business virtue.

The conversations of Michael Grant with David Travis and then with his father were not in any sense devious or dishonest. These were men doing, in this instance, their best both for themselves and for their company. The encounter between Oldershaw and Colley was different in flavour. They, too, were men attempting to get a job done, but their approach was overshadowed by the frustrations and fears with which each was variously afflicted and, in Oldershaw's case, led him to broach conspiracy with George Lovelace, a similarly frustrated boss of a subsidiary.

The meeting which took place on the same day between Earl Sanger and Colin Hardy was yet again contrasting in nature. It was conspiratorial, certainly, but in no sense should it be painted an unrelieved shade of black.

Sanger, as so often, was fingering a document, neatly ordered, with the margins and spaces between the varied headings and sub-headings pleasingly arranged. He was a man in whom the very feel of a good document induced a feeling of wellbeing.

'We can't employ this guy,' Sanger told Hardy, who was surprised, since the prospective recruit was an American with a glowing record at Harvard.

'But we need him,' said Hardy. 'I'll never get through the work-load you've given me without help. Especially now the Lovelace business is taking up more of my time.'

Hardy's comment was perfectly fair. As a relatively new, non-executive director of Lovelace's he had forced the pace, according to Sanger's wishes, in pushing Philip Lovelace to get the snowmobile engine production line working ahead of schedule. He had succeeded. In less than two months, towards late September, the line would be pumping out a thousand units a week.

Michael Grant, he knew, was also happy about this, for the chief executive now had nine months in which to continue developing a sports car prototype before the Le Mans race came round again. But actual production of the snowmobile engines meant that marketing and selling plans for them had to be hurriedly produced, and that – since he was the marketing consultant on the Lovelace board – was tying up Colin Hardy. He did badly need help in all his other projects.

'Listen, Colin,' said Sanger. 'I didn't say you're getting nobody to do your legwork. I said not *this* particular guy, right?'

'Why?'

'Because,' said Sanger smugly, 'I had him checked out.

190

He got fired from his last job on Wall Street. He's been given the brush-off by five companies since then. He smells.'

He tossed the document towards Hardy, stood up and hitched his trousers as if that were the end of the discussion. While Hardy read, Sanger got himself water in a paper cup from the dispenser in the corner.

'But, Earl, *why* did he get fired? Nothing here about that.'

'Who cares? Musta been a good reason.'

Hardy was not satisfied with so curt a dismissal of his question.

'We ought to know *why*,' he said. 'These agencies are useful, but they're not always right. Don't you remember the man who was blacklisted on Madison Avenue because he got fired, and later they found out it was simply because he refused to have his fingerprints taken when some idiot in the organisation decided it should become standard company procedure?'

Sanger shrugged. 'We haven't got the dough to do a depth job on a simple recruitment like this. Anyway, I don't think fingerprinting unreasonable. Do you?'

Hardy was non-committal. 'Depends what kind of business the company's in. I think Big Brother's getting too important these days. Too often, when data storage isn't dangerous, it can be downright stupid. The *Express* had a piece last week.'

'Yeah?' said Sanger sceptically.

'A woman aged 107 got a letter addressed to her parents who'd been dead 60 years. It wanted to know why she wasn't at school! All because some numbskull computer programmer had forgotten that human age can be, though it usually isn't, a three-digit number.'

Even Sanger laughed. But he still said, 'I'm not interested in fairy tales, Colin. I'll take the agency's opinion. And don't think because any goddam idiot can make mistakes that what I'm trying to do here to tighten up our security is invalidated.' Sanger, at Michael Grant's behest originally, had been working on Prospero's counter-espionage systems for more than a year. It was a task he enjoyed, too obviously.

Hardy decided he would not press the recruiting point –

for the present. He tried diversionary tactics. 'This might interest you then,' he said.

Sanger flipped the pages of the brochure which Hardy gave him. It was coloured garishly enough to have come from a package tour company, but the words on its cover read *Electronic Surveillance and Ancillary Equipment.* He smiled, noting the words *Export Only* on the brochure. Then he began to read about the equipment, sold apparently for purposes innocent enough. But it took no genius to see to what other uses the stuff could be put.

ALL-ROUND SOUND COLLECTOR TRANSMITTER – fascinating, useful, entertaining, instructional for all ages. Reveals an unsuspected new universe of sound about you. Highly recommended for indoor and outdoor use. Everything from baby-sitting to bird-watching. Will pick up a speaker's voice in a meeting room for improved hearing by the audience up to 1,200 ft away.

Sanger smiled again. Irony appealed to him. He flipped further. The brochure recommended a transmitter built into a wristwatch: *the perfect tool for note-taking at conferences.*

It got better. *Especially handy for plant inventory* was the come-on line for a transmitter contained inside a ballpoint pen.

There were briefcases with tape-recorders in the locks, activated by the fastening device; microphones posing as coat-buttons or matchboxes or sugarcubes; and (a Sanger favourite) a range of 'infinity transmitters' which, replacing the microphone of a telephone, will transmit over the open line everything spoken in a room once the number is dialled – from anywhere in the world.

It could be construed, indeed – despite the wording – as a complete arsenal for industrial espionage. The prices did not appear unreasonable. Briefcases from $250 to $750, the top-price item made of exquisite hand-tooled leather; a very pleasing earring microphone with matchbox-sized transmitter at $170.

Sanger asked, 'How does it compare with the Jap company?'

'Nothing to choose between them, pricewise,' said Hardy. Then he grinned, his Punch-nose seeming to grow more flushed and wicked, back to his normal sarcastic form. 'But myself, I prefer European quality. Better made, I think.'

'Horseshit,' said Sanger. 'Keep them in the safe. I'm not in the mood for buying just yet.'

Hardy knew what that meant. Until the episode of the police raid on Prospect House was decently in the past, Sanger had to play it comparatively pure.

'You know, Earl, I prefer using people to machines anyway. More reliable. And usually cheaper.' He laughed. 'I've got that bankroll photograph when you need it.'

'I'll need it,' said Sanger, and the humour was gone from his voice. 'At the right time.'

He was no man to omit the exaction of revenge, where it was deserved. He had, more secretly, discovered within the past week who had set up Prospero for the police raid. Without telling Hardy why he wanted the task done, he had – partly for insurance, partly for revenge – asked his assistant to arrange a small job for him.

In the bar of an hotel in Switzerland three days earlier a senior executive of the offending company had found himself attracted by a beautiful and apparently available air stewardess. They had enjoyed several drinks together and, at one stage, the girl had begun rummaging in her handbag for a lipstick. As she searched she began to remove things from the bag – it was always in a mess, she said, smiling – and asked him to hold for a moment a fat roll of Swiss francs. He did so. Finally, she found the lipstick, they drank some more. He was puzzled that she did not keep the assignation made for his room later that evening.

Sanger fully intended to find uses for the photograph of that unhappy executive holding the money.

'I hope you didn't pay her too much,' he said.

'They have a scale,' said Hardy flatly. 'I know the rules.'

To know the rules is, in truth, necessary. Many a secretary casually picked up and flattered, and ready in the end to copy a document or two for her friend, has been driven to panic and confession to her employer by being offered £5,000 for the job instead of a rich dinner and a good seat at the theatre. When the price becomes astronomic in her terms – whatever the secret is worth to a competitor – she may feel too sharply the pangs of sin and betrayal. The suggested enormity of what she is doing unbalances her.

Small bribes and kind words (especially to the sexually un-attractive) work more tricks than visions of Ferraris and holidays in the Bahamas.

Sanger leaned back in his chair, brushing imaginary dust from his cuffs. He appeared to have had enough of espion-age for one day. Hardy had been awaiting the moment for his big speech.

'Earl, here's something else that may interest you, assum-ing – as I have to assume – that we'll be leaving Debrais to young master Travis for the time being.'

Sanger scowled. He did not like the way Michael Grant had been able so easily to take over the negotiations with the French company which he had begun. But in the circum-stances he had been helpless. Michael could apply leverage through knowledge of the real state of affairs leading to the police raid. And Lord Bender had implied that for anyone other than David Travis to handle the on-the-spot negotia-tions would not please him. Sanger wanted no trouble with Bender.

'Don't push your luck,' he told Hardy.

Hardy could still smile. 'This you'll like. The Brandford bid for Kroos.'

'I read the *Financial Times* this morning,' said Sanger smartly. 'It's with the shareholders now. Something like 4 Brandford shares for every 7 Kroos, plus £2 cash. This bid values Kroos at around three million.'

'Nearly right,' said Hardy. '£2.50 in cash for every 7 shares – that's the only detail you got wrong.'

'So?'

'So, three million is ridiculously cheap.'

'Why?'

'We had a look at it six weeks ago, but there was no Prospero cash around to give us a chance to make an offer. We made the company worth nearly four million, perhaps more.'

'Are you sure?'

'Pretty sure. And I think I know where the hole is.'

'Yeah?'

'Part of the Kroos set-up is a building in South London. Run-down sort of area. But not now. It's slap in the middle of where a new hotel-office complex is planned. No one's revalued that building. It's leasehold, but it's got 33 years

194

to run. It's down in the Brandford sums at half a million. I reckon it's worth four times as much at least.'

'Holy Moses,' said Sanger, whose language under pressure of emotion was often naively high-school.

'We could make a much better counter-bid.'

'Do we have a holding in Kroos?'

'Peanuts,' said Hardy. 'Well under one per cent.'

'Get the resources group together for later today,' said Sanger. His voice bristled with excitement. 'If it looks right I'll call in Michael. Then maybe we'll start buying.'

'It'll need to be fast,' said Hardy.

'Don't worry,' said Sanger. He hadn't had such a good morning for the past three months. And when he was served, he was not ungrateful. 'Up the price in the next ad. you draft for an assistant,' he said. 'That way we'll get you someone faster.'

When Hardy had gone, Sanger demanded black coffee. The telephone call he was expecting came precisely at 3 pm. London time, which was 10 am in Washington, where it originated.

What Quant told Sanger about Ali-Chem's operation in Ecuador made the American want to hurl his coffee cup at the shaded window of his room. Not in anger, though. In exhilaration.

4

The Trident bounced sullen rain off its silver back as it hit the sea-fringed finger of land which forms the runways at Nice Airport. David Travis gripped his briefcase, looked out as the tarmac rushed by, and thought it was just his luck. Could the Mistral really rage on the Riviera in early August?

The sky was grey and the wind was bending the palm-trees silly as the hire-car crept, hissing, along the black promenade towards Monaco. The cafes were crowded, and the tents and awnings of the beaches flapped madly. The sea looked filthy, yellow and coated with a kind of scum at the fringe where it boiled around the stony shores. Further out it retained its green-ness, both light and very dark in patches. The hotels of Nice – the pink and white icing of the Negresco with its dainty domes, the West End, the Beau Rivage – were only names to him. Overall, he thought, looking at a dejected family trudging along in shorts with sodden newspapers covering their heads, it didn't seem very different from Bournemouth; too much concrete, too little sand, and people not very beautiful.

They began the curving switchback, past Cap d'Ail and the palatial villas of the overseas millionaires, which forms the last 15 minutes of the run-in to Prince Rainier's enclave. There were queues of cars at a succession of roadworks. Then, suddenly, as they began to descend a steep hill and David saw the rectangular harbour of Monte Carlo, with a great 3-masted sailing ship anchored plumb in the middle, and all those ridiculously luxurious white yachts of the very rich spread around its walls, the sun came out.

Merci, he said to himself, dutifully practising his French. He needed Claire Justine Debrais to be in a good temper.

He was staying for the first time in his life at the Hotel de Paris. A telex message from the Debrais office in Paris, telling him to go to Monte Carlo, since Mme Debrais had already left on holiday, had not mentioned accommodation. He thought he had better fix his own. Several flunkeys escorted him and his single suitcase to a room. He sprayed franc notes into waiting hands and hoped his trip would justify his expenses. Then he went in search of the yacht.

It was not, even among the hundreds of vessels tied up, easy to miss. It was pale green, streamlined, very chic and looked all of 300 feet long. When he gave his name to a languid-looking sailor at the gangway, he was told that Madame was swimming.

The pool of the Hotel de Paris is quite something – in the bowels of the hotel, indoors, sheltering behind a huge curve of sliding glass wall which gives out on to a pleasant terrace with a magnificent view over the harbour. The pool is large and curved also, its water deliciously warm. David stood on the stairs which lead down to it and wondered which shape might be that of Madame Debrais. The pool contained only half a dozen women, all moving very slowly in a curious upright stance. They pedalled through the water rather than swam, with puckered faces and withered limbs, wearing caps all of them and three in spectacles. The water was not allowed to touch their faces. He hoped he

196

wasn't going to be unpleasantly surprised by the Debrais woman.

He strolled as casually as he could towards the bar. When he mentioned her name, the barman pointed down the pool to where cane chairs and tables were arranged on a raised shelf. A woman in a white bathrobe, with black hair swept back into a braid and wearing large sunglasses, was sitting with legs extended on a beach-chair reading a book. An elderly man, gut hanging over swim-shorts, was with her.

David thanked the barman, slid him a five-franc note, afraid of under-tipping, and padded gingerly towards his quarry. She did not look up until he spoke.

'*Excusez-moi, Madame Debrais, Je suis David Travis, de Prospero de Londres.*' Awkwardly he bent down, extending his right hand.

The widow Debrais ignored it as she slowly put aside her book, removed her glasses and coolly appraised him. He let his hand return to his side, feeling foolish. She smiled lazily, almost studiously, turning to her companion.

'*Ah, Charles. Délicieux, n'est-ce pas? Il parle français.*'

David knew she was poking fun. He laughed. '*Un peu seulement. J'espère que vous parlez anglais.*'

She appeared not to mind. '*Un peu seulement aussi.*' She laughed again, speaking to the plump man who looked at David suspiciously through pig-eyes. '*Déjà prêt pour les affaires!! Regardes son porte-document. Les Anglais sont si sérieux!*'

Then she smiled with a hint of apology. '*Nous sommes en vacances, monsieur. On n'emporte pas du travail à la piscine. Mais, je vous comprends – et je vous pardonne.*'

She waved a hand indicating he should sit down. If she wanted to amuse herself he'd have to put up with it. He'd rarely met a more self-confident woman. That's what a few million in the bank and a yacht at Monaco can do for you, he supposed. Her photographs did her scant justice. Her face was smooth and, he imagined, had been lifted at least once. The skin was nut-brown, down to where the robe hid it, and her legs were a similar colour, unflawed by awkward veins or hairs. That was why she wore white. When she smiled, her black eyes crinkled and flashed; her teeth looked very white and were uneven enough, with spaces between several of them, to be her own. She spoke now in English, perfectly.

'Will you have a drink, Mr Travis?'

He asked for Campari. Her companion snapped his fingers at a waiter.

'May I introduce the executive president of our Company, Charles Prat.'

David leaned over and shook hands. The movement took his viewpoint across the loose front of Madame's robe. He caught a glimpse of breasts most ample and as brown as her face. As he returned to his seat, he caught her eyes. Her expression told him she knew that his glance had wandered. There was mockery and, he thought, a hint of challenge in those steady dark eyes.

'I hope you will not even open that briefcase in the next hour, Mr Travis,' she said. 'In fact, I think we had better make you swim.'

'I haven't got my gear . . .' David began to say. He wasn't sure he wanted to be inspected quite so abruptly.

'Please,' she smiled. 'They have everything here. You must relax. You are too tense to talk sensibly yet. Go and change, Mr Travis.' It sounded like an order.

He gave in gracefully. 'I'll be five minutes.' But he was damned if he was going to be poured into an old pair of hotel reach-me-downs. He roared upstairs to his room, dumped his briefcase and grabbed the new Aquascutum beach shorts he'd bought for the holiday with Sheila. When he came back to the widow, she was alone.

'Monsieur Prat likes to nap in the afternoon,' she explained. Then she giggled. 'He always eats a little too much at lunch.'

David remained standing before her, and although his belly was no more than a pound or so over-weight, he was doing his best to hold it in. She looked at him with deliberate casualness.

'You keep yourselves fit, you English. All that squash and cricket and those ridiculous diets. We shall have to feed you with some good French cooking. Have your drink, Mr Travis, then we shall swim.'

He sat down and she kept her faintly jesting eyes upon him.

'And what do you do with Prospero, Mr Travis, apart

198

from making journeys to persuade elderly foreign women to sell their business at bargain prices?'

So she could mock herself too, he noted, as well as him. He believed also she knew precisely what he did at Prospect House, but he told her all the same.

'Good,' she said when he had finished. 'And who runs you?'

'I work for Michael Grant.'

'What about Mr – uh – Sanger?' She giggled again. 'I called him Dr Blood. It seemed right. Does he command you too?'

'No,' said David. 'He's another director.'

'I expected him,' she said. 'Charles – Monsieur Prat – seems to think highly of him.'

'Have you met him, madame?'

'Once. He was very serious, too.' She smiled. 'Shall we swim?'

She swung her legs off the chair-rest and stood up. Beneath the bath-robe she wore a one-piece swimsuit, moulded to her, white again. She knew that, at 45, bikinis are ridiculous, revealing the tell-tale flab of stomach muscles which no amount of dieting and exercise can keep looking as if they're 20 years old. In this suit, she looked magnificent; a Rubens Venus with a touch of Boadicea. She was heavily built, but tall enough for the full breasts and the ample hips and wide belly to seem precisely right. Like her lower legs, her thighs were flawless. On her right thigh, a small birthmark burned a deeper brown than the rest of the smooth flesh. David noticed that she was vain enough to pull one trick. The upper muscles of her arms were held taut, so that her breasts were pushed together, forming a deeper cleavage between them.

In the pool she crawled easily and expertly. He laboured beside her, hoping that his leg-thrash was as straight as hers. She gave it all her concentration until they had been up and down the pool half-a-dozen times, as if testing him. He was rather shorter of breath than she appeared to be. She stood up in the shallows, globs of water shining on her shoulders, breasts now hanging more heavily.

'You swim well, Mr Travis. It is pleasant to have a companion for the water.'

They swam some more. As they climbed out, she said.

'We have a price, Mr Travis. And we will not go below it. You have the power to agree details?'

'Of course,' said David, not really certain if he could make promises *tout court.*

'Satisfactory,' she said. 'I would like to get it settled. It has been hanging about too long. And I am anxious for certain other people in France not to know our business until we are sure. That is why I had you come here.'

When they reached their table, she handed him a towel and then turned her back on him. He assumed she expected him to act the valet. As he placed the towel around her shoulders and gently patted them dry, she stepped back towards him and he caught a snatch of her scent. Dior, perhaps, with chlorine overtones from the pool. He was wondering how far she wanted him to take the towel, but she decided that for him. As his hands finished with her shoulders, she moved smartly away and picked up her bath-robe.

'Where are you staying?'

'Here. In the hotel.'

'Discreet man,' she laughed. 'I think I would like to invite you to the yacht now I have met you, but perhaps it would be safer if you remained here.'

David said nothing.

'But we shall dine tonight, yes? Come to the yacht at six. We will go through the papers with M. Prat. Then a meal you will enjoy.'

After she had gone, he walked out into the sunlight on the terrace to see if he could spot her approaching the yacht. At last she appeared on the quayside. She was walking with an air of gaiety, swinging her beach-bag with exaggerated freedom. As she reached the gangway of the yacht she turned and waved. She knew he would come and watch her.

They talked at six in a stateroom-type space which was everything David had imagined it would be. The wood was dark and expensive. Drinks were revealed not by yanking open cupboards but by pressing buttons for panels to slide aside. The coverings of the long seats, set cunningly into the side of the cabin, were very feminine; beige and black blended cunningly. The paintings on the bulkheads – oh yes, there were paintings, – were the brightest of Mediterranean abstracts, filled with blue skies and yellow houses and knotted nets of red and black and green. She was not surprised when he asked for *citron pressé*.

'A clear head?' she said. 'Me too.' She assaulted the lemon with swift, almost brutal wrists. Like Prat, she drank Perrier water.

It was the easiest negotiation he had ever done. The price Prat named valued the Debrais company at around fifty million francs, something like four million or so pounds sterling. It was perhaps a million and a half francs more than the figures David had learned by heart from documents which, he had to admit, were basically the work of Sanger and Hardy. He mentioned his lower figure. For a moment, Madame Debrais threatened to look angry. But she said nothing as David softly suggested that he would like to see the individual components which made up the total. He flicked through the figures.

'The plant at Lyon,' he said. 'You make its book value twice what we do.'

Prat smiled. He might have known. 'That is because you do not understand about it.' His English was as good as the widow's.

'What do you mean?' said David.

'I mean it is about to be purchased by a company in Paris and then leased to us again. Their price is a very good one.'

The widow smoothed out the long white skirt which she was wearing, topped by a tight lemon silk blouse, black belted. The skirt was split damn near to the crotch. 'Naturally, we will produce the appropriate documents, Mr Travis.'

By seven it was all over. Negotiations are usually like that when one side is a courteous suitor, willing, but by no means bereft of other prizes to seek, and the other side is eager to be pursued, caught and decently bought. There was nothing tricky about the negotiating tactics of the Debrais people, despite Bernard Grant's views of the French. Gallic realism, David supposed, sensing that both the widow and Charles Prat knew he was well aware of their desire to do a fair trade with Prospero before their unloved French competitors began a crueller takeover campaign. David reckoned he'd trimmed around £150,000 off the top price Prospero had been prepared to pay.

Prat opened the champagne, which was already iced, like a man who had expected he'd have something to celebrate.

'To the future of our companies, Mr Travis. And to you and to Mr Sanger who made the negotiation so pleasant.'

They drank. Again, David had to agree that Sanger had done the real work. He'd had the easy end of the game.

'I'm hungry,' said the widow.

'Perhaps I could ring London first,' said David.

She laughed. 'In the morning. We will not change our minds. This is my holiday and you should humour me.' She was arch, like a schoolgirl almost.

He nodded and smiled. There was no point in upsetting her.

'Charles has to return to Paris this evening,' she said. 'So you may escort me. I thought we'd dine out.'

The car that awaited them was dreamlike; a Lamborghini Urraco, painted pale-lemon like her blouse. She drove very fast but not especially expertly and she told him they were going to the Chateau de la Chèvre d'Or at Eze village.

The sun was still bright and there was a blue haze over the grey rocks and shelved farmland as they climbed to 1,200 feet on the twisting roads. It was breathtaking, the village set up on a grey pinnacle of rock, fortresslike. They parked the car and walked through narrow streets beneath red roofs and a church tower with a clock to the restaurant.

He ordered drinks and she led him out on to a small terrace, with a miniature swimming pool, adjoining the restaurant. The sea, seeming miles below, was grey-blue, puckered like a tablecloth gently moving, and the sunlight lay across it like a golden shield, so dazzling it hurt his eyes. Although it was August, they had arrived early enough for there to be few diners evident as yet. The wind moaned gently, mixing with the soft bossa nova that came from concealed loudspeakers.

'It is very beautiful, is it not?' she said.

'Superb,' he said. 'It makes you understand why the Incas worshipped the sun.'

She smiled. 'You are a very thoughtful young man. Not too much like a businessman.' She sat on a low wall, unselfconsciously. She wore no stockings. The flesh looked almost black in the deep shadows cast by the sun.

'What does your wife say to all your absences, Mr Travis? I suppose you are married?'

'Yes.'

'Children?'

'One boy.'

'I have two,' said the widow. 'They are grown up now. The boy in America, the girl in Paris. They go their own ways. Since my husband died, I sometimes feel very lonely. Not aimlessly so, you understand. Life is good. I am provided for. I have good friends.' She smiled a crooked smile. 'Yes, Mr Travis, I have lovers too, when I need them . . .'

She stopped, wanting to talk, yet still uncertain of her companion, for all her easy self-confidence.

'I was asking about your wife, Mr Travis. She accepts all your absences?'

'She's learned to live with it. So have I.'

'She accepts everything? You are a most handsome man. Away from your home for long periods, well, you must have cause to behave like a man. This too she knows?'

David was embarrassed. It was a long time since a woman had spoken so directly to him.

'We don't talk about it,' he said. 'But we're intelligent people. I think we're reasonably happy, and I know what I want. I won't paddle round the world for ever at someone else's say-so. But for the moment it suits us.'

'You love her?'

'Yes.'

'In love with her?'

'Yes.'

'Then you will be all right. Mr Travis. An affair or two is understandable. Who does not have them? I was in love with my husband, Mr Travis. Heart and mind. He was a great man. Strong in the business of the world, but never cruel. And with me, gentle but never soft. I liked his fairness. I hated those who cheated him. To hate your husband's enemies, that is the test of love, do you agree?'

He shrugged. 'I'm not a woman.'

That made her laugh. She stood up, shrilling, and suddenly threw her glass out over the cliff, and the sun caught it like a raindrop as it fell. 'There,' she said. 'That was foolish, but I felt like doing it. I'm glad you came instead of Mr Sanger. He is – I don't know – cold. A good man, perhaps, but . . .'

He interrupted her, sensing that she wanted him to. 'A good man – but cold. Let's agree on that. I think we should order.'

She came and placed her arms on his shoulders. Then she kissed him gently on the lips, her mouth soft and the scent of god knows what aphrodisiac concoction from the golden salons of Paris about her. She was responding to his assumption of control, almost with gratitude. Although intelligent women who are placed in situations where they must for ever make their own decisions grow used to it and are as good at it as men, they enjoy being led by someone they respect and admire; provided each assumption of control still acknowledges their right to command should they wish to exercise it.

'Thank you, David,' she said. 'You make me very happy.'

When the waiter came, he ordered lobster thermidor preceded by cold consommé, and she simply followed him. She was in that kind of compliant mood. He chose very inexpensively – a recent Muscadet – and she flattered his choice of wine too. He worried a little that the bill was already pushing towards the 300-franc mark. It was strange that such small considerations still afflicted him when he had probably just saved his company £150,000.

By the time they had reached coffee she had told him more about her husband, and David had regaled her with the wonders of the Amazon as well as the details of his family living. They were in tune in the way that can sometimes happen between man and woman when the stage setting is right.

To David, the dinner still had much of the air of unreality of the threatre. There was that song about it – what was it? – yes, *If They Could See Me Now*, which Sheila and he had heard Juliet Prowse belt out in *Sweet Charity*. His mind flashed on a quick picture of Jack, who'd been his mate down in Falmouth all those years ago and who was now, he'd heard, running mackerel catching trips for tourists. Jack, fat and tanned, looking fiftyish in a seaman's jersey when he was only David's age. Happy, undoubtedly, within one community's definition of happiness. If Jack could see him now, his old friend would indeed believe it was like a shot from telly soap-opera or a scene from a play, the old kind, like Noël Coward used to write.

'God,' he said suddenly, laughing.

'What is it?'

'I was just thinking – forget it.'

'No. Tell me.'

'About where I was born.'

He told her that too. She seemed to want to hear.

'You have sailor's blood,' she said deliberately. It was as if she wanted to romanticise their evening.

He laughed: 'My father was a clerk.'

'Nevertheless,' she said, 'you came from seafaring people. I think I would like you to take out the yacht. Do you come often to France? Could it be arranged?'

'Don't be silly,' he said. 'A 12-foot dinghy's more my mark.'

'But you could come to France some time.' She would not be put off. The very rich never see the practical obstacles to their diversions, however frivolous. 'Have you other business here?'

'I might stop off in Paris on my way back. We do have a French partner in Ecuador.'

'Who are they?'

'SAEF. You must know them.'

Her hand hit the table so hard that the coffee slopped into the saucers. She was not drunk, but the wine gave her an exaggerated gaiety. There was a certain pathos about her determination to be happy.

'Of course I know them. One of their top men, Broussard, Armand Broussard, is a great friend of the family. He and my husband used to play squash in Paris together. They helped each other. If you have business with SAEF, then I am sure we can fix it so that you have time for a little diversion too.'

She leaned back and smiled. 'I think I would like to be driven home.'

He looked at his watch for a long time, wanting to avoid her eyes, for he genuinely liked her and the thought that she had lines to SAEF made him both elated and sad. He would have preferred to let the evening stand where it was.

'I'm not sure I could drive that monster,' he said.

'It's easy, David. Five-speed stick shift. Men know about

that surely?' She was teasing him. In a perfectly conscious gesture, she smoothed the blouse over her breasts. 'We will have time for a nightcap.'

He paid the bill. Over 360 francs. The drive back seemed endless. The Lamborghini wanted to leap forward over the precipices of the highway every time he touched the pedal. Robbed of the ability to do anything but concentrate on his driving, he had no time to judge her mood.

No one was in sight on the yacht. She led the way aboard, walking sternly upright, but swinging her hips. He followed her to the same cabin and it was loaded with silence, the lap of water around the hull seeming very loud.

He said yes to cognac and with great care she poured out two measures into glasses larger than he had ever seen. She gave him his, and said, 'Drink. All of it.' He did as she bade him and, with the hot liquid adding to his self-confidence, just stood there wondering what she expected him to do next. She took his glass and put it down.

'Aren't you ever going to kiss me?' she said.

The taste of the brandy was still on her lips. Her body was soft and heavy. Her arms entwined him very gently, but her hands were hard. They searched out the muscles of his shoulders, his hips, his back, his waist. She ran them down the outside of his thighs, and as their mouths parted he buried his face in the black hair, kissing her ears.

She broke away and led him by the hand through a door and into a cabin with a large bed, covered with a black quilt. 'Undress in there,' she said, pointing to a smaller door. 'I wish to be ready.'

When he emerged he was surprised to find her lying across the bed, limbs outflung, still dressed. 'I like my clothes to be taken from me,' she said, 'and, if you wish . . .' She picked up a riding whip.

Beneath the skirt and blouse she was naked, and her whole body was an even shade of brown. Only the very rich, who have the time and the motive, and are able to buy the climate, can tan their skin that way. Almost coyly she pulled her hair, long and black, between her breasts which hung heavily, the nipples raised high and deepest brown. She swung her body across him.

Above the bed, a mirror was set into the ceiling. He thought how slug-white he looked against her. Fascinated, he watched her bending, dimples in her back where the vertebrae reached the swell of the buttocks. She was winding her hair about him, then waving her head from side to side so that the strands brushed and stimulated him gently. She was experienced, certainly, wanting to please him, but there was also in her demeanour an element of innocence; she seemed nervous, full of quick smiles and sudden gestures, a woman who needed the reassurance that she was loved as well as desired. He wanted desperately to be tender, warming to her, so that when she suddenly said, 'Hurt me, David,' pushing the whip into his hands, lowering her body on to him, he flicked only half heartedly at her. It seemed enough, and in the mirror he could see that at each stroke the brown suddenly became white and then filled with a sulky roseate tinge.

She became very excited, snatched the whip from him, and rolled over, moaning and writhing, and when he lowered himself gently at her, she went berserk, arching her back, screaming. Long after it was finished for him, she was trembling, and there were pinpoints of sweat shining from the whole of her trembling ripe copper body. Finally she lay still and the tears streamed down her face.

'What is it?' he said.

'I am happy, idiot. Happy. When I meet a man like you, I am always reminded – forgive me . . .'

He was too involved with her, for her, to do other than accept her words with gratitude. He felt he liked her, understood her.

'You are good,' she said. She rolled on her front, twisting her neck to look upwards at the mirror. There were misty, not ugly, marks still on her.

She got up and walked across the cabin with natural hauteur, hips swivelling and the breasts shaking but not drooping. She poured more brandy and turned to raise the glass. 'Do come back. I will arrange it.'

They lay together and smoked cigarettes. 'Armand Broussard,' she said, suddenly troubled, 'may not be as useful as I thought.'

'Oh,' he said, idly, but far from uninterested.

She giggled. 'He has been a naughty boy. Now he may wish to have the appearance of virtue.'

'In what way?'

'He has been mixed up with some of those Parisian politicians in a little game,' said the widow. 'One of the newspapers is on to them. Muckrakers. He will not be discovered. He is too clever. But he must be careful.'

She paused to sip her brandy. She lifted a breast and examined the nipple as if afraid it might be less than perfect. David said nothing. He thought back to an evening little more than two years ago when he was still new in London and Alison Grant, Alison Bennett as she was then, had been on the public relations staff of Prospero.

He had spent one night with her only. No one else knew, though Sheila his wife had had her suspicions. He recalled how easily he had spilled everything about himself then. Pillow-talk, it really was that way.

What was it in men – and, now he was learning, in women – that made them confide in, sometimes, virtually unknown bedmates once they had satisfied their physical appetite? Was it simple vanity, or the emptying, through sex, of the pent-up strength of discretion? It could be the plain need to share secrets with another person. Human beings, in his experience, were not good keepers of secrets. It was as if knowledge unshared had no tangible value. He waited, confident and shamefaced at once.

'Armand asked me to join his scheme,' said the widow. 'But I had not the time. He is on the board of a property company. They invite small savers to invest. With inflation, property has been the best hedge in France.'

'In England too,' said David.

'His company does very well for those who subscribe. Never less than 10 per cent interest.'

'Good,' he said.

'Perhaps. But the interest for subscribers is nothing compared with the capital gains which Armand's company has made for himself and his board. He does business with a number of smaller property companies. Each one has an associate of his controlling it, and some man of substance, perhaps a politician, to give it respectability. The smaller companies do most of the buying of property. Then they sell at a much higher price to the parent company. The subscribers provide the money to buy at the higher price. The smaller companies make big profits – and they are filtered back in many ways to the men who run the top company.

208

It is neat. It was even legal for a time. Armand wished me to come in – for the sake of my husband, he said. It was soon after he died. I was too confused even to care. I declined. Now I am glad.'

'Why?'

'I could have been in trouble.'

'But Armand Broussard?'

'As I said, he is too clever. The newspaper stories will end the business, but he will not be touched. No one can prove the links between him and the smaller companies.' She laughed. 'He will survive, but maybe he will not wish to be reminded of what I know by my asking him favours.'

'You're very important to him,' said David. 'And it's all in your head.'

She smiled. 'Not all. One of the men he used in a smaller company once worked for my husband. There are papers that show it. That man is now in Israel. It is better for his health. And for the health of Armand.'

Her interest was fading. As she mentioned the name of the man, boasting too that the lawyer in Paris who held her private papers was the most discreet in France, she played meaningfully with his body.

He did not leave the yacht until almost five the next morning, by which time her eyes had fallen into disintegrated shadow and her body was bathed in sweat, the flesh sagging. He felt terrible. She told him again and again that he was magnificent, as if she needed to reassure herself that none of the men she chose as lovers could possibly be less than very adequate. Or perhaps it was simply that she liked David as much as he liked her; and in her life now, she sometimes made love with men whom she did not especially like.

5

'Have you heard from young Travis?' It was Lord Bender on the telephone.

'Yes,' said Michael. 'He came through earlier this afternoon. He's done well. Only a few ends to tie up. And a very good price indeed.'

'Excellent. How did he seem?'

'Very tired,' said Michael.

Bender laughed. He was dependable, moral, responsible, but a realist. 'Of course. I'm glad we decided to send him. It wasn't Sanger's kind of job. Not dealing with a woman.'

'Whatever do you mean, Benjamin?'

'Travis has many talents. I believe that dealing with women is among them.'

'Come on, Benjamin. No games.'

'I assure you I'm not joking, Michael. I wanted him to go. That Debrais woman has a certain kind of reputation.'

Michael could scarcely believe his ears. What did Bender, dry and quiet old Bender, know about that kind of thing?

'And you never told me?' he said.

'Why should I, Michael?'

'I don't believe it.'

'Believe what you wish, dear boy. I'm just glad it's come off so well.'

They talked some more, about investments and about Ecuador, and as they were finishing their conversation the light on Michael's desk flashed. He buzzed twice for the secretary to come in. She pushed a piece of paper at him with Sanger's name on it. He said goodbye to Bender and invited the American in.

Sanger was never very good at hiding pleasure. His mouth sat in a composed and satisfied way, the upper lip thrust aggressively forward. His fair hair seemed to bristle more uprightly, which was perhaps even true, since the racing blood within him would have been washing rapidly around the roots. The very hornrims on his nose appeared to gleam more challengingly. He looked like a man who should have carried a warning about danger from his live rail.

'You've come at the right time, Earl,' said Michael, feeling he had to establish some kind of advantage.

'You said it,' said Sanger.

'Debrais will be all right.'

'Great,' said Sanger, but without enthusiasm.

'He said – and I don't mind saying it too – that it was a piece of cake with all the background you'd done, Earl.'

'What's the catch, Mike?'

'No catch, Earl. No problems. I'm just saying thanks. Credit where credit's due. It's an old English custom.'

'And the hell to you too,' said Sanger, but he relaxed

and smiled. Each man would remain on guard, but they were willing to be kissing cousins the while.

'David isn't a grabber,' said Michael. 'You trust him and he won't let you down.'

'Okay,' said Sanger, 'so give him a prize. If I helped, fine. And you'll not forget to tell the board, huh?'

Michael ignored that stab. He said: 'The price will please you, Earl. Well under fifty million francs.'

'Too high baby.'

Michael explained about the factory in Lyon. Sanger was unmoved.

'If – I say *if* – that's right, then it's not a bad price. Not good, but sure as God not bad.' Sanger smiled wickedly.

'What did you want to see me about, Earl?'

'Ali-Chem, Mike. I've gotten the picture. Those double-dealin' bastards. And Corsino. He's a shyster.'

'What's this all about, Earl?'

Sanger began to explain. About the price the American chemical corporation were paying for their stock in the Ecuador petro-chemical company. About the delayed payment. About the special privileges they still retained in the Ecuadorean market until the petro-chemical plant was built.

With every sentence, Michael felt better. It was a good day. He said nothing, just kept on nodding and putting on a judge's face. After ten minutes, he could wait no longer.

'Earl, thanks a lot. Your sources check out with ours. I agree, Ed Corsino is a bastard.'

Sanger took a moment for the message to sink in. Then, he said, 'Hey, Mike, what are you messing with me for? You *knew* all that?'

'Yes, we knew. But it's valuable to have it checked out.'

'Screw that,' said Sanger angrily. 'What kind of company is this that I don't get told?'

'It was being confirmed,' said Michael.

Sanger whipped off his glasses and polished them furiously. 'The hell you were, Mike. You know the rest too, I suppose?'

'Nothing else that matters,' said Michael. 'Is there more then?'

'You bet your sweet ass there's more.' Sanger already looked to have recovered his humour. 'Those clowns at Ali-Chem have got another deal on the side. Corsino knows all about it. So does your goddam chum Cantania. It's the only way they could persuade Ali-Chem to come in.'

'What deal?'

'Have you heard about a new site for a plant further down the coast, south of Esmeraldas, Mike?'

'Yes, I've heard. I told you, surely.'

Sanger laughed, a snort of derision. 'Yeah, I forgot. You told me. Well, that site was the leverage to get Ali-Chem in. The main petro-chem plant is going mostly to make PVC. For PVC, you need chlorine. Ali-Chem don't aim to import it – like hell they're gonna import it! They'll make it on the spot, using local salt.'

'Well,' said Michael, 'maybe we should have known – but what's wrong with that?'

'They wouldn't make chlorine there unless they could make it cheaper than in the U.S. of A. And, Jesus, they'll make it cheaper. Labour's cheap, number one. And number two, they'd be expected to use a non-mercury process if they made it in the States. It's kinda noxious. So what are they gonna do? In Ecuador they'll use a mercury process, and they'll pour the waste right into the sea.'

Michael was beginning, vaguely, to get Sanger's point. And that's dangerous?'

'It sure ain't healthy. The mercury'll turn up in their goddam fish. It's shit, Michael, real shit.'

'The Ecuadoreans won't take that, surely?'

'They will,' said Sanger. 'Don't you read the papers, Mike? All the under-developed countries don't give a good goddam for the ecology nuts. They think Nader and his boys are all part of a plot to get everyone to buy American cleaning and filtering equipment one day. Will Cantania worry about a few dead tuna fish when he's gonna make more profit?'

'I wouldn't say profit was his prime motivation,' said Michael.

'Okay, Mike, believe what you damn well like. But I'm telling you he won't get fussed about a little fouling up of the Pacific when he's got two million hungry mouths to feed. Be realistic.'

'But it's so unnecessary.'

Sanger shrugged. 'Ali-Chem have had a bad two years. They wanna make a comeback for their stockholders. This is one way to do it. If Ecuador allows the deal, to persuade Ali-Chem to put dough and U.S. expertise into the country, Ali-Chem won't spend more than they have to.'

Michael slid deep into his chair. 'Ed should have told us all this.'

'Don't be crazy, Mike. He'll have taken his percentage on that quiet little deal for sure. And I don't think that's the only thing he's screwed you on, Mike. I'm beginning to see some of the figures for the whole deal. Boy, did he add a percentage once all the members of the consortium had put in their prices!'

Michael was angry now. 'Who's giving you all this information? Is it Martin?'

'Hell, no. I'm not tellin'. Not yet. But, Mike. You and me are gonna have to work together. The board won't want to hear all this any more than they wanna know about the police raid, huh?'

Michael knew it was true.

'Don't look so goddam sick,' said Sanger, cheerfully. 'I think I've found us a way to get in on that Kroos take-over. And we've gotten ourselves something we can put the arm on Corsino with now, right? And Ali-Chem if we need to.'

That also was true; but Michael thought it was a hell of a way to do business.

6

Sheila Travis had heard three hours earlier from David that he would not be back from the Riviera yet. Instead of flying to London, he was taking a plane from Nice to Paris. He could be there at least 48 hours.

She felt frustrated. She missed him on absences like these more, she thought, than ever she showed. It meant, too, that their vacation was going to be delayed. She had hoped they might leave, *en famille*, to drive to the north-east coast of Spain that Saturday. The cross-channel ferry bookings were made. Now she was told by her husband to trade them for a reservation a fortnight hence.

She stormed out of the house, leaving Karen in charge, as soon as she'd eaten her lunch of cold meats and salad.

She'd drunk the best part of a bottle of wine with it. Her headache raged.

She took the car to the new shopping development, parked it, and went first to the grocery supermarket. She bought one or two packages – soap and cereals – aimlessly, without any particular heed, seeking to justify the use of her time. Then, walking swiftly across the car park as a spot or two of rain began to fall, she found herself in the toiletry section of the department store. The salesgirls were in hiding, as only salesgirls can keep themselves hidden when attendance to their manicures or their conversations about the previous evening are threatened with interruption. They did not think it proper to interfere with the customers.

Sheila picked up a package of Dior toilet water. No one came. The two girls at the end of the counter were talking closely. Impulsively, she placed the package in her open shopping bag and moved on. A scalp massager, electric, lay in a box lined with glossy satin. She pretended to examine it. The girls giggled. Sheila put that in her bag too. Then, quietly, her heart pounding, feeling a flush in her face, she turned and walked towards the open doors.

The rain was coming down hard. She paused in the doorway and pulled her coat-collar around her throat, then began to run for the car. Footsteps squelched close behind her. She looked over her shoulder. The man reached out and grasped her arm. She tried to snatch it away, but he was very strong. He stopped her running and she could feel the rain trickling down her neck as they stood looking at each other.

'Excuse me, madam. But I must ask you to come back to the store.'

'What the hell for?' she shouted. 'Leave me alone.'

But he still held her. 'Madam, let's not be silly. You know and I know. Or do you want a scene?'

Then, quite suddenly, the fight went out of her. What was the use? As they walked back to the store she felt very cold. Although her eyes stayed dry, inside she was weeping. With shame and anger that she could have allowed herself to be driven into a trap so obvious, so needless, so futilely stupid.

7. THE PRICE OF POISON

1

THERE isn't much in the whole United States of America that's more beautiful than the woods and hills around the town of Sharon in North-West Connecticut.

In winter, the snow may mantle the ground from before Thanksgiving Day, and it isn't much disturbed. Even getting up some of the gentle hills to the isolated and studiedly simple mansions of the New York pace-setters, the visitor may find that his automobile grinds uselessly at the snow and ice until progress ceases. But everybody has a snow-plough. Digging out the unwary is good winter sport.

In the fall, the leaves turn that startling New England red which looks hot enough to burn your hand off and is the most spectacular autumnal sight of anywhere in the world.

In the summer, it is a place for camps and camping, though not so concentratedly as the wilder climes of Massa-chussets and New Hampshire to the north. The occasional small lakes are good to swim in. Here come the uncertain offspring of the Eastern seaboard middle classes despatched for a few weeks to that ancient American institution, summer camp, whilst their parents ponder over stiff martinis what in hell to do, during the remainder of the vacation, to amuse the young minds they scarcely understand. The woods of this part of Connecticut are filled with deer and opossum, racoon and skunk, which, in season, may be killed with gun or, by seasoned trackers, with bow and arrow. Sharon is the very heaven of the American outdoor dream.

The small girl who this day wandered alone through the trees, seeking the birds with her eyes, was everyone's idea of the American idyll's eight-year-old. She was leggy and bronzed. A front tooth was missing, so that when she smiled it was delightful, and her face was freckled. Her hair, arranged in twin braids, adorned with ribbon, lay down her back, auburn against a red-and-white check blouse. She was

215

elated, because in five days she would see her father, who had been out of the country since before Easter. Her father she loved. She was cross, too, because her elder brother had been more than usually obnoxious to her. He had gone off to play baseball with some other kids and she reckoned that was a pretty boring thing to watch. That was why she was exploring the woods. She liked their coolness. She was proud of herself that she was not afraid of the dark shadows between the trees.

She followed a path that was fairly well-trodden. She was a lion-catcher in the African jungle – she had recently seen *Born Free* – and she would find a cub to nurse for her own. There was the lion, up ahead, at ease under a tree, its tail flicking away flies in the afternoon heat.

The lion turned out to be a heap of tattered brown cardboard boxes, surrounded by a mess of brown paper. She had heard about litter-droppers. They weren't nice. Angrily, she pushed at a box. It toppled over and several thin white sticks of stuff, a bit like chalk but crystalline and kind of glittery, just a few inches long, fell out. She remembered the candy cigarettes her father had brought her home once from a trip abroad. Nice. Sort of grown-up she'd felt, pretending to smoke them.

She picked up one of the sticks. Sniffed. Not much smell, but kind of sweet. Candy? Tentatively she bit off a little. Quite nice. Not great, but okay for a quiet afternoon and a lion-tracker. Must be candy. She went through a mime of lighting the cigarette, then started chewing. She stuffed a few sticks into her jeans.

What was the buzzing? Curiously, she looked around. A cloud of flies hung over a deer lying asleep in the grass. Quickly, she crept up to the animal, hoping she would not disturb it. Her feet were almost touching its nose, before, instinctively, she realised it would not move. Its eyes were wide open, glassy, like the heads she'd seen on the walls of the camp recreation hall. The mouth was open too, flies upon the tongue.

She started to run, crying and afraid.

For a man who was used to dealing with overseas contracts, flattering the local politicians, keeping his mouth shut, pushing the job through on schedule, Martin was saying a lot.

'Minister, I don't give a damn. How can I do a job of work for you if I don't know what's going on?'

He was annoyed about that chlorine plant. Not only for what it represented, which was bad enough; it wasn't even that Corsino, Cantania, Ali-Chem, all of them, had deliberately kept him in the dark. The final straw had been that it was Quant who'd told him two days ago what was going on down the steamy coast from Esmeraldas. What the hell was that prissy punk doing with information so big when he, as overall project director, didn't know?

Cantania, with the usual glass of whisky before him, sat squarely behind his mahogany desk and looked unperturbed.

'I am sorry, Mr Martin, that you are so upset. But,' he insisted, 'it is an operation totally separate from the plant you are building . . .'

'Yeah, maybe. But you figure to link it up in the end. And Ali-Chem are involved. And now some of the best labour is gonna be taken off my project. It's just ain't – well, ethical.'

Martin knew it wasn't a strong case. It was his pride, not his efficiency, which had been damaged.

'It was necessary for the national purpose to have the chlorine process,' said Cantania.

'Sure,' said Martin. 'Do you know what purpose that chlorine waste will serve? It'll foul up your fish.' The strawberry mark on his face burned very brightly.

'An exaggeration, Mr Martin, as well you know,' said Cantania coolly. 'The Pacific is a very large ocean. I think that Ecuador can put up with a few dead fish when the reward will be several hundred millions of dollars in the nation's purse.'

'But . . .' said Martin.

Cantania cut him short. 'Have you ever flown over the rain forests, Mr Martin? A foolish question. I am sure you have. When you look down at all those trees, all those millions of square miles of untamed useless territory, has it never made you wonder what the environmental prophets of the more comfortably placed nations are screaming about? First, let us use up some of the bountiful resources of our continent to fill empty bellies. Then we may start worrying about conserving them.'

'You can do both,' said Martin. 'Why foul yourselves up in the process of getting rich?'

'I doubt it, Mr Martin. Not while your corporations are, as I think you would say, calling the shots. Ali-Chem had a price. I judge that – for the time being – we are willing to pay it. If I kill some of the tuna – well let us say that is a few fish less for the boats from California to put into their nets. Even our coastal waters are not our own. There are laws, conventions; but we cannot stop all the Americans who sail south and commit trespass.' Cantania twisted his mouth and sipped whisky. 'Not even now we have bought Colonel Vargas his gun-boats.'

Martin was silent. There was not much more he could say. He looked at Cantania's silver hair shining in the gloom of the quiet room. The Minister smiled sadly, his shoulders bowed wearily.

'Believe me, Mr Martin, I am touched by your concern. But the decision is mine, not yours. Please go and build your plant. I have problems enough with Colonel Vargas.'

The telephone rang. Cantania lifted and listened.

'They have an urgent message for you at the consortium headquarters,' he said.

Martin drove recklessly, taking out his anger on the car. His leave was due to begin on Friday. But he didn't want to walk out with this mess unresolved. Could he resolve it though? The place for that was probably New York or Chicago or Washington rather than Quito. Maybe he could persuade Ali-Chem to reconsider the design of the chlorine plant or find some way to force them to. He rubbed his ginger hair roughly, hurting his scalp, by way of punishment for thinking so stupidly. He was as much caught in the inevitable web of circumstance as any of those poor bum Indians squatting in the gutter.

A cop in blue-grey uniform and white steel hat blew a whistle and motioned him to stop. The cop stood very proudly on a small raised dais that had advertising signs pinned to it for Lufthansa. He held the car whilst four truckloads of soldiers went across the intersection, bouncing madly as the vehicles rode the cracked roadway. Why the hell didn't that smug bastard Vargas send a few more of those guys up to the plant? Martin was getting tired of wasting his scarce labour force filling in holes made by the inexpert, but distracting, explosions of the guerrillas.

3

The news was better, 48 hours later, as the limousine carried Martin north towards Connecticut on the Saw Mill River Parkway. Not the news about the plant as Esmeraldas. For all he cared about that right now, it could be taken down bit by bit and dropped into the Amazon or given, as prizes for perseverance, to the guerrillas.

The airport police at Kennedy had told him that Cherry was going to be all right. She'd had a good night. The convulsions had stopped and she was out of coma. When he telephoned the hospital, the doctor said they'd washed every bit of poison out of her. The doctor described the process. A thin rubber tube pushed down the throat, water flushing into the stomach. Martin retched at the thought. Was that any way to treat a kid?

'We've given her cascara – but it's quite nice, Mr Martin. Flavoured with licorice. Kids like it.' Big deal, Martin thought. 'And bicarbonate of soda. That's an alkali, you know. It counteracts any acidosis.'

For a doctor he'd been quite forthcoming. He had told Martin most things, frankly.

'It was lucky she was able to show the people at the camp where she'd found the stuff before she started vomiting and the delirium set in. She was worried about the deer. It was dead, of course.'

'What in hell's name was this stuff?'

'We call it meta. Metacetaldehyde. It's white and crystalline. Gets used in slugkiller, mixed with bran. And they make it in little sticks as a convenient substitute for methylated spirit for heating purposes. I've heard of dogs and ducks eating the slugkiller before. With kids it's mostly the sticks. They think it's some kind of candy.'

'How come it was lyin' around in the woods?'

'Yeah, well – the sheriff's working on that.'

'He'd better be.'

'It could have been worse, Mr Martin. We think she only ate one or two sticks. As few as half a dozen, say 300 or so grains, can kill an adult.'

Martin had persisted. 'Come on, doc. What was that stuff left there for?'

'We think it was a dumping job.'

'Why dump it?'

'The boxes were wet. Maybe they were in a flood or a fire or something – hosed, you know. That would make the sticks crumble. They'd be useless to sell. So they'd be dumped.'

'But they just can't dump stuff like that anywhere.'

The doctor was very patient. 'No. Of course not. Usually a waste disposal trucking company gets that kind of job. There are special tips.'

'So they put it in the woods.'

'We don't know why, Mr Martin,' said the doctor. 'It's a disgraceful thing. But don't worry about Cherry. We're sure everything's going to be okay now. Really.'

The words didn't stop Martin being worried still as the automobile cut through a light evening mist. But he wasn't panicky as he'd been on the plane, unable to sleep, drinking too much. Anger was taking over. He kept asking the driver what kind of people it was who dropped crap like that around the countryside for kids to mess with.

'Yeah,' said the driver yet again. 'This country's fulla creeps, ain't that the truth. You was lucky, mister. It was in my newspaper. They said there was enough of that shit lyin' around up there to kill twenty, thirty people.'

'Jesus Christ!' Martin knew, but he pretended to himself it was a surprise. That way he fuelled his indignation.

'It ain't the first time, neither,' the driver continued. 'Some of these truckin' guys just wanna make a fast buck. Any place to dump the stuff will do when no one's looking.'

Martin fidgeted. 'Can't you make it any faster?'

'Sure can't, bud. I'm doin' 65 now, and that's 10 too fast for this here section.' The driver tried to make it more cheerful. 'It's great your kid's gonna be okay.'

Martin grunted, impatiently. He picked up the newspaper beside him and read it again.

S.E.C. spokesman denies
premature dropping
of monopoly inquiry

KERRIDGE STEEL
STILL SILENT
AS STOCK SLIDES

$250,000 gift to
Republican funds
under scrutiny

The story said that a Democratic Senator had been digging the dirt about the takeover, a month or so back, of a largish steel company called Talsey. The buyer was Kerridge Steel. It had seemed probable that the Securities Exchange Commission in Washington would disallow the deal as being against the public interest – too large a hunk of the steel business in Kerridge's hands.

Then, the heat had gone out of the situation. Quietly the takeover happened. The Senator wanted to know why. He had also dug up the fact that, so he alleged, a cool quarter of a million dollars had been paid a week earlier into Republican Party funds by Kerridge Steel.

Martin could not even get hot about the 5-dollar loss which the stock had suffered on Wall Street the previous day, although it was part of his contract that he had a fistful of stock options in the company. He was too concerned about Cherry, too puzzled as to where all this left the job in Ecuador.

There was a long piece about Kerridge and his hideaway in the Palisades. There was not one word about Ed Corsino. But that goddam guinea Corsino was in there somewheres, Martin knew, like a worm in the woodwork. When he'd made sure Cherry was okay, he'd go to see that guy. He ought to ring the Englishman, Grant, too. He had a prospective ally there, he was sure. He could do it from Sharon – after he'd got his hands round the neck of the bastard who'd dumped those boxes of poison sticks.

221

'You're looking very tired, Michael,' Bernard Grant told his son. 'It was very unwise to put off your holiday. Besides, it's not fair to Alison.'

Michael would not get angry with his father. Christ, he *was* tired. But there was too much happening for him to be able to take a holiday. Bernard, used for years to taking the strain himself, still had the habit of forgetting that now, the buck stopped here, in this room, Michael's.

'Alison's all right, father. She understands. A quiet hotel on Exmoor is probably better for pre-natal composure than Albufeira anyway.'

His father sounded unconvinced.

'I suppose you'll be wanting to fly to America tomorrow too?'

'Not tomorrow, father. Tomorrow I'm due to see the people from SAEF.'

'They're coming to you?'

'Yes.'

'You should let me go to see Kerridge. I could handle that.'

'Father, please. We've been through it all before. You simply don't know enough of the detail. You've not been out to Ecuador. You've never even met Martin. How can you cope with all that?'

In the coming weeks he would need to keep his father firmly in line. 'Look, Dad, I appreciate what you're trying to do to help. But this part of it I've got to see through alone. Anything else, all right. I'll be glad of your help. But Ecuador has to be my baby.'

'Take me with you, then.'

'I need you here. Earl is coming with me. He saw Kerridge last year. And he knows that scene.'

'I just hope it works out.' Bernard Grant was no more than mildly sulky. He knew his son was right. And he was guarding, like a charm, Michael's careless surrender to him of the right to look after other areas of Prospero business in the present crisis. He had ideas in that direction following a conversation he'd enjoyed at the house of a political friend three days ago.

'Those damned Frenchmen have become friendly all of a sudden, haven't they?' he said.

Michael forced out a smile. 'They're rather more co-operative since David Travis called on them in Paris last week. Besides, they're as worried as I am about the news from America. They'll want to stick close to us from now on. If anything fouled up Kerridge Steel, they'd be in trouble too.'

'What in heaven's name has that young man's wife been up to?'

'It's difficult to get at the truth. But I'm assured there's a very good chance of an acquittal. We've briefed the best man possible. Apparently she'd drunk a lot of wine at a time when she was taking sleeping tablets. I hope to God they're sorting themselves out now on holiday. She's a nice enough woman. But I don't want her screwing up David. We need him too much.'

'Can they leave the country with a court case in the offing? I didn't think that was on,' said Bernard.

'I've given sureties. And the bail was pretty stiff.'

'How much?' Bernard was no man to miss one digit which might ultimately find its way into the organisation's books.

'Two thousand.'

'I hope he's worth it, Michael.'

'Of course he's worth it, father. Apart from the Debrais thing, he seems to have persuaded SAEF to come across with a cash loan if we need it.'

Bernard paused in adjusting the knot in his deep turquoise silk tie. 'Which we doubtless will. Debrais may be good business, but where do you expect Harold to conjure the money from for that?'

Michael patiently explained. Euroloans were still not difficult to arrange for propositions as promising as the Debrais takeover.

'I think we should have a short meeting of those executive directors who aren't away tomorrow afternoon, father. Following my meeting with SAEF. Will you take the chair?'

It was a timely gesture. Michael was reassuring the old man that no plots were being laid.

'Certainly,' said the elder Grant. 'I don't think we need Lionel Westbrook, do you?'

223

'No. I don't even believe we need Harold. He's only down at Dartmouth, but I don't want to break his holiday – not if you agree, that is.'

Again, the sop was well directed.

'I think you're right, Michael.' Bernard was beginning to feel quite conspiratorial. Himself and his son, arranging things, together, just as it should be. Equal partners. There was Sanger, of course. He'd have to come. And Prosser. But Prosser would do as he was told. As for Sanger, two Grants against one of him should be sufficient. But in the Kerridge business, it sounded as though Michael had got Sanger on his side. Why else would he take Sanger to America?

Later, his mind at rest, Bernard sat in his own room staring at the Dufy on the wall opposite him. Was that not a miracle, the blue of the corn and the red outline of the horse? Such strange use of colour, yet so true; so honest to the artist's vision. A masterpiece. How right he had been all those years ago to pay what everyone had said was a ridiculously high price for the painting. It had given him more pleasure than half a dozen good fat business deals, and now it was worth six times what he had paid for it. Dufy reassured him about his own judgment whenever (which was seldom) he felt like doubting it. In this mood, very deliberately, he lifted the telephone.

Vernon Morton took the call in the merchant bank which Prospero had used for the past six years, and which had provided a natural springboard from which he might bound into a place on the Prospero board. It had been a quiet day; the Stock Exchange dead, only a boring baron at the luncheon table, and no takeover business in sight. August in the City usually is moribund.. He'd heard that someone – and it wasn't Brandford – had been buying Kroos stock that morning. But not in large quantities. It could mean nothing. He was glad to hear Bernard on the line. It might presage activity.

'Vernon,' said Bernard Grant once the formal pleasantries were over. 'I think you can tell your friend that we'd be interested to know what he has in mind for the Lovelace site.'

'He'll not make the price very high. Not yet,' said Morton.

'Not a penny under a million,' said Bernard; even at his

most serious his face remained blandly cherubic, free of lines, except for the curling, revealing wrinkles that skirted his eyes.

Morton laughed. 'Even for you, Bernard . . .'

'No, I'm serious, Vernon. I gather there's a strong chance the Hampshire plan is going to be revived.'

'Gossip, Bernard. They dropped it like a hot potato a year or more ago.'

'Hush, dear man. Circumstances have changed, according to my Westminster friends. The conservationists made the thing impossible before, true. But now that the motorway route has been agreed, the area round the Lovelace factory is going to be much changed anyway. There's so much noise coming from London firms wanting to get out of the high-rent areas, they've got to make some more land in the south-east available for industry. And for homes too. The Department have been tipped the wink that this time there'll be less opposition if they choose an area close by the motorway. Since Lovelace's already exist as an industrial plant, it's good sense for everybody simply to use that as the hub of a new trading estate.'

Morton gazed down on his ample middle. The watchchain draping it rose and fell with the excitement of his breathing. 'Supposing you're right, Bernard, that figure's still high.'

'It'll be worth double in two years.'

'Then why should you want to sell?'

'Money in the bank, Vernon. We're overstretched. Tell your friend if he'll agree our price now, take a bit of a gamble, we'll give him a firm commitment that he can be the buyer at the time of his choice.'

'Michael will be furious,' said Morton, cautiously. 'It's his thing, that company.'

Bernard Grant huffed. 'It's not the only damn place in England for building motor cars.'

'You make it sound so easy.'

'Nothing is easy,' said Bernard. 'Least of all, making a capital gain of 100 per cent minimum on a deal in two years. Michael will accept it, or he's not the man to run this organisation. You leave him to me, Vernon. Just see if your people will put their money where their mouth is.'

The crudity of speech was Bernard Grant's ultimate weapon. It had shock value.

'You really mean it?'

'Certainly,' said Bernard. 'Tell them they have my personal word on a commitment. By the time I've sorted out this Ecuador balls-up, we may need all the cash we can get.'

He delivered a brisk lecture on guerrilla philosophies and the folly of believing in destruction as a prelude to recreating any society.

'Damn fool young men. Girls, too, I hear. God knows what the world is coming to.'

But in truth, Bernard Grant realised that to pull Ecuador and guerrillas into the argument was only a convenient excuse. Once he had been a real estate hustler. The reactions of such a dealer still flickered deep within him. And that part of his character found the prospect of a quick profit over the Lovelace site quite irresistible.

5

There were thirteen of them in the room, waiting for the arrival of the man from Quito. Remains of maize cakes and eggs lay on plates, set strangely beside water-bottles, blankets and guns. The walls were blankly white, two small stools and a bare table the only furniture.

All of them, including Francisco, the leader, spoke in hushed voices. Not that there was especial need for caution at this hour of the afternoon when even policemen – unlikely visitors in the village at any time – would be taking a nap. But the soft word was their habit. Men who have been running for months wear furtiveness like a badge.

Outside, the sun had frozen the day. The light lay on parched buildings in brutal wedges. The shadows, blackest black by contrast, looked solid enough to have been nailed on to walls and earth. Shutters were closed, where there were shutters. Mostly, tiny windows were masked with scraps of cloth or carpet. Dogs lay like corpses in street shadows and when a skeletal cat, choosing the safe moment to investigate a trash-can, knocked off a metal cover, it clanged loud enough to have every hand in the room reaching for a weapon.

The look-out reassured them, but they were slow to start speaking again. They knew they were taking a chance, coming to a rendezvous so near to the road that linked Esmeraldas and Sant' Domingo de los Colorados. The village lay five miles east of the highway, 60 miles south-east of the petro-chemical plant site, according to the creased army map they used. But they were tired of the high plateau which had proved so unfriendly and so unprofitable to them.

They had had enough of tearing feet and hands on parched ravines and sharp boulders, crossing icy streams, shivering in the bitter nights, eating filthy food. The Indians up there had proved little interested in their message – when, indeed, they had been able to communicate with the tribes through the one or two dialects their Indian studies at the universities of Ecuador had taught them. Francisco had put forward the prosaic reason that the landowners of the country, less harsh and more benevolently paternal than those of Colombia, Bolivia and Chile, had left the Indians not so ripe for the doctrines of revolutionary land seizure as might have been expected. That was not very Marxist of him.

There were other problems in the mountains. The lines of communication with their groups in Quito and Cuenca and Esmeraldas were ridiculously long when the leader was holed up in the wild and inaccessible Andean valleys. Maintaining communications had been the main reason why seventeen of their comrades had been lost – three killed, seven captured, one dead of God knows what disease, and six missing. So disappointment had given a measured desperation to their new mode of operations. They would risk the soldiers and the police if the living could be easier, the strikes against chosen objectives more effective.

The privations they had suffered had not aged them, nor given them that toughly muscular and leathery look which guerrillas wear like battlepaint in movies and posters. The myths of Castro and Ché Guevara die hard. The guerrillas in this room, well-trained and intelligent scions of the middle and upper classes of Ecuador, with two Colombians and a Brazilian thrown in, simply looked thin, gaunt of face and younger than they were. The mixture of levis and cast-off combat jackets they wore was not especially different from the casual uniform of the under-25s anywhere in the moderately civilised world. Only their hard eyes, bright as those of lizards, and their guns and ammunition proclaimed them as men of action.

Oh, but they were not play-acting soldiers, nor foolish. They had learned a certain wisdom in the past year. At first, they had followed the rites which softer, sillier young people, the weekend revolutionaries, can afford the luxury of practising in, perhaps, Columbia University, New York City, or the London School of Economics. They had honoured the death of Ché in October. They had held almost ceremonial readings from his diaries and those of other cult figures. They had studied the tactics of campaigns in Guatemala, Brazil, Venezuela, Bolivia. They had argued endlessly about the role of the Marxist revolutionary in a capitalist society.

All that was over now. They had formed their own philosophy, and it had no room for heroes. Ché and the others they dismissed as archaic soloists, building legends but changing little except the economics of the political poster and paperback industries in more developed countries.

They wanted no big gestures, no advertising, for that method had brought only disaster.

The first direct raid on the petro-chemical plant site at Esmeraldes had cost two dead and three prisoners, whose confessions to Colonel Vargas had betrayed their headquarters and set back the building of the cell at Quito University by six months. So now, the guerrillas had managed to insinuate five men into the work force at the Esmeraldas site. Quiet sabotage was much more rewarding.

They had tried to convert the Indians, whom the guerrilla manuals preached were the seedbed of revolution, waiting to regain the land stolen four centuries ago by the *conquistadores*, but they had been rebuffed, ignored or even actively betrayed. So now they were returning to their own class and to the bored ranks of the lower class *mestizos* to find recruits. If the Indians did not want a revolution, then one would have to be manufactured for them.

They were, henceforward, aiming to work within society rather than against it – on the fringes, certainly, and outside the law, but choosing their targets with care. If they could make money they would; kidnappings for ransom had, inevitably, been suggested, though none had yet been essayed. There had been contact with one or two priests, since there was ample evidence that the younger clergy of the Catholic Church were not going to get on the wrong side of any revolution that might sweep out capitalism in South America. One of the less enthusiastically Marxist young men had even suggested a secret approach to Jesus Cantania with the offer of a deal whereby Colonel Vargas might be assassinated in return, ultimately, for pardon for the guerrillas. Cantania was believed by two or three in the band to be not beyond saving; a liberal with a conscience who might, under pressure, turn Marxist.

This view was not generally accepted, but its protagonists were not rejected by the rest of this guerrilla group as they would certainly have been a year earlier when the antics of Arabic and Japanese madmen were much discussed, even admired. Francisco's leadership kept them going, but some in the band secretly wanted to return to their families, to work within the known political framework.

How, though, does a guerrilla who has lost the taste for the outside life stop being a guerrilla?

In many minds there was the thought that, with enough money, they could move to another, more welcoming society and work for the cause from there whilst living open, even prosperous lives again. So they carried on their war against the targets they jointly disapproved of in Ecuador, and the momentum of being a unit kept them together; but there was always the thought that a big money prize could solve their dilemma.

And they would kill to get that prize; they had been trained for that. They had been more concerned, often physically ill, about killing in the first days. Now, they did it more by reflex, with some regrets but no pain. The judgment of a more conventional society could be that currently they were as much bandits as freedom fighters.

Through the silence outside the room came the sound of a car. Lightly, four men sprang to their feet, snapping the catches on automatic rifles as they slid on either side of the two doors to the room. The automobile's overheated engine croaked and died. By the time the knock came on the larger door, every man was pointing his gun at the iron-studded wood.

The look-out led in the comrade from Quito who wore, rather showily, a bush-hat. There was also a woman, her white blouse stained with sweat and dust. Apart from that she was very presentable; large-breasted and large-hipped. Not a man in the place, except for the homosexual with steel glasses, failed to fancy her. They did not have women very often.

'—Who is she?' asked Francisco.

'—I though you should question her,' said the comrade from Quito. '—She has been living with Vargas.' He spat.

Francisco, tall and surly black-haired, nodded and limped over – heritage of a stray army bullet in the first raid on Esmeraldas – to embrace the comrade, who swigged endlessly from a wineskin as he talked, detailing the names of recruits to the cell in Quito. They now had two contacts in the Ministry of Defence.

'—And Cuenca?' said Francisco.

'—Those tyre plant workers are pigs,' said the comrade in the bush-hat. '—The union has put up a notice at the entrance to the works. *Communism Stops Here.* They have no spunk, those people. We have four good men inside, but their words fall on deaf ears.'

Francisco checked the breech of his gun was empty and pointed it at the floor, clicking the trigger. '—Tell me about the American ambassador.'

'—Forget him, comrade. He has six soldiers with him wherever he goes. And two FBI men posing as trade delegates. Both are pistol champions. You would need all you have here' – waving his hand at the roomful of men – 'and twenty more to be certain of taking him. Every one in Quito now takes precautions.'

'—Including Vargas, I suppose,' said Francisco.

'—Especially Vargas,' said bush-hat, spitting wine on to the dusty floor. He was not quite the class of Francisco's other companions. Nor was the woman, who sat quietly on a stool. He nodded towards her. '—She will tell you.'

'—Yes. He has eighty soldiers at the house. Once there were a dozen. He is very pleased with himself.'

'—Why?' asked Francisco.

'—He boasts as once he did not. To me. He trusts me, I think. Else why would he have let me return to my village for a few days, which is where I am supposed to be? He wishes to show how clever he is.'

'—Why to you?' said Francisco.

230

She shrugged, pulling the blouse around her breasts as if suddenly cold. The men watched her, fascinated. '—I do things for him. These days he beats my ears with words instead of my body with leather.'

'—He does not like women,' said Francisco suspiciously.

The woman covered her bosom again with her arms. '—He has never made love to me, but he uses me to amuse him.' She explained how; some of the young men wished they could be so fortunate.

'—His boasting. Tell us more,' said Francisco.

'—He has bought warships in Europe. He is expecting a dozen helicopters from overseas this month. He will use them to find you. They carry guns. Like those of the Americans in Vietnam, he said. And he is negotiating for tanks with the British.'

Francisco turned to the man from Quito. '—What does Cantania say to all this?'

'—He is happy, comrade. What else? While Vargas can play soldiers, he does not interfere with Cantania's plans. The work at Esmeraldas goes forward despite all that our men can do. And Quito is full of rumours about the other site on the coast. That will belong to the Americans, they say, not to Ecuador.'

It was Francisco's turn to spit. '—More profits for the gringos. And for the pigs like Perez.'

Most of them knew Perez. With some, he had been a contemporary at university; others remembered him from the days when they too had been visitors to the Unicorné and Maxy's, before boredom and disenchantment set it.

'—We should kill Perez,' said the guerrilla with steel glasses, whom Perez had once, years ago, called a bull with no balls.

'—Cantania. He should die before Perez,' said a second.

The comrade from Quito removed his bush-hat. Sometimes, he thought, these heroes with guns were short on realism.

'—In the capital many believe that Cantania plays a double game. They say he will milk the gringos for everything he can get and then seize what they have built.'

He paused, wondering if he dared, then continued. '—There are some in the city who do not agree with attacking the petro-chemical plant. They would like us to strike directly at Vargas and his soldiers. They see Cantania as a man to be encouraged.'

That was as far as he would go. He could not say that there were comrades in Quito who muttered that planting dynamite on towers at Esmeraldas was too easy; that the real test for the activists would be more direct confrontation with Vargas's troops. To knock out the tanks or guns which controlled the country would more tangibly aid the future revolution than destroying installations which one day could be useful to a new leftish regime. It also, so such comrades averred, took more guts.

'—We have considered that viewpoint,' said Francisco. He clicked the trigger rapidly at the scruffy floor. '—We have plans. And we will not touch Cantania.' He looked fiercely at the zealot who had spoken earlier of killing the Minister.

'That is sensible, I think,' said the man from Quito.

'—Troop movements. Have you any news? If we had more information, we could attack more.' Francisco knew he had to score a point for his band to restore their pride. '—So far the comrades in Quito have failed us.'

The messenger produced a folded paper from inside his coat. '—Here are the plans we know of. Part of a battalion is moving down to the Esmeraldas site from Quito next week.' He smiled gently. '—They could be ambushed.'

Francisco studied the paper. '—Good. What else?'

'—The man in charge of the plant, Martin, he is away at present. In America. His child has been ill.'

Francisco grunted. '—Martin is a fair man, according to our information. He must not be harmed.'

He rose as if the messenger had been drained of usefulness. He pointed his gun at the woman. '—She will return? To Vargas?'

The man from Quito nodded.

'—Then let it be tonight. We want no suspicion.' He looked around at his men. Francisco recognised that in this situation, one woman might cause other problems. Sex was divisive; and exhausting.

'—Make sure we have further news of the site at the coast. I wonder what Cantania is up to there,' he said. '—And be certain we know swiftly about the slightest slackening in personal security for anyone of importance. Money we need. A kidnap would be the best way of getting it.'

Then he left the room, and the comrades clustered round the man from Quito. His news, however third-hand and gossipy, was the only contact they had with their largely well-to-do families, whom they might despise intellectually, but for whom they still retained threads of love.

6

Martin never found the man responsible for poisoning his daughter. He spent four days in Connecticut, worrying the local Sheriff, but the boxes containing the poison sticks proved too anonymous. The local trucking firms who carried such cargoes were all able to account for the destinations of any recent chemical waste.

'Musta been from outa state,' said the Sheriff, who wanted a quiet vacation. 'Those New York guys are different from the people round here.'

So when Martin finally rode down to New York City again, his frustration was intense. He came looking for trouble. In this way are major events sometimes moved and shaped by minor.

He found Michael Grant and Earl Sanger at the Drake, waiting for Corsino. The sticky late-August heat of New York did nothing to improve his temper.

'I'm not arguing with that guinea bastard,' he told Michael peremptorily. 'I want to see Kerridge. That's the company I've got my contract with.'

'Kerridge is sick,' said Michael. 'He can't come.'

Martin snorted and rubbed his brightly burning strawberry mark. 'Screw that for a diplomatic illness. He's just waiting for the heat to go out of the Washington situation.'

'Nothing's been proven about that,' said Michael. 'Ed said on the 'phone that Kerridge pays over money every year to the Republicans. It's coincidence that a quarter of a million was transferred just when SEC were looking into the Talsey takeover.'

'Yeah,' sneered Martin. 'So I read in the papers. Who's gonna believe that load of crap?'

233

Sanger stirred. He'd got to quieten this guy down. Whose money did Martin think he was getting uppity about?

'Listen, Del,' he said. He forced lips over teeth in a thin smile, which made his eyes bulge beneath the hornrims so that he looked almost comically aggressive. 'We can't afford to rock the boat. If Kerridge and Corsino get into a mess, it'll affect all of us, yeah? We gotta get that plant built.'

'And what about the other plant?' said Martin heatedly. 'The one Ali-Chem are building? No one told us about that.'

'None of our business,' said Sanger smartly.

Martin looked at him darkly. 'Poison is everybody's business, Mr Sanger. Do you know they're aimin' just to throw all that shit in the sea?'

Michael motioned Sanger to be quiet. 'We know, Del. And I'm seeing Ali-Chem about it. Maybe we can make them change their process.'

'And maybe we can't,' said Sanger, who wasn't going to be shut up. 'For all we know, that's the crunch for them. It only figures as a deal if they can have that extra stake in the territory, on their terms. We can't run the risk of having them pull out.'

Michael said: 'Would they do that, Del?'

Martin got up and walked across the hotel room. 'Nope. There's too much in it for them whatever happens on the chlorine process. If they pull out, then someone else will step in. They daren't.'

Sanger had lost any pretence of trying to stay pleasant. He jumped up too, snatching off his glasses. 'That's just wishful thinking, Martin. They've paid over nothing yet. They're smart, those Ali-Chem guys, right? We can't risk fouling them up.'

Martin didn't get angrier. He just looked at Sanger like something that had crawled out from under a stone. 'They'll have to change, Mr Sanger. Or I'll screw them someways. You'd better believe it.'

That evening, Michael rang Corsino and made their morning meeting one hour earlier. He conceded this point to Sanger, even though he didn't like misleading Martin. They badly needed to know what attitude Corsino and the Ali-Chem man would adopt before Martin injected his uncompromising viewpoint into the debate.

Corsino, for all his smiling and his hard handshake,

looked tense next morning. There were pale yellow thumb-prints under his eyes, and he kept adjusting the thick muscles in his neck by flicking his chin. Sanger scarcely believed it. Corsino had developed a twitch.

He came, too, with a flotilla of aides, as if they might cushion him from any blows which the Prospero people directed at him. It reminded Michael of the meeting – deep in the past, it now seemed – when the consortium contract had finally been signed. Sanger was thinking of something else: the preliminary meeting early the previous year when Corsino had, he now realised, totally fooled him.

How clever Sanger had thought himself, sorting through the list of people who were big enough to partner Prospero in the consortium – and, equally important, had the power and the ruthlessness and the means to deal with an operator named Gelson who knew enough about Corsino's shadier deals abroad to threaten to torpedo the whole project. In the end, only Kerridge had fitted the bill precisely, but Corsino had seemed very reluctant for Sanger to try to bring the giant American steel company into the consortium.

That, Sanger realised in retrospect, was Corsino's genius. All the time he had been urging Sanger forward, reading his fellow American's character correctly, knowing that the more he blocked Sanger's ideas, the more Sanger would want to pursue them. Corsino, Sanger deduced, had known damn well that Kerridge could squash Gelson, the black-mailer, like a fly. With his own large holding in Kerridge Steel, not obvious to Sanger at the time, Corsino had planned all along for the business to go in that direction.

Sanger could now see how Corsino had dropped crumb after crumb of information, casually, into his path, leading him cleverly towards Kerridge. Then, Corsino had used the veneer of apparent reluctance to do business with Kerridge as a lever to gain total freedom in negotiating on behalf of all the partners. That was why Corsino, it now trans-pired from the figures which Quant had supplied, was able to screw hefty commission out of every individual contract within the main contract.

Sanger had a lot to make up on Ed Corsino for sure. How the sharp hate those who are sharper. Sanger tapped a pen against his teeth as the meeting began, waiting for a chance to bite.

'We'll bring in the guy from Ali-Chem when we're ready, okay Mike?' said Corsino, trying to appear accommodating. Michael Grant nodded. Ali-Chem was only one of his objectives today.

They spent the first ten minutes listening to Corsino as he detailed every move of the Talsey takeover and the circumstances surrounding the gift to the Republicans.

'All right, Ed,' said Michael finally. 'But I see the *Wall Street Journal* has got Kerridge Steel marked down another 4 dollars this morning. Suppose the SEC unscramble that takeover?'

Corsino grinned, appearing confident. 'Not a chance, Mike. It's just politicians' talk. And this ain't election year. In a month this whole stink will have died.' But he still twitched his neck.

Sanger probed. Corsino waved away his arguments as if the words were gnats, troublesome, but of no real account.

'Right, Ed,' said Sanger grimly. 'May I Mike?' He caressed a clean blue folder . . .

'Yes,' said Michael.

Sanger slid across the folder to Corsino. 'This is how we make your commission on this deal stack up, Ed. Looks to us as if you've gotten yourself one helluva cushion in there. And we don't like that kind of ball game. Not when we've been screwed on everything that's gone into Ecuador so far.'

Corsino opened the folder. There was a hush in the room. Then he smiled as if he could hear soft strings in his head, but all Sanger could hear was the sound of automobiles grunting and grinding and honking on 56th Street.

'Maybe I'd argue a bit around the edges,' said Corsino. 'But hell, it's legal. You liked the price when you signed, didn't you, Mike?'

'I don't like it now,' said Michael. 'And we'll fight you on this, Ed. I'm not standing to see Oldershaw lose us money when you're taking so much.'

Corsino's grin was almost insolent. 'Ain't much you can do about it, Mike. A deal's a deal. The price was fixed. And I hear that SAEF are helping you out now. What the hell are you complaining about? Don't let's play games.'

'You played games with Ali-Chem,' said Michael. 'I want changes made in that chlorine plant process.'

'Okay, okay. Talk to the man when he comes in. If they don't mind, why should I?'

'You kept that deal secret,' said Michael.

'Why not?' said Corsino. He jerked his chin across his tie. 'Do I have to make a goddam confession of everything I set up? Don't forget I took all the risks. I spent the time down there in Ecuador not knowing if I'd even get back the price of my air fare. I worked on this for two whole years. I set up the game and then invited you in to play. If now you don't like the rules, then I'm not gonna blow foul. If you got somethin' to say to Ali-Chem, then say it.'

The man from Ali-Chem was young and sharp and eager. He was five minutes into explaining the problems of changing the chlorine plant design, and Corsino was smiling and hadn't twitched once during that time, when the door to the suite burst open. Martin stood there with a girl secretary holding up her arms in front of him like she was practising to be a traffic cop. He shouted at the smoky room. 'What's this kid telling me? I can't come in? To hell with that. What's going on?'

Michael smarted under the honest gaze of outrage which Martin beamed on him. 'I'm sorry, Del. There was a change of plan. We've only just got to the part dealing with Ali-Chem. So you've missed nothing that matters.'

It sounded unconvincing, even to him. But how could he have explained to Martin that he and Sanger feared the engineer's emotions might ruin the chance of pushing Corsino and Ali-Chem the way that Martin wanted?

Martin's liking for, even loyalty to, Michael was strained to the point of explosion. In the quiet of that room, they waited. Then he loosened, hunched his shoulders, sat down and said softly. 'Okay, so I'm here. I'm listening.'

The man from Ali-Chem continued. If the Ecuadoreans themselves didn't mind, he said, why shouldn't Ali-Chem give them the kind of plant they wanted.

Martin made no sudden movement. Almost lazily, he climbed to his feet and stuck out a short stubby forefinger. 'You build that plant without cleaning up all that shit, and I'll smear you through every newspaper that'll listen to me.' He swung towards Corsino. 'And I know a thing or two about you, buddy-boy. You just do like I say.'

Corsino twitched twice, his eyes blazing with anger. 'Who

the hell do you think you are, Martin? You ain't nuthin' here. Just a hired hand, that's all.'

Martin began to move to Corsino. 'Sure, Corsino. We're all hired hands. I'll do most things for you guys, but I ain't havin' poison poured out from plants I know about. I rang about my kid this morning, did you know that? She was sick all night again. That shouldn't happen to any kid just because creeps like you are pushing for a fast buck.'

Corsino slammed his fist on the table. 'What are we listenin' to this guy for? Just because his fuckin' kid can't take care of herself he thinks he can foul up a deal worth a quarter of a billion bucks?'

He lifted his fist. It was a big fist, the dark hair matted with perspiration around the wrist. But it was not as big nor as angry as the fist that caught him squarely in the mouth. The rest of the room was frozen like a tableau as Corsino pitched backwards, somersaulting over a chair. Martin sprang towards the fallen figure, and fell on it fists flailing.

It took four pairs of arms to pull him away, and Corsino scrambled slowly to his knees, shaking his head. Blood oozed from a cut at the side of his thick lips.

'You bastard,' he said to Martin. 'That's the end of the line for you, buster. You can go work for someone else.'

Michael Grant had remained apart from the group around Corsino. Now he stepped forward, pale, towering over the American.

'Oh no, Ed.' he said. 'Del stays. You shouldn't have said that. By God you shouldn't have said it. I haven't lost confidence in him, but I've damn near lost it in you. Just you play it straight from now on, Ed, or I swear I'll pull this whole house down around your ears.'

Corsino could scarcely raise a sneer, but he said: 'Quit foolin', Mike. You'd never dare.'

'If you think that, Ed,' snapped Michael, 'you don't know me very well.' Then he turned and led Martin by the arm from the room. At the door he paused and jabbed a finger at the young man from Ali-Chem, who had failed to get lost in the scenery surrounding Corsino.

'I'm not aiming to be unreasonable,' he said. 'But you make sure you can do something for Mr Martin. We'll talk tomorrow.'

8. LESSONS IN SURVIVAL

1

DAVID and Sheila did not return from the Algarve until September was well advanced. In the years afterwards David would recognise their two-and-a-half-week break as a major watershed in their marriage. Not *the* major one, for who can decide where such single and exclusively crucial points are reached? Marriage is a succession of calms and crises, whose apparent magnitude has nothing whatever to do with their actual effect. In the wrong context, annoyance at the colour of a dress or the lack of a courteous word may be as traumatic as a blatant act of unfaithfulness, by which is not meant sexual infidelity only; that is only a shorthand method of measurement by which certain societies assess sins far more deep-rooted and subtle.

It was a time of shamefaced reconstruction. David discovered that it was surprisingly easy to overcome the tug of annoyance he experienced at Sheila's indiscretion in the supermarket. He had his own reasons for feeling guilty. It was not the physical side of the episode with Claire Debrais which worried him, but the sense that he was cheapening both body and brain by the predictable use he now made of them in such situations. He was too sharply close to this particular success to allow his long-term philosophy – that the ends of profit, employment and satisfaction for the many people in Prospero justified the means – to erase his personal unease.

He also felt, although the emotion would not last, that he had recently been too unfair to Sheila. This was a question of degree, and certainly was not specifically linked with his sexual infidelity. He knew he should give her, tangibly, more care and more time and more love.

He tried to grasp the meaning of the incident in the department store; there had, of course, been dozens of similar cases. He looked at his wife and at himself, and easily went along with the idea that both of them were victims of the pressures created by today's society. Hadn't that society really killed the myth that nice girls grow up to marry nice men who smoke pipes and wear solid tweed suits? For that matter, he asked himself, where were the nice girls? Those who, proclaiming freedom, hung their lives loosely, tended to disintegrate totally; and the ones who, fearful of over-naive commitment, played it cool, ran the risk of freezing to death.

He had no answers; only compromises, one of which was a belief that apologies for thoughtlessness, jealousies and selfishness, either spoken or played out in actions, were essential between partners in modern marriage. People were now too aware of the possibilities of failure in themselves and others and therefore no longer assumed that one could go through life certain that everything would be all right. Continual examination and adjustment of the human machinery was essential, and premeditated abasement of the ego had to be the oil of wedlock.

For her part, Sheila was ashamed that she had let David down. The stupidity of her actions dismayed her. Endeavouring to explain them to herself, she was intelligent enough to come up with honest answers. Human nature needs challenge, is suspicious of an excess of comfort. Her life lacked challenge, the chance to prove itself. To steal (either scent or sexual experience or even the visions induced by marijuana) gave her the opportunity to demonstrate that she could still act independently. She understood, with some sense of shock, that she had perhaps unconsciously desired to be discovered in the department store, as she had also badly wanted David to see her dabbling with pot. It was her way of becoming conspicuous again. For too long she had been forced to direct all her energies into supporting her husband's life-climb, so that when, increasingly, he seemed to be flying free of her, she was left without purpose or importance.

She knew, however, that none of this justified the ridiculous melodrama she had forced David to take part in. Inevitably, he was humiliated by the involvement of Michael Grant in the court proceedings. To be caught shoplifting was a bungling way to signal her distress to David. She was, after the initial numbness, full of good resolutions about her life and theirs. She felt she owed him something even more acutely than he did her.

Their holiday, thus, was almost embarrassingly filled with giving. It overflowed with gestures of love and care which were made at first with exhausting premeditation and only after a few days flowed naturally, springing from the deep mutual affection that had been the basis of their mating in the years before. They never left each other, as if fearful that absence might cause further disintegration. They ate, walked, swam, sunbathed, read, kept silence, talked, and bedded together like honeymooners. Karen came too, to relieve them for a few hours each day of the chores of child-care, twitching her backside at the boys on the beach and going off to the disco most nights to tempt them again.

David found simple pleasure in building castles for Kenwyn, now approaching his second birthday, on the beach, or in rolling balls back and forth into the channel of the boy's outspread sand-covered legs. Sheila and he walked one day past Krazy Golf on the promenade at Armação de Pera. They watched fathers playing sons, knocking balls up concrete ramps and through tunnels and over sandy ditches, and he thought that the parents had everything on their side. If son beat father, then paternal pride in offspring's prowess could have its fling; if father beat son, then there was a subdued glow of pleasure that the old touch could still overcome the raw energy of youth. He couldn't wait for the day when he and Kenwyn could engage in such contests.

He explained his feeling to Sheila and she smiled, but there were many experiences they did not discuss. They learned again during the holiday that silence can be rewarding. Their lives back in England made too small an allowance for silence, which these days the developed nations feel impelled to fill with bristling hunks of noise. One evening they were alone in the villa Michael had lent them, reading.

'David,' said Sheila, 'I want to talk about it.'

'Talk about what?'

'Me. Supposing I'm found guilty. I must be, mustn't I?'

'Don't worry, girl. You'll get off. The solicitor thinks so. You'll plead not guilty.'

'But, David, I knew what I was doing.'

'You *think* you knew what you were doing. There's a difference.'

'Balls.'

'If they don't believe you, the defence will be good enough to have sentence suspended.'

'Okay.' She didn't want to worry him, but she had to talk. 'I'm sorry, David. I just felt so, you know, bloody small.'

'I know,' he said. 'It won't happen again. I've been away too much.'

'It's good on our own. We all need more of you. I'm better that way.'

He looked at his fingers as if he'd just discovered them. 'Me too. But you know how it is. I know what I'm doing.'

'What, love? What?'

'Money, sweetheart. I'm not staying in Prospero. Only till I've got enough in the bank to go it alone.'

'I don't know whether to believe it.'

'Why won't you?'

She was trembling a little. 'What will money give us? A bigger bloody car or something?'

'Independence,' he said. 'So's I can put two fingers up to whoever I want to. That's real freedom. Not frigging around screaming about democracy.'

'You should join the Monday Club. Or the John Birchers.' But she was joking, wanting to encourage him so that his words might reassure her.

'Sure,' he said. 'But it's true, isn't it? I work hard, I make money, I'm independent. Others may want to loon around, not have much, stay bound to someone or something – their union, their boss, their weekly allowance from father, even the dole. Fine, if that's their choice. But don't let them come on my back, then, that's all. You know what all those Hampstead trendies really mean when they're twittering about the greed and the cruelties of the capitalist? It's not his money or his instinct for acquisition then gets them – it's his independence. He doesn't have to wait in line for whatever it is they think at that moment it's right for him to have. I'm sick and bloody tired of listening to fat-bellied slobs telling me what's good for me. And all those sodding Oxbridge socialists who vote for comprehensives in the

House and quietly send their kids to private schools. They squeak in their tiny frustrated way about the wickedness of the bourgeoisie like nineteenth century curates telling us masturbation can turn the brain. They ought to go and see the pickets down at the docks roughing up the guys who don't agree with them. If that's the way it's moving, then I'm going to earn enough to build us a nice little castle where no one can touch us.'

It was, partly, the Portuguese brandy talking. But she didn't mind. All she said was: 'Okay – but don't stay too long with Prospero, then. Or away from me. Mean it, David.'

'As long as it takes,' he said.

'All right. As long as it takes.'

'Forty-five is the deadline, I hope. Forty if I can. Don't think I'm impressed by big organisations. I'm not. What guys earn has nothing to do with it. The more they earn, in a way, the more dependent they are. They'd be like heroin addicts deprived of their stuff if the money supply was turned off. Organisations for the young are all right. Teaches you size, teaches you about people, teaches you a sort of discipline. Once you've got it, who needs organisations? Use your talents and your discipline for yourself. Does that sound right?'

Sheila nodded. 'So?'

'So all we can do is keep trying. I'll be as good a lad as I can. Keep with me, love. I'll help. Whatever you want to do.'

'I'll help too. But don't make Prospero a life's work, love, please.'

'Okay,' he said.

But both of them knew that nothing would change dramatically, for human beings do not change in that way. They seek the pastures of their personal visions, resting sometimes on the lower slopes when they are forced to and sometimes when they are not, if they are either wise or kind. They compromise in order to exist, but they are rarely deflected; certainly not after the age of 30.

David and Sheila, flying back to London from Faro, could still not have enunciated, however, the most important aspect of their time together. It was simply that every crisis survived, as they had survived theirs, strengthens a relationship. The flabby body of sentiment and sex (or convenience) which starts a marriage, develops muscle only when it is strained, stretched and singed with the fires of doubt.

Michael Grant remarked on how well David looked when they met for the first time since his encounter with Corsino in New York.

'How did that go?' David asked.

Michael told him. David whistled.

'And now?'

Michael pushed the hair from his forehead and smiled a twisted, puzzled smile. 'God knows, David. About all that's certain is that Martin's back at Esmeraldas and working. The guerrillas seem less active at the plant. Construction's going pretty well.'

'Has Kerridge crawled into action yet?'

Michael threw a cablegram across the table. 'That's the sole answer I've had to five cables and twice as many telephone calls. The old man's disappeared from sight.'

The piece of paper simply said: QUIT WORRYING STOP OUR DEAL STANDS STOP KERRIDGE.

'But the Senator and his crusade?'

Again, Michael gave his know-little smile. 'Don't ask me to explain the mysteries of American politics. The story's dropped out of the papers. Seems it takes time to get a Washington investigation going. Frankly, we're not anxious to see Kerridge in real trouble. I just want that plant to get built now, without distractions.'

David was remembering what Michael had said ten minutes earlier; about pulling out of the whole deal if Corsino tried any more tricks. That, at least, was what he thought Michael had said.

'Corsino,' he said. 'What's Corsino doing?'

'You wouldn't believe it, David, but for the first time in his life he's running scared. He came to see me the day after the bust-up with Martin. Offered me a 35 per cent stake in his ultimate commission in exchange for a flat cash payment now of half a million U.S. dollars. I said okay, I'd think about it, provided he didn't get into Martin's hair and provided he did what he could with Ali-Chem, which would cool down Martin anyway. Martin's too bloody important to all of us now. We can't afford to have him do anything stupid.'

'Will Ali-Chem change that chlorine plant?'

'They're doing a feasibility study. A decision's promised by next month.'

'Sounds to me like a smokescreen,' said David. 'There's nothing we can do about it if they tell us to go take a running jump.'

'Nothing,' Michael agreed. 'All I'm trying to do is to keep Martin working in the belief we're doing all we can with Ali-Chem.'

'Which we are,' said David.

'Right. Maybe Martin will cool down. His kid's perfectly okay now. But I don't want him leaping off the job to tell the great American public how wicked Ali-Chem are. I agree with him, in fact. But it wouldn't do anybody any good except for a few columnists it'd make good copy for.'

David leaned back. 'So we wait?'

'We wait, David. The longer nothing happens, in a sense, the better. Just so long as the plant keeps getting built, fine. Earl's got lines out in Washington, so that we know if the U.S. government's going to squeeze Kerridge or Corsino.'

'What about our money? Are we still getting it?'

'Yes. Mark you, there's a snag to it.'

'What?'

'Everything in the garden's lovely for Cantania only so long as Vargas is kept happy. He's getting more ambitious. His warships are on station. Now he wants tanks and more helicopters.'

'Jesus,' said David. 'There are enough choppers in Ecuador for all the armies in South America. Hundreds of them. Working round the clock . . .'

'For the oil companies,' smiled Michael. 'Vargas wants his own. Big choppers. Full of artillery.'

'I suppose the ones we make are too small,' said David. Prospero had, for several years, controlled a company manufacturing helicopters used mainly for passenger and observation work.

'Luckily – or unluckily – yes. If they weren't, I imagine Vargas would be squeezing Cantania to get a few out of us for free. I'm glad I'm in no position to have to take that agonising decision.' He wiped his eyes with long strong fingers. To David, he looked very tired. 'The point I was making is that the more freedom Cantania has with pushing ahead on the plant, the stronger Vargas grows. Or should it be vice-versa? I lie awake nights wondering what happens if Vargas gets so strong he thinks he can chop off Cantania's head and get away with it. They sure as God hate each other.'

Michael yawned. David waited for the anecdote his boss obviously wanted to tell. 'It would be funny if it weren't so important. Years ago, some randy air force major who was a cousin of Cantania's seduced a girl who was a niece of Vargas. The major disappeared one night and everybody thought it was a political kidnapping. It wasn't. He came back minus his balls. A doctor in the Vargas clan had done the job. Vargas is supposed to have been among the kidnappers.'

David half-laughed, a brittle humourless sound.

'Yeah, I feel like that, too,' said Michael. 'But it still makes me insomniac.'

'I'll take my chastity belt next time,' said David.

'I don't want you to go to Quito again yet.' Michael smiled wearily. 'Just up to Staffordshire.'

'Thanks.' David chanced a sardonic tone, but Michael appeared not to notice.

'You shouldn't be away from Sheila again,' he said seriously. 'Not for a few months. Can you stand the strain of home cooking for a bit?'

It was his way of asking how Sheila was.

'She'll be okay,' said David.

'I gather the hearing's in a week's time. I'm sure we'll get her off.'

'Thanks for everything.'

'No, David. It's you I should thank. For Debrais, for Ecuador, for a lot of things. You've had a tough time. I'm grateful. Oh – and SAEF, well, SAEF are just dandy at the moment. We're going to need them before we're through with Kerridge and company.'

The rest of their talk was minutiae. Michael checked through a number of files before he got to one called Kroos and David heard, for the first time, about Sanger's plan to make a bid for that micro-electronics company. Prospero had, quietly, been buying shares. There seemed no particular hurry about a bid, since Brandford had now withdrawn their first offer and the market was quiet again.

'How is Earl?' asked David.

'Playing ball with me at present,' said Michael. 'Even said you hadn't done a bad job with Debrais.'

'Praise indeed,' said David.

'Too true.' Michael's eyes were yellow around the black-grey pupils. But they burned very brightly. He must believe he's winning, David thought.

Michael thought no such thing. But he'd come to the piece of news which, in its way, excited him most.

'I want you and Sheila to come to Brands Hatch on Sunday. The Lovelace car is running. The last serious race in Britain this year.'

'Will it win?'

'It bloody well might, David. George has done a fantastic job. It was the right thing to let Philip get on with the snowmobile engines. The production line's going great guns. It's given the old man a clear run to get on with the car. I drove it down at Goodwood – just slowly – and it was like a bird. But for God's sake don't tell my father.'

'Sure.'

'I've even persuaded him to come and watch on Sunday too. It should be quite a party. We've got Koringen signed for Le Mans.'

'That's good,' said David.

'He's a marvellous catch. It cost us plenty.'

They were at an end. David rose.

'By the way, what was it you wanted me to go to Staffordshire for?'

'Bill Oldershaw. What else? You got on okay with him in Ecuador. I want to know what you feel about him and the set-up right now. His costs have gone through the ceiling. Don't look alarmed, I guessed they would. But I'm more worried about his relations with the computer people. Too much of his stuff has been faulty. They've had to have a couple of shipments back – bad workmanship, bad measurements. And it's costing us a fortune flying out parts to keep up to our schedule. Bill says it's the fault of the computer people.'

'I'm no engineer,' said David. 'Why not send someone who is?'

'We've done that, David. Bill's right. The computer guys *have* made some cockups. Wrong programming, as usual. Rubbish in, rubbish out. But that end's sorted out, I'm assured. What we need now is to persuade Bill that we love him, that he's got to get this job through. He's grown so used to blaming Quant and company for what's gone wrong, he may think he can do it for ever. He's been in a sulk for months, arguing with everybody, screaming at his managers. Just try and cool him, David, and tell me what you think about the mood of the factory. One thing's for sure – if he doesn't stay in line during the next three months, we could lose every penny of profit making good our mistakes out at Esmeraldas.'

'I'll buy it,' said David. 'But I can't say I'm keen.'

'At least it's England,' said Michael.

2

Even Sanger came to Brands Hatch. He had no objection to seeing Michael Grant's toy in action. If it won, it would deflect Michael's interest further from some of the deals Sanger wanted to keep to himself. If it lost, he would smile and imply that he'd been right all along. Meanwhile, the motorcycle engine line was producing so well that he was flying to Chicago two days hence to finalise contracts with two manufacturers of snowmobiles in the States. The engines would go inside glass-fibre bodies, mounted on ski-runners, and drive these elegant playthings of the moderately affluent around the snow slopes in the coming winter. That was profit in hand; and Sanger understood profits today rather than the uncertain hazard of glory (maybe with profits) tomorrow, which was all that winning sports car races could mean.

Jesus, he'd been told it was noisy – but as noisy as this? Sanger tried to make small-talk with Alison as they stood in the paddock, buttoned up against a thin drizzle, watching George Lovelace flat on his back peering at the Special's suspension with the engine whining through the several-thousand revs barrier. He shouted, stuffed his fingers in his ears, and all she could do was smile and shrug. He looked at her swollen body under the heavy camel-hair coat. He was sure old man Grant wouldn't like it, her being there only a couple of week's away from being due.

Suddenly, the engine died and her voice came through. 'Looks good, doesn't it, Mr Sanger?'

How the hell did she expect him to know? Sanger peered through slightly-spotted spectacles; rain, like other natural phenomena, was sometimes a damned nuisance to Earl Sanger. The car looked okay, he supposed. Very sleek, with a vast central sweep of curved windscreen, a single king-size wiper set on it. An external rear-view mirror poked up from the windscreen area, set on the end of a tall pole like a submarine periscope. The steering-wheel looked very small beside the sizeable centrally-placed seat and the surrounding strap harness. Behind the driving compartment the line of the car dipped and then flattened into a long swooping tail which ended in twin fins. Perched atop the rear section was a narrow white aerofoil, angled and vivid against the darkish green of the body. He understood that this strip of metal was meant to keep the car pressed hard on to the road at high speeds.

'I think George has been looking at the Porsches to get those fins,' said David Travis, who had joined them.

Sanger nodded glumly. He didn't know much about that either, but he wasn't going to show his ignorance to Travis. He was thinking that the car might look nice, but he'd read that large-scale involvement in a racing season leading up to Le Mans could cost in the region of a quarter of a million pounds. He was going to ask for the precise Lovelace costs at the next board meeting.

David reached out and pulled Sheila gently by the hand. 'Alison,' he said, 'I think you've met Sheila before.'

He knew she had; but he always felt awkward talking to Alison on occasions such as these, although he hoped he didn't show it. They had a secret between them, he and Mrs Michael Grant, one which they mentioned only with their eyes. What did Alison think now about their night together and the awkward ending of their relationship, as if once they had experienced each other they quite liked the taste but couldn't be bothered to go through the awkward preparation of the recipe again?

'Hello, Sheila. Looks like you had a great holiday.' Alison seemed genuinely warm.

'Marvellous,' said Sheila. 'Thanks so much for thinking of us when you couldn't go.' David thought Sheila was good too; neither too flustered, nor too pushy, in what was a tricky situation for her. Alison must know about the court case. The boss's wife could so easily have made a wrong move, excessively solicitous or faintly cool. She erred in neither direction, although Sanger's look implied that he didn't know why senior executives' wives went round nicking – or being suspected of nicking – assorted artefacts from department stores. David had had none too easy a time at the office, either; he'd overheard a conversation in the men's room about young guys who get too big for their boots, then look what happens to their wives . . .

'England was better for both of us as it turned out,' said Alison. 'Did Kenwyn like it?'

God, David thought. She remembers the name too. Flattering. Maybe to himself.

The two women drifted away. Cars only held so much for them. Michael walked up. 'David, Earl – I'd like you to meet Lars Koringen, our driver.'

David knew that the Scandinavian driver, fifth in the Formula one rankings the previous year, was slim and blond. Neither characteristic was apparent in the man who now stood before them. He was short, scarcely up to David's shoulder, and his driving overalls hung loosely on him. He looked like the invisible man. Beneath an all-scarlet helmet, with clear plastic visor and protective chin guard, his whole face was swathed in a sort of crepe bandage. Only his sharply blue and humorous eyes showed. He was also like a walking billboard. Apart from his name and blood group (ORh+) embroidered on it, there must have been mention of a dozen products on his breast and upper arms, with Esso, Biostrath and STP among them. He peeled of his soft white gloves and put out a hand.

Sanger was blunt. 'Is the car any good, Mr Koringen?' They were paying the guy enough to be able to ask straight questions.

'Very fine,' said Koringen, muffled through his flame-proof bandages. 'She was sliding a bit on the tighter corners, Mr Sanger. But that was probably me. In practice yesterday the oil system wasn't perfect. That too is cured. I think she will do well. When I want power, oomph.' He flung out an arm expressively.

'The opposition's not as strong as we would have liked,'

said Michael. 'Only a couple of Porsches. One Ferrari. Several Lolas, but not the best drivers. I think Lars will win.'

The Scandinavian shuffled his shoulders in embarrassment. Behind him George Lovelace was beckoning. It was time for the car to be driven through the Brands tunnel to the pits. Koringen fiddled with his helmet. He had nothing more to say. A girl, all pelvis, in tight white trousers, with sunglasses shoved on top of her long blonde tresses, despite the rain, watched him go. Her eyes looked frightened.

'Who was that dame? Some goddam camp-follower?' asked Sanger as they stood drinking in the Grovewood Suite, which is the place for V.I.P.s at Brands. Beyond a panoramic glass window, they could see cars being wheeled on to the track. An engine came to life with a shattering explosion.

Michael laughed. 'Christ, no. His wife. Didn't you see her clipboard and stopwatches?'

'I thought these guys played around,' said Sanger.

Michael laughed. 'You've been watching those old movies again, Earl. They're more interested in money than sex nowadays. And in staying alive. They're workers. They've got their union like everyone else, and they use it to make race-tracks safer – more barriers, fewer hairy bends, better medical equipment. I don't blame them.'

'I like the banners, Michael.' Bernard Grant, who had kept his promise to come to the race and had watched the paddock preparations without comment, smiled out of the collar of an old-fashioned but, on him, highly dramatic fur-collared topcoat. It almost covered his ankles.

'I thought we might as well let people know we were involved,' said Michael. Away to the left, a succession of banners said: *LOVELACE, a Prospero Company*.

On the track, a green flag dropped, and the cars departed slowly in a wail of sound and a thin gauze of blue smoke. They were led by a Jensen saloon car, which would guide them on a gentle lap before releasing them at full throttle into a rolling start. One car remained, however. The driver had his hand raised. Three men ran to it and, finally, it left with a push start to the ironic cheers of the grandstand crowd.

'How many times do they go round?' asked Bernard.

'Fifty laps,' said Michael, who knew that Bernard could

251

use the correct terminology if he chose to. 'That's about 130 miles. Have some champagne, father?'

'Not now,' said Bernard, who had no need of the lift of alcohol when he was enjoying himself so much. He had let Michael enjoy his sport by not making a major issue of the Lovelace takeover. Now he intended to be a little awkward, a little unimpressed. That damn car didn't look any better than the rest. Could it really win?

Alison leaned towards him. 'Let me tell you as it happens, Bernard.' She knew what the old man was doing. The green in her eyes flashed and he knew that she knew. He still wanted to tease her.

'What did that Scandinavian fellow – Kor – what's his name – mean when he said the car might break, Alison?' He was only pretending to whisper, stage-acting. 'Does it really snap in two?'

'Not really, Bernard. More or less means anything that goes wrong. Oil system failure; a piece of the gearbox breaking; couplings going; the clutch coming apart; suspension adrift. Anything really. And crashes, of course. They do crash sometimes.'

She spoke the words creamily, but the edge of warning remained in her voice. She was authoritative about cars too. She had made herself so, even though her limit of interest in four-wheeled power-boxes was only a few degrees more extended than that of most women. Cars are for male Fangio fantasists, not for females, despite the way in which women tend to tag along with sports-car buffs. They follow that path because they know that automobiles can excite male hormones and flatter male egos, which can in turn mean that men become more pliable in the service of women. Alison had read somewhere of women in whom the sound of racing engines howling on straights could induce orgasms. This she would like to see proven medically since, in the end, she believed it nonsensical. Cars to her were mildly interesting. But, because they were one of Michael's passions, she had made herself fiercely interested, able to talk the language. It was part of what being a wife entailed.

She is good for Michael, Bernard thought, looking at her pink cheeks and flaming hair. A good daughter-in-law. He could not have done better. He might continue to irritate Michael privately this day, and others; that was part of the

252

game. But, he now decided, it was really not worth extending the sport to Alison. He needed her and her child.

'I understand. Thank you, my dear,' he said.

After seven laps, the Lovelace Special was fourth, perhaps three seconds behind the leading Porsche. Brands, full of twists and turns, wasn't the best of tracks for its high top speed to give it an edge. At Brands you need good gear performance and manoeuvrability rather than sheer speed. The wet surface was slowing the pace too. The cars banged past the pits in a ghostly spray.

'Looks like they're surfing,' said David to Michael.

'We took a chance on wet-weather tyres, like most of them,' said Michael. 'I hope to Christ it keeps on pouring.'

'How quickly would you need to change to dry-weather if it stopped?'

'It depends. I expect Koringen's wife would be shouting soon enough if we didn't.'

'Is it true a Ford racing engine costs almost ten grand?' asked Sanger, who flinched as he saw the Lovelace hurtle towards the sharp bent-pin corner which his programme said was called Paddock. He could literally see corporate profits going up in smoke if the car went out of control.

'About that,' said Michael. He gripped the seat in front of him as if it were a steering-wheel. His left foot tended to flick, change gear in time with Koringen, his right foot, though, pressed the wooden floor beneath him harder and sooner than the Lovelace driver was doing as he came out of the curves.

'He doesn't push it much, does he?' he whispered to David.

'It must be bloody difficult out there,' David said.

'Still,' said Michael grudgingly. 'He won't win if he doesn't shift when his extra power counts.'

Yes, he was critical. He still retained, from his own race-driving days ten years before, something of the last vestiges of the amateur tradition. They'd been a little less careful in those days, a little more rakehellish, a little more . . . perhaps the phrase should be *in love* with racing. There were drivers who took a good stiff glass or three of Scotch before they went out to race at Le Mans, young guys selling their London flats to buy the Bentley they wanted to race, the odd man at Lloyd's entering under a false name so his disapproving boss wouldn't know – that sort of thing. Modern drivers could be too like computers at times; too much concerned with side-benefits, too little in love with racing.

Down on the pit counter opposite he could see Koringen's wife, hunched and still over her clipboard. A nice girl, that; but alternating between screaming and staying unnaturally silent. She had dead eyes, too. Strange. Michael Grant could not see her eyes now, or else he would have noticed they were alive with fright. And she sat so still because she was, as always on these occasions, paralysed with apprehension. Her clothes were already soaked with sweat as well as rain. Four times she had been physically sick, vomiting up her fears, after Lars had won especially tight races. She believed he was driving only at nine-tenths, sometimes eight-tenths, these days because of her. Michael Grant had as yet no idea how badly she wanted Lars Koringen to live.

Eight-tenths proved to be good enough on the day. When the cars came round at the end of the twentieth lap, the Lovelace was in third position and a Lola was missing. *He's out at Hawthorn Bend, dropping a lot of oil,* said the bright announcer's voice.

At the start of the twenty-seventh lap the leading Porsche finished racing too. Michael almost saw it happen. He was watching Paddock Bend, where the stop lights of the cars burned bright red in the grey haze as they braked. The Porsche began its spin just as it began to go down the dip. Almost at once he saw stewards waving yellow flags. The car hit the earth bank. *The rear suspension's broken, I'm afraid,* said the announcer. *Very bad luck for Tony. He's okay. Walking back to the pits.*

With only four laps to go, the other Porsche went past the pits with its engine clattering ominously and a stream of black smoke from the exhaust. Next time around the Lovelace was in the lead, easily. The Porsche crawled into the pits. Not many minutes later the Lovelace had won.

At the small celebration party afterwards, Koringen looked pale. He was suitably modest. 'There was very little to beat,' he said quietly to Michael. 'But I am glad – glad for Lovelace. That car has promise.'

Shortly afterwards he left, his small blonde wife clinging

to his arm as if afraid he might disappear through a space in the floorboards.

Michael Grant was very pleasant to George Lovelace, ill at ease in an old-fashioned blue suit, with fluff-filled turnups on the trousers. 'Marvellous, George,' he kept saying. 'I knew we could do it.'

Privately, he had reservations about the car and about Koringen's lack, as yet, of commitment; the Scandinavian had acted like he was driving for the fee, nothing else. But what is a leader's duty other than to congratulate, motivate, spread a little happiness when victory is in hand? Michael played the part.

George Lovelace had reservations too. 'Aye, it's coming along. I'm glad you're pleased.' He knew he had to get more speed. Where dared he lighten the damn thing further?

Gingerly, he sipped the champagne he didn't much like. The victory settled one thing: Bill Oldershaw could go whistle for a few months on that idea of stirring up trouble with the Prospero board. George Lovelace wasn't going to stick his neck out now, not when things were going so well. The hell to that.

Bernard Grant overdid his role. He strode about the room being too nice, too lordly to everyone. He had always had this weakness for winning. He enjoyed it so much this day, he allowed himself to forget momentarily that Lovelace's had won at something he was supposed not to be interested in. He told himself he was only making up for being visibly, if mildly, offensive to Michael earlier in the afternoon. But in truth, he was excessively ebullient now because he had shown that his organisation could – even at motor-racing – once more be a winner. He felt, too, that if they had to beat anyone, it was very satisfactory to beat a motor-car made in Germany. Bernard could never forget the past.

Earl Sanger duly enjoyed the best of all possible worlds as he had anticipated, before the race started, he might.

'Great, huh?' he said to David Travis. 'It might even help me sell a few more engines in the States.'

'How many are you hoping for?' said David.

'Well, maybe ten thousand or so in the first year. That would be going some, though.' It was a deliberate under-estimate. Sanger would never be so unwise as to come back from any assignment having sold less than he had said he could sell. Where could the pay-off be in that?

'Good luck, Earl. It'll mean a lot if you can bring that off. When do you leave?'

'Tuesday.'

'Doing anything else while you're over there?'

'Nothing much.' And that, too, was a gross understatement. Sanger had one particular and burning idea of what he might do in America apart from selling snowmobile engines. David didn't press him further, however. He was too concerned in watching Sheila and Alison together. The girls had been talking all afternoon, so it seemed to him. He was afraid that they might start getting confidential. He drifted towards them.

'David felt the same about it,' Sheila was saying. He caught her eyes. They *looked* neutral enough. No sting to them.

'About what?' he asked.

'That film last week,' said Sheila.

'I think,' he said guardedly, 'it was overrated.' He wanted no arguments.

'Right,' said Alison. 'I couldn't believe in the relationship between the men at all.'

'What was the junkie chemist shop supposed to mean,' said David. 'It had no relevance to the plot. Just a chance for some fancy camera angles. Myself, I prefer Alistair Maclean movies. But early ones. *Guns of Navarone* or *Ice Station Zebra*, yes. *Puppet on a Chain*, no. Nasty, that one. Definitely nasty. All blood and no guts.'

Both women laughed. 'He's a simple soul,' said Sheila.

'Simple,' said Alison, 'he is not.'

They all laughed again, but David worried about that. There was too much knowingness in the words.

He need not have worried. Driving home, he picked up the subject of Alison with Sheila. His wife was warm about her, relaxed, unbitchy.

'I've never really talked with her before,' said Sheila quite simply. 'She's nice.'

'What did you talk about?' said David.

'Everything. But not you, if that's what you were hoping for.'

Sheila's easy smile and the pressure of her hand on his

256

knee removed any suspicion in David's mind of an ulterior motive behind the words.

'Could we ask them to dinner?' asked Sheila. 'I mean, would it look too pushy?'

'I expect we could,' he said. 'Let's see.'

Really, it hadn't been as bad an afternoon as he'd feared. And Sheila seemed to be climbing out of her depression.

That night they made love with a lack of premeditation which was, in retrospect for him, the best thing that had happened for them in many weeks. The next morning he telephoned Oldershaw at the Brasserton plant. Instead, he got Colley.

'I'm sorry, Mr Travis. Bill left for Ecuador on Saturday. Didn't you know?'

3

Prospero made its formal takeover bid for Kroos, the microelectronics people, two days after Earl Sanger left on his engine-selling trip to the States. He set everything up before flying out. Prospero had, that week, achieved more than a 10 per cent share of the company, which had been publicly announced, as was required in the code laid down by the City Takeover Panel. The bid followed immediately. The terms offered to the Kroos shareholders looked irresistible.

The first intimation of trouble came in a story not definite, but intriguing enough to make the front page of *The Sunday Times* rather than its Business News the weekend after the Brands Hatch race. The clue lay in a sentence which began: 'A private meeting of senior executives of Kroos was held yesterday at the home of the chief executive of the company . . .'

Michael rang David at 10.30 that Sunday morning. David was scarcely awake, dragging around in dressing gown, searching for coffee beans to grind and ineffectively trying to cope with Kenwyn, who was grasping at cups and plates in a kitchen cupboard. They'd been to dinner locally the night before and Sheila was still abed, recovering from champagne which they'd both sworn must have come from bottles costing less than £2, whatever the label said. David shouted to Karen to take over as he settled down at the telephone.

'What does it mean?' he asked after Michael had told him about the newspaper piece.

'I got a whisper about it on Friday,' said Michael. 'I think it means that Bird' – he dropped in the name of Kroos's chief executive – 'is organising a resistance movement.'

'If the shareholders want our bid to go through, what difference will that make?'

'My information is that every director and senior manager who matters was at Bird's house yesterday. If the whole bunch of them take against us, we may be sunk.'

'Why?' David's brain wasn't working too fast, and Michael's impatience showed a fraction when he answered.

'Come on, David. There have been other cases. Don't you remember that takeover last year when half the key executives threatened to quit because they didn't want to work for the people who were buying their company? The Monopolies Commission accepted the argument that a walk-out on that scale would risk serious damage to the firm's efficiency. So they vetoed the deal.'

There was an awkward silence. David felt compelled to fill it. 'But we've no guarantee that's happening.'

'I'm fairly certain so, and frankly, if that's how the Kroos people feel – I mean, genuinely, deep down – there wouldn't be much point in forcing the deal through anyway. We'd be better off without them. We're not so flush with good people ourselves we can afford to lose overnight the guys who really run that company.'

'Why don't they like us?'

'God knows. The usual stuff about not wanting to be in a giant organisation, being able to run their own business best. You know?' Michael sounded very tired. 'Maybe they're right. But they don't realise what we can do for them – capital, new outlets, giving them a chance to expand.'

'Supposing you're right, what do we do about the bid? The city columnists seemed to think it was right for the shareholders last week.'

'It's still no good if those managers won't work.'

David heard him suck in his breath, wearily. 'I blame myself. I shouldn't have let Earl push up into it.'

Even David didn't think that was especially fair, either

to Michael or to Sanger. 'He doesn't make mistakes, Michael. He gets the figures right. He did on Debrais.'

'That's the trouble. Figures. He bothers about them, not about the people. He said he'd made a sounding or two. I'll bet, when it comes down to it, he didn't. If we get egg on our faces, that'll be the reason.'

'He's still away, I suppose.'

'Yes – like Oldershaw. I've had no answer to my cables to Oldershaw.'

'Perhaps he's out in the jungle.'

'More likely he's ignoring them,' said Michael. 'If he cocks anything out there I'll really clobber him when he comes back. He shouldn't have gone without telling us.'

'Maybe,' said David, chancing his arm, 'he knows we would have tried to stop him going if he'd asked.'

To his surprise, Michael only laughed.

'You're right. And, if he's still supposed to be his own boss, how could we have stopped him? People. That's what's the trouble. Bloody people. Sometimes I wish I were running a grocer's shop.'

Michael's forebodings proved only too justified. Within two days a statement signed by twenty-seven of Kroos's senior executives was issued saying they were opposed to the Prospero takeover and would resign if the deal went through. That afternoon a swift meeting between Bernard and Michael Grant, Armfield, Bender and Morton agreed that they would see how the shareholders' acceptances went for a further seven days before deciding whether to continue with the bid.

In the event, seven days weren't needed. There was to be no conflict between the feeling of Kroos's executives and the people ranging from large institutions to elderly widows with holdings of a few hundred shares only, who owned the equity of the company. Acceptances of the bid ran at one-eighth the level which had pertained before the Kroos statement, and when the chairman of another insurance company who owned a 7 per cent stake in Kroos rang Bender at his Mondor Insurance offices to tip off an old friend that they would give the thumbs-down to the Prospero bid, the decision-makers at Prospect House agreed to forget the whole thing. They ignored a long Telex of dissent from Sanger, who had heard of the debacle too late, and Bender deliberately told his secretary to say he was away when she announced, late on Thursday afternoon, that the American was calling from Buffalo, New York. Instead of talking to Sanger, Bender went back to scratching the stubble of hair on his right temple and considering the words he would say to Michael Grant at ten o'clock the next morning.

It was a long time since Bender had been in Michael's office. His usual beat at Prospect House was between the boardroom and Sir Bernard's room. Michael sensed the meeting was special. Bender was pale and serious, a small heap of man in a slightly larger heap of clothing; but then, Michael reflected, when did Bender not look pale and serious? He would not have been pleased had he known what was in Bender's mind. The chairman of Mondor Insurance considered that the boy appeared distinctly strained. Michael pushed his hand too often at the fall of hair across his forehead; his fingers bent and unbent too many paper clips; and his eyes were strained, definitely strained, around the pupils.

'That was a disaster,' Bender said.

Michael replied uneasily. 'Not a disaster, Benjamin. Unfortunate, yes. But not serious.'

Bender seemed to grow smaller inside his tent of cloth as if tensing muscles for the big punch.

'I'm sorry, Michael. Symptomatic. It makes us both look foolish. The City thinks we have not done our homework, and that is bad for confidence. Makes us look like amateurs. If you don't know you can win, don't play.'

'It looked good.'

'To those who knew only half the story perhaps.'

'Earl recommended it. We were all agreed.'

'Mr Sanger, yes. He tries too hard.'

'Can anyone try too hard?'

'Yes,' said Bender curtly. 'If one's motives are wrong, trying too hard is dangerous.'

'What were his motives, Benjamin?'

'To prove again that he is faster, better, more ruthless, more profit-orientated than you. Knowing that, you need to test every proposition he makes the more carefully. You must control him, Michael.'

Michael smiled, despite the tension, perhaps because of it.

'You know Earl Sanger, Benjamin. How does one control him in some of his moods?'

Bender wasted no words. 'Then he must go.'

'But that's not possible, Benjamin. Whatever his faults, he's an important part of the organisation. In certain situations, he supplies some of the toughness I lack.'

'More ruthless than you, yes,' said Bender. 'Tougher, if you mean firmness of resolution when you know you are right, I doubt.'

'Let's not split hairs,' Michael said. 'I still don't think we can do without him. And we'd still have to persuade a majority of the board to agree with us.'

Bender pouffed, as if the control of a board ought also to be within the competence of any chief executive worth his salt.

He was not to be deflected now. He had already been through all the arguments. He turned the screw.

'If he stayed, then you could not. It's not that he has no virtue, simply that the contention between the pair of you is bad for the organisation. We may defer the decision, but barring unlikely miracles, it will remain to be made, month after month.'

Michael looked at the cool clear determined eyes of Lord Bender. They told it. Deep into his sixties, Lord Bender had no need of spectacles. It wasn't even that he scorned such weakness; he simply didn't require them. The body didn't matter, nor the slightly askew look of Bender's shoulders. The eyes were the man – decisive and uncompromising.

'I won't accept that now, Benjamin. But I'll consider what you've said.'

'I expect our price will slip,' said Bender mournfully. 'Investors don't like losers.'

'We'll get it back,' said Michael.

Bender rose to leave, duty done, willing to be sociable. 'How is your wife?'

'Well, Very well. Any day now,' said Michael.

'Remember me to her,' said Bender. 'I hope everything goes well. I'd like to be invited to the christening.'

'Of course,' Michael said. 'And thank you for what you've said. I value your advice, you know that, even if I can't always take it.'

Bender simply nodded. 'Don't forget,' he said. 'Him or you.' Then the small heap of clothes moved swiftly and silently through the door.

4

Oldershaw paused beside the Thames at the end of the long walk he'd given himself from his hotel in Bloomsbury and looked up at the shiny pinnacle of Prospect House, bouncing back the sunshine of a warm late September morning. Against the moving clouds it looked as if it was toppling towards him. That's the way he felt about the link of Brasserton's with Prospero now, without need of the natural illusion. He wondered if he'd ever get out from under.

The fact that he'd grown used, over the past six years, to coming to London didn't make him like the place more. It was full of pinnacles like these, exuding steely power over people in every corner of the country. He preferred dark Midland walls and corrugated iron roofs and the ability to make his own decisions. He wished he'd realised all that when old man Grant, smooth-talking and persuasive and full of promises, had made the pitch to him to take over Brasserton's in the early sixties. These days, he was agreeing in his mind, though rarely in words, with Colley; they should have tried to make it on their own. What he had just been through in Ecuador only made him more desperate.

'It's not bloody fair,' he told Michael within a few sentences of beginning their meeting. 'No one ever suggested we'd have to change our valve designs so much when this contract was fixed. We're having to buy more and more licences from the bloody Yanks.'

'You wanted the contract, Bill. Let's not waste our time arguing about whether that was right or not.'

Oldershaw might not have heard. 'I suppose it suits Martin's book. Working with designs he knows and people he knows. Americans stick together.'

'Can you do it, Bill? Never mind what's in the way. Can you get that contract completed?'

Michael only half-heard the next two minutes or so of Oldershaw's speech, which did not give him the direct answer he wanted. He was worried about Sanger. Where was he? Once he'd sent the cable that the Kroos deal was off, four days ago, he'd expected every morning to find Sanger bursting angrily into his office, fresh off an overnight jetliner from New York. Instead, silence. It was unnerving; and exhausting. Each day Michael had built himself up for the Sanger assault, then found only anti-climax when the American did not appear.

'Perez is more concerned saving his own neck than looking after our interests,' Oldershaw was saying. 'Keeps telling me that fewer people stick by their word now Vargas is on the scene. They're scared to be seen doing his uncle favours in case Vargas wins out. Slimy bastard.'

Michael was not certain how useful it would be to ask, but he still made the gesture. 'What's your view of the Cantania-Vargas thing, Bill? Our information is that it's less tense now Vargas has got what he wants.'

'Only *part* of what he wants,' said Oldershaw sourly. 'He's greedy. I wish we'd never gone into that damn country.'

'For God's sake stop that kind of talk.' Michael was close to shouting. He knew it would do no good. He was almost ashamed, yet could not stop the words. 'We're there. And we can't change it. *Now* – straight answers, Bill. Can you do it?'

Oldershaw looked at him very evenly and put his square-ended fingers deliberately on the table. 'I'll finish that bloody job on time if I have to kill everybody at Brasserton's with overtime to do it. But then . . .'

'But then, what?' said Michael.

Oldershaw hesitated, a man who'd suddenly seen he must slam on the brakes. 'Nothing. Then I'll take a holiday.'

There was silence. A helicopter clattered outside, tracking the river. At last, Oldershaw said, 'I hear David Travis was up while I was away.'

'He expected to find you,' said Michael.

'What else did he find?'

'A lot of men wondering where their boss had gone – and why.'

'I'm within my rights,' said Oldershaw.

'Yes,' said Michael. 'Provided you don't forget you're also accountable for your actions.'

Oldershaw nearly went over the edge at that moment. But he wasn't ready yet. Ecuador had frightened him. He hoped Colley could solve some of the problems on the valves he'd brought back in his suitcase. He swallowed, tightened lips over teeth, and went on with his report about the work at Esmeraldas. But the anger in his eyes could not be switched off as easily as words.

Sanger, when he entered Michael's office at much the same hour three days later, was not angry. He had the cocky look of a man who knew he was no loser. He listened with scarcely a word to Michael's recitation of the Kroos debacle. Finally, he shrugged.

'If we're on the look-out for take-over opportunities as often as we are, we're bound to have some failures.'

'It's rather more important than that, Earl. We were made to look like fools.'

Again, Sanger shrugged. Michael wondered whether the American was really so cool, or simply disorientated after stepping straight off the plane. Either way, Sanger was not usually so icy if he was truly worried.

'So I set up the deal, sure. Then it hits snags. That's life. If the board hasn't the guts to fight it through, how come you crap on me from a great height?'

'People, Earl. You didn't check on the people.'

'The hell with people.' Sanger was scornful and becoming more steamed up, true to type. 'With the real estate value of some of that property Kroos are sittin' on, who cares about the people? If they don't want to work for us, they can go some place else. It's a free country. We could still have come well out of that deal.'

'Doubtful – and you know it,' said Michael. 'Anyway, what would people think of us if we rode roughshod over the opinion of every damn executive in that place? Organisations like ours have problems enough without getting public opinion up in arms.'

Sanger didn't lose an ounce of his scorn. 'We're so goddamn worried about our image these days, business'll stop altogether soon. Why should we let Commie politicians call the tune? The deal was right for us, and for the people at Kroos, if only the guys who run the place didn't have their heads in the sand.'

'Okay,' said Michael. 'It's not worth spending our time arguing. Perhaps you'd better tell it all to Benjamin.'

'What's that supposed to mean?'

'He wasn't best pleased.'

'I suppose your father wasn't either?'

'Leave him out of this, Earl. I'm more concerned about Lord Bender. I wouldn't say his view of your future in Prospero was exactly encouraging.'

Sanger leaned back and laughed. 'Look, Mike, I don't give a damn if no one wants to hear what I've brought back from America.'

'It'll take more than a few thousand motorbike engines sold to change Benjamin's mind,' said Michael.

Sanger didn't seem to be thrown by the crack. He was in a good humour, and he even kept his hands away from plucking at the thin gold buckle of his belt. 'I got 25,000, if you're interested. That's getting on for two million dollars-worth of business, baby.'

'I'm impressed, Earl. But I wouldn't count on it impressing our major shareholder.'

'On that, I pass, Mike. That's only my flush. Wait till you see my full house.'

'Yes?'

'Aces on Kings.'

'Surprise me.'

'Okay. I've been to see Ali-Chem.'

'Big deal. I suppose they're going to change that chlorine plant.'

'Nope,' said Sanger. 'But they might.'

'Why?'

'They're our chums,' said Sanger, using again the quaint English idiom he'd picked up and delighted in displaying. 'And I made them so. And don't forget it.'

'Tell me, Earl. I'm tired of games.'

'Okay, Mike. Straight.' Sanger wanted some drama now. From a thin black leather briefcase he drew out a coloured brochure. He slid it across to Michael.

'Snowmobiles. Good design, huh? What makes 'em? Two things, basically. An engine and a body. We make the engines. Who makes the bodies? People who make glass-fibre, Mike. Ali-Chem makes glass-fibre.' He leaned back, enjoying every moment. 'They were really friendly when I put the business their way.'

'How did you do it?'

'Not difficult. D'you remember that movie, *Sweet Smell of Success*, where Tony Curtis sees the proofs of next day's column by the big showbiz writer – that was, uh, Burt Lancaster – and then cons a guy he knows has got a good mention that he can fix it so's the guy makes the column?'

Hell, Michael thought, he's never talked this way before.

'Great movie, that,' said Sanger. 'Well, first I already *knew* that an Ali Chem subsidiary had made a bid for the work, which wasn't surprising. It's a natural kind of business for any glass-fibre company to pitch for. But I knew for certain because I saw a confidential report the snowmobile guys had.'

'How?'

Sanger grinned. 'They didn't know I was interested in Ali-Chem. And guys talk. Especially after a few martinis.'

Michael didn't comment, just waved a hand for Sanger to continue.

'So I went to Ali-Chem, told them I had a chance of putting several million dollarsworth of business their way. No one refuses to talk to you when you put that kind of proposition to them. Then I went back to the snowmobile guys. There was still a snag. The Ali-Chem price wasn't the lowest.'

Michael had stopped being half doubting, or even sardonic. He nodded and Sanger went on.

'I said we'd knock two per cent off our unit cost if the glass-fibre making was put Ali-Chem's way.'

'Was that wise?'

'Sure. We can still make a profit. I'd marked up around 30 per cent anyway. We're in the clear. Even if we aren't, I figured some leverage on Ali-Chem was worth buying. I also got to act as broker for them in England over some special licences they want. I'm owed a favour or two.'

'I don't suppose you've any guarantees that Ali-Chem will keep *their* side of the bargain,' said Michael. 'Now they've got their contract, how do we know they won't just laugh if we ask for favours?'

'That's a matter of my judgment,' said Sanger coolly, and he looked so confident that Michael could not believe other than that there was further knowledge inside the chunky crew-cut head opposite.

'Good,' said Michael. 'I accept that. You've done a bloody marvellous job.'

'Right on,' said Sanger, only now snatching off his spec-

266

tacles to polish them. 'Do you think Lord Bender will fix it for you and the board to fire me now?'

Michael couldn't help grinning, just for a moment. Sanger was a bastard, mean and gritty, but by God he was a competitor. Sanger never complained if the fighting drove him to the edge. He'd always bounce back, sweating, and pull something. A survivor, Sanger, a man to keep the muscles of those around him in tone. Prospero would not be able to stand him for ever, but Sanger wouldn't be leaving yet.

'Yes, Earl,' he said. 'You stay the right side of the law – our law, I mean – and I don't think Benjamin will put the knife in this time. But next time – who knows?'

9. ALL THE GOOD LOSERS

1

THE men whose skill it is to sniff out incipient business failure – newspaper reporters, investment advisers, debt collectors – twitched their sensitive noses only gently at first. The figures in the stock prices columns hinted, yet did not reveal; there were but a few lines of comment in one or two newspapers.

Michael Grant had particular cause to remember how it began. Alison was almost two weeks overdue before she gave birth to their son, Peter Robert Nathan, in mid-October. He had been too concerned about her health to worry with more than eight-tenths of his brain about Prospero; and anyway, the organisation had had a relatively trouble-free period following Sanger's return from the U.S.A. There was no major alarums from Ecuador, from France, from Bill Oldershaw, from any of the several score of companies for which, ultimately, he was responsible. Even Lord Bender, apparently mollified by Sanger's American successes, had remained quiescent.

Bernard Grant reacted to the birth of a grandson predictably. It was he who, a fortnight after the event, staged a cocktail party for the Prospero board, their wives, and certain selected senior executives to celebrate his good fortune, since this was how he viewed the arrival of Peter Robert Nathan Grant. He gave the party at his house, which was only fair, since both his son and daughter-in-law would willingly have done without the palaver.

The twenty-seventh bottle of champagne had been opened, small talk was wearing thin, and the late-October mists of that Friday eveing had long since enshrouded the Georgian frontage of Bernard's house in Kensington when Lionel Westbrook, the marketing director of Prospero, found himself alone with Michael in a corner of Bernard's library. He leaned with his elbow hard against a first edition of Samuel Butler's *Erewhon*.

'Great party, Michael,' said Westbrook. 'Bernard does these things beautifully. I'm so glad for you and Alison.'

'Thanks,' said Michael. 'I must get her home soon. It's taken a lot out of her.'

Westbrook didn't take the hint. Instead, he leaned forward with that leaden air of confidentiality which the moderately inebriated affect. His elbow slid off the bookshelf and a few spots of champagne hit the carpet but, fortunately, not *Erewhon*.

'Didju see the *New York Times* today?'

'No,' said Michael.

'Have a copy sent over in the afternoon, every day. Friends of mine.' Westbrook tapped his nose. There was sweat on his face and the wide pink tie he wore with a grey, chalk-stripe suit was loosely askew.

Michael was not particularly impressed, but his mind recoiled from having to judge the man before him. He felt responsible in part for the way in which Lionel Westbrook had lost direction in the past year. Had he been unfair, using Westbrook's skills and loyalty, and then, by refusing to satisfy Westbrook's expectations of high office, causing one of the organisation's intelligent executives to give up trying?

Perhaps Westbrook's disintegration was proof that Michael had been right to doubt his judgment and stability. But the sense of lack of loyalty, of culpable responsibility for Westbrook's condition still clung to Michael's mind like a cobweb, influencing nothing, but unsettling to the touch.

For a moment only, therefore, did Michael allow himself the rather spiteful luxury of silently criticising Westbrook. Who but Westbrook would find the time, or the inclination, to dip into the *New York Times* daily? Weren't *The Times*, *The Financial Times* and the British heavyweights enough?

'Kerridge Steel aren't doing so well,' said Westbrook. 'Down eight dollars yesterday. Five the day before. The *New York Times* says it's due to cash-flow problems.'

'Dow-Jones has been sliding this past fortnight,' said Michael. 'I don't expect Kerridge is any different from the rest.'

Westbrook looked exaggeratedly crestfallen. 'I'm still going to make a few inquiries on Monday.'

'Thanks, Lionel. I'd be grateful.'

'I'll bet you something's up, Michael.' Westbrook sounded desperate to be proved right.

'Yes – well, look, I must see what's happening to Alison.'

As he went to find her, he made a mental note to ask some questions himself – before Monday, though he was certain that Sanger would have been in to see him before now if Kerridge Steel were afflicted by anything other than the general Wall Street blues. Nothing serious, so the financial editors said: just a technical downturn following an exaggerated boom during the summer.

Bernard was already helping Alison with her topcoat. Michael had rarely seen his father look so happy. The old man touched Alison's arm with the gentleness of a connoisseur handling an eggshell teacup. Michael did not want to intrude on Bernard's moment. He turned and saw Sanger.

'Earl,' he whispered. 'Lionel says Kerridge Steel is having a rough time on Wall Street.'

'Yeah?' Sanger sounded surprised. 'How rough?'

'Down thirteen dollars in two days.'

Sanger shrugged. 'That guy cries wolf too easy. But I'll check if you like.'

'Don't bother, Monday will do.'

They said no more. Michael moved again towards his father and Alison. Bernard was saying 'I'm so very happy for you, my dear. Do come and have lunch, both of you, soon.' Then, very confidentially, 'What you have done for me you will never fully know.' As Michael and Alison left the house, Bernard was blowing his nose with untypical force. Michael smiled wryly, remembering when Bernard had told him he was growing sentimental.

That weekend, Michael could not raise any of his friends in New York City. On Monday, at 4 in the afternoon, he received a cable. Kerridge Steel had opened that morning 10 dollars below the Friday price. Half an hour later Sanger came in looking grim.

'Dammit,' he said. 'Who woulda thought Lionel would put his finger on it? Kerridge is in trouble, Mike. Big trouble.'

When *Fortune* and the *Wall Street Journal* and the *Financial Times* came to write their analyses of the Kerridge affair later, it must have seemed to the reader not at all difficult to understand what had gone wrong with the corporation.

First, there was the trouble with Crewe's, the sub-contractor to whom Kerridge Steel had entrusted the job of building the towers and vessels for the Ecuador plant. It had been an unwise choice. That year, Crewe's produced a thumping loss. It turned out to be a badly damaged company, slow on the research and development side, doing only an indifferent job with the steel pumped out by Kerridge mills. Kerridge Steel had been forced to revive Crewe's with infusions of money in order to keep the work going.

Second, Kerridge Steel itself was not nearly as strong a corporation as its balance sheet had, a year or two back, suggested. The figures had looked good, the financial pundits declared, with adequate profits, increasing turnover, and full order books both for the organisation's steel mills and the several other companies which the conglomerate ruled.

Closer examination showed that the good position was partly based on stocks of finished material held by Kerridge Steel (which might or might not be sold) and on work in progress, for which cash had not yet been paid by customers. The stocks turned out to be over-valued; and too much of the work in progress was linked to fixed-price contracts, and inflation was slowly eating away at the profit built into these until it disappeared altogether. What was worse, Kerridge Steel was committed to massive development expenditure on new technical projects – all of which sums were recorded in the balance sheet as assets instead of being written off. Too many of these research projects had been abortive and, therefore, valueless.

All of this might betoken an inefficient business organisation, and to some extent this was true. But the situation has happened before with large organisations – especially those headed by men who once started in a small specialised way and, as growth occurred and they grew old, lost the personal grip they once held and were forced to delegate their powers to others who cared less. Kerridge Steel were not notably inefficient. It simply had bad luck.

There was something else, too; something crucial. The frailties of an organisation are often disguised when it is very active in its dealings. If money and shares are being moved around all the time, if takeovers and other deals are being made, then the corporation tends to be thought of as

271

thrusting, go-ahead, profitable. It is, as it were, an act of financial legerdemain.

When the Kerridge deal to take over Talsey, a smaller rival steel company, was questioned by a troublesome Senator, a brake was put on the corporation's dealings. No one seemed anxious any more to do business with Kerridge Steel until the various sneaky questions which were being put were resolved. These included not only the size of Kerridge's donation to the funds of the Republican Party, but also the structure and costs of the consortium deal they had in Ecuador – Kerridge's largest overseas contract.

Business confidence in the Kerridge operation waned from that day. Investment analysis looked more closely at their position. Such a freeze, such questions, such evaporation of confidence can be fatal to an organisation which depends on continual movement.

As usual, even the deepest analysis in newspapers and magazines did not reveal every fact. No one explained, for instance, that the choice of Crewe's as the largest subcontractor to Kerridge Steel had resulted from nothing more complicated than Corsino's greed. The commission – or, not to put too fine a point on it, bribe – he had been promised by Crewe's was larger than that suggested by any other competitor for the contract. A goodly share of that loot now rested in a numbered account in a Panamanian bank.

All of this, however, lay in the future. On that late-October Monday afternoon when Michael Grant learned that Kerridge Steel stock was falling fast on Wall Street, and Earl Sanger arrived with his own version of the bad news, both men were still scrambling after the truth.

Michael's first reaction – and in time to come he would learn from this, even smile to himself about it – was to turn to his father. To his surprise, Sanger did not demur. Before they walked towards Bernard's room, however, Sanger laid the most important information he had on the line.

'Too many companies have gotten impatient about the time Kerridge Steel is taking to pay its bills. Now they're getting nasty. Pushing, asking questions, talking around Wall Street. One bank Kerridge's use won't pay out on their cheques. They'll be forced to make a public statement.'

'I'll have to get over there,' said Michael.

'*We'll* have to go,' said Sanger meaningfully.

'Yes – all right,' said Michael. He wasn't sure whether he'd take Sanger. But at this moment he needed the American badly. 'Earl make a snap judgment for me. The consortium as a whole must be responsible for the completion of the contract, mustn't they?'

'Top of the head, Mike, I'd say that because Kerridge Steel is the leader, and Corsino set up everything through them, *they'd* be held responsible in the first instance rather than the whole consortium. But that's pure guesswork. Ask the goddamn lawyers.'

'Whose lawyers, though?' said Michael. 'Ours? Kerridge's? Or the Ecuador Government's?' He was deliberately pessimistic. 'If Cantania's got any sense, he'll make sure his people say we're responsible as well as Kerridge. What good can it do them if they hammer Kerridge alone? Assuming Kerridge is short of money, it'll be a waste of time.'

'I'd still like to hear what the lawyers say,' said Sanger.

'Okay, that's fair enough – but we can damn near work it out ourselves.' Michael couldn't keep the edge of impatience from his voice. 'One way or another they'll get us. First, the petro-chemical company will claim the contract has got to be completed by the consortium and it's not their responsibility now. We signed the goddamn thing.'

'And so did SAEF.' Sanger couldn't help smiling nervously. Someone else was in trouble as well as Prospero.

'We'll deal with SAEF later,' said Michael. 'My point now is that the Ecuadoreans are going to involve us *all* in this. They'll insist that every member of the consortium – Kerridge, SAEF, ourselves – is responsible for the completion of the contract. Suppose we tried to say it wasn't on. They'd simply enforce the penalty clauses in the contract for non-completion on time and we'd have to pay up that way. For Christ's sake, Earl, that plant's over halfway built now anyway. They'd just hold on to it – and all our stocks of equipment there – and refuse to pay out any more money. Our losses would be huge and our international reputation would probably go down the drain into the bargain.'

'Maybe we could find some other corporation Stateside to take over the Kerridge commitments,' said Sanger.

'At this late stage, I doubt it,' said Michael. 'The whole

structure's too complicated, too interdependent, I'd guess. To replace Kerridge's miles of steel with someone else's, to make new arrangements with sub-contractors — Christ, it would be a nightmare. It would hold things up so long, I expect the Ecuador people could slap in penalty clauses against the whole lot of us.'

They paused, the pair of them, eyeing each other without hope, their rivalry forgotten in an alliance of distress.

'You know what you're saying, Mike?'

'Yes, Earl. I know what I'm saying.'

Bernard Grant knew what his son was saying too. When he'd finished listening and asked some questions, he said, 'If things turn out to be as bad as they might be, you believe we daren't let Kerridge Steel go bust?'

'Yes, father.'

'I agree with you.'

Bernard was surprisingly subdued. Michael expected him to huff and puff. Instead, he just sat there with his fine lips drawn tightly together, occasionally pouting them rather like a sulky child, fingers playing gently with the strings of the small Hepworth bronze on his desk. The figure had often, Michael suddenly realised, been his father's substitute for worry beads.

'That could be extremely expensive,' said Bernard quietly.

'We'll have to find a way that isn't,' said Michael, though not with conviction.

'You're both responsible,' said Bernard. His son could not expect to be excused, but he wanted to spread the blame to Sanger, instinctively feeling that such an action might in some way absolve Michael from the worst of the trouble.

For once, Sanger's eyes were glazed with defeat. His jaw hung slackly, like a fighter who didn't want to finish the round. He had, without difficulty, sidestepped any blame for the shakier details of the contract. But he could not expect now to avoid being hanged with responsibility for the original notion of involving Kerridge Steel with the Prospero Group. It was he who had sought out (or, as he now knew, been encouraged to seek out) the aged American, he who had made the recommendations to the board, returning across the Atlantic brandishing Kerridge's name like a flag of victory.

His voice was hushed, suspiciously cracked. 'Like Mike says, Sir Bernard, we'll work something out.'

Bernard pressed a button on his desk. 'Ask Mr Armfield to join us now if he's free.'

Michael flashed a challenging glance at his father, but Bernard simply said, 'You need him, Michael. We all need him.'

'I think SAEF will help if it comes to money,' said Michael.

'I should hope so,' said Bernard as if he'd already punched a few millions from them into the equation he was formulating. 'They stand to lose almost as much as we do. We will still have to find many millions, I don't doubt.'

'All of this assumes Kerridge Steel is really screwed up,' said Sanger, snatching at any hope there might be.

'I think,' said Bernard, 'we must view the future in the worst possible light, Earl. That way we shall be forearmed. Agreed Michael?'

'I'd like to hear what Harold says, father. But let's assume the worst – yes, that's sensible.'

Harold Armfield, arriving in haste, peering at the world through goldfish-bowl glasses as if he continually expected it to invade the privacy of his mental balance sheet, could say nothing from which Michael might take definite comfort. But he helped. He was rational, cool, quiet; and Michael's admiration for him grew by degrees in the next half-hour.

Armfield might have spiced his words more liberally with prejudice had Sanger not been present for, in truth, he did not particularly enjoy doing business with foreign companies. He still remembered with distaste his first business trip to New York.

It was the banks that horrified him. He had been used to gloom and grilles and dark brown counters in Britain; to conducting respectful conversations, almost as a beggar, in private rooms. He felt ill at ease in the American banks where squads of crewcut young men and full-skirted women sat at desks behind long open glassless counters in long open halls. There was hardly a private room in sight. There were displays of flowers in the banks, who promoted dog shows and ice skating exhibitions to pull in customers, and poured out trashy canned music to ease the pain of cash transactions.

Ice skating! It wounded him. And the lack of privacy inside the banks was even worse. Was it not blasphemy to be speaking of money so openly in those vast temples of pleasure? The eagerness of the executives to help him lay hands on the banks' money seemed indecent to his surburban London mind.

He'd recovered from the shock, of course; learned to live with it, as everyone learns to live somehow with change, even if loss of dignity is involved. But he'd never accepted the correctness of the new order. That an American company had let them down now did not surprise him.

'First,' he said, 'we have assets to sell. But we don't wish to do that. Agreed?'

Everyone nodded, knowing they would have to endure a preliminary warm-up in any Armfield lecture. He was, by his own standards, brisk about it, however. Finally he said, 'If we go to the Ecuadorean petro-chemical company and ask for money, I assume they'll say no. Or they may say – and it's the Ecuadorean Government who'll have the last word – that if they provide money, they must be given a guarantee of some kind.'

'By the banks?' said Bernard.

'By the banks, Bernard,' Armfield confirmed. 'They'll want commercial banks to guarantee them their money if the deal goes wrong. And a bit more besides, I fancy. In that case the banks in turn would want a guarantee from the consortium members. A guarantee based on our assets.'

'Risky,' said Bernard.

'There's something else,' said Armfield. 'I'm not sure the Bank of England would be happy about that arrangement. They certainly wouldn't want sterling to be turned into Ecuadorean currency if things went wrong and the guarantee was called in.'

They all sucked on that for a moment or two, like a bitter lozenge that might help a cough but could not cure it.

Then Armfield went on, shuffling the pack of possibilities. Bernard mentioned his Government and Whitehall contacts who might be persuaded to intervene discreetly if the Bank of England proved difficult. Sanger, recovering slowly from his initial shock, emphasised his friendship with Ali-Chem. He reminded them that Ali-Chem theoretically owned a chunk of the Ecuador petro-chemical company they would be negotiating with, and Kerridge himself a further 15 per cent. All of them knew, however, that decisions would stem from the government in Quito alone, so Michael set rather bigger store by the verbal assurances he had received from SAEF, after David Travis's timely visit to Paris, of the utmost co-operation in future between the French company and Prospero.

'I wonder if co-operation equals a few hundred million francs,' Bernard observed with a sardonic smile.

'They are very friendly,' said Michael; and only he of the four men present knew why. Would he ever, if it came to it, use the power of blackmail David had given him over Armand Broussard?

And so they all spoke and agreed or disagreed and kept some secrets, and when they were exhausted with speech and the burden of risks that any feasible way ahead would entail, all that they had left was a list of alternatives. It was too early for decisions.

'The next move is obvious,' said Bernard. 'America. To see Kerridge.'

'My girl's already booking the tickets,' said Michael.

'No,' said Bernard.

'What do you mean, father?'

'Not for you, Michael. For me.'

Sanger was bursting to speak. But he left it to Michael. 'Father, you haven't met Kerridge.'

'Nor, I understand, have you. Only Mr Sanger has.'

'But still . . .' said Michael. He wanted to mention the word *coronary*, but somehow dared not.

'There are some things which only a chairman can do,' said Bernard. 'This is one of them. Your place, Michael, is in Paris or Quito. And your duty, Earl, is to tell me every relevant factor about your friends at Ali Chem. I'll need to see them too.'

'Look, father, I know what you're saying, and I appreciate it . . .'

Bernard Grant suddenly rose. He looked taller than his six-foot plus, his eyebrows bristling, and decision – but not anger – hardening his eyes. 'Let's agree it, Michael, without any silly business of board meetings. This I have to do and you, I know, understand that. Kerridge is mine.'

He walked to the window and looked out on the misty

evening that was already suffocating the river below. 'Kerridge and I are of an age, more or less,' he said. 'Perhaps we'll even talk the same language!'

2

By the time they removed the bandage from Martin's eyes, his irritation was already vying with his sympathy for the people who had tied it.

He was tired of this kind of play-acting. Why couldn't these overgrown kids recognise a friend when they found one? And didn't they realise that he was taking a risk as big as their own by flying down to Cuenca for the meeting?

He was certain he hadn't been followed. The company plane from Esmeraldas to Quito was secure enough. But then he'd had to switch to the scheduled SAETA service, flying south by Viscount just after dawn, low over patchwork fields and brown-striped sierra and, finally, the rolling green hills that encircled Cuenca.

The airport police, he thought, had looked him over too long and too closely. Still, after all these months, they searched every passenger thoroughly for arms.

Martin was being irrational. Sensibly, he could not expect guerrillas to accept him and his liberal sympathies at face value. He had let it discreetly be known that he wanted a meeting with them. He hinted at information in his possession. Now, as he should have anticipated, the guerrillas would test him. With the blindfold off, the room was too dark to see more than shadowy figures at the far end of it.

Martin could not, however, be expected to behave rationally. During the flight he'd begun to doubt the balance of his own mind. The stewardesses on the plane were the prettiest and the most civil he'd ever seen, darting about like friendly tropical birds in their light and dark uniforms, flashing their plump thighs as they pressed stewed apples and meats and salad and cakes and endless cups of coffee on him. All for a 45-minute flight, too. Jeez, they'd even offered him a cigarette – and lit it. They seemed happy enough, and so did the passengers, twittering over their parcels and their kids. What in God's name was he getting mixed up in the politics of this place for?

Even on the ground, the people looked untroubled. They were poor; but they smiled a lot. And they ran around the market, amid the plenty of fruits and meats and seeds, as if they knew what they wanted to do and were glad to be doing it. He'd stood on his hotel balcony, looking down on the market crowd – a mass of panama hats and the brilliantly coloured shawls and skirts which all Indian women wore – and thought he'd never seen anything more right, more natural, more purposeful. Up at the tyre factory, a visit to which had been part of the cover for his journey from Esmeraldas, one of the managers said, 'I don't know whether to thank God for the oil or not. It will ravage this country.'

In the end, though, the man had smiled. 'I expect you know, Mr Martin, that this city used to be world's largest producer of panama hats. When the world decided it no longer wanted them, what could we do but make tyres? I am glad you're buying them. It is not easy for us. One-third of the tyres in Ecuador are, probably, contraband – from Colombia. Three-quarters of the city buses here, we know, run on contraband tyres. And what can we do about it? All the smugglers need to do is to persuade the customs officials at the border not to put their seal and signature on the import permits. Then each permit can be used ten, twenty, thirty times.'

The manager shrugged. 'So, I suppose the oil is good. Perhaps this time it will be fairly shared. It is another chance. But I fear Cuenca will be ruined. It will grow to 300,000 people by the year 2000.'

Cuenca, with domes and shady squares and churches and the sweetest smell of any city he had known, was to Martin perfect. A jewel. Watching and listening during the morning, thinking as he napped in the afternoon, Martin grew ever more confused about the needs of the city, the country and, above all, his own decision to intervene in the way these might be decided. When, after dusk, a car called for him and the pantomime of the blindfold and the long lurching drive began, his anger sprang more from frustration with himself than from tenable objections to the guerrillas' methods.

'We are glad to see you, Mr Martin.' The voice spoke perfect English.

Martin said, 'Where the hell am I?'

'You must know we cannot tell you,' said the voice.

'Okay, if that's the way it is. But it's not exactly easy for me to be here either.'

'We appreciate that, Mr Martin. And we are grateful. Please sit down.'

Martin saw the chair. He groped for it, lowering his aching body, and peered across the room. There were three of them. Now he could see, from the glowing embers of the fire, that they wore hoods and nylon stockings beneath them, covering their whole faces.

'I don't want to stay long,' he said.

'We have heard good things about you, Mr Martin,' said the central figure of the three.

'Yeah, well okay. Here's what *I* have to say. You blow up things at my plant, right? It's not getting you anywhere. We're pushing ahead. Nuisance value, sure. But it don't change things. I'm not here to tell you what I think about all that. None of my business. But there's something you ought to know. Down on the coast, south of my plant, another site's being prepared. That's the goddam stinking thing you ought to be bombing.'

He told them everything he knew about the chlorine plant that Ali-Chem would operate.

'If we agree with you . . .' said the only guerrilla who had spoken so far.

'You've gotta go along with me,' snapped Martin, acting as if it had scarcely occurred to him that he might be in danger. 'It's your country that plant is going to foul up.'

'Your point is taken,' said the voice. 'And we are grateful. What more could you let us know?'

'You tell me how, and I'll find a way to let you know every move they're gonna make?'

'Why, Mr Martin, why?'

He told them that people who did that sort of thing were animals. Excreting. He told them he'd done a dozen jobs around the world, not asking questions, but that poisoning earth and water was different. And finally he told them about Cherry.

Then he got up and one of the men, walking soundlessly, came and put on his blindfold again.

When he had gone, Francisco and the others took off their masks.

'—He is to be believed?' said Francisco.

'—Yes,' said one of his companions.

'—I'm not sure,' said the other, who wore steel-rimmed glasses.

'—He is to be believed,' Francisco said again, and this time it was a command.

The other two men were silent.

'—No harm has been done. We have other ways of finding out if what he said is true,' said Francisco.

'—We could have held him,' said steel-glasses.

'—He is not important enough,' said Francisco.

Steel-glasses growled, hesitantly. But he would not openly disagree with the leader. Francisco spoke again.

'—If he is trustworthy, we will need his information. If he is not, then we can wait until he comes again.'

He lifted a revolver from his belt and clicked it at the floor as he always did when he was thinking about violence.

Martin, meantime, was driven circuitously towards his hotel. He had done it. Now his mind was free to worry some more about what the hell was happening to Kerridge Steel back in the United States.

3

Even Kerridge, who had left so many communications unanswered in the past few months, did not refuse a meeting with Sir Bernard Grant when he was told by his New York office of the Briton's Telex message requesting it. Even several managers in that office felt relieved there was going to be *some* action. Of late it had been a gloomy long-faced place.

The price of the corporation's shares was now at an all-time low. A succession of meetings during the past fortnight, with worried executives scurrying between New York City and Kerridge's home in the Palisades, had so far failed to find the size of funding necessary to keep Kerridge Steel moving. No one was going to put money behind his operation until the threatened Washington investigation was settled. And analysts hated the fact that the health of Kerridge Steel depended so critically on the contract in Ecuador.

Early November snow flecked the landscape when Bernard Grant was driven up from New York City to see Kerridge. The chairman of Prospero had never before seen at such close quarters the industrial wasteland of New Jersey on the west bank of the Hudson River. In the grey gloom, foundries and chemical plants glowed with devilish brightness. The earth, rimed with snow, looked dead. The piles of scrap metal which too often formed a frieze to gas stations and motels, brashly shining with neon, somehow gave them an air of impermanence. This world looked as if it were being slowly eaten up by rust and suffocated with garbage. He was reminded of Dante's Inferno.

The foothills of the Palisades ought to have uplifted him, for they are prosperous with skiing stores and antique shops and neat wooden houses, refreshed with the beauty of woods and streams and tumbling slopes. But, half-drugged with the heat-blast in the car, looking at forests painted black and menacing by the leaden sky, Bernard could think only of Ibsen and decay.

He had been well-briefed on the Kerridge house, so he was not surprised when the limousine hissed down a long wet and silent drive, overhung by dripping trees. No wonder so many of those early American billionaires, the robber-barons, had proved eccentric. To build their palaces in such gloom-laden isolation invited the onset of a certain cast of mind.

Who was the railroad man who had built a private track up into these hills so that he could ride his solitary coach down to the city? No matter. Bernard's prejudices about some traits of American business received ample confirmation as he surveyed the land where capitalism's early warlords had chosen to live during the years when the American dream of making it was young and relatively unchallenged.

He could not prevent an inner smile as he was led through the house by a manservant in wing collar and striped pants. A real live butler, dear God. More English than the English. The house was like that too. Moss faintly marked the pillars outside and the great hall behind the double-doors had hammer-beams, shields, suits of armour, a log fire crackling and a strong smell of wax polish. The atmosphere was so baronial, he half-expected to see hounds champing at bones.

Kerridge awaited him in a room which had books and dust and leather chairs enough to be reminiscent of the libraries of the older clubs of Pall Mall, except that the old man's view was not of wet London streets. The American sat brooding in a rocking chair and through a huge uncurtained window Bernard could see a tumble of pine trees falling down to a lake. He rose to greet Bernard, grunting with the effort, and the Chairman of Prospero, who had come prepared to be tough, had no heart to feel anything but sadness for the man before him.

Kerridge's body was frail, a gnome's, the head scarcely reaching Bernard's shoulders. His legs were bent like those of someone martyred by arthritis. His shoulders sagged. Above a scrawny throat, his face had disintegrated.

Bernard knew the face that had been there. As he remembered the many photographs, it had been etched and cratered and scarred with deep lines of determination; an unforgetably ugly face. Now the tension in the skin had gone, and the flesh hung in thin folds over the bones. The nose – that famous straight, long, unbloated Kerridge nose – protruded like a tent-pole around which the canvas had collapsed.

'Sir Bernard. Good to see you.' Kerridge lifted a waxen hand, ice-cold.

'Thank you Mr Kerridge. I've been looking forward to our meeting.'

'You'll stay to lunch?'

'That would be nice,' said Bernard. Then he smiled, the charm working at full power. 'Provided we're still on speaking terms in two hours' time.'

Kerridge wheezed into laughter. It made him cough. He sounded out of practice at laughing. He flopped back into his chair, waving Bernard into another.

'*Touché*, sir. But then I reckon you and I had better get on together. What's going to happen to this whole damn mess if we don't?'

Bernard smiled again, then crossed his legs carefully to retain the crease in his trousers. Kerridge's suit hung on him without shape.

'I agree,' said Bernard. 'I imagine we both have an interest in keeping our minds free from prejudice.'

'I thought your son might be with you, Sir Bernard. I hear fine reports of him.'

'No. We considered it would be better if you and I talked alone in the first instance.'

'Damn right, sir. My people wanted to come. Ed Corsino too. I told them to go to hell.' Bernard noticed for the first time that, despite the decay of the body, Kerridge's brown eyes burned hot. 'Still and all, I would like to have met your son. They're useful, sons.'

'Yes,' said Bernard, smiling.

'I have three daughters. Fine girls. But they can't help a man in a business like this, now, can they?'

'I suppose not,' said Bernard.

The gilt-handled doors of the library opened. The butler came in bearing a tray.

'I thought you would like some coffee, Sir Bernard. And cognac too if you want it. It's a day for liquor. Since my illness I'm not supposed to have it. But around eleven o'clock in the morning I feel the need of it. It warms me. My doctors would kill me if they knew. But what do those damn quacks understand about the way a man feels inside?'

'No brandy, thank you,' said Bernard. 'But coffee, yes. Black. No sugar. I hope you're feeling a lot better, Mr Kerridge.'

'Fair. Just fair,' said Kerridge. 'It's these damn pains that kept me away from the job. If I'd been there kicking the asses of the fools who work for me, all this wouldn't have happened. That's what comes of having no son. My business was a family business. Did you know I was just an apprentice in a steel mill when I was 14 and I owned that mill by the time I was 23? Then it all grew and grew, and I had to take strangers in. Outsiders, Sir Bernard. It's not the same. The *feeling* goes out of it.'

Kerridge lowered his loose lips on to a brandy glass and sucked up the liquid. Bernard wondered how seriously to take Kerridge's homespun recitation. This lament for the lost virtues of small-time business seemed scarcely compatible with the character of the man who had driven Kerridge Steel to a position among the top 100 corporations of the greatest commercial nation on earth. Maybe Kerridge was playing games with him. Perhaps the old man was stumbling into senility, which could also account for the way his conglomerate had become so mis-managed.

It was as though Kerridge could read his mind. Suddenly, the American slammed a hand on the arm of his rocker. 'Dammit, Sir Bernard. You must think I'm a fool, rambling on this way. I'm not a fool. And I'm not going crazy. It's just that – well, these last few years I seem to have lost interest. I let people like Corsino climb on the wagon. We all make mistakes.'

He ran a finger around the rim of the glass. 'Have you ever wondered what we half-kill ourselves for, Sir Bernard?'

Bernard shrugged. 'Men have the urge to build. You make one building, then you want to see if you can better it. You go on and on. It seems to take on its own momentum. I've no answer beyond that, except that you want to leave behind something for the world to remember you by . . . Why did Shakespeare write plays or Bach write fugues?'

'So's they could eat, if I remember my history,' said Kerridge conclusively. 'I'd got everything I needed to eat, drink and be merry for the rest of my life by the time I was thirty. But I didn't stop.'

'You can't, can you?' said Bernard. 'When you've got to that point, too many people depend on you.'

'That's just a rationalisation, Sir Bernard.' Kerridge was talking to his own lap. 'We have this itch we can't explain, the thing that keeps us going, and so we try to justify it. Lately, I'll be damned if I can. My family don't need my money, not any more. The people who work for me would probably be better off if they were in a smaller set-up where they knew the boss and the lines didn't all get crossed up by accountants and lawyers. And as for what the world thinks of what I've created – well, I expect my obituary will be about yet another man who got too lazy, too old and too greedy.'

He glanced up at Bernard. There was humour in his eyes as well as heat. For a moment Bernard did not know what to say. This was nothing like the conversation he had envisaged having. Or was it?

Part of his mind said that this was really why he had come instead of Michael. Kerridge and he had been through

285

the same school. There were times, also, when he had thoughts not so very dissimilar to Kerridge's.

'Well, Sir Bernard, all this is not what you came to talk about.'

Bernard smiled. 'I'm not so sure. But let's save philosophy for lunch. Figures would spoil my digestion.'

Again, Kerridge wheezed his laugh. 'You're a damn poor liar, sir. From all I hear you handle them well enough at breakfast as well as lunch.' He passed a hand into the wreckage of his face. 'I want to be square with you. No point being otherwise.'

For an hour they talked corporate structures and figures, Washington politics and pressure groups. At the end of it, Kerridge looked more like a collapsed tent than ever.

'Sixty million dollars is a lot to be asking,' Bernard said finally.

'Forty million we can raise.' Kerridge stabbed a pale bony finger at the papers in his lap. 'I've told you the companies I'd sell off. Further than that, we daren't go. Dammit, you know the reasons. If we're seen to be running scared for much more, the whole goddam shoot won't be worth a nickel. There'd be no confidence in us.'

'Twenty million is a lot of money,' said Bernard evenly.

'I know.' Kerridge was growling for the first time. 'You'll be putting out a lot more money to save what you've already sunk in Ecuador. It's a risk. But if I were in your shoes, Bernard,' – at Grant's suggestion his title had been dropped – 'then I guess I'd be saying it was a chance that had to be taken.'

It was the nearest Kerridge had come to making a selling pitch at Bernard. Even Kerridge knew he hadn't much of a story.

'I doubt we'd raise the money on the market,' said Bernard. 'Not when the banks knew what it was for. And my board will scream. We'll probably have to sell assets ourselves.'

'The French people will maybe help.'

Bernard turned the palm of his right hand upwards. 'Who knows what SAEF's attitude will be. Is there no hope in Washington?'

'After the Talsey business, no one will lift a finger. That can still blow up into something nasty. I hear that the Ex-Im

286

Bank are chasing Corsino too. They've looked into his Ecuador costings, and they think he inflated the figures so's he could get a much bigger loan from them.'

'Corsino, yes. I still don't fully understand about Corsino,' said Bernard doubtfully.

'He's the front man for a syndicate who have a large shareholding. Nothing more to him than that.'

Bernard looked too eager for a fuller answer. Kerridge grunted. 'He hasn't got anything on me. He's not a blackmailer, if that's what you imagine. No pictures of me with little boys or whores who have imagination. They tell me there's a lot of that about. Not me. Nothing so corny. I wouldn't give a good goddam if he had. It's much more complicated. He came on the scene, oh, maybe ten years ago. He knew people with money to invest when we were desperate to expand. He set things up. He could also pull strings in Washington. So gradually he insinuated himself. You know the kind of man?'

'In England we perhaps control them better.' Bernard felt he had a right to be magisterial.

'You need to have the best people to lobby on Capitol Hill,' said Kerridge defensively. 'And money is put together in this country in strange ways, Bernard. Even I am not sure precisely where Corsino's associates get their money. There are, you know, organisations, syndicates.'

'You mean the Mafia?' Bernard was incredulous.

'No, not necessarily.' Kerridge seemed to shy away from the word. 'That's just a name they use in newspapers. Oh, it exists, of course. It's a useful – well – umbrella word. But there are many organisations, legal as well as criminal, that agglomerate money without reference to the Mafia. I've never thought of Corsino as strictly a Mafia man, though there are plenty of respectable businesses controlled by them now, of course. But he has associates with contacts all over the United States.'

'What kind of contacts?'

'Contacts who control people. I mean men who can force others to do as they wish.' He looked at Bernard as if he were seeking some kind of absolution. 'I'm not proud of that, Bernard. It was convenient to know Corsino. He got things done. Only in this past year have I begun to discover why and how.'

'He has a position in your company?'

'None, officially. But he became the fixer of so many deals, my corporate officers got used to working with him. I let him operate almost by proxy.'

'If we put in money, we could want Corsino out,' said Bernard quietly.

'That would not be easy.'

'Nevertheless . . .'

Kerridge slumped further into his chair. 'It's possible. Just possible.'

'There would be other conditions. I think we would want to take over your holding in the Ecuador petro-chemical company. It might be useful to have some voice there if we're assuming the real direction of the consortium.'

'I've no objection.'

Bernard rose suddenly, stretching himself. Beyond the window a deer was rubbing itself against a tree. 'Too much business is bad for my legs. I get cramp if I sit too long.'

He could not satisfactorily explain why the presence of Kerridge drew such admissions from him. Normally he would never have betrayed his infirmities to others. Probably it was that Kerridge was so manifestly worse off than himself that he felt he could safely allow his companion to win a point or two in the game of joint misfortunes. Or, more simply, he believed afterwards that he was responding solely out of pity, sympathy, kindness – he could not fashion the exact word.

No more could Bernard completely decide why their conversation had moved to such a conclusion. He was pushing Prospero deeper into involvement with both Kerridge Steel and the Ecuador adventure than was prudent. What would the board – and especially Bender – say? In extreme circumstances, Prospero could raise such sums as had been talked about. But at what price to the shape and prosperity of the whole organisation? Bender, he was certain, would challenge that price. He had no idea, at this juncture, how the deal which he and Kerridge were discussing so calmly could be fashioned in detail. He knew only that it was possible somehow. And that was enough. The whole morning had a curious logic to it which he felt, but could not have expounded.

Kerridge stirred. 'Your other conditions, Bernard? Are there more?'

'Yes. But I'll need more time to consider them. I think we've talked enough.'

He walked over to examine the faded spines of some of the books. He selected one and opened it. 'You have some beautiful things here. I'd like you to see my own first editions.'

'Odd,' said Kerridge. 'Now I've more time, I don't seem to read so much.'

Bernard was uneasily reminded of what he himself had found to be the case since Michael had taken over as chief executive. He smiled, nodded his head, then moved along the shelves to where a worn wooden ladder stretched down from a shelf above.

'Move the ladder – don't go under it, please.' Kerridge's voice was cracked with alarm. Bernard turned sharply to see the American standing, claw-hands extended.

Awkwardly, Kerridge pushed the folds and crevices of his face into a kind of smile. 'I'm sorry, Bernard. It's well, I worry about ladders. Unlucky.' His voice became even more sheepish. 'No use tempting fate.'

Bernard thought of the Greek shipowner he'd met who would only do major deals on Tuesdays, for no specified reason. And of all the men who, denying superstition, would yet scarcely cross the road on Friday the 13th and would touch wood when they spoke of misfortunes which had never afflicted them.

Not superstitious, no; but anxious to make a discreet investment in the bank of good luck, just in case. Men who argued that it did no harm to be on the safe side. Men like that. Including himself.

So he smiled back at Kerridge and said, 'Of course. I didn't notice.' He was glad he'd been warned.

'Do you feel like lunch?'

'Not much,' said Bernard.

'Damn right,' said Kerridge. 'I've no appetite these days. I'm sick and tired of the greenery they give me to feed on.'

He pointed painfully at the window. 'Fine trout in that lake, Bernard. Do you fish?'

They talked no more figures. They sat in their chairs and spoke of people liked and disliked, and of things which they'd enjoyed doing outside their professional lives. Bernard at last drank some brandy, which was not like him. Usually, in victory, he found that Evian Water was enough, since the juices secreted by his body were sufficiently intoxicating. Liquor for him was customarily an accompaniment of defeat or depression.

'Here's to us,' said Kerridge, raising his glass as the clock struck one.

'Here's to us,' said Bernard and both of them drank with the gusto of losers who no longer care very much about what they have failed to win.

4

The tanks, three of them, moved in before daybreak. Their guns were trained on the two blocks which the students had draped with banners carrying various slogans of which the most common said ALI-CHEM POISONERS.

Three hundred troops supported the armour. As the sun pierced the mist trails of a Quito dawn they stood yawning, shuffling their feet, uncertain what they might need to do. From the windows of the campus blocks, faces surveyed them. The sullen motors of the tanks, the squeak and clank of their tracks, had woken most of the students. Colonel Vargas looked upwards, thumbs stuck arrogantly into the shiny leather belt that encased his stomach.

The show of force was his decision. There had been no violence the previous day, only chanting and marching and some windows broken with stones thrown by a few of the students. But he remembered the riots of a year ago which had led to the university being closed for six months. It had been a mistake, in his view, to open it again so soon. Cantania was one who had argued strongly for the reopening, after a cadre of new senior academics and administrators had been installed. Cantania had pointed out that forty-three known activists from the faculty staff and student body would not be allowed back. Weak as usual, Cantania. The flushing out of trouble-makers had not been thorough enough. In his pocket, Vargas carried a list of fifteen names whose owners were, he believed, inside the two blocks. If he could take those fifteen, he would be satisfied. This time a policy of overkill was necessary. That way, Vargas was certain, he would prevent serious rioting.

The windows were already reflecting the sun painfully into his eyes. It was time. He lifted a loud-hailer to his mouth and began stating his terms to the students. Five minutes later, three men and two women came out through a door in one of the blocks and walked, hands raised, towards the tanks.

It was never clear, afterwards, whether there had really been a gunman on the fourth floor of the other building or not. Vargas was able to produce in evidence a Springfield .30 rifle with telescopic sights – the sniper's tool the world over – which he claimed had been found stuffed beneath the mattress of a bed close to a fourth floor window. But of a marksman there was no sign, either dead or alive. What was certain, however, was that a single gunshot cracked across the campus when the five surrendering students were around thirty paces from the tanks. It could have been a sniper. It could, just as easily, have been a nervous soldier.

There was an aching kind of pause after the shot, every actor in the scene freezing for a split-second before the adrenalin, drug of fear and mindless agression, swept from their glands. Then the machine guns of one of the tanks opened up. There was a flurry of rifle fire. Within a minute the shouts of officers and NCOs stopped the barrage.

Again, silence. The five students were flat on the ground, two men seeking the hopeful shelter of the concrete, one woman bleeding from a leg wound. The others, one man and one woman, were dead.

Screams, at first of fear, broke the silence from inside the building. Then a baying of anger joined the sound. But the students did not rush out to do battle. Held in check by the fear of bullets, they watched, still making their sullen noise, as the troops slowly moved in towards the fallen bodies.

Two hours later, just before the Cabinet meeting which declared an emergency in the capital, Cantania erupted into Vargas's office. His silver hair, usually slick, was wild and uncombed. The scars on his left cheek were fringed with stubble like wounds so new he dared not shave. He was not now a man surrounded by silence, which was the atmosphere he customarily cultivated.

'—Murderer! You have done this deliberately. How can we hold them now?' His long pale fingers stretched towards Vargas, flexing in a mime that suggested strangulation.

Vargas, rooted in his leather-padded desk chair, let his black eyes absorb Cantania's loathing. His plump, swarthy face glowed still darker. But he spoke with measured calmness.

'—We would not have been able to contain them at all had we not acted swiftly. My task is to maintain public order against the enemies of the state. I have fulfilled it.'

Cantania shouted. '—I am seeing the President before the Cabinet meets.'

'—Do. And remember I am responsible to him, not you.'

'—I shall urge your dismissal.'

'—He will support me. We were fired upon.'

'—That is not my information. Your ridiculous response to a simple unarmed demonstration invited trouble.'

'—You civilians, what do you know?' Vargas's scorn scorched the air.

Cantania ignored the jibe. '—They were objecting to *my* plans for the nation, to something I believe can only uplift the people – but even I would not have acted like a barbarian.'

Vargas fingered the two rows of medal ribbons on his combat shirt. He only wore them when there was action. '—There's the irony, my dear Cantania. I happen to agree with some of the students. I think your stinking chemical plant is a disgrace. Why should we pollute our native land to make money for foreigners? That is what *I* would call ridiculous. Yet I have to shoot these people because they carry their dissent to the point where they attack the forces of law and order. That is what duty means, Dr Cantania. I understand it. You do not.'

For Vargas it was quite a speech. Cantania swung round abruptly and strode towards the door.

'—It is your plant we must persuade the President to stop, doctor, not my soldiers,' said Vargas to the back of Cantania's head.

'—Impossible,' shouted Cantania.

'—You make it too easy for the guerrillas,' cooed Vargas. He was winning and he knew it.

No planes were permitted to land at Quito that day.

Michael Grant, flying in from Miami to push Cantania for assistance or forbearance in the crisis precipitated by Kerridge Steel, assumed it was the weather which caused the diversion to Guayaquil. He had managed to reach Bernard by telephone in New York City during his three-hour stop-over in Florida. His father had said only that conversations with Kerridge and with Ali-Chem were going well. He was not to worry, just extract as much as he could from Cantania.

The air was smoky with humidity as the plane floated over the snaking brown rivers and marshlands around Guayaquil. Pink and white houses stood isolated on the drier patches of dull green land, freckled with bushes, and Michael wondered how the hell the inhabitants got at them when they came home from work. Here the equatorial position of the country produced a landscape which reminded him of Lagos in West Africa. He imagined he wasn't going to like it very much.

At the airport it was teeming with rain, and there were soldiers everywhere, surly and impatient. It took ages for everyone to be examined. Despite the plane's diversion, a man from the local port authority met him, courtesy of Perez. Quickly he told Michael what was happening in the country. No fighting, except for stray explosions attributed to the guerrillas; just a general clampdown. No internal flights to Quito at present. Michael would have to wait a day or so until a passage to Quito could be arranged.

He had to take off his shoes and socks and paddle through almost a foot of water to the official's car. A porter splashed in the rear with his bags. Then they drove along a roughish kind of road, in and out of lakes of water, through which Indians and others waded with the air of people who expected nothing else. The official pointed out with some pride a soccer stadium and a basketball arena. The English team had played at the former during a tour a few years back, he said.

The evening lights were being lit as they hit the centre of the city. The streets here were good, the buildings grey and modern. They went along a wide avenue that skirted a promenade with pleasant trees. Beyond them were boats moored and water as far as he could see.

'The River Guayas,' said the official proudly. 'Here we

293

have built the finest port on the west coast of South America. The World Bank loan is repayable over 20 years at interest of only 5¾ per cent – very low. Ships of 30,000 tons and more can use it. A quick turn-around, Mr Grant no quarantine.'

. He was like a walking fact-book, and proud with it.

'I shall be honoured to conduct you around it tomorrow if you wish.'

Michael looked as enthusiastic as he could and watched a crowd of people, clothes dripping, fighting to get on a bus.

That evening he spent a fruitless hour at his hotel trying to telephone Quito before the man returned to take him to dinner. The next day he was afflicted with a blinding headache and heavy sweatings. He called off his visit to the docks; the official sent grapes and a letter of sympathy. The following morning he was only just struggling out of sleep when the bedside telephone rang. Del Martin's voice, determinedly cheerful, announced that Perez and he were downstairs in the lobby.

The three of them had breakfast together.

'Not a chance of seeing Cantania today,' said Martin. 'We wanted to check out on some consignments coming in. Including one of Oldershaw's – almost the last. So I thought we'd better come to you. We got special permission to take the Excalibur out of Quito.'

'How's it really going, Del?'

'For the first time I'm happy,' Martin smiled, very brown beneath his tight-cut ginger hair. But Michael wondered why the American at once pushed fingers at the strawberry mark on his face, which usually meant Martin was uneasy.

'You mean that?'

'Sure I mean it. Even your guy Oldershaw has caught up with the schedule. It was useful him comin' out here a few weeks back.' He grinned more expansively. 'Trouble with Oldershaw is he's too much of a perfectionist. He got a few things wrong with his stuff, but nothing he can't cure. Still it was good to see him. Sure, I had to stop him almost bustin' some goddam official down on the waterfront. But we did it. Perez here has been very helpful.'

Perez bent his head modestly. 'It was a pleasure, Mr

Grant. We are here to serve.' Michael wondered how expensive service had come this time.

'Why so much improved, Del?'

'Well, for one thing a job like this has a kind of rhythm. It seems nothing's going to work out for a spell, like you'll never make first base. Then, suddenly, it all begins to fit and you're hitting home runs every time.'

'For example?' asked Michael.

'Okay. For instance, the guerrillas have stopped bothering us. Partly that's Vargas and his soldiers. But mostly it's because they've found another target. They're playing hell down around that Ali-Chem site.'

Martin said the words with almost savage relish.

'Ali-Chem are still working out how they can make changes, Del. My father's in the States now, talking to them.'

'Your old man? Well, thanks. But those bastards soon won't have a goddam site at the rate things are happening. And serve 'em right. What a bloody stinking thing to do.'

'None of our business, really,' said Michael. 'But they could have been more diplomatic.'

'Everybody's business,' said Martin. 'They'd better change it.'

Perez looked distinctly ill at ease. He dropped a spot of cherry conserve from his toast. As it hit his white suit, he surveyed this personal pollution mournfully. 'Mr Martin, you must not speak so publicly of these things. My uncle, you understand. He supports that chlorine plant.'

'He knows the way I think,' said Martin curtly.

Michael had to play umpire. 'All right, Del. I know how you feel. But we've got to get *our* plant built without any more hassles. Besides, I need the support of Dr Cantania.' He bowed his head towards Perez.

'Check,' Martin growled. 'But it won't get built, that place. Not unless they change it. Now, what in God's name is goin' on with Kerridge?'

Briefly, Michael explained the situation, but he gave it an optimistic gloss. Between them, Prospero and SAEF would hold the consortium together – provided Cantania would help too.

'You mean we're gonna get paid after all?' Martin was in the mood for jokes, recklessly so. 'And Perez here will get his commission?' Perez looked even more mournful. Ten per cent – or twenty or thirty in certain special cases – was no subject for levity. He dropped more conserve, and dabbed desperately at it.

Martin stood up smartly. 'Come on, Mike. Let's go visit with the guys at the docks. Ain't a damn thing else you can do until tomorrow.'

Outside, the rain of the previous day was only a memory. The sun reflected oozily off shining green leaves and striped awnings and lamp-posts on the promenade. There were pleasure boats afloat, a blue-streaked sky, and shoeshine boys smiling as they worked in the gardens by the water. It felt almost like a seaside resort except that there were great hunks of vegetation floating down the river and, at one street corner, he saw soldiers lounging against an armoured car.

The road to the port cut straight through marshland. A Mercedes 600 had been sent by the dock authorities.

'Funny,' said Martin. 'They call this the Avenido Quito, don't they, Perez?'

'Indeed, yes. It goes all the way from one end of the city to the port. When we return I will show you the family tombs in the cemetery. Mausoleums, Mr Grant, but they are very beautiful.

Michael raised his eyebrows at Martin, who pursed his lips. 'Yeah,' said Martin. 'Beautiful. Just look at that land, Mike, wet and lovely. Bananas, cocoa, coffee – you name it. They call the Guayas basin the breadbasket of the nation. It's a pity more people don't have their bellies filled with what's in the basket.'

'Be fair, Mr Martin,' said Perez defensively. 'Our child death-rate has gone down dramatically. We will feed every-one – if the guerrillas will let us.'

'Yeah, okay,' said Martin, and Michael wasn't sure if Perez appreciated the irony.

They made a detour to see the lock through which ships passed to and from the port, via a series of creeks. A rusty steamer was moving through and they watched it for a few minutes, waving away mosquitoes which were thick here-abouts. Out of the mangrove swamps came a dug-out boat, painted gaily in red and blue, paddled by men, both very dark-complexioned, although the women and children with them were much paler-skinned.

'What are they doing?' asked Michael.

Perez smiled. 'A day out in the town, Mr Grant. Many of the families here are cut off by water.'

Every person in the boat was grinning at them. Again, Martin had that same doubting feeling he'd had down in Cuenca. Who was he to get mixed up in trying to shape the country's future? Angry with himself, he pushed the thought aside, but the *mestizos* didn't stop smiling as they came ashore.

They drove into the main port complex. The driver flashed a pass at various official-type men en route, but no one took much notice. On the quayside a gang of around 30 dockers, some stripped to the waist, others in ragged cotton T-shirts, were carrying boxes from trucks labelled BANANERO into the hold of a ship.

'Used to load 'em in stems,' said Martin. 'Now it's boxes.'

Inside one of the long low storage sheds, Martin showed Michael hundreds of crates piled to the roof. 'That's our stuff, Mike. Every goddam bit of it. You're gonna have quite a plant.'

The official whom Michael had met on his arrival joined them. They spent an hour talking to various of his friends in the port buildings, being loaded with statistics and pamphlets. At last, Martin led him out into the open air. He whispered to Michael, 'Don't believe everything you hear. Those guys don't run this place. Vargas presides over the committee that does. It's stuffed with admirals. And a Cardinal, naturally.'

The Mercedes was waiting. They climbed in and it rolled past the cranes and fork-lift trucks out on to the Avenida Quito once more. The driver put his foot down hard.

There was not much traffic around, and it was surprising when the driver suddenly stabbed savagely at the brakes as they approached a stationary car. The Mercedes halted, engine murmuring. The driver turned and lifted a hand on to the back of his seat.

The gun he held looked so small, maybe 7 or 8 inches long. A Colt .45 automatic. Very snug, gleaming grey, formidable.

'Not a sound, gentlemen. Sit perfectly still.'

From the stationary car beside them, two men emerged. They squeezed into the back seats with Michael, Perez and Martin.

Then they too produced revolvers, older and uglier and bigger Smith and Wessons. One of them prodded a barrel against Perez's ribs. '—Out,' he said.

Michael saw Perez, looking almost comically frightened, slide into the other car. Immediately yet another man came to the Mercedes. He got in and, as the car began to move again, he held up in his right hand not a gun but a hyperdermic syringe.

10. A TRAP FOR EVERYONE

1

PEREZ was returned, damaged; a bruised thorax, a split nose, one tooth missing. The guerrillas did not like profiteers. Martin came back too, with just a needle-mark in his arm to show where he had been pumped full of pethedrine to keep him quiet. Martin they did not want. Michael they did. The ransom price was set at half a million American dollars.

Three weeks later, as a Trident jet carried David Travis down to Orly airport in Paris, it had still not been paid. David felt as angrily helpless as he had all those months ago when he stood with the injured Indian beside the Aguarico River in Ecuador. What he was going to do in France was, of course, indirectly connected with Michael's plight. But it seemed strangely irrelevant. He wanted to be out there, in Quito, doing something more active and obvious to help Michael. That, however, was now in the hands of Bernard Grant. David hoped the Chairman would have more success with the apparently implacable Vargas than had earlier envoys.

He glanced below towards the dark-grey apartment blocks which stood like sentinels guarding the hatbox-shaped fuel tanks on the ground. There were myriad rows of light-posts, sprouting up like the antennae of insects.

Would it be easier to find someone who'd been kidnapped here in France or in Ecuador? There were so few damn houses in Ecuador it ought to be easier there. But then the men at Vargas's command were unlikely to be as skilful, rough and ruthless as the French security forces. He'd read a lot about how armour-clad the French were in the struggle against the O.A.S. – all those former Corsicans called *barbouzes*, beating and torturing their way towards making the Republic a place fit for de Gaulle to live in.

David bet Vargas wished he had a few hundred *barbouzes*

on call to let loose on the guerrillas who'd proved tricky enough to keep Michael out of Vargas's way for three weeks. Would they really kill him if the money wasn't forthcoming soon? David tried to push that thought completely out of his mind. He could not imagine life without Michael Grant, not now. He realised, almost for the first time, the bond that had grown between them.

It had started as business; David climbing the ladder, resignedly accepting the rungs on which he found himself, the people he rubbed elbows with or tugged forelocks at. Imperceptibly, it had grown into a relationship quite different. It wasn't just that he believed Michael to be the best leader Prospero was likely to get. He cared what happened to Michael in a way divorced from their job relationship. He thought they would be friends for ever.

He had no time to dissect the over-simplification of that assumption. He was too engaged in worrying whether Bernard would be able to fix the ransom. Vargas was the problem, refusing to countenance so easy a surrender to the guerrillas. Who, in Ecuador – including Vargas – would be safe, once the pattern of kidnap and ransom paid was established? So Vargas had been reported in *The Times* as saying. Meanwhile, Prospero had the money ready. SAEF had said, secretly, that they would help, as the French company had also promised assistance in the arrangements to prop up the ailing fortunes of Kerridge Steel. It was the details of all that which David was here to work out, the last assignment which Bernard Grant had handed out before he'd flown to Quito. David was flattered that Bernard had given him the task. The old man seemed to trust him.

A car, provided by SAEF, swept him from the airport towards the city centre. Even on this busy November morning, you could see past the new apartment blocks to the Eiffel Tower on the left and the multi-coloured hill of Montmartre, topped by Sacré Coeur, on the right. The driver pointed out the landmarks as they went: the cannon and the old tank on the Esplanade des Invalides, the Foreign Office with the huge notice DEFENSE D'AFFICHER cut into its walls, the gold-tipped railings of the National Assembly building, the Hotel Crillon and the Admiralty. They drove from Left Bank to Right, into the gardens of the Tuileries.

He didn't enjoy the statuary in the Tuileries; the figures were in such attitudes of prayer, thought and agony it reminded him too much of human beings being tortured. Nor did he welcome the information that the British Embassy people always laid roses at the Joan of Arc statue on the anniversary of her death. He was too concerned whether Michael might die.

His hotel, deliberately chosen for its unobtrusiveness, was not far from the Opera. He rode up alone in a minuscule elevator. There was more than an hour before he would need to leave to meet the men from SAEF. He wanted to check through his background papers again. Inside his room, sitting cross-legged in a chair, was Claire Debrais.

'Hello, David,' she said. 'I wanted to make sure.'

He smiled nervously. 'Sure of what?'

'Sure we met. Sure we could talk. Just sure.'

Her choice of words was ironic. He'd never seen any woman look more sure of herself. She gleamed like hard steel. Every detail about her was perfect. Her suit was dark green, with silver buttons. Beneath it, her ample breasts were upheld inside a spotless white blouse, pulled just tight enough to be astonishingly ambivalent. No man could not have wanted to touch her there; yet he would not have dared to disturb all that perfection. The legs were flawless inside nylon; her face had a subdued glow; her black upswept hair shone. She looked as if she ate little boys for breakfast.

He dumped his case, took off his topcoat, and sat down. To offer her a hand seemed foolish; and more than that he would not gamble on. Kissing – hand or cheek or lips – seemed out of the question.

She smiled, just a fraction. 'I think you have some explanations to make.'

'I'm sorry, Claire. Really. Since I got back after Monte Carlo it's been hell.'

Imperiously she waved a hand, gloved. She had the kind of aristocratic demeanour he could only think of as pre-Revolutionary. 'Not that, idiot. I understand. You must choose your time to come back. Don't be ridiculous.'

'What then?'

'You are pigs, all of you, you businessmen.' She spoke flatly, the voice of a woman who had come to expect no better. 'Why are you now conniving to sell my husband's company?'

For a moment David was unable to reply. The talks that Prospero had been having in France were supposed to be as secure as the Crown Jewels. He stalled.

'How did you get into my room, Claire?'

'David.' She swung her legs open and stood. 'Please don't treat me like a child.'

'It's nothing like you think . . .'

'I know,' she said simply. 'For God's sake, let's not start lying to each other. We don't need to. We don't have to live together, and only that kind of pressure justifies having to tell lies. We are free and we should be honest. What is the point, otherwise?'

He shrugged. 'All right.' He was going to tell her, straight; and he justified the action by asking himself whatever reason there could be for continuing with Prospero, or any other company, if he was going to behave like a Sanger.

'It wasn't the plan,' he said. 'When I talked with you, we were buying you out in order to run your company. Now things have changed.'

'What things?'

'Don't be naive, Claire. You read the papers. Michael Grant may die if we don't get him out. And, in case the other reason isn't clear, we're looking for a few millions to bail out Kerridge Steel.'

'Prospero is a huge enterprise, David. You could snap your fingers and raise such money. Besides, SAEF is helping you. That's why you're here.'

From the way she looked at him, he sensed she knew everything: including the gentle use – it could scarcely be termed blackmail, but just a hint dropped discreetly as a feather – he had made of her revelations about Armand Broussard.

'I'll not make excuses,' he said. 'I believe what I did was right – right in the long run for all the people involved. I have to think about people.'

'I should – oh, I don't know – I should feel like killing you. I don't believe you need the money. And you used me, used what I told you about Armand. I felt like a whore.'

He could not help putting out his arms. As he touched her, the muscles of her arms grew tense.

'I'm not good at the sincerity bit . . .'

'*Hein?*'

'I mean – I don't know how to make you believe . . .'

'I will listen, David.'

'Michael Grant is a friend,' he said. 'I don't want him to die. Nor do I want there to be a revolution in Prospero. Both are possible. We must get the money for him and for Kerridge Steel. Even with SAEF's help, we need millions. And if we do it by selling old assets, the big shareholders won't stand for it. Michael will be out, dead or alive. I happen to believe that would be disastrous, for thousands of people. We can only protect him by unscrambling the deal I worked out with you. It will give us spare capital and it won't look so much like selling Prospero's established assets. It's the only way, Claire, believe me.'

'And Armand?'

'I swear I'd no idea you knew him or about him. But once you'd told me, well, all right, I did use it. I'm not particularly proud of doing so. There were good reasons, that's all I can say. Why do you think I haven't been in touch with you? I felt a bastard. So . . .'

'So?'

'If you want to, kick me in the balls and go out the way you came.'

She was standing, looking out of the window. She turned slowly, her eyes wide with wanting to believe him. Then the eyes narrowed, looking into him as if they were trying to scour every part of his mind for falsehood. At last, her shoulders sagged and she was a *grande dame* no longer, just a woman who had grown tired with searching for honesty that had no percentage attached to it.

'There's no point in doubting, is there, David? If you're lying, then I pity you more than I pity myself for being deceived. And that would have to be revenge enough.' She paused, seeking something to say. 'You – you are all right?'

'Fine.'

'And your wife?'

It was a strange question, until he remembered how much they had talked about their families in Monaco. He remembered, too, that she knew nothing about Sheila's court case. It had ended swiftly, only 10 days ago. Sheila had received an absolute discharge from the court. There were still a few malicious quips to be heard at Prospect House about the affair; but David could take those. In a way, it pushed him closer to his wife. He loved her, yet he was still, ridiculously, not out of love with Claire, and both of these affections had an element of pity in them.

'Yes,' he said. 'Sheila's fine too.'

'Will you save him – Michael Grant, I mean?'

'We might. His father is out in Quito now.'

'Is there anything you should be doing now which might help him?'

He glanced at his watch. 'In 45 minutes, yes.'

'Then make love to me, please. For 45 minutes.'

It was, ridiculously, better than in Monte Carlo, despite the cold-bloodedness of the beginning and the total alienation in their surroundings. It was as though their bodies were emphasising what their minds wished to believe in. He knew, too, that this would probably be their last meeting; and so did she.

2

Michael Grant saw sunlight for only thirty minutes or so a day. It slunk in through a small window perhaps 20 feet up one of the walls of the room in which they kept him, at around 10.30 each morning.

The window, minute in size, was too distant for him ever to consider attempting to reach it up the smooth wall. He had been told, anyway, that he would be shot if he tried. An armed guard, always hooded, face in shadow, sat with him constantly. He had no idea where his prison was.

Whenever the sun shone, he stood in its warmth, sucking in the goodness with the fervour of an Inca of old. For much of the rest of the time he walked round and round the room, which measured perhaps 20 feet by 12 feet, believing that somehow this would do his body good. There was nothing arduous or unpleasant about his confinement, but he had never before realised the acute despair which lack of liberty gives to those who are imprisoned. Or perhaps the word is desolation. This was compounded not only of being ignorant how long he might remain in the hands of guerrillas, but also of apprehension about how they might handle him.

It was all very well they had not yet inflicted pain on

him, that they appeared civilised – even friendly at times – and continually stated in muffled tones that they wanted money rather than his life or his screams. But when would their patience run out and his life be a necessary forfeit in order to maintain the credibility of the whole guerrilla blackmail against the Ecuador Government?

Besides, there were those among his captors who disliked him, and they plagued him in small ways. The small one, whose steel glasses glinted within the recesses of his hoodmask, had a whole repertoire of tricks.

One morning, bringing in Michael's breakfast, steelglasses deliberately tilted the tray so that a glass of milk slid from it and spilt on the captive's trousers. There was no more milk. Worse, there were no more trousers. The clothes Michael had were already stained, filthy, hardening with sweat. The milk, creating its own sour stench as it dried, made him feel dirtier. It was a subtle form of humiliation. Thus is degradation hastened.

On other occasions steel-glasses came and sat in the room whether it was his turn for guard duty or not, saying nothing, busying his fingers in filling the magazines of automatic weapons with bullets, very slowly. Michael could *feel* him smirking, even though the face was in shadow, each time he announced that there was still no news of the ransom being forthcoming, implying that the descent towards death was accelerating. He was a gloater, one of nature's torturers.

In the circumstances, sunlight was important to the captive. Sunlight reminded him of Alison, sunlight on her hair, sunlight in her movements. He dreamed of her, worried about her, tried to remember the face of his child. Conversation, though, was even more important than sunlight and mental images, and fortunately there were many among the guerrillas who talked with him – men who appeared almost embarrassed that they had a prisoner at all, not knowing what to do with him, not wanting to kill him. Michael quickly realised that these exchanges were his best hope against melancholy. He sought to understand the motives and the minds of the guerrillas.

Francisco, their leader, was the one with whom conversation went on longest and probed deepest. His was the sole name Michael knew. Francisco, a lawyer's son, was never

305

embarrassed by the situation. He was *chef* because he was the most realistic of the band. However he might privately wish his situation could change, he knew that the only hope for survival of any of them was to keep the band together until a decisive opportunity for flight across the border arrived. For that, money was needed. He was determined, somehow, to get the ransom paid.

On the evening of the twenty-third day after Michael's capture, he entered the room and sat down.

'You must write a letter, Mr Grant.'

'What am I to say, then?'

'That you have only one week left to live.'

Oddly, the news had no particular impact upon Michael. When you are uncertain of life from day to day, a week seems a very long time.

'Nothing has had any effect on Colonel Vargas so far. Why should this?' said Michael.

'You will write it to your father.'

'What can he do?'

'He is in Quito. He will persuade Vargas. He must.'

Michael had not yet been given this information, although Bernard had been in Ecuador for over a week. With the over-optimism of those who must snatch at any hope, he smiled. The knowledge of Bernard's presence somewhere near made him feel that everything was going to be all right. He wanted only to do anything which could help Bernard, and this urge sprang primarily not from his desire to live, but was more a form of gratitude to his father for assuming, again, the lost role of protector.

'I'll write,' said Michael. 'But in my own language.'

'So long as it is persuasive. We do not wish to kill you, Mr Grant. But if necessary, we would.'

'What would my death achieve, *chef*?'

Francisco shrugged. 'We have been through that before. It would be stupid of the Government to force it upon us, but it would show them we are serious. That is necessary. One death is not so important.'

In this strangely unreal conversation, that did not sound an unreasonable proposition. Michael waited, encouraging Francisco to continue.

'So many have died. This country was founded on blood. Like most in South America.'

'But this is a different time now. Values change.'

Francisco was prepared to debate. 'The men who control this society do not change. And they must be changed. Violence seems the only way. The descendants of a few hundred Spaniards from four centuries ago should not be allowed to inherit this country like princes.'

'Your family is among them. You've told me.'

Francisco fingered his face. Even inside the hood Michael could see he was, unlike many of his companions, unbearded. 'I am proud of the Indian blood that is in me, Mr Grant, as you well know.'

Indeed, Michael did. Amerindians do not grow much facial hair and European blood is often today proclaimed in South America by a wearer's moustache, imitating the pointed beards and whiskers of the old *conquistadores*. Francisco was either naturally unhairy or regularly used a razor to perpetuate the romantic light in which he saw himself. He had scornfully referred to the carefully shaped moustache of Palindo Perez on several occasions.

'If I remember my true ancestors, why should I be concerned about one life?' Francisco continued. 'The invaders slaughtered thousands when they came. Even when the leaders of the Incas became docile Christians, they were betrayed and tortured and killed.'

Michael knew the facts, Francisco had told him often enough. The wife of the Inca, Manco, stripped and beaten and shot to death with arrows in 1539; Manco himself later stabbed to death by seven Spaniards as they played horseshoe quoits with him; the last Inca, Tupac Amaru, beheaded after a hasty and unjust trial. Francisco did not tell Michael that in the first and last cases it was Indians who had done the killing – members of the Cañari tribe, who disliked the Inca supremacy, and always supported the Spanish invaders. He felt that until his prisoner knew more history the information could only be misleading.

'The Incas were conquerors themselves,' said Michael. 'That, too, you have taught me.'

'That was different,' said Francisco. 'They were people of this continent, natural leaders. They created a way of life which was *ours*. The Spaniards were foreigners. Even many of their own philosophers believed they had no moral

307

right to subject the native inhabitants of the colonies to virtual slavery.'

Francisco paused, groping for a new fact with which to underline his point. 'Did you know, Mr Grant, that Indian women were forced to carry foals born to the mares of the Spaniards in litters during Almagro's march towards Chile?'

Michael was silent. He had no answers, few arguments. It was another world and the understanding of it would be a painful process. There were times when Francisco implied that he was descended from the Incas, and Michael did not know enough to be certain whether this could be so.

'Well?' said Francisco, irked by Michael's silence.

'How can I argue with you, *chef*? You have good reason to be bitter. I understand more now.' He had, in previous conversations, challenged the morality of basing contemporary terrorism on historical atrocities. But this seemed no moment to press the point.

'You will write the letter now,' said Francisco. And Michael nodded, smelling the fresh sweat of his body even above the several other stenches which he had about him.

3

The letter came to Bernard Grant by way of Martin secretly. The American did not reveal why he was used as go-between. But he was overwhelmed with relief that the guerrillas had shown again they were willing to give him a special position.

His sense of anguish had come close to panic pitch during the past weeks. Michael's kidnapping had been in no way connected with Martin's earlier approach to the guerrillas. But that did not prevent the American from feeling that if Michael were murdered he would be partly to blame. His dealings with the guerrillas were transformed into a sense of direct treachery against Michael. Martin felt guilty by association.

Bernard Grant was low in spirit, appalled at Cantania's apparent powerlessness and at his own inability to move Vargas or to get the President to say other than that the decision of the Cabinet must remain paramount. So he did not hesitate to discuss the letter with Martin once he had read it. He had formed, within a few days, much the same opinion as his son of Martin's competence and basic decency. And he was moved by the American's obvious distress at Michael's plight. Martin read the words in silence.

I AM WELL. BUT THE RANSOM DEMAND IS SERIOUS. THEY SAY THEY WILL WAIT ONLY ONE WEEK MORE. DO WHAT YOU CAN.

MICHAEL.

His first reaction was impulsive and irrational. 'They'll have to let us pay it. We'll go to Vargas now.'

Bernard remembered his three previous interviews. 'He won't agree.'

'He must,' said Martin. 'Even that bastard's got to change some time.'

'What difference will a note make?' said Bernard. 'Vargas has already taken their threats seriously. You know his arguments for not doing what those damn terrorists want. I can't even be sure that my own Government is particularly anxious for me to pay up.'

Martin was colder, more determined. 'Then we'll have to do what they want without Vargas's agreement.'

'And how do you propose I produce a suitcase with half a million dollars inside it, stuck here?'

'There must be some way,' said Martin. 'Flown in from outside the county. A contraband route. Something like that.'

To Bernard, it sounded like the fantasy of espionage movies. Martin observed his expression of doubt.

'How much risk will you take, Sir Bernard?'

'I want my son,' said Bernard flatly. 'I don't care how it happens. Nor what it costs.'

'You'd better mean that. I may not be talking of just half a million and a few incidental expenses.'

'I suppose you know all the contraband runners.' Bernard razored his voice with more hostility than he felt.

'No,' said Martin. 'But I'm damn sure Perez does.'

'Perez? He'd never dare. Why should he help us? Cantania is his uncle.'

Martin thoughtfully rubbed the red mark on his face. Then he said: 'In a way, that's the point.'

They invited Perez to go for a ride. Martin was afraid to talk anywhere within the consortium building or in Perez's office. So was Bernard. Neither of them knew much about bugging, nor whether the Ecuadoreans were sophisticated enough to fix such traps. But they had to be sure.

Perez sat nervously in the Oldsmobile as Martin drove out of Quito in a light drizzle. He had no idea what the American and Michael's father wanted. He kept sweeping at his moustache nervously. Since the guerrillas had snatched him he'd become twitchy. His nose still sported a plaster across the bridge, and the skin around his right eye remained bruised dully blue and yellow.

They stopped by a grove of eucalyptus trees on the road that led south to Ambato. The rain had stopped, and the scent of the trees, awakened by moisture, was overpowering. Bernard had a headache and he continually felt short of breath. The thin air of the high plateau made him feel old and that, in turn, made him only more desperate to succeed, less careful of the price. Was it imagination that made him suspect pains in his chest? The dread of his coronary, the Christmas before last, chilled him. He smoothed his lapels. What would normally have been a gesture of vanity was now an unpremeditated way of easing his mind, of preparing himself for the most important negotiation of his life.

Perez laughed incredulously at first.

'You are joking, Sir Bernard. I am deeply sorry for what is happening. Michael is my friend.' Martin thought, oh Christ you oily creep. 'But, Sir Bernard, I cannot possibly help you in *that* way. It would be more than my life was worth . . .'

'You won't have much of a life left if you don't,' said Martin before Bernard, flicking his tufting eyebrows angrily, indicated that there must be only one negotiator.

'Senor Perez. Please. I am asking you this seriously. I do not wish my son to die. Your contacts are good enough to get that money to me.'

'This is madness, Sir Bernard. Even if I could arrange something through the contraband men, how could you expect me to take the risk? It is against the interest of my country. It would be treachery to my uncle . . .'

Perez was prepared to make further patriotic and familial noises. Bernard cut him short.

'No,' he said. 'You would be helping your uncle.'

'Nonsense,' said Perez. 'How?'

Bernard paused, breathing quickly. His chest hurt, no doubt of it. This was the moment when the persuasion pitch began; the salesman's supreme test.

'Dr Cantania's whole political career – let us say his credibility – depends upon driving the petro-chemical plant at Esmeraldas through to completion. And soon. There have already been delays enough. Should he not succeed he will be finished as a political force. He has staked his whole reputation upon that plant and what it means for Ecuador. You have heard his speeches . . .'

'But, Sir Bernard . . .' Perez began.

'Let me finish,' snapped Bernard. 'If Dr Cantania is overthrown, where will you be? You depend upon his power and his favour. Colonel Vargas will eat you as he will eat your uncle if the Esmeraldas project is a disaster.'

'But the plant will not be a disaster,' said Perez, eyes eager at the prospect of easing the pressure. 'It is in the final stages.'

'I shall withdraw my support,' said Bernard. 'Everything. No more money will be forthcoming. Every expert at the site whom I control or can persuade will be withdrawn.'

'You are, forgive me, only one part of the consortium, Sir Bernard. The leaders are Kerridge Steel . . .'

'Kerridge Steel can only exist now with the money I'm putting into the operation,' growled Bernard.

'Then you would lose all your profits, Sir Bernard. I don't suppose you've yet been paid for all the equipment you've provided.'

'No,' said Bernard, growing calmer with every minute as he laid out his stall. 'I haven't. But the promissory notes covering the stage payments are reasonably up to date. I'd be prepared to take my losses.'

Perez grew more excited. 'You'd be sued for breach of contract. The sums could be huge.'

'That's a chance I'd have to take. With my son's life as part of the whole equation, the outside world might well

311

consider the question of court cases as a blasphemous irrelevancy. And by God, I aim to tell the world tomorrow if I don't get action from you, Perez.'

'There are other companies we could turn to for the job to be finished.'

This time Martin, explosively interrupting, would not be silenced. 'Crap, just crap. Don't you know that? This job has gone so far now with the present partners, it can't be unscrambled – not unless you're gonna wait years for the plant to be finished. It's got to be driven through the way it is. We depend on you, Perez, and your government – but sure as God you depend on us too. What international corporation do you think is going to want to get involved in the game at this goddam stage? Especially if they thought it was dangerous too. They wouldn't risk losing top men to the guerrillas by kidnapping or just plain killing. Use your brains, Perez.'

Perez tried to look as if he were massaging his mind. 'If all that you say is true, why not go to my uncle? Why involve me?'

'That's too dangerous,' said Bernard. 'If your uncle began to work the strings, Vargas would know for certain. Do you want to risk that? If your uncle is found out, you're finished in this country.'

'The risks are huge for you too,' said Perez. 'I am not convinced you are serious about taking them.'

In the distance they watched a peasant, dressed in blue trousers and a grey poncho, slowly skirting the white walls of a hacienda. The heavy deliberation of his movements somehow decelerated the conversation. Bernard's next words fell on Perez like boulders.

'Please, Senor Perez, believe me. I mean what I say. I would damage myself and my business. But I would not hesitate to destroy you and your uncle in the process. Totally.'

Perez raised a pale fingernail, carefully manicured, to his mouth and nibbled at it. 'I'm not sure what I could do . . .'

'Listen,' said Martin. 'That ain't all.'

Perez turned his head sharply. There was a cold distaste, almost hatred, in Martin's voice.

'I can wreck that plant. Easy.' Martin tried to brush away the redness on his cheek. 'Oh, and I'd do it too. No one could ever blame me. Things go wrong all the time in projects so involved, so technical. But that ain't the end of it. If you don't do this for us, Perez, I think I'd kill you.'

Even Bernard had not expected to hear that. He sat rigidly, embarrassed. Perez jerked his hand away from his mouth, the fingernail bleeding, and there was silence. The rain had begun again, drumming dully on the roof of the car. Bernard wondered about Perez: whether fear for his life was the paramount emotion, or alarm at the calculation of percentages lost in a world where graft was just another item that had to be budgeted, like nuts and bolts or computer time.

'I will see what can be done,' said Perez at last. 'And if it is possible, I would suggest gold rather than dollars. It may be more negotiable.'

Then they drove back to the city without speaking, the screen wipers flailing at the rain. Bernard's body felt painless, free and floating.

5

In three weeks and three days Alison Grant lost six pounds in weight. Feeding her son each day, she became increasingly melancholy. The child, so she imagined, looked like Michael already. In his face she traced every contour of the father and wondered whether the boy would need to be her substitute for the man.

Sensibly, not wishing to distress Bernard further, she agreed not to fly to Ecuador. But the waiting was hell. Everyone at Prospect House was dutifully, and embarrassedly, sympathetic. But no one *told* her anything, not the details. They had the misguided sense of chivalry within which so many large organisations attempt to embalm the intellect of women. Finally, she rang David.

'How did you get on in Paris?'

'Fine.' Pause.

'David, don't stop there, for God's sake. Explain. Everyone clams up on me.'

'Not on the 'phone, Alison. It's tricky.'

'Will you call in on your way home?'

Pause. 'Sure – if you really want me to.'

'Of course I want you to.'

'Okay. Around seven.'

He sat down with her in the window that overlooked the Embankment. The home-going cars laid streaks of light on the wet road. She gave him a martini and sipped one herself, hungrily.

'It must be bloody awful for you,' he said.

'Not nearly so awful if I knew what was going on.'

She looked at him almost piteously, no fire in the grey-green eyes, her whole body in an attitude of collapsed submission. The slacks she wore were paint-streaked, the shoulders of her sweater marked with fallen hairs and dandruff.

'Okay,' he said. 'Paris was good. SAEF will help with the ransom money if necessary. And they're getting their government to put pressure on Quito. We couldn't have got much more.'

'Thank you, David. I'm grateful, very grateful.'

He shrugged, embarrassed still. 'It wasn't difficult. I want Michael back too.'

Now she smiled, sadly but with genuine warmth. 'I believe you do.'

'Come on, Alison. He means a lot to me. He's more than just a boss. You must know that.'

'Yes, I think I might even be a bit jealous.'

It was a remark meant to put him at his ease, to lighten the tension. It succeeded. They both smiled, warily but spontaneously. David spent ten minutes telling her everything he knew about the negotiations for Michael's release.

'It doesn't add up to much,' she said.

'I suppose not.'

'No one's done as much as you. Michael told me five or six weeks ago you were able to put pressure on SAEF in some way. Something to do with a political scandal.'

'Something like that,' he said.

'And a woman?'

'Yes.'

'Meaning what?'

'Look, Alison, don't push me on that.'

'Sorry. Honestly. It's the state I'm in. I don't give a damn how you've done it.' Then she saw his face. 'Sorry again. Do you?'

He didn't know what to say. Did he care? Could he really sustain every example of dubious morality by arguing that the end justified the means? He knew only that he was becoming very weary of confrontations which demanded such decisions.

'Christ knows,' he said, and she divined his anguished confusion.

'I understand, David. It's a bloody awful life.' Yet in her mind, beside the warmth and gratitude she felt towards him, lurked the thought that Michael, surely, would not have been so imprecise. To take the right decision demanded toughness of spirit. Had David got that?

His reply made her slightly ashamed of her suspicion. 'No, it's a good life. I don't want everybody to love me, so long as I can live with myself.' Then, typically, he added an unserious tone to his speech. 'I know what I'm doing. But you have to talk as if you don't sometimes. Good for the soul, they tell us.'

He rose to leave. 'Thank you,' she said. 'Thanks for everything.'

'That's okay.'

'I think we're better now – you and I, I mean.'

'Maybe we are.'

'I was glad about Sheila,' she said. 'The court decision, I mean.'

'Perhaps you'll come – well, I mean, when Michael's back – would you like to come to dinner?'

'Oh Christ,' she said. 'Please let him come back.' She put her hands, suddenly, to her face as her control collapsed. He put his arms around her and for two or three minutes she simply allowed the tears to come.

Then, her shoulders slowly subsided and she looked up at him. 'Please, David, pray for him. I don't pray, not ever, you understand, but now every night, every damn night.'

'All right, I'll pray.'

He didn't like leaving her, but she insisted that he went at once. He felt miserable, yet relieved. It was good to have a relationship with her again, one whose dimension and limitations were known by both sides.

6

As David rode the train into Surrey, Lord Bender and Earl Sanger met across a peaceful table in a private suite of the Savoy Hotel. Sanger played with gleaming cutlery on the starched tablecloth. No one would disturb them for half an hour, at which point dinner would be served and he would have finished the small pitcher of martini which stood before him.

Bender drank water, plain old London tap water.

'It can't go on much longer, Benjamin. You know it.'

'It'll have to.'

'Dammit, be reasonable,' said Sanger. 'Harold's okay to hold the fort for a guy who's on vacation for a coupla weeks. But it's getting serious now. Mike's been away well over a month.'

Sanger took a large draught of martini, wiped his lips with the back of one hand. Bender said nothing. Hunched in his chair, he regarded Sanger closely.

'All right,' said Sanger, unwilling to delay coming to the point any longer. 'I don't like saying it any more than you, Benjamin, but how do we know he'll make it back here at all?'

'I've considered that possibility,' said Bender.

'Everyone's sorry for Mike, but we can't let Prospero fall apart.'

'No,' said Bender.

'Well, we need to take some decisions.'

'I presume you mean that this is your application for the post of chief executive?'

Bender spoke coldly, wanting to make Sanger squirm. But that was only because of his abhorrence of the thought of death, and his distaste for the American. Not that distaste at a personal level would influence any business decision by Bender. He would do what was right for himself, his shareholders, his employees, perhaps even for God, Queen and country too. The problem of what would happen to the leadership of Prospero if Michael Grant did not return had rarely been out of his mind.

Sanger was not deterred by Bender's tone. Indeed, he was cheered. The noble Lord was getting the point.

'If you want to take it like that, then okay. I'm only saying we can't go on this way. In your heart you know it too.'

Bender looked stern. He did not enjoy references to his heart. It reminded him of mortality, and Bender was a man who believed it to be important for many people that he stayed alive.

'I'm aware of the problem, Earl. I don't wish us to make any hasty decisions, that's all.'

Sanger stayed cool. 'Who else is there but me?' He honestly believed that, too.

'I'm not inclined to disagree with you if we look only at the present board. But we could recruit outside.'

He might not have spoken for all the notice Sanger took of him. 'Even if Mike comes back, how can you support him as top man? Not if you're really doing the job for your stockholders. This whole Ecuador deal is a disaster.'

'You supported it too,' said Bender.

'I don't disagree. But it's not the commitment that was wrong – it's the way it's been carried through. Do I have to bore you with all these details again?'

'No,' said Bender. 'It's not been perfect, everyone knows. But it's doubtful whether it calls for a vote of no-confidence in the chief executive.'

The conversation had reached the point to which Sanger had, reasonably and without overplaying his hand, been leading it.

'There's something you don't know.'

'What?'

'Quant, the computer guy who's working for us at Esmeraldas, flew into town yesterday.'

'Yes?'

'He says it's extremely doubtful whether the process control system for that damn plant is gonna do the job it was supposed to. It's too technical for me to explain fully – but if that's true, the petro-chemical company will crucify us.' He pushed a hand through the stubble of his head, then tugged at his belt as he got up. 'Would that be a no-confidence matter, Benjamin?'

There was a gentle knock on the door. A waiter's head appeared.

'Come in,' said Bender. 'For once, I'm hungry.' Then he

looked up at Sanger with the same coldness as before but his head was nodding as he spoke. 'Yes. I think that would be. You play a mean game, Earl.'

7

One week later, with Bernard Grant still in Ecuador, the rump of the Prospero board sat around their glass table in Prospect House waiting for Bill Oldershaw. Harold Armfield had acceded to the demand from Sanger and Bender that a committee of the board should discuss the state of the Ecuador contract with the head of Brasserton's. But the discussion moved to wider issues as the four of them – Armfield, Bender, Sanger and Vernon Morton, the plump merchant banker – were delayed while Oldershaw extricated himself from a traffic snarl-up somewhere close to the end of the M1.

Armfield had insisted that Morton should join them. Not only did this give the meeting a more heavily financial complexion, but Morton was a friend of Bernard's. Today, Bernard was going to need friends.

'When *is* he coming back?' Sanger was insistent. 'He doesn't seem to be getting anywhere over Mike. Surely he should be thinking about the organisation too.'

Armfield took that as a criticism of his own ability to manage Prospero in the absence of the Grants. And he was right.

'The organisation is in good shape, Earl,' said Armfield precisely. 'Or perhaps you have omitted to study the latest trading accounts?'

'Sure, sure, we know all that,' said Sanger. 'But look at our price on the market. Everybody knows how shaky the whole Ecuador thing is now. They're waiting to see what happens to Kerridge Steel. I've said it a dozen times already.'

'You have indeed, Earl.' Armfield's voice was sharply sarcastic. 'But we must wait for the Chairman. He is our negotiator on that.'

'That's what bugs me,' said Sanger. 'We can't wait any longer.'

'It appears we can,' said Armfield. 'Kerridge are moving equipment out to Ecuador again. Dealings in their shares have not been suspended, as everyone imagined they would be. And their bank is making money available to them. Immediately, there are no problems.'

Sanger knew all that was true. What he had failed to discover, despite all his sources in New York City, was why. His frustration showed as he spoke again, a little too loud.

'Yeah, that's dandy. But what the hell has the Chairman committed us to out there? We still don't know.'

Bender stirred. 'I'm worried about that too, Harold.'

He said no more. But the implication that Sir Bernard Grant might, on occasions, still view Prospero as a one-man business, and himself as emperor, was there.

Armfield glanced towards Morton, seeking support. He wanted to defend both Bernard and Michael, despite his own doubts.

'That, gentlemen, is surely a question of confidence in Bernard's judgment. He has cabled us that the arrangements discussed with Kerridge will be satisfactory for us. That, as far as I'm concerned, is that. In the Kerridge negotiation, the Chairman has my confidence.'

Morton nodded vigorously. There was no comment from either Sanger or Bender. Sanger decided to try another point of attack.

'Supposing,' he said, 'Oldershaw has really screwed up that job. Supposing his valves and all the other stuff won't function properly – as Quant fears. What the hell then? We'll be crucified, whatever we've done about Kerridge Steel.'

'Perhaps that young man Quant is busy building an alibi for himself,' said Armfield.

Again Bender stirred tetchily. 'Let's forget whose responsibility it is or isn't. Earl has a point.'

Armfield was not a man inclined to real anger. Irritation, yes; sarcasm, too, under stress; but he was not given to explosions. Now, however, it took a real effort of the will to contain his anger. He was becoming very tired indeed with Bender's position of too-easy power. There had been a great change in Armfield's attitudes during the past year or so. Since Michael had made him the second most important executive officer in the corporation, he had grown much closer to both Bernard Grant and his son. They had played fair by him, had given him his area of power and respected it. Armfield was appalled to see Bender seemingly aligning himself with Sanger. It was an unpretty kind of treachery, that; ungrateful to Bernard, who had performed so well for Bender's customers down the years. And Bender's continual niggling was a criticism of Armfield's competence to fill the top executive seat in Michael's absence.

It was anger that now decided Armfield to make his move. He had nursed for months one piece of information against this day. Ideally, he had wanted to use it, if necessary, when both of the Grants were present: to demonstrate to them his loyalty, his competence and his foresight. Regretfully, he decided that he must deny himself the pleasure.

'The situation Earl envisages would be regrettable, but not disastrous,' he told Bender in his softest and most menacing tones. 'At the very outset of our dealings in Ecuador, I arranged for a professional indemnity insurance. If our equipment fails technically to do the job it was designed to do – provided it's not our bad workmanship – we will be covered. We'll make no profit, certainly, but we'll recover our outlay.'

'Why the hell wasn't the board told about this?' Sanger blurted out the words, frustration thwarting his sense of balance. Had he been concerned primarily for the health of Prospero, he should have been congratulating Armfield rather than continuing to be petulant. 'Did Michael or the Chairman know?'

'I'm paid to do my job,' said Armfield icily. 'That was a financial precaution I deemed necessary, and it was within my area of responsibility. I do not consider it essential to bore the board with details of that kind.'

Sanger glanced at Bender and was about to speak again when Armfield cut him short. 'That will do, Earl. I am chairing this meeting, and I'm saying that the subject is closed.'

Oldershaw walked in. No knock, no ceremony, no words. He carried a large suitcase and he scuffed his way to a spare seat facing Armfield. Then he stuck his locked hands defiantly on the glass table before him and glared around him.

'Good morning, gentlemen. Hadn't we better get on with this session of the Star Chamber?'

Armfield looked at him warningly. 'That's not the attitude, William.' He was like a headmaster. 'We're here to help if we can.'

Oldershaw puffed his cheeks and exploded them derisively as if the idea that any of these London slickers could help a black-nailed engineer was the richest of sick jokes.

Yet he still said, 'All right. I'll accept that. But why do I have to come down here to explain myself?'

'You used organisation funds. We have a right,' said Armfield. 'It's normal, you know that, William.'

'Just because it's normal, doesn't mean it's right. Or fair. I could have raised funds on the name of my company if need be.' He threw a packet of papers on the table. 'There you are. We've wasted a bloody week we can ill-afford getting all that gunge down for you. It's not reasonable.'

Armfield regarded Oldershaw with some sympathy. The little engineer looked ill. His eyes were yellow and the skin around them dark and puffy; he could scarcely control the shaking of his hands. In fact, he'd had only three or four hours' sleep a night for many weeks. Armfield knew he'd made a mistake. He should never have allowed Sanger, with Bender, to bully him into calling Oldershaw to London for a meeting like this. Oldershaw worked better if he was left alone, given the illusion of freedom.

The board took one of Oldershaw's documents apiece. Then Oldershaw began to lead them through the figures, riding the questions – occasional and cold from Bender, frequent and hot and invariably critical from Sanger. There were obvious shortcomings in the way that Brasserton's had serviced the Ecuador people. Armfield noticed that supply had often fallen behind requirement. He saw how Brasserton's cash-flow had been ill-managed. He could not miss the number of replacement orders – presumably for defective equipment – which Brasserton's had been forced to make. The bills for air freight made him shudder.

Yet, throughout the steamy half-hour of questioning, he felt impelled to defend the man. Oldershaw made no attempt to disguise where things had gone wrong. His answers, like the document he'd produced, were honest. It had been an incredibly difficult operation. Brasserton's had made mistakes. But they'd put them right. The profit on the job would, ultimately, be much less than expected. There would, however, still be profit. And the job would be done.

Finally, Sanger said. 'My information is that the process control operation may not work.'

'Balls,' said Oldershaw.

'Hold it, Oldershaw,' said Sanger. 'These are experts saying it.'

'That snotty-nosed kid Quant, you mean?' sneered Oldershaw. 'I've designed more valves in my time than he's had hot dinners.'

'He's our project manager,' said Armfield, trying to control Oldershaw. If Oldershaw shut up now, the peace might just be kept.

'And he shouldn't have been,' snapped Oldershaw. 'There's only one man in the field I trust, and that's Del Martin, even if he is a Yank.'

'I suppose you know all about computers,' said Sanger, sneering in return. 'It's your goddam valves that's given all the trouble. Sheer incompetence.'

Oldershaw shot to his feet. The chair behind him toppled over. He looked as if he might scream his head off, but he didn't. He spoke very tightly, cool with fury.

'I know enough about computers,' he said. 'Oh, yes. A real gutful. And you, you stupid bastard, wouldn't know a valve from a paper bag, so when I say what I know, then don't you bloody disagree. Because you don't know anything.'

Armfield snapped. 'That's enough, William. I'll not have brawling. And you, Earl. Get off his back.'

'I've finished,' said Oldershaw. 'But for one thing.'

He bent, and from the suitcase he pulled out two valves – pieces of shaped and moulded metal almost identical, around a foot long. He held one in each hand, aloft. He shook his right hand.

'This is a valve, Mr Sanger. I made it three years ago. It's beautiful, perfect. That was before we were forced to reorganise our production at Brasserton's, and before we had all those bloody computer men in to tell us how to do the job.'

He shook the valve in his left hand.

'This one was made six months ago, before I had the chance to put things right in my factory. It's misshapen, the tolerances are all wrong, the metal's flawed. It's a bloody disgrace. That's what computers did for me, Mr Sanger – computers and all the damned interference I've had from

London. Yes, I know all about computers. But it's going to change, Mr Armfield. When the Chairman's back I'm going to demand that this organisation treats us differently. And there are a lot more managing directors out there in the operating companies who'll be with me.'

He glared at the four Prospero directors, challenging them to interrupt him.

'And now I'm going. I can't see you've much else to learn from me, and I'm damn sure I haven't much to learn from you. But just have a look at these when I've gone, Mr Sanger – if they're not too dirty for you to soil your hands on.'

He tossed, really tossed, quite deliberately, the valves on to the glass table. The sound was abrasive and hard, but the glass, shivering for an instant, did not break. The metal lay there, dead, one of the valves showing just a trickle of oil, as if it were bleeding. Oldershaw didn't bother with the suitcase. He just walked out.

He was still shaking, with a heady mixture of fear and exhilaration, when he reached George Lovelace on the telephone ten minutes later.

'Christ, George, I needed to talk to you. Christ, I did.'

'What's up, lad?' said Lovelace.

'I've done it, George. I've bloody done it.'

He explained. For five minutes.

'Bloody hell,' said Lovelace. He sounded more scared than enthusiastic. 'Did you mention my name?'

'No,' said Oldershaw. 'Just said there were a few others who felt like me.'

Pause. Then Oldershaw again. 'Are you there, George?'

'Aye.'

'Well?'

'Hell's teeth, lad,' said Lovelace. 'You were a bit strong.'

'Had to be, didn't we?'

'Didn't *you*, lad. It's not the way I would have chosen.'

Oldershaw spoke through the fingernail he'd begun to bite. 'All right, all right. So. I'll carry the can for what I said. But it doesn't change what we've all got to do. Now's the time.'

'I'm not sure.'

'Come on, George. You promised. I can get at least two other signatures on the letter to Bernard Grant.'

'You should have told me beforehand,' said Lovelace. 'I'm not ready. These cars of mine are going like the clappers. I can't risk mucking about just now.'

'But, George. You *promised*. Any time after mid-November you said. Dammit, George. You can't bugger about now.' Oldershaw's voice rose from high-pitched anger to even higher-pitched pleading, whining almost.

'No, Bill. I'm sorry. But no. Why didn't you tell me?'

'But George. For Christ's sake.'

'No, Bill. Look, I've got to go. Will you be at the Christmas party?'

'Fuck the party – and fuck you,' said Oldershaw.

He got into the Rover 2000 and fumed in the pre-Christmas crowds that snared him like a fly in honey. By the time he broke clear and hit the Hendon Way it was dusk. Sleet began to fall, through mist. It took him another half-hour before he burst through on to the motorway proper.

He drove like a maniac. He was half-singing, half-sobbing to himself. *Bastards. Bastards all of them. Can't trust anybody. Rotten lousy bastards.* He stayed in the fast lane, horn blaring, headlights undipped, speedometer around 90.

The M1, leading north to the midlands and beyond, is a strangely deceptive motorway. Its curves are leisurely, but if you hit some of them at really high speeds, they can quickly seem as tight and difficult as a right-angled corner on a slower highway. Not far north of London there is one such curve, a long right-hander for cars travelling north. There's a brickworks near it and, incongruously, black and white cows in the fields at most times of the year.

Oldershaw didn't see any cows. Nor had he observed the twin flashing amber lights which had been switched on for 5 minutes or so before he reached the curve. His speed was 85 and he could see quite clearly, except that there was an excess of moisture, which he would never have admitted were tears, in his eyes.

Suddenly, though, he could see almost nothing as he struck the pocket of fog which makes the M1 among the most hazardous of fast tracks in Britain. In a panic he stabbed at the brakes. The car went into a skid, began to half-broadside along the wet road. Ahead of him he could hear a succession of dull sounds mixed in with the screech of metal upon metal. It was like some of the sounds at Brasserton's, but with none of the harmony of noise that his beloved lathes could create.

The car stopped broadsiding. It began to spin and spin, and it went on spinning until the side on which Oldershaw was sitting, hands rigid with fear on the wheel, struck the back of a huge truck carrying milk in bulk.

His hands were still on the wheel and his face was miraculously unmarked when they pulled out his lifeless body one hour later.

11. KILL AND BE KILLED

1

NONE of the guerrillas slept for more than a few minutes on the night the plane was due to take off, even though they had been on the move, under cover of darkness, for five days and were raw around the eyes from lack of rest.

Their route back to the village which had once served as their base when they were raiding the plant at Esmeraldas had been a circuitous one. Twice, by pre-arrangement, they were driven in a truck for a few score kilometres along highways; the first time on the rocky road going west from Quito to Santo Domingo de los Colorados, the second on the smoother run when the route turns north from Santo Domingo towards Esmeraldas.

But these rides had been a rare respite. Mostly, by night and day, they avoided the highways. On the first part of their journey that had meant picking their way through ravines stuffed with boulders, fighting currents as they forded streams and rapids, climbing walls in stony fields where poverty-line Indians scratched out a living. The days were warmish, since the altitude of the high plateau tempered the equatorial heat, and the nights were very cold. It rained a lot, for December is still within Ecuador's wet season. They ate maize, fruit and small lizards, roasted over screened fires.

Unpleasant as the journey at 10,000 feet or so had begun, it was easy compared with the trek beyond Santo Domingo. Here, closer to sea level, they faced terrain which was lush and tropical. It wasn't as bad as Amazonian jungle, but it was deterring enough.

The rains beat down almost incessantly. Where the land away from the roads was uncultivated, trees and creepers grew thickly. And even the banana plantations weren't easy to cross, the vegetation dense and green and three or four times a man's height. The mud was deep and clogging, so that their calves ached with the effort of dragging themselves through it. Their sweat, drawn out by the warm humidity of the air, mingled with the rain that soaked their clothing.

They tried not to think too much of the snakes which they knew might be curled around the stems of bananas hanging from the palm-like plants just above their heads. Sometimes they saw snakes and avoided them. They did not see the scorpions and tarantulas which they also knew hid in the greenery, although ants and termites in columns were sometimes visible on the ground. Most of the insects they felt, however – ticks and jiggers and borrachudos and sweat bees. It was not possible to avoid their bites.

There were times when they were so tired that the urge to dump their guns was strong. They kept up their spirits by thinking of the burden which each one of them carried in a rucksack on his back.

The gold, shipped in by a contraband route according to arrangements made in Panama by Perez at the request of Bernard Grant and Martin, had been divided between the sixteen men in the group. At around $65 an ounce, the $500,000 ransom money had bought more than four hundredweights of the stuff. One whole hundredweight – over $100,000 – had been the fee to the contraband men for the escape plane. What was left gave each man upwards of 20 lbs to carry towards a kind of freedom, to be used (such was the theory) to pursue the fight against the Government of Ecuador from a place beyond its borders. It got heavier and heavier as they slipped and stumbled towards their rendezvous.

Still, they had finally reached the village. Now they sat, backs against white-washed walls, saying little, too exhausted to sleep, waiting to start the last stage to the strip, closer to the coast, where the plane would be waiting at midnight.

Francisco surveyed his companions. It had been all right while it lasted, but he wondered whether, once out of Ecuador with their gold, the resolution of these men for the cause would remain. Even with himself, he was no longer as sure as he had been. What sustained him now was a personal hatred for the pigs of the administration, like Vargas and his friends, rather than an unquenchable belief in what

327

might replace them. There were times when he regretted that he had not chosen to work against the institutions of state from within the system, instead of assaulting it so directly from the outside.

Two of the group were picking unenthusiastically at the steak they had been given. It was hard and blue-veined, under-cooked, spotted with blood. Even after the lizards, he hadn't been able to touch it, sticking instead to the thick maize soup and maize cakes which (like chips in England) come with everything at a lower-class level in Ecuador.

His comrade with steel glasses had a cheek bulging as he sucked and chewed. Francisco suspected he was on coca again.

Scarcely stuff for the revolutionary, coca. It was the oldest drug of the Amerindians, leaves picked from bushes on Andean slopes and mixed with lime, producing smallish quantities of cocaine when chewed.

In the present circumstances Francisco could scarcely object. Coca deadens the sense of fatigue and hunger. And steel-glasses had often claimed that it was a link with their Indian brothers.

God, he ached, and his skin was still raw in places with sunburn. There were weals on his shoulders where the straps of the rucksack had cut into him. His lame leg throbbed. It would be good, somewhere south of Ecuador, to live without a gun. He brushed pointlessly at his trousers, stiff with caked mud.

His watch said 10.50. In ten minutes, the radio message would be sent which would free Michael Grant from a cell carefully hidden behind a funeral parlour in Quito.

In the end, Francisco had liked Michael Grant. He had understood what Francisco was talking about, had come to see that there must be change in a society which still left Indians to starve and freeze on the high plateau, or enticed them into a steamy coastal climate which killed them. Francisco was more than ever sure that the persuasion of men like Grant, who were not evil, should have been the way for the radicals to operate in Ecuador. But then, if the guerrillas were not violent, how could the Michael Grants of the world be put in a position where they might be made to listen?

Francisco sprang upright, carbine poised, as fast as a disturbed snake, when he heard the sound of the truck. Four other guns were aligned with his. The gentle knocking at the door reassured them, and when they saw who it was, guns were slung and the whole party moved quietly out of the room with their burdens of gold.

'—Is the plane down?' Francisco whispered to the driver as the truck moved off.

'—Down, yes. Waiting. All the flares are out.'

'—Fuel?'

'—It has fuel enough. Now be quiet, please. I must concentrate.'

The truck proceeded slowly, without lights. The atmosphere was almost luminous, not difficult to see through once the eyes were adjusted. After perhaps half an hour, they halted. There was nothing except strange shapes of trees and the assorted screechings of night creatures. The driver flashed his headlights three times. Somewhere up ahead flashed an answering light.

'—We walk now,' said the driver.

He eased the truck to the side of the road. From the disturbed foliage, water dripped on the guerrillas as they got out.

They followed the drive in single file, instinctively keeping at the verge of the road where they could swiftly find cover. They may not have been trained soldiers, but they had learned their lessons well.

Finally, they came to the truck that had flashed back at them. Beyond it, trees no longer obscured the horizon. There was open land, squelchy beneath their feet, and clearly outlined against the sky, the plane.

Despite the strict orders which Francisco had given, there was a murmuring of relief behind him. For some of the guerrillas, infamous last words, as Vargas was to put it.

The land was suddenly awash with light, searchlights swivelling. Down on the ground fast, bags of gold flung to one side, safety catches off and a collection of carbines, sub-machine guns and self-loading rifles answering the annihilating crossfire which the waiting troops laid down. But where were the guerrillas to shoot, except at the lights?

Francisco got one searchlight; his companions killed two more. But in truth they stood no chance. Two tanks fired at almost point-blank range, mortar shells followed, three static machine guns rattled.

Nine men died, six were injured and lived. Somehow, slithering and rolling and tumbling away from the lights, Francisco encountered blessed darkness. He pressed himself to the earth, took one last look through the smoke at the fallen bodies, and then scrambled his way through the trees a hundred metres or so away.

2

Michael remembered the syringe. They produced it in the morning, while he was taking his bath of sunshine from the window.

Now it was dark. He peered around and shouted with pain as his skull struck an impediment. More carefully he raised his hand again. He was in a narrow street, close to a wall.

He felt too heavy, too befuddled, to do more than lie there. Two Indians passed him and did nothing, imagining him to be one of the hundreds who sleep in the doorways and niches of Quito at night. A dog found him, sniffed, and peed at his feet. At last, a truck approached, and with an effort Michael raised himself and clawed one hand at the beam of its headlights.

Bernard Grant, who had flown back to London a week earlier, on Martin's advice – and, also, to attend Oldershaw's funeral – was in Quito within 36 hours. He knew about the ambush of the guerrillas. He knew he might be flying into trouble. He no longer cared. He had to see Michael.

Martin met him, which was something of a surprise. He half-expected to discover Martin in gaol and, perhaps, himself along with the American soon after landing. But the customs and passport formalities were merely formal. He saw Martin waving to him.

'How's Michael? All right?' Bernard's words were clipped and fragmented from exhaustion.

'Coming along fine, Bernard. Really fine. I've been to see him three times.'

Martin sounded cheerful enough. Yet the American was rubbing his face as if he wanted to put a hole in it. Bernard misinterpreted the sign as concern for Michael, whereas

Martin was wondering how much longer he'd be allowed to walk around free. Cantania had summoned him and talked blandly about inquiries being made into the incident of the guerrillas and the release of Michael. The consequences of that he was willing to face, but how much else might be discovered about his earlier contacts with the guerrillas?

'I want to see him. Now,' said Bernard.

'Sure,' said Martin.

'Look,' said Bernard. 'I don't understand why you're here. Can you get out of the country?'

Martin shrugged. 'They've taken my passport. But that's all. Cantania was quite friendly when I saw him today. Full of getting the plant finished. I don't know what the hell to do except wait and see. Cantania is waiting for you and me, by the way, as soon as you've talked with Michael.'

Bernard was amazed at the coolness of the American. Driving towards the hospital, he asked Martin, 'How much does Cantania know, d'you think?'

'Everything or nothing, Bernard. There's something strange going on there.'

'Is the plant still getting built?'

'Sure. I did a revised schedule yesterday. If Brasserton's keep their promises on the redesigned valves, we should be finished by June next year. Say, Bernard, I was sorry about Bill Oldershaw. He was a good guy.'

'Yes,' said Bernard. 'A tragedy. We shall miss him. He was so reliable. Dedicated. But I've made sure that Brasserton's will be well looked after. You'll get your valves.'

'I don't know what you did with Kerridge's Bernard, but they're moving well too. I gather you're in that company in a big way now. What's the deal?'

'Later, Del. Please.'

His son lay in a quiet private room, with walls so white they hurt his eyes, cared for by nuns who dressed like nurses. Martin left the two of them alone. Bernard embraced Michael with a warmth which took both their minds back to the days of Michael's childhood.

Never, paradoxically, had Bernard been happier than in the weeks of his son's captivity. Once more, he had become the leader of their lives. He it was who could save Michael. He, too, could save Prospero. He had not for many years felt that kind of exhilaration, springing from the realisation of danger, of responsibility and, above all, of being needed crucially both by his son and by the organisation he had painfully constructed down the years.

So there was now, in the meeting of the two men, a degree of emotion in the counterpoint which was virtually unique, certainly in terms of their recent experience. Michael's face was haggard and pale, but the eyes were warm and confident.

'I feel great now, Dad. Honestly. I'll be out of here in 48 hours. Just getting a bit of strength back in my legs. There's nothing really wrong with *me*. It's you I'm worried about.' He forced out the words. 'Your heart, Dad . . .'

Bernard smiled and put out both hands to hold his son's. He could not speak. There were, and he was not ashamed, tears hanging just below his eyes.

'Dear God,' he said finally. 'It's good to see you. I've never felt better. My heart? Sound as a bell.'

'But . . .'

'No qualifications. I'm fine. You're lucky, Michael, like me.'

'I'm still not clear why they let me go. What's going on, Dad?'

Bernard looked around the room meaningfully and waved a hand at Michael to indicate it would not be wise to talk here.

'Leave it, Michael. It's complicated.'

Michael pointed a finger at Bernard, raised his eyebrows, and nodded his head back and forth – a mime asking if Bernard had been heavily involved. Bernard nodded vigorously in return.

'I see,' said Michael. 'Thanks. Is Alison all right? And the baby?'

'They want you very much,' said Bernard, deliberately side-stepping the question. Alison had in fact been far from well. 'She's the happiest woman in London now.'

'I thought of her all the time.'

'Yes.'

'And you.'

'I'm glad.'

'It taught me a lot.'

'They didn't hurt you?'

'No. They were really rather good to me, all things considered.' Michael glanced about him, but still did not hold back. 'I don't agree with their methods, but they've got quite a case about this country. There's a hell of a lot that's wrong.'

'We'll talk it over later,' said Bernard.

'Yes. But listen. What have you done about Kerridge? Martin says it's all fixed. How?'

'We can save that till later, too.'

'Dad, we can't. Come on, now – you'll do me far more harm leaving me lying here wondering what in God's name is happening than by giving it to me straight.'

'There's nothing to get alarmed over, Michael . . .'

'Please, Dad. I'm not a kid. Perhaps what's happened has done both of us a lot of good – for the future, I mean.' He put out a hand and squeezed Bernard's arm. 'We're all right, now. I know it. But don't spoil it. Let's talk.'

His father looked up from beneath the extravagant eyebrows, impatiently wiped at the last drying spot of moisture on his face and saw that Michael meant it. He was satisfied. For the past eighteen months there had been a superficial equality between them in the governing of Prospero. Now, there seemed a chance that the equality might become real. Michael's words had signalled that he accepted his need of Bernard.

His son tried to ease the way by turning the question. 'Am I still chief executive, father? Are you still chairman?'

Bernard exploded into laughter.

'Of course, dear boy. Of course.'

'But what about Sanger? And Bender? They must be blowing their minds if you've committed the organisation to a huge rescue operation for Kerridge Steel. Aren't they screaming for my head?'

'They were,' said Bernard, now serious. 'But I've come up with a formula.'

'What?'

Bernard drew a deep breath. This damned altitude was not his idea of fun. 'No corporate funds are involved, Michael. I've committed the whole of my personal holding in Prospero to Kerridge.'

'My God,' said Michael. 'How much?'

'It was going to be eight million pounds. Now it's nearer ten.'

'But you're mad, father. You could be ruined.'

Bernard, incredibly, was still smiling. 'Nonsense. Provided Kerridge shares pick up again, I should get my money back. I might even make on the deal.'

'But, father – it isn't fair to you. What about SAEF and the others?'

'Oh, they've helped. But it was a big rescue operation, Michael.'

'I still don't see why . . .'

Bernard interrupted him, the smile unfaltering. 'There was no other way, Michael. Bender and Sanger would have torn you limb from limb, believe me. I had to keep Kerridge going – and without weakening Prospero.'

'Father, you've hazarded damn near your entire personal fortune to keep me in the driving seat. I still say you're mad.'

Bernard smiled even more broadly. 'No, not mad. I believe that Sanger and Bender between them would ruin Prospero if they gained control. It wouldn't be the company I built.'

'But, father, if you've lost your holding, they're stronger than ever.'

'Not really. Bender could always have outvoted us if things went wrong. He held the key before, and still does. So there's no change. You remain as chief executive and now you must produce performance that will persuade Bender to let you stay there.'

Michael looked down, ashamed. 'All that money. Your own . . .'

'Money isn't so important, Michael. And I keep telling you – it's not lost yet.'

'Father,' said Michael. 'You're making me feel dependent on you again. I'm grateful for what you've done – but I'm not sure I like it.'

'Rubbish,' said Bernard. 'We're finished with all that, aren't we? Playing the game for position, all that? Yes, you depend on me partly. You can't escape that, nor can I. Let's simply accept it. But then you know that I depend on you too. I need still to feel I have a role in Prospero. And you and Alison and the boy – oh yes, I depend on that as well. In the last few weeks I've learned a lot. Danger clears the mind marvellously.'

Bernard's frankness was compelling; Michael felt forced to speak obliquely.

'How did you get on with Kerridge himself?'

'We understood each other, Michael. We had things in common. Both of us know about horse-trading. The bargaining wasn't unfriendly.'

'I should think not. He must've been damn glad to see you.'

Bernard smiled slowly. 'Oh, yes. But I did lay down conditions.'

'Like what?'

'Like getting rid of Corsino.'

'You're joking.'

'No, Corsino is out. Once he was under a cloud in Washington, among other places, he had no more use as a fixer. No one would have bought a second-hand car from him, let alone a major deal.'

'But Corsino represents big interests, a lot of the money that was in Kerridge's.'

'I know that too,' said Bernard. 'Very funny money as well. I've heard the Mafia mentioned. Not that I believe it, and neither did Kerridge. But whoever Corsino was fronting for, they must've had their business heads screwed on. They recognised that a discredited front man would be no use to them either. There's been no reaction at all to the dropping of Corsino. Last I heard, he was staying in Panama City, taking a long vacation.'

'What other conditions, dad?'

The dusk was gathering when Bernard left the hospital with Martin. They found Cantania in his gloomy office, seeming surprisingly at ease. He was drinking Scotch, of course, but that was so much a usual part of Cantania's scene that to Martin at least it betokened no sign of excessive strain.

'Sir Bernard, we are delighted your son is safe. Thank you both. Thank you for everything.'

Martin and Bernard exchanged wary glances.

'I'm not sure I understand you, Minister,' said Bernard.

Cantania stroked his glass. 'But you must, Sir Bernard. You organised the gold for the guerrillas. It was extremely useful.'

He was enjoying their discomfiture.

'We anticipated that if we were obdurate for long enough, you would move on your own behalf. It was only to be expected of you as a good father. So, when it happened, my nephew, Perez, told me – a good, dutiful boy, Perez – and I told Colonel Vargas. I doubt whether that dolt would ever have got to grips with the guerrillas had he not been given that information.'

Bernard beamed a look of extreme distaste towards Cantania. 'If we accept what you say, you were playing with my son's life.'

'Not at all, Sir Bernard. The guerrillas wanted gold, not blood.'

'And what do you propose to do now?' asked Bernard.

'Nothing, my dear Sir Bernard. Everybody is happy. You have your son. I have my plant well on the way to completion. And Colonel Vargas gains the satisfaction of having broken up a dangerous band of terrorists.' He smiled. 'The fact that the terrorists were about to quit our territory he conveniently ignores. But I would not wish to rob him of his moment of triumph.'

It was Martin's turn to glower. 'I thought you hated Vargas's guts.'

Cantania considered the phrase. 'A little extreme, Mr Martin. He is no friend of mine, nor I of his. But the realities of politics can create strange alliances. Doubtless you have frequently found the same in business, Sir Bernard?'

Again he waited while the point sank home. Bernard relaxed. Cantania was in the driving seat and, Bernard sensed, wasn't going to run the visitors down. He would simply enjoy it for some minutes more. Bernard knew the feeling.

'For the time being I must run with Vargas,' Cantania continued. 'That is the condition of my survival and of achieving my immediate ends. I need his – well, lack of hostility. And the incident of the terrorists has shown him that I can be useful to him. We are used in Ecuador to marriages of convenience.'

Martin was still smarting. 'Those goddam contraband men. They double-crossed us all down the line.'

Cantania leaned forward, eager to continue his lesson. 'Certainly not. They endangered you in no way whatsoever. You will even, Sir Bernard, get some of your ransom back.

Not all of it, unfortunately. Certain of the fees payable have now been banked by people outside these borders. But all the gold which the terrorists were carrying will be returned to you, with certain deductions for expenses of state, and for the share which the one terrorist who escaped took with him.'

'Why did they double-cross us?' growled Martin, still not satisfied.

'No sensible man in the contraband game would run the risk of making himself completely *persona non grata* in this territory,' said Cantania smoothly. 'We can never completely eliminate smuggling, so we often turn the blind eye and make sure we can control its volume. The big men in contraband know the rules. To handle terrorists as cargo would break them. So they were quite willing to co-operate with us.'

Martin glanced at Bernard. What else was there to stay for?

'I'm told your son will be well enough to travel this week, Sir Bernard.' Cantania was smiling almost warmly. 'I expect you'll be wanting to get home for Christmas.'

'Naturally, Minister.'

'And you, too, Mr Martin.'

'You've got my passport,' said Martin sullenly.

'Ah, yes. We were afraid you might rush off in a panic, Mr Martin. And you're too good a man, too essential to the plant. Now that you understand the position, we'll be delighted for you to take a break in North America.'

Cantania was stretching out a hand. Bernard had no option but to take it, and in truth he felt no particular hostility towards the Minister. Cantania had turned a shaky poker hand into a winning one. He commanded respect if, as yet, Bernard would not give him admiration.

'If Mr Martin's construction timetable is adhered to, then I think we might have cause to drink champagne together around June next year,' said Cantania. 'We will arrange a completion ceremony – for you and your people. I shall be delighted to invite you as my personal guest.'

'Thank you, Minister.'

Cantania turned to shake hands with Martin. 'By the way, Mr Martin, I have some further news for you. Ali-Chem have submitted an alternative design for their chlorine plant. No pollution.'

Martin looked blank.

'I though you would be pleased?' questioned Cantania.

'I'm pleased,' said Martin suspiciously. 'But why the sudden change?'

'Because I told them to change,' said Cantania smoothly. 'It is part of my agreement with Colonel Vargas. Neither of us could stand any more activity from terrorists around that site, or any more screams from students.'

'But you told me it couldn't be changed because it was part of the agreement with Ali-Chem.'

Cantania shrugged. 'You do not understand, Mr Martin. An agreement with a foreign corporation is one thing. The needs of my country are another. I will do anything to help Ecuador, anything. That is what being a minister of the republic means.'

'And Ali-Chem will play ball?'

'They are realists. They are so far committed, they would not wish to lose their investment entirely. Besides, they want to have a firm base in Ecuador for their Andean Pact operations. They know they have plenty of competitors dying to leap in. So they have little choice.'

He placed both hands on Martin's shoulders. 'Come, Mr Martin. Look a little pleased about my news, please. You got what you wanted.'

Martin looked hard into the black eyes which had moved in very close to his own.

'Okay,' he said. 'I'm pleased.'

He never did find out then, or later, precisely how much Cantania knew about his dealings with the guerrillas.

3

Christmas in England was white. Michael and Alison stayed in London, with Bernard joining them for the two main days of the holiday. After the heat and rain of Ecuador, it was beautiful to crunch the snow underfoot on the Embankment.

On the afternoon of Boxing Day, the three of them went walking in Battersea Park, although Bernard was loth to leave the child, whom he had gone to sleep nursing in an armchair after Christmas lunch. The cold air made his daughter-in-law glow with health. To him she looked more beautiful than ever, copper hair tumbling across the white fur of her topcoat. She had recovered quickly from the bleak weeks without Michael. She would be good for his son down all the years.

For no reason he could think of he said: 'Bill Oldershaw would have enjoyed this. He liked the winter.'

Michael, arm warm inside Alison's, nodded. 'I'm sorry, Dad. It shouldn't have happened. If I hadn't been away . . .'

'Not your fault, Michael. Harold told me Bill Oldershaw was under great stress that day. Sanger and Benjamin pushed him hard, but in the end he pushed himself even harder. Bill was always like that. Conscientious to a fault.'

'Is that fair? He was being made to do something he didn't want to do.'

Bernard shook his head. 'No, Michael. He used that pretence as his shield, once he found he'd bitten off more than he could chew, but Bill was as ambitious as any of us. He told me once he wanted a production computer in his works more than anything else. Oh, he coveted that Ecuador contract, all right. It was like the seal on his success as an engineer, out there playing ball with the international giants of the world. Our sin was in not recognising that he wasn't the man to cope with it. For that, I blame myself.'

'But he did good work,' said Michael. 'Oh, he made mistakes, yes. He put them right, though. By the time he died, he'd almost made it. That was the tragedy.'

'He killed himself making it,' said Bernard. 'No success in business is worth that. Never let any of our people do that again.'

'I'm learning, father. In all kinds of ways.'

'Thank God for that,' said Alison, and neither of the men minded. They stopped by some shuttered kiosks; ice-cream, candy floss, potato crisps, fortunes told, photographs taken. Beyond them were the skeletons of roller-coaster rides and carousels.

'The boy will love these when he grows up,' said Bernard. 'Pray God I'm alive to bring him here.'

'You'll outlast us all,' said Michael.

'Funny thing about Bill Oldershaw,' said Bernard. 'The

largest wreath was from his local bowling club. He had a passion for the game. Won dozens of trophies. I never knew.'

4

The interview with Earl Sanger, Bernard saved for the second day of the new year. The clean snow of Christmas had been pounded into dark yellow slush as the world awoke to business again after the protracted holiday. While the American was taking his seat, suspiciously, Bernard commented how sad it was that snow got spoilt.

'That's the way I've always known snow,' said Sanger. 'Where I was raised it turned dirty in the air.'

'Where was that, Earl?'

'Ohio. They grow steel mills there. The air used to be so full of cinders, people thought they were the state bird.'

It was a grim joke, which Sanger had used before. Cinders, as well as brick streets full of rotting houses and boozing parents and street fights with blacks or polacks were some of the interesting facts about Sanger's Ohio steel-town life. His background had made him less squeamish than most about the methods he employed to get out and stay out of that particular environment. Sanger expected to fight tough, rough and, if necessary, dirty. Time had not yet mellowed him, though it might.

Bernard's smile was thin. 'You've taught us a great deal, Earl. We should be grateful.'

Sanger was momentarily baffled. 'I don't think you need much teaching, Sir Bernard,' he said. He was still wondering what the old man was up to as Bernard leaned, confidentially, across the desk.

'Earl, we want you to leave London.'

'What does that mean?'

'We want you to resign from Prospero.'

'The hell you do. What are you trying to pull?'

'It will be for the best, Earl. In your interests, I assure you.'

Sanger was on his feet, tugging at the waistband of his trousers. 'I'll go when I'm good and ready. What does Bender say? You can't push me around . . .'

Bernard held up his hands placatingly. 'Please. Do sit down. Hear me out.'

Grudgingly, Sanger resumed his seat. His spectacles had become slightly misted. He began to polish them energetically.

'I have a proposition,' said Bernard. 'Lord Bender knows all about it.'

'Yeah?'

'Indeed yes. In a week's time, if you agree, you will be announced as the new president of Kerridge Steel.'

'That's ridiculous,' said Sanger. 'What about old man Kerridge?'

'He'll become chairman of the board.' Bernard smiled as graciously as he could.

'I still don't believe it.'

'You'd better,' said Bernard. 'Because it's true.'

'Old man Kerridge would never . . .'

'Mr Kerridge had no alternative,' interrupted Bernard. 'I insisted. Otherwise, my personal fortune would not have been available to ensure the survival of his corporation.'

Sanger still could not believe it. Did Bernard Grant hate him so much he'd put all that dough on the line just to be rid of him?

'Hell,' he said. 'I don't know a thing about steel.'

'There are plenty of people in that company who do. And steel is only one part of what it's about. It's more a conglomerate now, like us. What the company needs is good management. It's got to be knocked into shape. I think you're the man to do it, Earl.'

'I suppose the rest of your damn board agrees?'

'Lord Bender, yes. My son, yes. Armfield and Morton, too. The others won't argue.'

'Supposing I say nuts.'

'Come, Earl. That's surely unlikely. You'll be the head of one of the leading corporations in your country. A salary of one hundred thousand dollars a year to begin with. A fistful of stock options for you. A three-year contract. It's the chance you've been waiting for.'

Sanger realised that if he was trapped, it was a tender trap. He eyed Bernard for a moment; then he laughed.

'You've got me by the balls, haven't you? But you're not squeezing very hard.'

Bernard smiled too, more warmly. 'I think we understand each other.'

'You'd vote me off the board here, wouldn't you, if I said no?'

'Think of it as a great opportunity,' said Bernard blandly. 'What have you got to lose?'

'Nothing, I guess. But you have, Sir Bernard. You're risking a chunk of money . . .'

'I believe the risk is limited. With you to look after my investment, I think I might do very well. Very well indeed.'

'And if you don't, I don't,' said Sanger. 'If Kerridge Steel isn't pulled round, my stockholding won't be worth more than a few nickels.'

'I'd never quite seen it in that light,' said Bernard.

'Sure you hadn't,' said Sanger, smiling ironically. 'You just wanted to give your most promising director a good promotion.'

'Then it's agreed?' said Bernard.

'I'll think it over. But I'm not likely to say no to a hundred thousand bucks a year.'

'Good,' said Bernard. He rose, extending his hand. 'I think it's the right move for you. I've never thought you were really happy with our English ways, Earl.'

Sanger lingered, suddenly looking troubled.

'Was there something else?'

'Nothing much. I was just wondering about the quarantine laws. I've got this cat, see. I wouldn't like to lose her.'

That same evening, David and Sheila Travis dined with Michael and Alison.

It was a happy occasion. Lars Koringen came too, his face tanned beneath the fair hair which he'd grown longer. He'd been out in Australia, enjoying the sun and the easier pressure of the races there after a heavy year of Grand Prix and sports car contests. His wife, smaller even than he, with long blonde hair down a jet-black evening dress, seemed more relaxed.

Michael talked quite easily about his experiences in Ecuador. He clearly didn't want to cast himself as suffering hero.

'Will your plant get finished on time now, Michael?' asked Koringen.

'No reason why it shouldn't.' Michael smiled. 'A year ago, Lars, that would have been enough. Now it isn't.'

'What do you mean?' said Koringen.

'It seems ridiculously inadequate just to build a plant and take your profit and go home again.'

Koringen did not understand. 'That is business, is it not? You told me that the plant will create hundreds of jobs. And it will bring new wealth to Ecuador. Isn't that what you wanted?'

'Yes, Lars. But wealth for whom? God knows where the money will go. I'm not naive enough to believe I can do anything to change society out there, but somehow I want to do something more *direct* than helping to turn out plastic buckets and shoes and fertilisers.'

David tried to help him. 'You've done enough, Michael, God knows. Those who are soldiers fight. Those who are doctors heal. And you – well, you create wealth and the opportunities to work. You can't do everything.'

Michael appeared to have heard only one part of David's speech. 'Perhaps you've hit it, David. Maybe we could build a hospital, or a clinic. Something like that. We could make a gift . . .'

'That would be good,' said Koringen's wife. 'Too many people cannot get help when they are sick in places like that.'

Koringen smiled upon her. 'Maria was born in Sicily, Michael.'

'There were few hospitals in Sicily,' said Maria simply. 'Not for my family.'

'Let's think about that, David, shall we?' said Michael. 'Find out about costs.'

'All right,' said David. Alison was smiling at him; so was Sheila. He hadn't realised Michael was so determined about the Indians.

'It's going to be a good year,' said Michael. 'I feel it in my bones. We'll do well at Le Mans, Lars.'

Koringen bent his head and, for a moment, David saw the apprehension flash in Maria's eyes. 'That car gets better every time I see it, Michael. I'll do my best.'

'Here's to you and the car.' Michael raised his glass of cognac. Koringen lifted his ginger ale. Even when he was first in a Grand Prix, he ignored the celebratory magnums of champagne.

343

The Koringens left at midnight. The others gathered round the log fire. Michael poured out more cognac.

'I wanted to say it when you were here, Sheila,' he said. 'God knows what I'd have done without David this past year. He's been bloody marvellous. Always there, always helping. With SAEF, with Debrais, with everything. I know it hasn't always been fun. This year's going to be different. We'll kill ourselves otherwise.'

Sheila was not sure how she ought to respond. In the past fortnight she'd seen more of him than she did in any usual two-month period. She was grateful for the efforts he'd made to carve out time to be at home, to go to parties, to take her to the theatre. They'd grown closer too in the shadow of Michael's time of captivity.

Yet she knew it couldn't last. You didn't change the nature of a man, or the style of modern business, so easily. She'd grown accustomed to what was expected of her and of what she might expect of life. It was, she told herself, a kind of growing up. And it had nothing to do with happiness. Those who believed that the end of living was happiness were infants. What she looked forward to was something other than happiness, something deeper, for which she could scarcely find a name. Perhaps it was fulfilment.

'May I tell them?' she asked David.

He nodded at once, understanding her need to give an oblique answer to the invitation for confession which Michael had offered.

'I'm thinking of going back to school,' she said. 'I'm rusty. But if I take a two-year course, I reckon I could be some use as a teacher one day.'

'What about Kenwyn?' asked Alison. 'Are you planning any more kids?'

Sheila pondered before answering. How could she make them understand that if kids happened, then that would be okay, but that both David and she agreed – almost without discussing it – that to have children in a rush now, deliberately, as some kind of glue to stick their marriage together in case of accidents, would be disastrous? She wasn't even sure whether the teacher training course was a good idea either. She knew only, as did David, that she had to attempt in some way to signal her independence, to touch a working world which was separate from her husband's.

She said: 'If I got pregnant, I'd have to think again. But I don't want to hang around any more. I was asking myself the other day exactly what we had an au pair *for*. It seems pointless if it's just to give us the chance to make a few more parties.'

'It sounds right if that's what you want to do,' said Michael. 'How will Kenwyn take it?'

'Who knows?' said Sheila. 'That's the trouble. But I can't imagine that having me as a sort of decaying cabbage will do him much good. We'll just have to try it.'

David thought it was time to lighten the atmosphere. 'I'm taking up golf, to fill the time when she's doing her homework.'

'I'll need you to coach me.'

'I can fit in both. You're always telling me I'm not interested in anything but work.'

'I'll get Michael to carry your bag,' said Alison. 'Living in a flat I can't get him to grow chrysanthemums or have a dog or sculpt in the garden and all those other exciting things that tycoons are supposed secretly to yearn to do. You really are very dreary, Michael – just being interested in people and arithmetic.'

They all enjoyed the irony, and David was especially grateful to Alison for awarding him, as it were, an oral commendation for devotion to duty which Sheila had heard. His life, during the past month, had settled into a kind of rhythm which provided time for almost everything he wanted to do. It gave him space for sharing with Sheila, for endless talk, for music and books and walks in the snow as well as Prospero.

But it wouldn't be like that for ever. The years would be an endless succession of crises followed by calms, when hours and days and weeks might divide his wife from him. He would have to learn to live with it, and so would she. They would each need an inner strength which, at times, could sustain them without help from each other.

And what, he wanted to say out loud, was so wrong with that? He had never understood what was supposed to be so damn sacrosanct about fishing and messing about in boats and collecting rare stamps and drinking beer in pubs and all those other pursuits which some people wore like a badge that was intended to tell the world WE KNOW HOW

TO RELAX: SEE WHAT COOL, WELL-BALANCED, CIVILISED, INTELLIGENT PEOPLE WE ARE.

It was meaningless, all that. Living was people; living was what you did best; living was the speed that suited you, and speed was nothing to generalise about. If some people needed to build bridges between themselves, then there were times when others needed to blow them up. What was it the old libertine in that poem by Louis Macniece had craved? Yes – that was it – 'after the event, the wish to be alone.'

The fire was almost dead. He hoped Sheila understood his mind as well as he did himself. And he promised himself, since New Year resolutions had again been forgotten, that he would try to understand hers.

'We'll all go to Le Mans,' said Michael. 'It should be a ball. On Prospero, David, both of you, you've earned it.'

5

The two Indians who walked across the cobbled streets around the central square of Parque Calderón in Cuenca, past the bored blue-jacketed traffic cop, attracted no attention. They were dressed in the normal way for people of their class – the man wrapped in a poncho, with black hair partially obscuring his face as it fell from beneath a floppy-brimmed panama hat; the woman in white blouse, long red skirt and blue shawl, gold rings in her ears, her hair worn in black braids to her waist and topped, like his, with the inevitable panama.

He carried a basket; but then who, in Cuenca, does not carry one? On her back she humped a sack, which made a change from the usual bundles of children.

The lush trees in the square stirred, the white marble of the surrounding buildings gleamed in the late sun, as they passed groups of people moving towards the cathedral. In a narrow street, the Indians entered a doorway.

In a dark, cool room upstairs, they laid their burdens down with care. Then the man quietly opened a shuttered window so that a thin wedge of light came into the room. Within the building it was so silent, they could hear the susurrant sound of the people in the square below. Not too many people, not very much noise, but enough for the modest occasion which was approaching.

The woman had now dropped her shawl. The man, even at this moment, could not help admiring the upper half of her body. It was extravagantly full, the curves and the softness suggested beneath the loose blouse. She was still very beautiful, even though her face was scarred. She did not smile these days, for that would have shown her broken teeth.

Vargas had done that to her, blindly furious when he discovered that she had had dealings with the guerrillas. He had snatched a soldier's rifle, swung it by the barrel, smashed her face. Then he had thrown her out. She was no longer dangerous, no longer useful. He was even tired of humiliating her.

The man smiled at her with gratitude. She had been faithful enough; both to the cause, for a long time, and to him personally during the past few months, despite the danger. She had been protector, fixer, mother, mistress. Had he been capable of love at this time, he would have said he loved her.

Together they knelt. On the floor, as they opened wrappings of cloth with great care, lay brown wood, dull blue metal, long thin barrel, magazine, bullets. When he had finished assembling it, the man's hand stroked the gun almost lovingly.

He lay flat on the floor, edged his way towards the window, opened the shutters a little further and sighted the rifle at one of the buildings opposite. It was an L1A1, standard issue to many armies in the world, heavier and less accurate than the Lee Enfield .303 which it had largely replaced. But it is accurate up to 300 metres in the hands of a fair shot and, because it is semi-automatic, can maintain a fast rate of fire. Guerrillas like it because it's easy to maintain and service.

Outside the light was going. The woman handed him a fat tube, perhaps a foot long and a couple of inches in diameter. This he fixed to the top of the rifle and peered through it. Truly remarkable. Bystanders below appeared big and clear, almost illuminated, in his sights. Called an image intensifier, it was the very newest piece of equipment for hand-picked troops, able to intensify natural light between 45,000 and 80,000 times. With it, marksmen can pick out targets in the dead of night. It made easy work of the glowing early dusk. It had cost him 30 ounces of gold.

The woman left him silently, checking that the stairs to the alley behind the house were clear. Francisco, now lying on cushions, body well supported, waited. He thought of his companions, still blaming himself for their deaths. It had been an act of unpardonable vanity as well as selfishness to believe that he could lead them out towards a softer life. He was glad that the nucleus of their cells of sympathisers still remained in the cities. It was more dangerous than ever for him to work now, but his mind burned the more intensely in its single-mindedness. He would be sensible, certainly. But only after he had done today what he had to do.

Below, in the square, voices grew louder. A limousine stopped close to the cathedral. Vargas stepped out, knee boots gleaming, medal ribbons ablaze on his green tunic. There was a scatter of officers close to him, and a cardinal in red. He stood chatting on the cobbles, smiling. For many months he had arranged all outside appointments in the early evening, feeling safer in the gathering darkness.

The first bullet was damaging but not deadly. It struck Vargas in his thick muscular neck and he coughed uncontrollably, spraying blood over the man nearest to him. The second hit the skull. His head exploded, fragments of blood and bone showering the cardinal.

It was over too quickly for the noise in the square to cease even for a moment. Before Vargas's lifeless body had fallen, Francisco's fingers were already closing the shutters with slow and careful movements.

12. THE TASTE OF VICTORY

1

'MICHAEL, you're a bloody old fraud.' Sanger was laughing, really laughing as he spoke.

Michael Grant forced himself to concentrate closely on Sanger's words, savouring sound not sense. It was Michael's discipline, his way of avoiding any temptation to anger. At this, perhaps their last proper conversation before Sanger left for the United States, Michael wanted to keep the temperature low. In the months ahead, to ensure that the Ecuador contract ran smoothly, he would need Sanger's co-operation.

'No, Earl,' he said. 'We want to build that clinic. There's no catch.'

Sanger was predictable. He must be practising, Michael assumed. The idiom he had used was very English. As he had been abrasively American to gain contrast with his surroundings in London, so Sanger would use elements of Englishness once back in the States. They would give him distinction.

Yet Michael wasn't certain he was being entirely fair. Perhaps with the necessity for conflict to some extent re moved, Sanger was genuinely changing and softening. There was certainly more warmth, less acid, in the American's humour

'I'll believe you, then, Mike,' said Sanger. 'Some people might think that getting soft on the Indians was a convenient cover for not making a decent profit out of the job.'

'So I've heard.'

'Things aren't so bad in Ecuador,' said Sanger. 'Not like Peru. Did you know women there still pull the ploughs at ploughing time?'

Michael pushed back his chair, squinting as a commotion of February sunshine invaded his office. 'What I'm doing out there is what I think is *right* to do. I've seen those people at close quarters. How could I live with having a stake in the country and doing nothing to help?'

Sanger said, 'That conscience of yours again.'

Michael bridled. 'It's a good business decision too. The people have got to be won over to Cantania's side before the guerrillas become too strong.'

'Francisco's really in business again, they tell me.'

Michael shrugged. 'What do you expect? After what happened to his friends . . .'

'Killing Vargas was a dumb move. All Francisco's achieved is a campaign against him that's twice as hot. Cantania's backing the army with everything he's got.'

There was no denying that, Michael thought. Someone ought to write a book about the psychology of the South American military and politicians. Virtually no country in the subcontinent failed to maintain a large army, using anything up to a third of the national budget. Yet those armies rarely fought big wars. They skirmished locally, their presence controlled nations, more or less. But mostly they simply existed. It was this lack of real function which, he believed, turned so many military men towards seeking control of government and commerce and, as with Cantania now, turned civilians towards armies as their natural allies. Career soldiers had to believe they could play a constructive role in their nation's life when they did so little as fighters.

'Cantania has to use the army now, whether he believes in it or not,' said Michael. 'Otherwise we'd never get our plant finished.'

'The army's winning, though.'

'You know they are, Earl. Inside four months that plant will be finished.'

'Yeah,' said Sanger. 'But that won't be the end of it. You've got that stake in the petro-chemical company to look after. Rather you than me. What did your old man take Kerridge's holding for?'

'It's a cheap investment, Earl. We could do very well.'

'Provided Cantania stays your chum, Mike. If he doesn't want you, he'll just kick you out. Have you been reading his speeches lately?'

'I've read them.'

'He sounds like a supercharged Vargas. All that stuff

about Ecuador's national destiny and controlling her own resources. I'd be worried if I were you.'

'I'm concerned,' said Michael. 'But not depressed. I think I can handle Cantania.' He couldn't resist a final thrust. 'Anyway, Earl, you should be worried too. Kerridge Steel is still in Ecuador too. And your prospects are linked with ours. It's our money you're using.'

Sanger wouldn't rise to the bait, although he did take off his spectacles and hold them up to the light, searching for dust on the lenses. Then he chuckled.

'Sure, sure. Your old man's dough. I aim to give him a good return on that money one day. But not from Ecuador. I've got other fish to fry. Fancy the goddam British bailing out a U.S. corporation. It just ain't natural.'

Michael took it as Sanger intended. 'Maybe we'll show you a thing or two more.'

'Like that car of yours, huh? Will it win?'

'It'll win,' said Michael tersely.

'Wanna bet?'

'Why not?'

'Evens. A hundred dollars a side.'

'You're on.'

It was a ridiculous wager. Any car could be the hottest favourite for Le Mans – which the Lovelace Special wasn't – and still come unstuck. But Michael took the bet. His pride had been needled, and he recognised with a shock that part of the equation was pride in his adopted country as well as pride of self.

He *had* to win, or at least do well, at Le Mans for other reasons. Another condition Bernard had made for saving Kerridge Steel, and securing Michael's future as boss of Prospero along with it, was that Lovelace Motors should, later that year or early next, give up their old home in Hampshire. Prospero, Bernard had pointed out, could make a big profit out of selling the site to a developer. Michael had not yet dared to tell George Lovelace. If Lovelace changed homes, the old man would need the uplift of victory for his car to sustain him.

Sanger was on his feet. 'I've a lot of clearing up to do.'

'Are you still planning on taking Hardy to the States?'

'Sure. Along with my cat. I'll need someone I know there

to watch out for knives at my back. And Hardy thinks he'll have more dough to bring up his five kids there.'

'Good luck to him,' said Michael, and he meant it. He didn't care for Hardy's independent cynicism, and he would always suspect the man's loyalty. Besides, it would make it easier to give a seat on the board to David Travis once Sanger departed. David had earned it. Equally importantly, they needed new blood on that board; and it was necessary for Michael to have some of his own men around him at the summit.

'I'd like to pick up Derek Quant too, once that Ecuador job's finished.' Michael couldn't help smiling. Sanger too was gathering allies.

He stuck out his right hand. 'Well, Earl, good luck. I suppose you've got what you wanted.'

'You could say that,' said Sanger. 'And so have you, you cunning bastard.'

Sanger knew the moment to put his signature to the peace terms.

'I wish it could have worked out, you and me,' said Michael. 'But thanks, anyway. Thanks for everything.'

Sanger nodded. He walked to the door before he spoke again.

'By the way, Mike. You remember that C.I.D. raid?'

'Of course, Earl. Not one of your better moments.'

'Yeah, I remember. But at the time you did say you'd kill the guys who set us up.'

'Perhaps I did.'

'Sure you did. But you've done nothing about it.'

'No,' said Michael. 'Later, it didn't seem very important.'

'I've done something.'

'What?'

'I thought it would be my going-away present for you. I got a photograph of one of their top guys taking a bribe. I've typed out an explanation of what it all means and I'm sending copies, anonymously, to Scotland Yard and to the papers. That could be interesting.'

'They'll never fall for that.'

'Who knows?' said Sanger. 'Anyways, I did my best.'

'Yes, Earl,' said Michael. 'You always did your best.'

*   *   *

The interview with Sanger was one of the few happenings of that spring which, in later years, Michael would remember in detail. It was a strangely quiet and placid period after the almost melodramatic events of the previous year.

David Travis got his directorship, the pace at Prospect House was more measured, and his living with Sheila the easier as a result. She was registered for a teacher training course due to begin in the autumn. That gesture helped to sustain her pride and damp down her doubt during the spring and summer.

Events in Ecuador, obstinately and surprisingly, refused to go wrong. The plant at Esmeraldas ground towards its completion. Cantania stayed in command, Francisco stayed free, and Martin paid two visits to London, Bernard having persuaded his son not to return to Ecuador yet.

Michael did not omit to display his gratitude to Harold Armfield. He even dared – picking up a judicious hint – to send Armfield three dozen Fragrant Cloud rose-trees to mark his 57th birthday in March. Armfield was delighted; Bernard glowed with the understanding that his son was learning so well. For his father's 68th birthday, Michael bought a Lowry, one of the few English moderns Bernard liked.

Bender remained quiet, satisfied that Bernard had bought security for Prospero; his ears went flat with pleasure when, in late April, Armfield began to forecast the best first half-year's trading results for three years.

Only once did Michael, in the golden spring, clash seriously with his father. The car was doing so well in the races which constitute the run-up to Le Mans that he made one last attempt to change Bernard's mind about moving the Lovelace operation. He could scarcely leave George Lovelace in doubt much longer, for the news might leak; yet he still did not want to distract the old man from producing a winning car.

'For God's sake, Michael,' said Bernard, 'we'll build them a superb *new* plant. Can't you make motor-cars *anywhere*?'

'George will be upset. He's like that. This may mean the difference between the car winning or losing. And if we win, it could make your profit on the site look small beer once we start selling cars as a result.'

'*If* you win. *If* you sell cars,' said Bernard flatly. 'I want to take our profit more safely.'

'All right, father, but think of the *man* in this equation.'

'Don't tell him directly. Start suggesting he's done so well you want to get him better facilities. Ease him into it. And remember, I've given my word.'

'You shouldn't have done that, father.'

Bernard shrugged. 'I doubt if I could have organised the money for Kerridge without it.'

Michael held out his hands in a gesture of reconciliation. 'All right, father. If that's the way you saw it at the time, what can I say now? I'm still very sad there was no alternative.'

Bernard smiled gently. 'May I tell you a story?'

'Go ahead.'

'You know who Harold Armfield worked for before he came to us?' Michael nodded. They both remembered the active hereditary peer. 'He told Harold to arrange for the sale of a certain company without its managing director knowing. And he said' (here Bernard put on an exaggerated, pinched upper-class accent) '*My uncle said, he said it. When you've got a pig in the poke, get rid of it. Yes, get rid of it.*

'So Harold said to him, nicely of course, *Shouldn't you be getting the managing director of the company to do all this?*

'And Harold's boss said. *Do you know what his problem is? He's fallen in love with the pig, that's it. Fallen in love with the pig.* He was a man, Michael, who believed that the repetition of phrases somehow gave them more validity.'

'I don't agree with the message, father, but I take your point,' said Michael.

'I didn't mean it to apply directly to you, Michael – but wait, I haven't finished, dear boy. So Harold asked, *Surely that's loyalty, sir. And isn't that an admirable trait?*

'And do you know what that old devil said? *Admirable, yes. But inconvenient. Damned inconvenient.*'

2

On Tuesday, 9 June, Michael Grant sat outside the committee room, which lies in the centre of the pits, opposite the main grandstand, at the Le Mans circuit, and stared at the small black plaque set into the wall across the tarmac.

It bore a golden cross and the date: 11 Juin 1955.

The light was fading. A few practising cars banged past. He couldn't understand the cast of his mind. When he'd raced here before, it had been only a few years after the plaque was set up. He hadn't thought of the accident then, hadn't noticed the plaque.

Now, however, he kept seeing in his mind the newsreel shots of 11 June, 1955, when Mike Hawthorn and Fangio were dicing and another car, braking in the pits straight, had slewed off the track and wiped out 88 lives in the crowd opposite where he sat. Supposing a car should go wild in four days' time? The track was so narrow at this point, the people so close.

The loudspeakers were still playing: *Yessir, That's My Baby.* An accordion sound, too. Still, it was better than the Taverne Munichoise in the so-called Village area behind the pits where, in an immense marquee, you could sup in *Roll Out the Barrel* from two stone-faced trumpeters and a drummer in lederhosen while the eaters downed pork and sauerkraut and bubbly beer. Roll out *ze* barrel, in fact, sung in broken English like an old-time movie about the Wehrmacht.

Further down the pits, walking past the long-tailed Porsches and the short-tailed Porsches, past the Ferraris and the Stingrays and the sole Ligier – all in various stages of automotive undress – David Travis came walking. Michael watched David stop by one of the Japanese cars. Damned Japs. They were still writing knocking ads about Lovelaces.

Still, that was a minor annoyance. The Lovelace had come first at Thruxton at Easter, second in the BOAC 1000 kilometres at Brands and, finally, had been a clear leader in the Nurburgring 1000 before a broken gearbox had put it out of the race late on. It could scarcely have been a better run-up to Le Mans. Michael was puzzled now that he didn't feel more elated.

'Any news?' he asked David.

'Sorry, nothing good. I'm worried.'

Michael forced out a laugh. 'Christ – not you too. What's up?'

'I've been talking to Lars. There's talk that the French police have been asking about Green.'

Michael's eyebrows lifted hurriedly at the mention of the

top driver for the second-string Lovelace. 'Asking what, for Christ's sake?'

'He's supposed to have been charged with some driving offence – for an accident, I think – a few months back. He never turned up for the hearing. That's the story.'

'Is it true?'

'I don't know, Michael. I've telexed London to see if there was any story in the papers.'

'I'm bloody sure there wasn't. If it's true, he's for the high jump. Why the hell didn't he tell us?'

David shrugged. They looked at each other evenly.

'The stupid bastard,' said Michael.

'You'd drive, wouldn't you – if necessary, I mean?'

'We can't do this thing with only one bloody car.'

'No, Michael. I know. Cheer up, then. You'd enjoy it.'

'But would the car?'

David said, 'It'll be okay. I thought that's what you really wanted.'

'Yes,' said Michael. 'That's what I wanted.'

*　　*　　*

Going back to the hotel, Michael felt physically sick. In the lobby, two men in dark suits awaited him. They showed him their papers and a warrant for Green's arrest. They wanted to know when he'd last seen Green. One of them asked if Michael was feeling ill. He said no; it was just the uncertainty.

He wasn't unsure for long. Lars Koringen came pounding down the stairs. Even had he wanted to stop his words, because of the policemen, he'd launched them before he had time to think.

'Green's gone, Michael.'

'Gone? Where?'

'Who knows? His room's bare. All his luggage, his gear, everything – it's disappeared.'

'We believed that might be the case, Mr Grant,' said one of the cops.

'Oh, sod it,' said Michael. 'Sod everything.'

They ate at the Hotel Ricordeau in Loué that night, almost 20 miles from Le Mans, because Michael insisted it was the best food in the area and, from tomorrow on, everybody would be entirely concentrated on the race. David suspected that Michael wanted not to sit around thinking. Koringen came with them, and Koringen's wife, but not Lovelace. And even that was not unusual. Mostly the drivers stay holed up in their own private camps during the week of the 24 Hours, cut off from temptation and distractions and the noise of cars in the streets – all those Fangio fantasists who pour in by the tens of thousands and fill this modest provincial town with hairy-chested decibels for a couple of days and then depart, sated.

There is no temptation in the Hotel Ricordeau, unless it be the special aperitif of strawberry liqueur, French vermouth and champagne, which is supposed to clear the stomach to receive the food, and no sin except gluttony. The décor is sternly French provincial – clean and serious; the host limps about with a walking stick in white chef's uniform; the hostess is plump, determined, black-garbed, bespectacled; the sounds are those of steady mastication and the mouse-squeak of cocktail almonds on the teeth.

David was the only one who did justice to the food, following wild boar pâté with a magical mixture of scrambled egg and truffles. But he needed not to wonder why his companions – and especially Michael – had driven 20 miles to eat so spartanly. It had been confirmed earlier that Green had left Le Mans by private plane.

Koringen spent most of the time checking out with Michael the work which had been done on his car since the Nurburgring race – so different from Le Mans that George Lovelace had been going flat out to change the Special's suspension, gears, brakes and, especially, the contours which would govern aerodynamic effects at high speeds.

'Thank God we've no problems at scrutineering,' said Michael.

'Satisfactory,' said Koringen unemotionally. That was Lovelace's pigeon, not his.

'They get more fussy every year. Not much chance of putting one over on them now.' Michael was striving to be cheerful. 'Do you remember the guy who boasted he'd put lead bars in his car?'

'No. How, Michael?' Koringen's tone was still flat.

Michael laughed. 'Inside the seat cushions. He took 'em out after the scrutineering. Cheeky bugger!'

Koringen shrugged. 'He was cheating.'

He was indeed. The job of the scrutineers is to inspect each vehicle to ensure it complies with the complicated race regulations. They'd not been intended to find the lead bars, which had temporarily increased the weight of the car. Since the placings in the Index of Performance at Le Mans are awarded on a formula which includes weight (the heavier, within limits, the better a car's index is likely to be) it was, in fact, an act of dishonesty to remove them for the race.

Michael was not regretting the absence of opportunities to cheat. He was sighing for the days when Le Mans was more free, more easy; when the whole affair wasn't so serious, so commercially orientated, so joyless. There was still a faint smile on his face. He was remembering the driver who was forced to drink coffee by his mechanics during a pit stop and found that the cup contained a fuse to substitute for one that had just blown in his car, replacement of which at the pits would have offended against the regulations of the time. Good days, those. Yes.

Koringen was speaking again. A good-hearted reliable man, Koringen; but joyless, definitely joyless. Like modern Le Mans.

'I am sorry about Green, Michael. You're determined to drive?'

'Yes.'

Koringen frowned. 'Michael – forgive me – but it is different today. Faster. Very much faster.'

'I know that, Lars.'

'I would not advise it. I'm serious, Michael.'

'We'll see. I'll take the car out tomorrow. Push it. Really push it.'

'When does your wife arrive?' asked Koringen, as if suggesting that Alison Grant might take a hand in stopping such madness.

'Friday.'

'Maybe you should talk with her.'

'Don't be silly, Lars. I can make my own judgments.'

And all the time the men spoke. Maria Koringen was looking at the table, her face ashen and the fingers at her lips trembling. David divined something of her thoughts.

Why is my husband so anxious to prevent the man who is making *him* race from also entering a car and travelling

358

at 200 miles an hour? Why is he so concerned about Grant's wife when every time Lars Koringen submits himself to the madness my sanity is eroded more and my whole body feels as though it has been violently assaulted? Why? Why is Grant so different from Koringen?

*   *   *

On Wednesday, 11 June, Michael Grant left their hotel and was at the race circuit before noon, even though practice did not begin until late in the afternoon.

Already there was a line of white Citroen ambulances, lace-curtained, in the area behind the pits where the teams set up their workshops – pieces of cars lying everywhere, piles of fat black tyres, chassis stripped naked, and girls in sunglasses holding long loaves and bottles of wine. Michael scarcely noticed the cars; only the ambulances.

He took the number two Lovelace Special out under the sad eyes of Koringen. He drove very steadily, holding himself ready for the changes in the course since he'd last tasted it.

The Chicane, a snaky right-and-then-left-hander built to slow down the pace just before the pits straight, he found especially difficult. It was too tight a corner, involving very fast changing down of gears before hitting it, which tended to distract him from taking the correct line. Third time around, trying to keep up his speed, he touched the protective safety rails on the first corner, shot out into the middle of the track in a shower of sparks, and almost lost control.

Even by his own modest expectations, his first drive was not encouraging. Koringen had lapped the previous day in around 3½ minutes; Michael's best time was 4 minutes 27 seconds. He hadn't touched 190 along the Mulsanne Straight, where a car as big as the Lovelace Special ought to make 220. The look on George Lovelace's face as he returned to the pits said that if he couldn't do better than that, he might as well not bother.

'It goes beautifully, George,' he said.

'Don't be frightened of it, Michael. It's safe as houses.' Lovelace stroked the green body.

'I know, George. I'm just getting the feel of it.'

He managed to get closer to 4 minutes the next morning

and finally broke through to a 3-57 lap. Koringen was driving the number one car better and better. At 3-23 or thereabouts for his average lap time he was well abreast of anything the Porsches or the Japs were turning on; and the Ferraris weren't doing as well as that. Towards Thursday evening, George Lovelace was beginning to smile. Over a weak Vermouth at the Club des Pilotes in the Village, Michael decided that the moment might never be better to open up to the old man.

'Really, George,' he said, 'if we do as well as we think we might, we're going to need that extra capacity at the plant before long.'

'Oh, aye,' said Lovelace. 'We'll find the room if people want the cars.'

'Not in Hampshire,' said Michael.

'Why not?' Lovelace looked as if only half his mind was attending to the conversation.

'We'd run into the engine-production area if we add anything significant to the car workshops at present,' said Michael, knowing his story sounded unconvincing. 'And we might have planning trouble if we want to buy more land. You've done so well, George, you need better facilities altogether.' He smiled, screwing one side of his mouth, to soften the words. 'Perhaps we'll have to think one day of moving out altogether, building you a new place somewhere else.'

'Moving?' said Lovelace. 'We've been where we are fifty years or more. People know us.'

'They'd know you anywhere.'

'I daresay. But moving – well, I'd have to think about that.'

Michael had gone too far not to push further. 'It could mean a great deal for the firm. You'd be able to turn out all the cars you wanted; faster and better.'

'I don't know as I want to build *too* many. We'd lose quality.'

'We could take care of that, George. More people, better people, to help you. Don't worry. If you've got customers, we ought to satisfy them.'

'Perhaps, perhaps not. We don't produce tin cans, you know. Now Michael, about that aerofoil . . .'

* * *

On Friday, Alison and Sheila arrived. David and his wife soon found themselves in one of the pavilions of the Village looking at a tower skilfully built on the grass from several hundred champagne glasses, mounted on plump racing tyres. A couple of girls in hot pants began to hand jera-boams of champagne to several men – brown and polished, TV celebrities – who then poured the liquid into the glasses at the top of the tower. The foaming champagne cascaded down the glasses, filling those at the top first, slowly reaching the lower ranks, much of it fizzing on to the grass. A murmur of approval came from the fifty or so people watching. The men went on pouring, the champagne continued to water the grass. Finally, more girls handed out glasses.

'There doesn't look like anyone here who isn't a PR person,' whispered David as they sipped.

'No.'

'We'll go in a minute. Everyone of these hustlers is looking for someone who's a non-hustler so's they can start hustling.'

'Very funny.'

'You can spend Le Mans in a haze of free liquor at any one of forty pavilions if you know the right people.'

'That's for me,' said Sheila.

One of the PRO's who David knew came up to them.

'Enjoying yourselves?'

'It's fine;' said David. 'But what a waste of good champagne.'

'Great gimmick, though,' said the PR man. 'It takes hours to build that tower of glasses.'

A hotpants girl in yellow, with Camel across her back, came up and offered them a free cigarette.

'Enough to drive you to drink,' said the PRO as she left. 'Now, if you'll excuse me, I've got to get my fretsaw.'

'Fretsaw?' said Sheila.

The PRO chuckled. 'Sure, ma'am. Some sod's gone and hung a banner right in front of mine. So when it's dark I'll weaken the supports a bit.'

'Let's go, love,' said David, taking her arm.

'And don't forget to do a test drive to your car-park place this evening,' said the PRO. 'Otherwise you'll end up in bloody Marseilles tomorrow.'

David and Sheila walked out of the pavilion, past the

wall mural made from the ends of champagne bottles, into the Village. There were thousands of people around now and dust hung in the air. The sound of voices mingled with music and the occasional howl of a car engine. The lights of bars and restaurants and show stands were on as the evening deepened. Everyone seemed to be selling something: beer, sausages, caps, belts, crepes, racing helmets, stickers, bread, bags, badges, insurance and perhaps themselves. And there was scarcely a piece of wall or a patch of sky which wasn't obscured by banners and bills. Castrol, Banga Expresso, Mobil, Coca Cola, Cibie, SEV, Marchal, Supra, Elf, Nutsy, Lucas, Gulf, Autolite, Dunlop, Slavia, Jambon, Olida, Bougie-KLG, Martini. David didn't know what many of the names meant or advertised.

'Was he serious?' asked Sheila.

'God knows, but the PR men make damn sure they get the best sites for their banners and things.'

'It's quite fun,' she said. 'Just to see, I mean. Will Michael really drive?'

'What else can he do?'

'He looked very strained.'

'It's a tough week.'

'No, I mean he looks as if he doesn't fancy driving. He thinks he's got to prove something to us.'

'Perhaps he has,' said David.

They walked hand in hand, fingers entwined. They showed their passes to one of the guards at a gate in a wire fence and moved towards the back of the pits.

'Alison doesn't want him to do it,' said Sheila.

'Has she said?'

'No, of course not. But she's frightened as hell.'

'Yes,' said David. 'So is Michael.'

*   *   *

At nine minutes to four on the Saturday afternoon in front of the massed grandstands, a man held up a placard bearing the words MOTEUR.

The engines of 50-odd cars, strung out in ranks of two on the track, revved and howled into life. Bonnets were finally clamped down, clouds of blue smoke whirled above the automobiles. The crowd, which had grown silent before this

362

moment of ritual, babbled along with the voice of the commentators on the loudspeakers.

Michael stood with Alison and David and Sheila in a box above the pits, watching. The plan was for him to take over the second car in three hours or so, when his co-driver had done the 60-lap maximum allowed for any driver in one spell. He'd felt it was better for half an hour to get out of the supercharged atmosphere of the pits, where George Lovelace was white as chalk and irritable, as he always was at the start of a big race.

Besides, and this surprised him, Michael wanted to be with Alison.

Le Mans wasn't the same, that was for sure. The old men who'd been there back in the days of Bugattis and Bentleys, the years of the Twenties and Thirties, might try to make it so, reciting their litany of most favoured names – Cunningham, Rodriguez, Mairesse, Oliver – and recalling the dices they'd had. But nothing could bring back the past. Today Le Mans was a festival of selling. He regretted that they'd stopped the famous running start, with the drivers sprinting across the track and leaping into their cars. Today there would be a rolling Indianapolis-style start, with the field making one slow circuit of the track behind a guiding Jensen and then unleasing themselves flat out as they reached the pits straight again.

The notice 1-MIN appeared on the placard before the waiting cars. The engines were ascending and falling down the scale, both powerful and shrill, as the drivers revved. Michael's hand found Alison's. He was sweating. Her grey-green eyes burned.

Koringen's Lovelace was close to the front, behind two Porsches, beside one of the Japanese cars. The Lovelace which Michael would drive was further back.

The 10-SECOND sign went up and suddenly the cars were away, booming and screaming, and then there was only the crowd, chattering like starlings.

A man from one of the tyre firms leaned in towards Michael. 'I think you're going to do it for us.'

'Hope so,' said Michael.'

David said: 'How many other cars are you on, apart from us?'

'The Japs, and the Ferraris. One or other of you ought

to come up.' The tyre man smiled sweetly. 'Winning is more important than being chauvinistic, they always say. But I'd sooner win on you.'

David couldn't help noticing how closely Alison clung to Michael. And how pale Michael looked, tiny pin-pricks of sweat beading his nose and forehead. He'd been like that all morning, ever since they left the hotel. It had been a noisy hotel, too; *the whole place shaking with mass adultery, as it might have been called in less permissive days,* David had observed to Sheila. Then they were shunted all round the town by cops in navy-blue battle-dress, with big white gloves and puttees, towards the Garage Rouge at the track.

It was as though the French had laid it on for Michael. No fewer than three ambulances, with sirens wailing, had passed them during the drive which had finally taken them to their parking place via a cemetery. Even the car park had small numbered markers in it that looked like tombstones.

He noticed that Michael kept glancing up at the sky. It was a windy day, sunshine and blue sky one moment, bruise-bellied rainclouds skating across it the next. For an hour before the Lovelace cars were wheeled on to the track, Michael and Lovelace and Koringen had debated whether they should put on dry or wet weather tyres. In the end they'd chosen dry. David hoped they were right.

The crowd's noise rose to a crescendo. Away, to the left, they could see the cars in view again, approaching the Chicane. They peered hard for the numbers 17 and 18, black on white fluorescent paint, surrounded by British racing green, which the Lovelaces wore. David saw the guiding Jensen suddenly swing right into the pits entrance, away from the baying pack behind it. A chorus of engines screamed higher and blurred cars pounded past them. The race was on.

After three laps, the Porches and the Lovelace with Koringen at the wheel were overhauling the tail-end of the field, where the slower GT cars lived. Koringen's 17 was solidly tucked in a few lengths behind the leading trio of Porsches, in fourth place, and the other Lovelace was alternating between 12th and 15th, caught in a tight pack of red Ferraris and white Japs and a blue Matra-Simca. David got used to the pattern of noise – the zoom of the big cars, the buzz of the smaller ones, and the savage howl of one

American monster, so different from the rest. Although the daylight was still perfect, the faster cars, including Koringen's, had their headlights on to warn slower ones of their approach.

Already, one or two cars had pulled in to the pits, rear-ends uplifted for engines to be inspected, windows swiftly washed by the waiting teams. One group was disintegrating, the driver gesticulating and bawling at the pit manager, who bawled back. It was going to be a 24 hour shouting match for a lot of people.

Michael said, 'You won't want to stay here too long, David. It gets very boring unless you're a driver or a man with tyres or money on the cars.'

Doing his best; trying to keep it light, David thought.

He looked at the packed stands opposite, the clothing as colourful as at a bull-fight arena in Barcelona. A bit like a bull fight, the whole affair. Perhaps they were waiting for the blood too.

Michael Grant took over the second-string Lovelace, number 18, when the rains began, just before eight. The car had to come in – like most others – to have its tyres changed. It was lying ninth and slipped to twelfth while the change was made; Koringen handed over car 17 at the same time, but hung on to his second position, since all the leading half-dozen cars stopped too.

'Not to worry, lad,' George Lovelace told Michael. 'You'll make it up.'

Michael pulled down his flame-proof bandage, kissed Alison, climbed into the car.

'Good luck darling,' shouted Alison. 'Go get 'em.' Her eyes refused to add conviction to the words. Hunched behind her on a pit counter, arms outstretched towards Koringen, Maria Koringen smiled as if in pity, then eased her aching sweat-drenched frame to the ground. The green Lovelace 18 slid along the pits, paused at the red light which warned of cars in the vicinity of the track, and belched smoke as it shot off when the light turned green.

'Four of the bloody Porsches gone already,' Lovelace told Koringen. 'And two of the Japs. We could do it. Any complaints?'

'Nothing,' said Koringen. 'But there's oil on the track

over at the Arnage corner, and more at the Esses. This rain could make it tricky.'

They went back to the box, David and Sheila and Alison, while the Koringens went off to rest in a caravan trailer. The doors to many of the other boxes were open, girls crowding round the champagne and food. Some had already given up the battle to look bright, interested and desirable and sat collapsed, shoes off, faces bored, while the men talked cars.

Lovelace 18 came round once, twice, thrice, and each time Alison instinctively put a hand out to David or Sheila.

She let her head fall, without warning. 'I can't watch. It's no bloody use. Walk me somewhere, anywhere.'

The Village was jammed, people jostling and eating and drinking to the sound of the squeeze-box music on the loud-speakers. Ancient gentlemen solemnly sat in pedal-cars shaped like equally venerable Ford-Ts and Bugattis, reliving reality or continuing their fantasies. As David and Sheila walked with Alison, saying nothing, they unexpectedly hit a relative pool of silence and heard crickets chirping against the whine of the cars on the circuit.

Alison stood fascinated by a booth in which stood a huge illuminated scoreboard. It gave the running order of the racers and, at the bottom, a list which so far contained the numbers of nine cars set beside the very final word: ABANDON. Neither 17 nor 18 were *abandons* yet; 17, indeed, was still in second place, trailing a Porsche, followed by Ferrari, Porsche, Porsche, Porsche, and then a Japanese.

An attendant started shifting figures around. To their disbelieving surprise the figure 18 was put into seventh position. But instead of straining to get back to their box, Alison just hung on for almost 20 minutes, as if wanting to live her hopes and fears – but mostly fears – vicariously. Then, decisively, she led them away. It was dark now, cops with batons that had torches at the end, waving an ambulance through the mob.

*   *   *

Michael followed the slight right-hand inclination of the road as he moved towards the end of the Mulsanne Straight, then began to change down through fourth, third, second for the right-angle Mulsanne Corner.

Christ; incredibly, he'd found it. He was going faster as it got wetter and darker, headlights carving through the gusts of rain. Last time around the signals on the Mulsanne Straight told him he was fifth, a lap behind the Porsche in front. The other Lovelace was still second.

He accelerated towards the dip before the sand-banked left-hander that led into Arnage. His movements were all together. He could feel nothing; only think that if he went on like this he'd catch bloody 17. He wanted to catch 17. Badly he wanted to. Show bloody Koringen.

His thoughts clicked past like shaky movie frames. He'd found it again just when he thought he'd lost it. He wasn't afraid any more.

Why didn't that stupid sod in the Porsche GT get out of the way? Stupid sod, move over.

He braked, veered left, swiftly corrected the start of a slide and tore over a blind hump, through a shallow right-left-right S, passed the White House on his left, and drifted right, going down the gears again, ready for the Chicane.

He bit at his face bandage.

Hold it, hold it, part of him was saying.

Don't lose it now. Not over-confident. Not now.

* * *

In the pits, George Lovelace stood fuming. 'Bloody fool, bloody fool. Why doesn't he take the signal?'

It was the third circuit that Michael had ignored the come-in sign on the Mulsanne Straight.

'He'll run out of bloody fuel if he's not careful,' shouted Lovelace.

The mechanics stood, hands on hip, idly. But when, at last, Michael came in, they sprang into action, ripping open the engine cover, jacking up the car, scrambling underneath, cleaning windows, avoiding the snaking gas-pump lines.

'You ran that bloody fine,' Lovelace told Michael.

'Riding my luck, George. I was too well together to want to stop a second before I had to. I knew how much gas I had. I mightn't get a streak like that again.'

He stood by the car, stretching his limbs impatiently.

'You going on?' said Lovelace.

Michael waved away the other driver. 'It's my night, George. Where's Alison?'

'Off somewhere,' said Lovelace. 'Concentrate on your bloody driving, son.'

*　　*　　*

A friendly neighbourhood official, wearing a tie with the motif 24 in an all-over pattern, drove David and the two girls along twisty country lanes, past a farmyard with flowers growing in beds inside worn tyres, to the end of the Mulsanne Straight. Alison seemed unable to stay for more than a few minutes in the pits area.

Cars here moved so fast, at up to 220 m.p.h., it was impossible to read their numbers. How could men go so quickly in the dark, when their headlights gave them only about 100 metres of vision in front of them? David marvelled. The headlights were so bright he could read his programme by them, but all around was trees and blackness and people watching and *pompiers* waiting for the first sniff of death.

'David, how long will he be out there?' Alison was shaking.

David put an arm around her.

'I'm sorry, love. There's nothing we can do. We'll stay with you. He's doing all right, really.'

All three stood there shivering. The noise of every car came high as it crashed towards them, then swooped to a lower pitch once it was past. People were close by them, talking.

'This is where the men get sorted out from the boys,' said a man, in English. 'Coming up to eleven o'clock, old son. Guys who've been out there three, four hours. They're in the groove, driving a bit automatically. They hit the Esses just a touch too fast, the top's greasy, just like now, and BOOM.'

He slapped a fist into his other palm.

'Let's go to the Esses, then,' said his companion.

'Not for me, old son, I said I'd meet this bird back at the Welcome Club. We'll see the Esses in the morning. Around eight it'll be like a bloody old car graveyard.'

*　　*　　*

Michael saw the flames as he came out of the Esses, just by the Tertre Rouge Corner. He trod on his brakes and crept past what looked like three cars, all blazing. His speed along the Mulsanne Straight was at least 10 m.p.h. short of what he'd managed before.

Past the pits, next time, the big yellow disaster light was flashing like crazy. At Tertre Rouge, the flames were out. The cars still running were almost queueing up to get past the blackened foam-covered wrecks of the crashed automobiles which blocked off half the track. Speeds were around 20 m.p.h. He could see something lying, black and very still, beside the track. Only bodies looked like that.

This time, he knew he hadn't got anywhere near 200 on the Mulsanne Straight. A Porsche went past him as if he were stationary, flailing spray, leaving Michael almost blinded. He determined to try and catch it.

At the Chicane, the Porsche didn't make it. It touched a guard rail. spun crazily, buried itself somewhere away to his left.

Michael had to brake so hard, his own car spun too. He was savagely wrenched about as he fought for control. Pains shot through his back and his legs.

He was astonished to find himself still at the wheel, pointing in the right direction, slowly sliding. He put his foot down again.

As he bent right, out of the pits straight, under the Dunlop Bridge, he felt he was sitting in blood. Hot blood. Christ, had he bust something inside? Or had he crapped or pissed in the car? Gingerly he put a hand down. Wet, warm.

He stuck it out for four more laps, going slower and slower, his foot seeming unable to press the accelerator with any strength. Just before midnight, he came into the pits. Lovelace had to help him from the car.

'Jesus Christ!' said Lovelace. 'You're sitting in a pool of bloody hot oil.'

'Bugger it, George. Bugger it. I'm sorry. I thought I'd got it too.'

George Lovelace thought that Michael was cursing the car. But the words meant something quite different.

*　　*　　*

Alison never saw Michael until they'd cleaned him up and his mind had begun to recover from the shock of self-recognition.

Her desire to keep away from the race had, half an hour before he came in, taken her to the fair. David and Sheila stayed with her, wading through the oceans of paper in the tunnel beneath the track that led to a carnival of hell.

The warm fatty smell of food and oil and car fumes was everywhere. Smoke rose. Chickens flared on spits. On the Tourbillon Rouge a man with a sexy voice encouraged more riders. There were flying rides, lucky dips for TV sets and radios, wrestlers with names like Catch Jackson, a big wheel, rock dance halls, Karting, Hully Gully, two-headed ladies. Tents all over the place, sleeping bags, thousands of people lying in the dirt among the pine trees, dust, mist across the moon, boxes of *frites* in too many hands.

By a notice that advertised Mass at 6, 9 and 11 a.m., Alison stopped and vomited.

'Oh, the stupid bastard,' she moaned. 'What is he trying to prove?'

*   *   *

Michael sat in a trailer, alone, sipping scalding hot coffee. His watch said almost 1 a.m.

He grimaced. The sound of the loudspeakers came through to him. *Numero Dix-Huit. Abandoné.* Christ, they needn't keep saying it.

He looked up and Alison was in the door. She looked paler than he'd ever seen her, black streaks on her face. When she ran over and almost collapsed into his arms, he could smell the vomit.

'Darling, what is it?' he said inadequately.

'I just felt ill,' she said. 'I'm all right now. What about you?'

'I'm fine. My backside's a bit tender. The bloody car's finished, though.'

'I'm not sorry, Michael. Don't expect me to be. Forgive me, love. I'm not made to be a racing wife.'

She began, very gently, to cry. 'I'm sorry, Michael. But, oh God . . .'

He rocked her head in his arms, hushing her gently. 'It's

all right. Honestly. I've done it now. I had to. But never again.'

She looked up at him, gratefully, but still not believing. 'I'd be better next time.'

'No next time,' he said. 'I promise.'

It would be a few weeks, perhaps longer, before she understood all that lay behind his words.

For a couple of hours out there, on the track, going faster and faster, the reflexes had worked again for him. He had forced himself to be a racing driver, with a driver's attitudes and single-mindedness.

The facade had crumbled as soon as the bad accidents happened. A driver, a real driver, would have gone on. They are trained – or perhaps it should be *numbed* – to do that, for how else can men ride on the rim of death and serious injury so consistently if they are not? Michael had too much else to play for now. He was a businessman, family man, too much aware of the scores of options in his life to go on acting the part of boy-racer once he saw the terrible dues he might have to pay. Life moves on. There was no turning back.

To Alison, three weeks later, he would say: *I've got to do the things I can do. It's no use mooning after the things I can't. Not any more.* And that would be his way of acknowledging that on the Mulsanne Straight he had, with slowly evolving and undramatic insight, learned truths about himself. For Michael Grant, as with other men, self-knowledge was the most important gift of life.

But now, he simply said to her: 'Let's go back to the hotel and get some sleep.'

'Don't you want to stay?'

'No. We'll come back in the morning. I want to be with you. Koringen can look after himself.'

'David says he's staying. I think we ought to take Sheila back. She looks like I feel.'

'Okay,' he said. 'He's a bloody good man, David.'

'He's a bloody darling,' she said. 'Him and Sheila. You're lucky.'

'So's he,' said Michael.

They went out into the night. It was icy now. A couple of men in red anoraks went past them.

'It's a pretty unremarkable race this year,' said one.

* * *

Koringen and Lovelace number 17 didn't, in the end, win.

He was in the lead for maybe an hour early on the Sunday morning, when the mist trails lie athwart the crimson horizon of Le Mans and the early-wakers can see the damage of the night all round the circuit. But then his oil system gave trouble, just as number 18's had done. A leaking oil tank was changed. Later he had problems with throttle linkage. George Lovelace and his bleary-eyed crew cured that too.

Throughout the sunny Sunday morning, with the crowds who had drifted off in the darkness regathering, Koringen and his co-driver pushed the Lovelace up from fifth place to second. And that was where the car finished – but it came first in the Index of Performance which, as the bright and burbling English announcer kept repeating, was worth 'a bag of gold' to the car that won it.

David slept on a camp bed, in a trailer, from three till almost nine in the morning. An hour later, Michael and the two girls joined him. They watched the cars, ate bacon and eggs, drank black coffee and Scotch, and felt they never wanted to leave each other for one moment.

At three o'clock, an hour before the finish, it looked as if nothing could catch the leading Porsche, provided it didn't break. The man from the tyre company popped in to see them.

'Bad luck, Michael. Still it was a good try. And I think Koringen's going to bring us joy.'

A woman came up and kissed him. As she disappeared, the tyre man said: 'All the truly cool are now leaving.'

At four o'clock, the crowds were on the track, beating past the *flics*, fighting to touch the winning Porsche and the man who had driven it. Everyone in the Lovelace camp was on the track too, hugging Koringen, drinking champagne. Koringen's wife had her photograph taken kissing him; then she leaned against the pit counter for a long time, shapeless as a body without bones, eyes that might just as well have been sightless.

It was, by the standards of many years, an unremarkable Le Mans, as the man had said the night before. Only one death on the circuit, six crashes, involving one or more cars; and, away from the track, 17 coronary attacks, perhaps a few hundred hearts broken in a romantic sense, somewhat fewer marriages irreparably damaged, several thousand examples of alfresco copulation, and a record weight of food and drink consumed.

George Lovelace, uneasy in navy-blue suit for the evening prize-giving, began by feeling elated but, as he poured cognac after cognac into himself, grew more and more depressed.

He'd got what he wanted. He hadn't won, of course. But he'd got the next best thing. At least half a dozen people came up to him to inquire when he'd have a car ready for them. In his speech, the official from L'Automobile-Club de L'Ouest, organisers of Le Mans, spent more time saying how delighted everyone was to see such a famous marque as Lovelace back in the ascendant than he did in complimenting the Porsche team which had won. George Lovelace had everything going his way.

But he was not happy. Philip, his son, hadn't even come to Le Mans. The boy was away in the States, sorting out another crisis on the snowmobile engines. Lovelace kept thinking about the move, less than six months off.

He didn't want to move. Hell, he didn't. Nor did he want to make a lot of little Lovelace cars for the sons of the rich.

When he got back to his hotel room, he sat on the bed, put his head in his hands, and thought about Bill Oldershaw. He wished he hadn't let Bill down last year. Bill was right.

You're a bloody old fool, Lovelace, he told himself. Those bastards have got you by the short-and-curlies.

3

Two weeks after Le Mans, Michael and his father walked slowly together around the colonnades of what was modestly called the *hacienda* of the Cantania family.

'I don't understand you,' said Bernard. 'First you make us buy that damned company when it was in a mess. Now, when you've scored a brilliant success with it – and got a very profitable sideline going into the bargain – you want to get rid of it. It doesn't make sense.'

'It makes sense to sell it now, when things are going so well. We'll get a good price.'

'And we could make even better profits if we kept it. We put the life back into it. Why give it up now?'

'Because it's not our style,' said Michael.

'What does that mean?'

'It means that if people aren't reasonably happy working for you, nobody will get any joy from the arrangement. No profits, no satisfaction. Nothing.'

'Who's not happy?'

'George Lovelace.'

Bernard snorted. 'He ought to be jumping with joy.'

'Lovelace cars may be back on the map, but if he's got to move the plant and make cars in much larger numbers, he doesn't want to know.'

'He'll have to move anyway. I've got that arrangement on selling the site.' Bernard looked fierce. 'I'll not go back on that.'

'You won't have to go back on it.'

'How do you work that out?'

They sat down together on a small wooden seat, overlooking a garden where a fountain played amid a splendour of white magnolia trees. One of the small yellow and black birds, common to the warmer valleys away from Quito, hopped near their feet: *gauirachuro* it was called, meaning the sound of voice or wind.

'I've talked with George, put a proposition to him,' said Michael. 'We can split the firm in two. Philip Lovelace is perfectly happy to shift the motor-cycle operation elsewhere. He hasn't got the attachment to that damned place George has. He simply wants to make money. If you leave George where he is, just building a few special cars like he always has, he won't need more than one-eighth of the site. We were only holding on to the land because of the expansion of the engine side and the belief we'd need some kind of car production line in due course. Surely it's possible to honour your promise on the land and still leave George with his corner of it?'

'Yes,' said Bernard. 'It's possible. Certainly possible. But if you find a buyer for the snowmobile engine business, who's going to want the bit George Lovelace is left with?'

'There are plenty of permutations. Maybe the buyer can't have one without the other. Maybe now that Lovelace is a fashionable racing marque, there'll be people who want to

374

sponsor George. Perhaps then we'd keep the snowmobile business ourselves. Oh, and there's another option.'

'I'm waiting.'

'The car bit of Lovelace stays independent. We give back part of the profit we make on the land to George to set himself to rights, or make him an interest-free loan.'

'You're joking,' said Bernard.

'No. George is bound to know in the end if we make a lot of money. It was his land before we took him over. He has a right to some of it.'

'No *right*,' said Bernard. 'It was *our* skill and *our* knowledge that made the land be fruitful and multiply.' Under stress, Bernard's speech often took a biblical turn.

'Even so, father, what's the point in leaving people feeling sore, in letting the world think we're that kind of company? It'll do us no good in the end. If people believe you're always trying to squeeze them, they'll not do business with you. A modest profit and a continuing growth business is better than a killing and no more customers.'

Bernard glanced at his watch and sighed good-humouredly. The bird had gone. All they could see now were three soldiers, talking at an arched gateway. There were soldiers everywhere.

'Whatever happened to you out at Le Mans, Michael? That was a damn fool thing to do, racing again. I thought you had more sense.' Bernard had been saying that for the past fortnight.

'I learned a little more about myself, father. Learned my limitations, if you like. It was worth doing.'

'And now you're trying to teach me my limitations.'

Michael laughed. 'I wouldn't be so damn presumptuous.'

'But you are,' Bernard insisted. 'Telling me what can be done in business now and what can't.'

'Those aren't *your* limitations,' said Michael. 'They're the rules the world imposes on you. And it's no use fighting them.'

'I've fought rules all my life,' said Bernard.

'And . . .?'

'And got myself a pile of money I've now had to throw away. Plus a daughter-in-law I love and a son I believe I'm proud of.'

'You'll have me in tears soon,' said Michael.

375

Now it was Bernard's turn to smile. 'I told you once you were growing sentimental, so I'll give that point to you. But you give me my point too. You're teaching me. Oh, yes, you're damn well teaching me.'

Bernard rose. 'Come on, Michael. It's time to see the Minister.'

* * *

They showed their papers to two soldiers, one at the end of the colonnade, one outside the door of the Minister's room. The drive from Quito airport to the *hacienda*, with Alison and the Travises, mostly along the Pan-American Highway, had already shown them the uneasy atmosphere in the country. There were two road-blocks, with guards who were not playing games. Many of the roads were badly cut up by tanks. Cantania was taking no chances with the ceremonial opening of the petro-chemical plant, due in 48 hours' time.

The last sizeable village they'd passed through had swarmed with soldiers, even though it was otherwise unremarkable, with Coke and Pepsi signs, young men playing handball, barefoot kids, babies carried on backs, young girls sitting outside houses weaving, and several large scrawled signs on walls that said VIVA CANTANIA. This was squirearchical country, in the old-fashioned sense, with Cantania top of the feudal heap. Indeed, he was more than a lord out here; more like an emperor.

In the morning, the Minister and his very beautiful wife had shown them the *hacienda;* about sixty rooms of it. Every one was stuffed with treasures – old painted beds, exquisitely carved furniture, paintings, fragile glass, murals, ornate objects in gold and silver, encrusted with jewels. In three rooms were piled up figures and fragments dating back up to 3,000 years; there was no space properly to display them. Crucifixes and virgins, beyond price, were everywhere. So were touches of humour, conscious and unconscious.

Out of one cupboard tumbled some boxes containing material used to renovate objects with gold-leaf: the trade name was THE MIDAS TOUCH. In the bar and disco used for parties by their children, there were eight-foot long

Auca blowpipes serving as decoration; the darts used with them, wooden, only about an eighth of an inch thick, didn't look strong enough to kill a man, as they could.

Best of all, Michael and the other guests had been intrigued by a Borgia crucifix made of silver. It opened up to reveal, in the hollow interior, a knife with 'Christ Bless Me' engraved on the handle. There were reputed to be many descendants of the Borgias in Quito, Senora Cantania explained.

God knows what all the stuff they'd seen was worth. How could you price it? Michael wouldn't have been surprised to hear six million or sixty million pounds as its value.

The room in which Cantania now awaited the Grants was as rich as all the rest. Cantania played with a silver knife, the handle set with emeralds. In a corner, amid the heavy furniture and dark paintings, was a Napoleonic bird-cage with stuffed birds that would whistle merrily once it was wound up with a key.

The Minister had grown plumper in the last six months. His grey hair was cropped shorter and he wore a green combat shirt, with button flap pockets and epaulettes. He offered Bernard and Michael whisky. In his drinking habits, at least, Cantania had not changed.

'You are now an important stockholder in the petro-chemical company, Sir Bernard, you and your son. You should know something which affects the affairs of one of the other foreign stockholders.'

'You mean Ali-Chem?' said Michael.

'Yes, Ali-Chem,' Cantania continued. 'They have, I fear, been disappointed. I have had to tell them that they will not be the prime petro-chemical producer within the Andean Pact area.'

Bernard waited for Michael to speak. 'But, Minister, I thought that was their main motivation in coming here.'

'So I believe, Mr Grant,' said Cantania. He was almost offhand.

'What did they say?' asked Michael.

'What could they say? They are here now. Their expertise and their capital is committed. They will need to become exporters.'

Michael had no particular love of Ali-Chem, but he felt

outraged at Cantania's casual attitude. 'They can't be certain of a market that way, Minister. Why can't they have what implicitly they were promised?'

Cantania shrugged. 'I did my best, Mr Grant. There were more important products for which Ecuador needed to have the manufacturing monopoly within the pact. I had to bargain.' He lit a cigarette. 'Believe me, Mr Grant, they were promised nothing – beyond favours within our borders until the petro-chemical plant was completed. They took a normal commercial risk. They have been disappointed in their best hopes. That is all.'

Bernard was thinking that, if he understood the situation correctly, the holding he'd taken over from Kerridge in the petro-chemical plant wouldn't be exactly a great profit-yielder in the future. He was glad that not one penny of Prospero money had been paid over for the stockholding yet.

'Nevertheless, Minister, they must feel almost cheated,' said Michael.

Cantania smiled thinly, no humour in his face. 'As I said, Mr Grant, I did my best. And you must understand, as I have told you before, that I act only in the interests of my country. I do not consider the interests of foreign corporations, except insofar as they serve Ecuador. You are in business for profits, are you not? Not for love or patriotism. And you will get your profits, Mr Grant, on your share of the consortium's construction work. I understand Mr Corsino was not ungenerous in fixing your margins. So why should you complain?'

'That plant will be meaningless if you have no domestic market,' said Michael.

'I think not, Mr Grant. It can export. It can be a symbol of our technical advance. And one day, I am sure we can reach an accommodation with our friends in the pact to use it as a subsidiary plant for the whole Andean area. But such arrangements will be domestic, of course, not involving foreign corporations.'

Cantania smiled again, this time victoriously, and all Michael could think to say was, 'We'll consider the implications for Prospero.'

'By all means,' said Cantania. 'Please take your time. And do not blame me over-much. Like you, I have limitations on my freedom to act. That is true of the clinic you wish to build also.'

'In what way?'

'We would like it, naturally. But it would not be wise, in the present mood of the country, to put the name of a foreign corporation upon it. It would be too obvious a target for the guerrillas.'

'I don't see that,' said Michael.

'I would not wish Ecuador to appear a pauper, Mr Grant. We have had enough here of monuments to the conscience of foreigners who make their profits from our resources.'

Michael was growing angry. 'We'll not build it, then.'

Cantania leaned back, exhaling the last mouthful of smoke. 'Please, you misunderstand me. We want that clinic, Mr Grant, but we do not wish the source of funds to be revealed, that is all.'

'Not much of a bargain, Minister,' said Michael.

'Then perhaps I can tempt you into thinking it might be,' said Cantania. 'We need helicopters of a kind one of your subsidiaries makes. Perhaps you would like to tender, Mr Grant. We would be very receptive.'

Bernard narrowed his eyes. The spiky brows above them bristled like antennae, reading the signals which suggested something might yet be saved from the mess.

'My son and I would like to consider that, Minister,' he said. 'Thank you.'

Cantania rose. 'I think we can leave details until after tomorrow. But an arrangement seems to me possible.' Outside the room there was a sudden rattle of automatic fire. 'Those damned soldiers. Always at target practice. No wonder their ammunition bills are so crippling.'

Michael silently agreed with his father. They would need to rescue what they could.

'How is the country, Minister? Do your plans go well?'

Cantania shrugged, and there was a gleam of genuine sadness in the eyes above the scarred and concave cheeks. 'So far as reality allows, yes. Two years ago I would not have believed I would have a voice in running the armed forces as well as the national resources side of government.'

'Pardon me,' said Michael. 'I was not aware . . .'

'Oh, technically the President looks after defence,' said Cantania. 'But he delegates much of it to me. Once Colonel

Vargas was gone, who else was there unless I was to allow another colonel to leap into power? I do not like the necessity for what I do, but my country needs me. If someone has to fight the guerrillas, it is better that it should be someone of my inclination, rather than a soldier who knows nothing.'

Michael nodded, automatically, but he was still dumbfounded. He'd never heard such pompous garbage. And Cantania sounded as if he believed it. Duty, the national need, the unfortunate exigencies which called for repression. He gazed upon Vargas's successor with an expression of blankness that masked distrust and a certain loathing.

'How strong are the guerrillas now?' asked Bernard.

'Strong enough. We have needed to enlarge the army.'

Michael found his voice. 'Francisco. The man who organised my kidnapping. Is he still in Ecuador?'

'Yes,' said Cantania. 'But we will capture him one day. And kill him.' Cantania sounded very tired. 'Enough of that, gentlemen. You'll want to rest before the car takes you to Quito.'

He offered each of them his hand. 'I thank you warmly for what you have done. We will all have a splendid opening ceremony. I shall pay tribute to you.'

As Bernard and Michael went through the door he called: 'Do not worry about your personal safety, by the way. Twenty of our most expert marksmen will guard your party night and day.'

*　　*　　*

'What'll you do, Del, now this job's over?' asked David Travis.

Del Martin ruefully rubbed his freckled shoulders. 'Hold on, son. It ain't over yet. I'll be here two more months at least. Opening ceremonies don't mean the workers can all pack up and go home.'

He grinned at the group around him, sitting beside the blue pool of the Hotel Quito. They were soaking up a little sun before flying to Esmeraldas for the next day's ceremony at the plant. The two girls were great. And he liked David and Michael and Bernard as much as ever, though he was worried that Michael was talking so loudly and so rudely about Cantania. Martin wanted only to have the job finished without further trouble and get the hell out of the place.

'That's ducking the question, Del,' said Michael. 'Where are you going in two months' time?'

'A good long rest, with the kids,' said Martin. 'Then, who knows. You wanna give me a job?'

Michael laughed. 'Could be, could very well be. But you don't want another of these, do you?'

Martin shrugged. '*These*, as you call 'em, is all I'm fit for.'

'But the hassles, Del. The bastards you have to work for.'

Bernard frowned at Michael. He was being unnecessarily undiplomatic.

Martin said: 'Bastards are everywhere, Mike. I've been through a few rough patches this time, true. But I still believe in what I do. So long as it's not making guns or explosives or anything of that kind, I reckon what I do can ultimately only help people in the places I work. The thing to do is get the development done, start the resources of nations working. If the wrong people control 'em now, they won't for ever. But let's face it – a kid who's starving in the mountains here ain't gonna quibble whether the food package he gets given comes from a guerrilla or a missionary or a government official in Quito. Just so long as he gets something in his belly or some clothes on his back.'

'All right, Del' – and this time it was David who spoke – 'but are the Indians *getting* it, whoever's giving it.'

'Cantania's done some good things,' said Martin. 'A lot of laws have got passed.'

Alison arched her eyebrows. She saw no reason to keep quiet. 'I was reading in a magazine the other day that there was a prospect of some kind of ecological doomsday if they stripped away too much of the Amazon forests.'

'Aw hell, Alison, I've been reading that article for the last ten years. No offence, ma'am, but what do these darn experts back in their cosy offices in Washington expect? The South Americans aren't going to leave the Amazon as a billion square-mile nature reserve, that's for sure. These people have got to *live*.'

'But what's happening could still be dangerous,' said Alison.

'Maybe, maybe not,' said Martin. 'I doubt if you or I

381

will ever know the answer to that. We've just got to go on listening to the best advice there is, then doing what seems fair and reasonable. I can't see how cutting down maybe a thousandth, or a tenthousandth, of the jungle around the Amazon is going to make much difference. I'm a mite more worried if my country, or yours, keeps on pouring poison into the seas around our coasts, or fouling up the air with chemicals.'

'You talk a lot of sense, Mr Martin,' said Bernard. Then he turned to Michael, humour crinkling his still firm-cut face. 'You ought to give him a job, Michael. They don't make them like him any more.'

Everyone laughed. Sheila put her hand in David's. How could she, who believed herself modestly intelligent, expect to weigh questions like this? How could David and Michael or even Martin, who seemed to know more than any of them? But they would have to go on trying, taking the best decisions they could, as David and she would need to go on trying.

She felt happier about that too. She could never expect to share in what he did fully; but she was enormously grateful to Michael for bringing her out here now. It gave her a perspective, an insight, and that was about as much as any modern executive wife could expect. She had gained some further knowledge of the language David spoke now, and the sharing with him would be the warmer.

The previous night she'd told him that the teacher-training course wasn't on. She was expecting a baby. David hadn't gushed, which would have shown his guilt, but had smiled slowly, embraced her firmly, and said: *God bless you, girl.*

Michael was speaking again. 'Could you stand England, Del? I don't think I'm going to push Prospero into this kind of overseas job again.'

No one could tell whether he was joking or not.

'I'm a rovin' man, Mike. Never could settle in the one place. And don't kid me about overseas contracts. You've got your feet wet now. Next time, you'll know better how to cope.'

'I don't know,' said Michael.

'Sure you know,' said Martin. 'You can't buy little moral packages, Mike. Business isn't like that. Nor can you always guarantee no risk. It ain't like you to want to push more goods out – whatever they are – just in your country, or in America or Europe.'

'There's poverty in Europe. In America too,' said David.

'Sure, sure. But how can it possibly compare with what it's like here? Or in India, or Africa?'

'All right, Del,' said Michael. 'That's one of the reasons I took on this contract. Look where it got me.'

'It got you a profit,' said Martin, not unkindly. 'And it got a damn good plant built here, where it's needed. Never mind who owns it. In time it'll help everybody who lives in this country.'

'Even accepting that,' said Michael, and this time there was the glimmer of a smile on his face, 'I still feel a bit like I've been raped.'

Martin bent forward, lowering his voice. 'These damn people have had a lot of practice at raping . . .'

David spoke softly too. 'But one day, the Indians'll . . .'

'One day the Indians or the guerrillas or someone else – God knows who – will have it all,' interjected Martin. 'Maybe we'll live to see the day even.'

'I'd like that,' said Michael.

'Yeah,' said Martin. 'Meanwhile all you can do is go on building, Mike, whatever business you're in. There's no use sitting on your ass, and no use getting obsessed whether you're always right or not. No one ever is. But don't stop building.'

Alison wanted to shout with the joy of having found an ally. She was puzzled at Sheila's need to experience something beyond David – something important to Sheila, it seemed. She herself wanted only to breathe with Michael, to live through him. Her faith and her loyalty were almost Jesuitical.

Martin jumped up. 'Jeez, I need a swim. Anyone join me?'

The two girls loosened their robes. David and Michael stretched their legs. Bernard just sat there, applauding Martin. He couldn't have said it better himself.

'Okay, Del, I'm not arguing with you,' said Michael. 'I'm a believer. But hell, the going's tough while we're walking towards paradise. What have we got *now*, except the

Cantanias and Vargases and Corsinos of this world, that's what I want to know?'

'Well,' said Martin, shaking his head, 'at least we've got each other, all of us.'

Then he turned and led them to the water.

* * *

The opening ceremony at the plant began well. Even the rains kept off, although it was humid enough to drench every non-South American who attended in sweat.

There were ambassadors from everywhere, four in silk top-hats. There was Sanger, smiling like a big success. A brass band sixty-strong played, and a thousand soldiers strung round the perimeter wire fence kept their trigger-fingers tensed.

There was also Cantania's speech, glittering with clichés, aflame with the future. The plant, he pointed out, had been finished ahead of schedule despite immense difficulties. Both the constructors and Ecuador could be proud, which indeed was true.

As he spoke, Francisco and the fifty men who had patiently waited in ambush on the route which Cantania was due to take were already creeping through jungle, returning to their hide-away in the banana plantations. They had been duped. Cantania, now much better versed in the dissemination of false information, had flown from the air-strip at Esmeraldas to the plant by helicopter, as had all of the chief guests.

Francisco, finger still on the trigger of his carbine, was disappointed, but not despondent, for he was fortified with the knowledge of his band's many successes in the past few months.

He knew there would be other occasions.